A River
in the Sky

Also by Elizabeth Peters

The Amelia Peabody
murder mystery series:
(Titles listed in order)
Crocodile on the Sandbank
The Curse of the Pharaohs
The Mummy Case
Lion in the Valley
The Deeds of the Disturber
The Last Camel Died at Noon
The Snake, the Crocodile and the Dog
The Hippopotamus Pool
Seeing a Large Cat
The Ape Who Guards the Balance
The Falcon at the Portal
Thunder in the Sky
Lord of the Silent
The Golden One
Children of the Storm
Guardian of the Horizon
The Serpent on the Crown
Tomb of the Golden Bird

The Vicky Bliss
murder mystery series:
(Titles listed in order)
Borrower of the Night
Street of the Five Moons
Silhouette in Scarlet
Trojan Gold
Night Train to Memphis

A River in the Sky

ELIZABETH
PETERS

CONSTABLE
London

Constable & Robinson Ltd
3 The Lanchesters
162 Fulham Palace Road
London W6 9ER
www.constablerobinson.com

First published by Avon Books, 2010

This UK edition published by Robinson,
an imprint of Constable & Robinson Ltd, 2010

Middlesbrough Libraries & Information	
MY	
009030291 5	
Askews & Holts	Mar-2011
AF CRI	£18.99

A copy of the British Library Cataloguing in
Publication data is available from the British Library

ISBN: 978-1-84901-288-1

Printed and bound in the EU

1 3 5 7 9 10 8 6 4 2

PEFC
PEFC/16-33-111
CATG-PEFC-052
www.pefc.org

To Pat and Allen Ahearn

Acknowledgments

Once again I am indebted to Dennis Forbes, editor of *Kmt: A Modern Journal of Ancient Egypt*, for reading the entire manuscript and catching several errors. Thanks as well to Dr. Donald P. Ryan for the material on Samaria, a subject on which I was less well informed than he. (And still am, despite his best endeavors.) As always I owe effusive thanks to my friend and assistant Kristen Whitbread, who made me work when I didn't want to and encouraged me with snacks and cups of coffee.

Foreword

Thanks to recent negotiations with the heirs of Mrs. Emerson, the editor is able to present another volume of her memoirs. (If the reader is curious about the chronological placement of this particular volume, the editor notes that *A River in the Sky* chronicles events that occurred in 1910, and thus follows *Guardian of the Horizon* [1907–1908] and precedes The *Falcon at the Portal* [1911].) In this case Mrs. E. has gone to greater lengths than usual to conceal the identities of various persons mentioned. This may be attributed in part to the delicacy of the political situation at that time and in part to Mrs. Emerson's wish to avoid lawsuits. Students of this somewhat obscure period may be reminded of actual events and/or individuals. The editor does not feel it is her responsibility to verify or deny such theories.

Chapter One

Emerson looked up from the book he was reading.

'The Old Testament,' he remarked, 'is a tissue of lies from start to finish.'

As I have said before, and never tire of repeating, my husband is the greatest Egyptologist of this or any other century. It cannot be denied, however, that he holds somewhat unorthodox opinions on certain subjects. Prejudiced he is not; his critical comments are applied indiscriminately to all the major world religions, and not a few of the minor ones. Ordinarily I do not bother to protest, since contradiction only inspires him to more outrageous flights of rhetoric. However, I had become bored with my own reading material – an article on negative verb forms in the latest issue of the *Zeitschrift für Aegyptische Sprache* – and considered what response was most likely to result in a refreshing discussion.

The weather was unusually warm even for August in Kent, and the roses in the garden outside Emerson's study drooped dustily. This chamber, the library in point of fact, is one of the most comfortable rooms in the house, a pleasant clutter of books and papers sprinkled with the ashes from Emerson's pipe and the hair shed by cats of various colors. We all tend to gather there;

Emerson's attempts to claim it as his own are sporadic and ineffectual. He only does it to stir up an argument when other sources fail.

The only other member of the family present that morning was Nefret, our adopted daughter. My son was presently on an archaeological excavation in Palestine; his Egyptian friend David, whom we regarded as one of us, had betaken himself to Yorkshire in order to be with his affianced bride, my niece Lia.

If I had been looking for support – which I was not, since I do not require assistance in my discussions with Emerson – I would have known I could expect no agreement from Nefret.

To look at her, one would have assumed Nefret to be a classic English beauty, fair-skinned and blue-eyed, with a glorious crown of golden-red hair. Yet her formative years had been spent in a remote spot in the western desert of Egypt, where the old gods were still worshipped, and she had served as High Priestess of Isis before we rescued her and brought her back to the land of her ancestors. Though I had endeavored to instruct her in the faith of those ancestors, I harbored no illusions as to my success. Early impressions are difficult to erase and from time to time she would say or do something that indicated she was more in sympathy with Emerson's views than with mine. Her frequent visits to the little pyramid we had caused to be built in honor of a young man who had perished in her service might have been occasioned by respect and fond remembrance; but it would not have surprised me to learn that she sometimes addressed a prayer to one of the pagan deities mentioned in the inscriptions. Curled up on the sofa, playing with one of the cats, she looked at me with an anticipatory smile.

I returned my attention to Emerson, whose smile was not so much anticipatory as provocative. I had decided on a flank attack rather than a direct assault.

'Good heavens, Emerson, are you reading the Bible? Are you feeling quite well?'

Emerson's smile broadened into a grin that displayed a set of large white teeth. 'Nicely done, my dear. I assure you, my health has never been better.'

As if to verify the statement he rose to his feet and stretched. Muscles rippled across the breadth of his chest and along his arms. They were admirably displayed by his costume; his shirt was open at the throat and his sleeves rolled above the elbows. His thick black hair was becomingly disheveled and his blue eyes shone with sapphirine brilliance. The sight of Emerson's splendid physical endowments never fails to stir strong emotions, but on this occasion I resisted the distraction since I was genuinely curious.

'Why are you reading the Bible, Emerson?'

'The answer to that question will become evident in due course, Peabody. Have you no comment to make on my original statement?'

'Well, as to that,' I replied, settling myself more comfortably, 'you know as well as I do that the statement is, to say the least, inaccurate and exaggerated. Don't tell me you have read the entire Old Testament. How far had you got?'

Emerson glanced down at the volume open on his desk. 'Genesis and Exodus,' he admitted. 'It gets damnably boring after that.'

'One does not read the Bible to be entertained, Emerson,' I said severely.

'Than why the devil does one read it?'

Before I could reply, an emphatic knock at the door preceded the appearance of Rose, who announced that luncheon was ready. Our very efficient housekeeper is allowed in Emerson's study only when it reaches a stage of questionable hygiene; she gave it a critical look, pursed her lips, and shook her head.

Emerson saw the look. Rising in haste, he said, 'Coming, Rose, coming at once.'

A formal meal, in such warm weather and when there were only three of us, was in my opinion a waste of time. Gargery, our butler, did not share this opinion, primarily because he seized every opportunity to listen and contribute to our conversation. (I do not encourage this, but Emerson has not the least notion of proper behavior with servants.) After serving cold ham and salad, Gargery inquired, 'May I ask, sir and madam, whether you have had a letter from Master Ramses recently?'

As I had often told Gargery, our son had reached an age at which that childish title was inappropriate. The name was equally inappropriate, but Ramses had been given that appellation in infancy because of his imperious manner and the fact that his swarthy complexion and dark eyes and hair appeared more Egyptian than English. (I have sometimes been asked to account for this resemblance. I see no reason why I should.)

I replied with a rather curt negative, and Emerson, who had finished his ham and salad, asked, 'What do you know about the Old Testament, Gargery?'

'It's been a while since I dipped into the Good Book, sir,' Gargery admitted. 'I remember David and Goliath, and the parting of the Red Sea, and a few other stories.'

'Stories is the word,' said Emerson. 'There is not a jot of historical evidence for any of them.'

This was aimed at me, not at Gargery, so of course I responded. 'If it is history you want, you had better skip on to the books of Kings and Chronicles. The historical validity of the Exodus has been much debated – no, Emerson, I do not care to debate it now – but the lives of the kings of Israel and Judah are based on solid historical evidence.'

Emerson pushed his plate away and planted his elbows on the table – a deplorable habit of which I have not succeeded in breaking him. 'Is that so, Peabody? Perhaps you would care to cite a few examples.'

Though I would never have admitted it to Emerson, it had been some time since I had dipped into the Old Testament. I promised myself I would do so immediately after luncheon. 'Do your own research, Emerson. You wouldn't take my word anyhow. Nefret, my dear, you haven't eaten a thing. You seem a trifle out of sorts these days. Is something worrying you?'

The disingenuous attempt to change the subject succeeded. Emerson, who adores his adopted daughter, glanced at her in alarm.

'No. Well . . . I miss the boys. Not that you and the professor aren't splendid company,' she added quickly. 'But with David in Yorkshire and Ramses off in the wilds of Palestine . . .'

'You have no one to play with,' I suggested.

Nefret returned my smile. 'I suppose that was how it sounded. Oh, it is perfectly understandable that David would rather be with Lia; they're madly in love and it will be some time before they can be married. But why did Ramses go haring off to Palestine? He might at least have the decency to write.'

'Mr. Reisner's offer to work with him at Samaria was a splendid opportunity,' I said. 'And you know Ramses has never been a good correspondent.'

'Well, sir and madam, I don't understand it either,' Gargery declared, serving plates of custard. 'Egypt is where we always work. Why did Master Ramses go off to that heathenish place?'

'The adjective is singularly inappropriate, Gargery, since we are speaking of the Holy Land, sacred to three great world religions. And,' I added, 'I cannot remember inviting your comments on the matter.'

Unperturbed by my rebuke, for he had heard similar remarks so often they had ceased to make an impression, Gargery declared, 'I worry about him, madam, and that's a fact. You know how he is.'

I did know how he was. Ramses had a habit, a propensity, one might say, for getting into trouble. It would take too many pages of this journal to compile a list of his adventures, which included being kidnapped off the top of a pyramid, being temporarily entombed in another, stealing a lion . . . But as I have said, the list is long.

Candor compels me to admit that certain of Ramses's escapades were due in part to the activities of his father and myself, for our dedication to truth and justice had occasionally brought us into contact with various criminal elements – tomb robbers, forgers, a murderer or two, and even a Master Criminal. To do myself justice, I must add that I had done my best to protect him as only a mother can. Certain of his narrow escapes were unquestionably the result of his own recklessness, and although he had settled down a bit as he approached the official age of maturity – which he had reached this past month – I had been forced to the conclusion that I was no longer in a position to control his actions. At least not when he was in a place where I could not get at him. It had occurred to me, upon occasion, to wonder whether Ramses had deliberately selected a place where I could not get at him.

'For your information, Gargery,' I said, 'the site of Samaria was once the capital of the kings of Israel, after the united kingdom broke into two parts following the death of Solomon, Israel being the northern and Judah the southern. The city was subsequently conquered by . . . er . . . various conquerors, ending with the Romans. The Roman temple on the summit of the tell – as such sites are called, being the remains of one settlement atop another . . .'

As I had expected, my lecture succeeded in boring Gargery to such an extent that he cleared the table and removed himself. It also bored Nefret, who asked to be excused, and Emerson, who declared he knew that, Peabody, and left the room. I knew he was going to the library to look up the information I had given in the hope of finding me wrong. He would not. I had been careful to stick to generalities.

As a rule it is not difficult for me to read Emerson's mind. However, speculate as I might, I was unable to account for his sudden interest in a subject that had hitherto roused only derision. I found time that day to refresh my memory of the biblical books I had mentioned. I did not doubt Emerson was reading them too, and I intended to be ready for him.

He did not refer to the subject again. When he informed me, the following morning, that he had invited two guests to join us for tea, my attempts to ascertain more information about them were met with evasion and, when I persisted, a flat-out refusal to say more. Rather than give him the satisfaction of demonstrating further interest, I did not pursue the matter, but I felt a certain foreboding. Emerson's acquaintances include Arab sheikhs, Nubian brigands, thieves of various nationalities, and one or two forgers.

I was therefore pleasantly surprised when the guests proved to be unarmed and harmless. They were an odd pair, however. Major the Honorable George Morley appeared to be in his late thirties or early forties. Of medium height, with thinning brown hair, he carried himself like the soldier he had been, but his well-tailored clothes failed to conceal the fact that the life of a country gentleman had thickened his waistline and certain other parts of his anatomy.

In contrast to the solidity of Morley, the other man gave the impression that a strong gale would blow him off his feet and send him floating across the landscape. His receding hair might have been white or very fair. His beard was of the same indeterminate shade, so that his face looked as if it were framed by a halo that had slipped its moorings. His eyes were of that pale shade of blue that, if physiognomists are to be believed, are characteristic of mystics and fanatics.

His name was equally remarkable. Morley presented him as the Reverend Plato Panagopolous. His garments were of somber black and he wore a clerical collar. I asked, with my usual tact, to which particular church or denomination he belonged. I had to repeat the question before he replied: 'I serve the Lord God of Hosts in all his manifestations.'

He contributed little to the conversation after that, except for murmurs of vague agreement when someone commented on the beauty of the August weather or the prospect of rain, but from time to time his gaze focused on me or Nefret, and a singularly sweet smile warmed his thin face.

Pouring tea and offering plates of biscuits and cucumber sandwiches, I wondered what the devil Emerson was up to now. As a rule he avoided English squires and otherworldly eccentrics like the plague. Nefret, as puzzled as I – and as bored – gave me a questioning look. I smiled and gave my head a little shake. 'Be patient,' was my unspoken message. 'Emerson is bound to burst out before long.'

I confess, however, that I was not prepared for the precise nature of the outburst.

'The Old Testament,' said Emerson, fixing Morley with a piercing stare, 'is a tissue of lies from start to finish.'

'Really, Emerson,' I exclaimed. 'That is very rude to our guests, who probably take quite a different view of Scripture.'

Morley laughed and waved a plump pink hand. 'Not at all, Mrs. Emerson. I fully expected some such view from the Professor. I am here to change his views, if possible.'

'Proceed,' said Emerson, folding his arms.

But before Mr. Morley could do so, Panagopolous leaped to his feet and began speaking in tongues.

Genuine, actual languages, that is to say. I recognized Hebrew and Latin, and what sounded like Greek; but his speech was so disjointed and his voice so high-pitched I understood only a few words. He might have been the reincarnation of one of the Old Testament prophets: eyes blazing, hair and beard bristling, arms flailing.

'What the devil,' Emerson exclaimed. 'He is about to have a seizure.'

'Don't touch him,' Morley said. 'He is not ill. It will pass.'

Sure enough, the spate of speech stopped as suddenly as it had come on. The reverend's bristling hair and beard settled back into place. He resumed his chair, and took a biscuit.

'Did you understand what he said?' Morley asked coolly.

'Gibberish,' Emerson said, even more coolly.

I realized I was staring rudely (if understandably) at the reverend, who was placidly munching his chocolate biscuit.

'Languages are not my husband's specialty,' I said, getting a grip on myself. 'I recognized a few words – names, rather. He referred, I believe, to the city of David and the conquest of Jerusalem by Nebuchadnezzar of Babylon.'

'Very good, Mrs. Emerson.' Morley beamed at me and patted his hands together in applause.

Emerson glowered at the reverend, who was working his way through the plate of biscuits with calm concentration.

'And is this your evidence?' Emerson demanded. 'The ravings of a religious fanatic?'

The parlor door opened a few inches. Expecting to find that Gargery, frustrated in his attempt to hear through a heavy wooden panel, had eased it open, I was disconcerted to see Horus squeeze through the opening.

We have a good many cats, too many, as some might say. They were all descendants of a pair of Egyptian felines we had brought back with us from Egypt, and they had bred true to type, being handsomely brindled animals with large ears and a high degree of intelligence. Horus was undoubtedly one cat too many. He was a bully and a philanderer, whose contempt for us was matched by our detestation of him. For some unaccountable reason Nefret doted on him.

Apparently he had learned how to open doors. After an insolent survey of the persons present he sauntered across the room and jumped up onto the sofa next to Nefret, shoving her aside so he could sprawl out.

'What a handsome cat,' said the reverend, whose chair was beside the sofa. 'Here, puss, puss, good puss. Would you like a biscuit?'

'Chocolate is not good for cats,' I said. The comment came too late; with a sudden lunge, Horus snatched the biscuit from the reverend's fingers and crunched it up, sprinkling damp crumbs over the crimson velvet upholstery of the sofa.

Emerson had had enough. Breathing heavily through his nose, he fixed Morley with a hard stare. 'I agreed to listen to your proposition, Mr. Morley – against my better judgment – because you claimed to have solid documentary evidence supporting it. Thus far that evidence has not been forthcoming.'

'This prospectus,' said Morley, removing a handsomely bound booklet from his breast pocket, 'contains a photograph of the scroll I mentioned when we last –'

'Photograph, bah,' said Emerson. 'I would have to see the scroll itself.'

'It is in extremely fragile condition, Professor, and cannot be carried about. Several learned authorities have inspected it and pronounced it genuine. You may communicate directly with them if you like.'

'Well, I don't like,' Emerson declared. 'So-called experts can be hoodwinked as easily as other men. Anyhow, I have no interest whatsoever in biblical legends, or in the Israelites, who were treacherous, bloodthirsty sinners, turning on one another whenever they ran out of Amalekites, Jebusites, Philistines, and Moabites to slaughter. Furthermore, the scheme you propose is unacceptable on several grounds.'

'What scheme?' I asked.

I might as well have saved my breath. Having regained his, after his long diatribe, Emerson continued. 'You cannot be unaware of the unsettled state of the area in question. Your scheme may – almost certainly will – inflame conditions that endanger the peace of the entire region.'

I got one word out – 'What' – before Morley interrupted. The narrowing of his orbs indicated rising temper but – I do him credit – though his voice was a trifle loud, his speech was measured.

'With all due respect, Professor Emerson, that is only your opinion. I have permission from the authorities to carry out my scheme.' He sipped genteelly at his tea.

'What scheme?' I demanded.

I can, when occasion demands, raise my voice to a pitch that is difficult to ignore. Morley started and burst into a fit of coughing – having, I deduced, swallowed the wrong way. Emerson, who knew the futility of ignoring it, replied in a tone almost as vehement as mine.

'The damned fool is mounting an expedition to Jerusalem, to look for the Ark of the Covenant.'

The ensuing silence was broken by Nefret's melodious chuckle. 'I do beg your pardon,' she murmured, trying to keep a straight face.

'Your derision is justified,' said Emerson. 'People have been looking for the damned thing for centuries. They are welcome to keep on looking for it, insofar as I am concerned; it is a harmless enough fantasy. That is not my point. My point is –'

'You have made it, Professor.' Morley placed his cup carefully on the table and rose to his feet. 'I will take no more of your time.'

Though as a rule I deplore Emerson's bad manners, I was as anxious as he to get our visitors out of the house. I had fully expected the reverend to fall writhing to the floor during his initial outburst. His present look was almost as disconcerting; looking up from his pensive contemplation of the (empty) biscuit plate, he inquired, 'Are we going now?'

I accompanied our guests into the hall. Morley took his hat from Gargery, who was hovering, and turned to me.

'If the Professor should change his mind –'

'He will be sure to inform you,' I said. 'Good afternoon.'

We shook hands, and I offered mine to the reverend. He met it with a surprisingly firm grip and a sweet, childlike smile.

'Good afternoon, Mrs. Emerson. Those were excellent biscuits!'

Gargery followed me back to the parlor, so closely he was almost treading on my heels, and began clearing away the tea things with glacial slowness.

Emerson went to the sideboard and poured the whiskey.

'Here you are, Peabody. We both deserve it, I believe, after that interview.'

'He can't have been serious,' Nefret exclaimed. 'Why on earth did you bother listening to such an absurd proposal?'

'I had my reasons,' said Emerson. He gave me a sidelong glance. 'They were excellent reasons. That is all I can tell you.'

'Can, or will?' I inquired. A few sips of the genial beverage had restored my composure and a few ideas were simmering in my head.

'Can,' said Emerson, with considerable emphasis.

'Sworn to secrecy, were you?'

'Quite,' said Emerson, giving me a meaningful look.

'Ah,' I said.

'What on earth are you two talking about?' Nefret asked.

'I am waiting for your Aunt Amelia to tell ME what I am talking about,' said Emerson.

'Oh, very well,' I said. 'Far be it from me to make you break your sworn word. You will not be guilty of that error if *I* tell *you*.'

'Precisely,' said Emerson, no longer attempting to conceal his smile.

'Please do, madam,' Gargery exclaimed. 'I can't stand the suspense much longer.'

There was no use ordering Gargery out of the room; he would only listen at the door.

'Confound it,' I muttered. 'Why can't they leave us alone? I suppose the meeting occurred last week, when you said you went up to London to work at the British Museum. What were you given this time? I don't want any more cursed emeralds.'

'I was given nothing, Peabody. Not even the threat of a title. Apparently the royal family only pays on delivery.'

'Royal family,' said Gargery in dying tones. 'Madam . . .'

I addressed Nefret instead of Gargery. She had been courteous enough to refrain from questions, though her wide blue eyes indicated her interest. 'Some years ago we were able to be of service to her late Majesty in a delicate family matter. Upon its successful conclusion she summoned Emerson to Windsor and offered him a knighthood – which of course he refused.'

I ignored the groan from that consummate snob Gargery and went on. 'She then presented him with that vulgarly ostentatious emerald ring which you may have seen in my jewel box. Apparently she passed on the story to her heirs, in case another delicate situation arose. This delicate situation, one may deduce, inspired the otherwise inexplicable visit today from Mr Morley. Now, Emerson, it is your turn. I hope His Majesty doesn't expect you to go looking for the Ark youself.'

One of the kittens wandered in and jumped onto Nefret's lap. Stroking it, she remarked, 'Does it exist? As I recall, from my studies at the vicarage, the Ark contained the tablets given to Moses on Mount Sinai.'

'The Ten Commandments,' I said helpfully.

'Yes, Aunt Amelia. But I thought the Professor didn't believe in Moses. Or the Exodus. Or –'

'That doesn't mean the fabled Ark is pure fiction,' Emerson

13

replied, taking, as was his habit, the opposing side. 'We know that Jerusalem was besieged and overrun by the Babylonians, who carried away its residents into captivity. There was time –'

'So you admit that not all the Old Testament is a tissue of lies,' I said. 'The fall of Jerusalem is mentioned in Second Kings, if my memory serves.'

'It is also described in the Babylonian annals,' Emerson retorted. 'An historical source, Peabody. As I was saying, there was time during the siege for the inhabitants to conceal their greatest treasures. The Ark was only one of them, though the most important. There were vessels of gold – an altar, candelabra, incense vessels, and so on. Who is to say they may not still lie hidden under the ruins of the Temple?'

'Do you believe that, Emerson?'

'Certainly not,' said Emerson, tiring of his teasing. 'Jerusalem was taken and sacked many times. If the Babylonians didn't seize the temple treasures, somebody else did. The Arch of Titus in Rome shows Roman soldiers carrying away some of the treasures, including a menorah. The Ethiopians claim the Ark was taken there by the son of Solomon and the Queen of Sheba. People have looked for it in Ireland, at Mount Sinai, and for all I know in Birmingham. Even if I believed there were the possibility of such a discovery, I would not countenance an expedition by an untrained amateur in a particularly sensitive part of the world.'

'Gargery,' I said in some exasperation. 'Will you please finish clearing the tea things away? The kitten is about to knock over the cream jug.'

Nefret removed the cat, and Gargery, who had abandoned all pretense of carrying out his duties, exclaimed, 'Then why don't you and madam go looking for the treasure, sir? You'd do a proper job of it.'

'Kindly stay out of this, Gargery,' I said. 'It is difficult enough to keep this family on track without your digressions. I cannot imagine what the Ark of the Covenant has to do with any of this, or why the British government should take an interest in the plans of an adventurer like Morley.'

'Would you care to have me explain, Peabody?' Emerson inquired in a devastatingly mild voice.

'That is what I have been asking you to do, Emerson.'

'Hmph,' said Emerson. 'I presume you are familiar with the present uneasy political situation in the Middle East?'

'I am not, sir,' Gargery said eagerly.

'Nor am I,' Nefret admitted.

'You really ought to make an attempt to keep up with modern history,' I said. Emerson, who had opened his mouth, closed it.

'Palestine is of course part of the once-mighty Ottoman Empire, which during the sixteenth century of the Christian era controlled the entire Middle East, North Africa, and parts of eastern Europe,' I explained. 'Like all empires founded on conquest and injustice, it could not endure; gradually its territories were lost and at the present time only the support of Britain and France, who fear the collapse of the aging giant would open the doors of the East to Germany and Russia, keeps the sultan on his throne in Constantinople.'

'Very poetically expressed,' said Emerson, who had been waiting for my breath to give out. 'To look at it another way, Nefret and Gargery, the aging giant is rotten at the core. Provinces like Syria and Palestine are racked with poverty and corruption. Britain and France don't give a curse about the misery of the people; what concerns them is that in the past decade or so, German influence in the region has increased enormously. When Wilhelm the Second visited Istanbul and Jerusalem, he was greeted as a conquering hero. The Germans are constructing a railroad line from Damascus to Mecca, and one is entitled to assume that they aren't doing it for altruistic reasons. If war should break out –'

'War!' Nefret cried. 'And Ramses is there, in the thick of it?'

15

'Stop worrying about your brother,' Emerson said impatiently. 'There won't be a war, not for a few more years. But it's coming, and Germany is already making preparations – such as that railroad. Very useful for moving troops and supplies.'

This speech was presumably an attempt to reassure Nefret. Not surprisingly it failed. 'War or no war, if there is any way Ramses can get in trouble, he will,' she said vehemently. 'If the situation is so unstable –'

'Nonsense,' I said. 'Samaria – the modern Sebaste – is nowhere near the area where the Germans are working, and Mr. Reisner is a responsible individual. Emerson considers him one of the most qualified of the younger generation of Egyptologists.'

'Hmph.'

'Or would, if he considered any other Egyptologists qualified,' I emended.

'He's not so bad,' Emerson admitted. 'Though one would suppose he had enough on his plate with his excavations at Giza and in the Sudan, without taking on another responsibility in an area he knows nothing about –'

'Reisner would argue that the basic techniques of excavation are the same in all parts of the world,' I said.

'Well, well,' said Emerson. 'Hmph.'

The ambiguity of this response ought to have raised alarm bells. It is not like Emerson to be ambiguous. In my defense I must say that I was more concerned with calming Nefret. 'George Reisner is a mature, dedicated individual who lives only for his work. Not even Ramses can get in trouble while he is in Reisner's charge.'

From Manuscript H

Ramses had been aware for some time that he was being followed. The night sky was overcast and the grove of olive trees through which he walked cast heavy shadows, but the faint sounds were unmistakable. He had been listening for them. He slowed his pace, ears pricked. When it happened, the attack was sudden and unexpected, for it came not from behind him but from close ahead. A slight stirring of the air and a change in the shape of the shadow across the path gave him just enough warning to duck. It turned out to be a bad move; instead of hitting him in the chest or shoulder, the missile struck the side of his head, hard enough to make him lose his balance and fall to hands and knees. Though dizzy and disoriented, he knew better than to stay where he was. He crawled off the path and among the gnarled trunks of the trees, where he lay still, listening and waiting for his head to clear.

Not a sound, except for the normal night noises.

'Damn,' Ramses said softly.

The pattern was like that of the last attack – a missile flung, a hasty withdrawal. The only difference was that this time there had been two of them, one following, to distract his attention, the other waiting in hiding. He had hoped this time to lay hands on the assailant, or at least get a look at him.

He returned to the path and switched on his torch. His lips pursed in a silent whistle when he saw the size of the stone that had struck him. It was as large as his head. If it had hit him full in the face . . . A deliberate attempt at murder?

Probably not, he decided. The fellow's aim wasn't very good, and if he had homicide on his mind he would have chosen more lethal weapons. The first stone had hit him in the back, hard enough to get his attention but doing little damage.

He picked up the stone and went on his way without encountering any living creature except a few of the village dogs. When he emerged from the trees he saw the lights in the houses of the village of Sebaste. There weren't many lighted windows; people in this part of the world went to bed early to save costly lamp oil. The brightest lights came from the house the Samaria

17

crew had rented for the season. Reisner was still at work. Ramses stopped outside the door and after searching his pockets found a grubby handkerchief with which he wiped the blood off his cheek.

When he went in, his superior didn't look up.

'You've been a while,' he remarked, adding a note to one of the papers on the table before him.

'Sorry.'

Clarence Fisher, Reisner's second in command, was lying on the divan. He sat up, stretching. 'What's that you've got there?'

I might have known, Ramses thought, that he'd focus on an artifact instead of asking, 'What happened to you?' The cut had stopped bleeding, but his cheek was smeared with dried blood, his clothes were dusty, and his hair was festooned with dried leaves. He handed Fisher the stone and sank into a chair.

'It's from the dig,' Fisher said, examining the remains of ornamentation on one side of the stone. 'Why were you there at this time of night?'

'I wasn't. Someone pitched that at me a few minutes ago, when I was walking through the olive grove on my way here.'

Reisner put his pen down and leaned back in his chair. His eyes moved over Ramses's disheveled form. 'Not again!' he said.

'Sorry.'

'No, I'm sorry.' Reisner's sudden grin bared a large number of teeth. 'The remark sounded somewhat callous. Were you injured?'

'Oh dear,' Fisher exclaimed. 'I fear I was also negligent in failing to inquire.'

The two of them converged on Ramses. Reisner pushed the matted hair away from Ramses's temple and ran expert fingers over the area. Most field archaeologists had to know something about medical treatment; accidents on a dig were not uncommon.

'You'll have a nice big lump tomorrow,' Reisner said coolly. 'How many fingers am I holding up?'

'I don't have a concussion, sir.'

'I expect you are only too familiar with the symptoms.'

Ramses couldn't tell from his superior's expression whether that had been meant as criticism, sarcasm, or a simple statement of fact.

'Yes, sir,' he said.

'You don't have to keep calling me sir.'

'Habit,' Ramses said. 'Hard to break.'

He got another of those toothy grins. 'I understand. I still have to fight the tendency to address your dad that way.'

Reisner went back to his makeshift desk, took out his pipe, and began filling it. Fisher, clucking remorsefully, handed Ramses a glass, which the latter accepted with a nod of thanks. Unlike his parents, who celebrated the end of the workday with a whiskey and soda – or two – his current supervisor kept a scanty supply of liquor for medicinal purposes only. Not very good liquor, either, Ramses thought, sipping.

They sat in silence for a few minutes, while Reisner fussed with his pipe and Fisher rummaged in the box of medical supplies. The small shabby room, the best the village had to offer, was illumined only by two flickering oil lamps. The gloom hid the ramshackle furnishings, such as they were, and the evidence of what his mother would have described as typical male untidiness – a pair of stockings draped over a chair, papers spilling out of the rough boxes they used for filing documents.

Reisner lit his pipe and puffed contentedly. 'You went out tonight in the hope of provoking another attack.'

'Well – yes, in a way. But I only wanted –'

'To find out whether the first attack was an aberration or part of a pattern. Fair enough. If there is trouble brewing we need to know. Have you any idea what could be behind this?'

'No. Perhaps you would prefer that I resign,' Ramses said.

'What the hell do you want from me, an apology?' Reisner clamped his teeth down on the stem of his pipe. Then he said

19

suddenly, 'You probably think I've been a little hard on you these past weeks.'

'No, sir.' The question almost surprised him into a truthful answer. Ramses was used to criticism. His father was a hard taskmaster; his frequent outbursts of temper had earned him the Egyptian title of Father of Curses. But Emerson doled out praise as readily as blame, and his shouts of laughter were as frequent as his curses.

Fisher let out a whinny of amusement. 'Don't take it the wrong way, Ramses. George is afraid your mother will scold him if anything happens to you.'

Ramses's jaw dropped. 'What does my mother have to do with this?'

'He promised her he'd keep you out of mischief,' Fisher said, with a smile that held a certain amount of malice.

It would have been hard to say who was more outraged, Reisner or Ramses. Ramses was too infuriated to speak, which was just as well. Reisner gave Fisher a hard stare. Then he let out a sudden bark of laughter.

'The truth is,' he said, 'your father intimidates me, but your mother absolutely terrifies me.'

Fisher joined in his laughter. Ramses was not amused. 'With all respect, sir, I am not a child.'

'Oh, for heaven's sake, don't be so touchy,' Reisner said irritably. 'If I had any complaints about you or your work you would have heard them. All I'm trying to do is find out what the hell is going on. We had no such problems last year. You are the only one of us who has been physically attacked. It smacks of a personal vendetta.'

'But I was here last year too,' Ramses pointed out. 'And I'll be damned if I can think of anything I've done lately to arouse resentment.'

'I can't think of anything either,' Reisner admitted. 'You're as familiar with the mores and sensibilities of Middle Easteners as I am.'

'More so,' Fisher murmured.

Reisner acknowledged the truth of the statement with a wry smile. 'Have you any suggestions, Ramses?'

Ramses shrugged. 'Somebody doesn't like my face. I'm not trying to make light of the situation,' he added. 'It's just that I haven't any sensible explanation.'

They sat in silence for a time. Finally Reisner said with a sigh, 'Neither have I. Just avoid solitary strolls from now on, will you? And – er – you needn't mention these incidents when you write the family.'

'I've no intention of doing so.'

'Good. Put some alcohol on that cut before you go to bed.'

It was a dismissal, which Ramses was happy to accept. Lying awake on the hard cot, he went over the conversation and began to see the humor in it. He wasn't the only one under his mother's metaphorical thumb. It was a large thumb attached to a very long arm.

Something else struck him now that he had leisure to think rationally. A personal vendetta implied a personal enemy, but it needn't be a new one. He had acquired a few over a short and misspent life; his parents had acquired even more. Did one of them bear a grudge strong enough to follow him here? He began going over the list but fell asleep before he had got halfway through.

I did not doubt that Nefret's concern for her brother was genuine, if unfounded, but I suspected she was exaggerating her distress in order to get her own way. Owing to Emerson's obduracy we had not settled on our plans for the winter season. Having been banned from the Valley of the Kings by the Antiquities Service,

Emerson refused to accept any other site, though several had been offered him. He had spoken vaguely of returning to Nubia, where we had excavated before. Nefret did not want to go back to Nubia. (Neither did I.)

'Well,' she declared, 'I don't really give a curse about the Ark of the Covenant or Major Morley. I am worried about Ramses. You know how he –'

'Yes,' I said, with a sigh. 'I do know.'

'I am going to write to him at once.' Nefret's chin set in an expression I knew only too well. 'And demand that he reply by return mail.'

'That may take weeks,' I said.

'Then the sooner someone gets at it, the better.'

She closed the door behind her with ominous softness.

'Now then,' I said, fixing Emerson with a stern look. 'Out with it. You have not told me everything.'

'I didn't want Nefret to hear.'

'Why not?'

Emerson got up from his desk and tiptoed to the door. That is to say, he was under the impression that he was tiptoeing. Seizing the handle, he flung the door open, peered suspiciously into the hall, and closed the door before returning to his chair.

'What you know of the matter thus far, Peabody, might be deduced by any informed person. What I am about to tell you is a state secret, known only to a few. It must go no further.'

Emerson's is not a countenance that lends itself to deception. The furrowing of his noble brow, the slight compression of his well-cut lips, and, most particularly, the movement of his hand to his chin, which he is wont to stroke when in thought, indicated that he was in deadly earnest.

'You have my word, Emerson,' I replied, as earnestly. 'And may I add that the confidence you have displayed in me . . . I will say no more.'

'Indeed?' The sobriety of Emerson's countenance relaxed into a smile. 'Well, my dear, I take you at your word. To answer your question: Morley is an additional complication to a witches' brew of a situation. If he starts digging around the Temple Mount he is likely to stir up trouble with the Jews and the Moslems, both of whom consider that a holy site. Someone needs to keep an eye on him and try to prevent him from doing something stupid.'

'And that someone is you?'

'I have a legitimate excuse for protesting his activities, Peabody, on purely professional grounds. He's bound to make a mess of the excavation, but until he does so there is no legal way of preventing him from going out there. What concerns the government is another matter entirely. The fact is, I spent only a few minutes with His Majesty. After the usual exchange of courtesies he left me to the Director of Military Intelligence and another individual, whose name was never mentioned.'

'How extraordinary.'

'It was a most extraordinary conversation, Peabody. These intelligence people – well, you know how they are, seeing plots and conspiracies all over the place. It seems there have been rumors of an uprising – not a violent affair like the Mahdist Revolt in the Sudan, but a carefully planned long-range project that may be years in the making. The object is the expulsion of foreigners from the Middle East and the creation of an Islamic state in Syria-Palestine.'

'Expulsion?' I repeated. 'That is a rather tame word. Are you talking about a jihad?'

'It may come to that eventually, Peabody. At the present time, military intelligence is chiefly concerned with the part Germany is playing in the region. It has been ten years since the All-Highest, as his fawning subjects call the Kaiser, visited Damascus and Jerusalem and declared himself the defender of Islam. The Turks aren't naive enough to believe his high-flown rhetoric, but they will use him to serve their own purposes. German agents are swarming all over the region, thinly disguised as explorers, engineers –'

'And archaeologists?'

Emerson nodded, and I exclaimed, 'We are doing the same, of course. Archaeologists make excellent spies. Please don't tell me that George Reisner is secretly working for British intelligence.'

'Then I won't. Come now, Peabody. In the first place, Reisner is American, with no loyalties to Britain. In the second place, he is the least likely individual of my acquaintance to let politics distract him from his work. Speaking of distraction, Peabody, you've done it again. Do you want to know why the War Office is interested in Major Morley?'

'I suppose they suspect him of being a German spy,' I said with a sniff.

Emerson's superior smile vanished. 'Curse it, Peabody, how did you know that?'

'Logical deduction, Emerson. The War Office instigated Morley's visit to us; the War Office doesn't give a curse about inept excavations; the War Office is obsessed with spies; ergo, the War Office suspects Morley of being one. A spy, that is to say. Utter nonsense, of course. I trust you informed them to that effect?'

'I haven't had a chance to do so as yet. I had planned to go up to London tomorrow.'

'I will go with you.'

'You have not been invited, Peabody.'

'Nevertheless, I will go.'

'Logical deduction informed me that you would say so,' said Emerson.

We caught an early train next morning. Finding ourselves alone in a first-class carriage, Emerson took advantage of the opportunity to explain to me the organization of the military intelligence services, and the meaning of various confusing initials. The DMO was the Director of Military Operations, which had, at the present time, several subsidiary branches. MO2 was the branch assigned to cover Europe and the Ottoman Empire, and the only one that concerned us. Emerson would have gone on to tell me about the other branches, but fortunately several passengers got into the carriage at our next stop and refused to listen to Emerson's strong hints that they go away. In fact I had heard all I needed to hear. Men like to create unnecessary organizations and give them impressive or mysterious names; this usually ends in increased confusion, and should therefore be ignored.

The new War Office building was on an imposing height in Whitehall, across from the old Admiralty. Emerson was expected, for he had telegraphed earlier. I was not expected. There was some little discussion, which I ignored. I had worn my second-best summer hat, trimmed with roses, and a new costume of crimson silk (crimson being Emerson's favorite color), and I suppose I made a rather unusual figure in that bastion of male supremacy. The men, even the clerks, might have ordered their somber black suits and their gray cravats from the same tailor and haberdasher.

Since Emerson refused to budge a step without me, MO2, and even the DMO, were forced to concede. An extremely nervous young person escorted us to an impressive office on the second floor, where we were met by an equally nervous young secretary. He began twittering at us but was almost instantaneously replaced by the DMO himself, General David Spencer, who came bursting out of his office.

'Mrs. Emerson, I presume,' he said, with a (very) slight bow. 'I was not expecting you.'

I studied him with some interest, since I had never met a DMO before. A long, sagging chin was more or less balanced by an unusually high forehead. Under heavy brows a pair of muddy brown eyes regarded me without pleasure.

'I believe I can provide a useful viewpoint,' I explained, switching my parasol from my right hand to my left and offering the former. 'I felt it my duty as a loyal servant of the Crown to be present.'

A poorly suppressed gurgle of amusement from Emerson rather destroyed the solemnity of my statement and wrung a critical look from Spencer.

'Come in, then,' he said grudgingly.

There was another person in the office, a slight, unimposing young man with protuberant blue eyes and a brown mustache. He rose when I entered and politely held a chair for me. I assumed he was the unnamed gentleman to whom Emerson had referred. By that time I had become a trifle impatient with unnecessary mystery, so I introduced myself.

'Mrs. Emerson. How do you do?'

'This,' said Spencer, forced into feeble civility, 'is Mr. Smith.'

'No, it isn't,' I said, arranging my skirts and my parasol. 'His name is Tushingham, and I met him two years ago following a lecture he gave at the Royal Academy of Science. How are your botanical studies progressing, Mr. Tushingham?'

Over a chorus of snorts from Spencer and chuckles from Emerson, Tushingham said, 'I did not presume to assume that you would remember me, Mrs. Emerson. Our encounter was fleeting, to say the least.'

'You mean you hoped I would not remember you. Never fear, Mr. Tushingham. My discretion is well known. Now let us not waste time, you probably have other matters to attend to and I mean to do a little shopping while I am in town. Major Morley is not a German agent.'

The general dropped heavily into a chair and stared at me. Tushingham seated himself and stared at Emerson.

'Does the Professor agree?'

'Oh, certainly,' said Emerson, standing behind my chair. 'He is a common garden-variety adventurer. Not that he isn't capable of making mischief. His notion of proper archaeological methodology –'

'What about the other fellow – Panagatopolous?' demanded the general.

'Panagopolous,' I corrected. 'If he is secretly working for Germany, or any other government, he is the finest actor I have ever seen, on or off the stage. You know, of course, of his role in Morley's project.'

'We investigated his background,' Tushingham said. 'In his native Greece he is considered to be part of the lunatic fringe of biblical scholarship – harmless and possibly mentally disturbed. I – that is, we – assume Morley is using him and his bizarre theories as a rationale to mount an expedition.'

'I am certain that is the case,' I replied. 'As for Morley, my husband and I are of the same mind concerning his motives. He isn't the first treasure hunter to be enticed to the Holy Land.'

'Quite,' said Emerson. 'Shapira, Parker –'

He would have gone on and on, and I was in a hurry to get to the shops, so I interrupted. 'Religious fanaticism and greed, singly or in combination, have been responsible for a number of explosive incidents in Jerusalem. One needn't invent German spies to explain this latest project, or wish to prevent it.'

Tushingham leaned back in his chair, ran his forefinger along his mustache and shot the general a meaningful glance. I had the distinct impression that he shared our opinion but had failed to convince his obsessed superior.

'Morley has raised a great deal of money from various wealthy, gullible individuals,' Emerson said. 'Surely that constitutes fraud, or at the least –'

'I'm afraid not,' I said. 'In our free society people are allowed to spend their money as foolishly as they like. You are wandering from the point, Emerson, if you will excuse me for saying so.'

General Spencer leaned forward, his elbows on his desk and his hands clasped. 'And what, Mrs. Emerson, is the point?'

I told him.

He still believes Morley is working for the Germans,' I said as Emerson and I left the building. 'Goodness, how dull these military persons are. Once they get an idea into their heads it is impossible to get it out. Mr. Tushingham, now –'

'Why didn't you tell me you knew Tushingham?'

This was such an unjust reproof I realized Emerson was in a surly mood – possibly because I had removed him from the general's office before he had a chance to enlarge upon his opinions. He had not offered me his arm. I took it and leaned upon it and replied, not to the question itself but to the annoyance that had prompted it.

'The lecture was on new varieties of wheat in the Golan Heights, Emerson. You refused to attend it because, as you so pithily put it, varieties of plant life are only of interest to you when they are on your dinner plate.'

'Hmph,' said Emerson. 'He's no damned botanist, is he?'

'Oh, yes, and a good one. Wasn't it you who mentioned that exploration and archaeology make excellent cover for spies? The same is true of other scholarly professions – botanists, geologists, even ornithologists. They provide a legitimate excuse for persons to poke their noses into places where they might not otherwise –'

'I did point that out,' said Emerson between his teeth. 'So you needn't lecture me about a subject with which I am thoroughly acquainted.'

28

His point was valid, so I abandoned the subject. 'There is a cab, Emerson.'

'So I see.' Emerson gestured, and the driver pulled in to the curb and stopped.

'Fine day, sir and madam,' he said, raising his whip in salute.

'Hmph,' said Emerson, helping me in. 'Take us to Victoria Station.'

'By way of Harrods,' I said. 'I have a great deal of shopping to do before we leave for Palestine.'

Chapter Two

From Manuscript H

From where Ramses stood at the top of the mound he could see some distance across the plain. It was a country of rolling hills and peaceful valleys, fields of grain laced by streams whose water caught the sunlight in a shimmer of sparkles, vineyards and groves of olive and fig trees. On the eastern slope of the hill a cluster of nondescript buildings marked the modern village of Sebaste. Behind him lay the ruins of the royal city built by King Herod in the first century. Reisner had identified the forum area, the road of columns that led round the hill to the forum, and the great temple Herod had raised to the glory of the emperor Augustus.

It was the latest of several cities that had occupied the same site, each built upon the ruins of its predecessor. Tells like this one were found all over Palestine, rising above the plain like the man-made hills they were. In theory it should have been possible to peel off each level of occupation sequentially, from top to bottom, with each successive level earlier in time than the one above. In actual practice, the separate levels were sometimes almost impossible to separate. New settlers had dismantled earlier structures and reused the stones, and dug foundations down through earlier strata, sometimes to bedrock. The result resembled a trifle that had been violently stirred with a spoon, mixing fruit and cake and cream into a hopeless jumble. (He had done that once when he was six years old, feeling that since everything got all mixed up inside anyhow, he might as well save time by doing it beforehand. The explanation, though quite logical, had failed to impress his mother.)

The only practical way of dealing with such a site was the one Reisner had adopted – digging straight down next to a foundation wall and trying to locate the dividing line between one occupation level and the one above it. Clearing then continued horizontally along that line. Ramses was waiting for Reisner to come and verify his belief that they had found an actual floor level. He wasn't allowed to proceed until the Mudir had approved his findings.

In fact, Ramses thought, he had little more authority than the skilled Egyptian workers Reisner had brought with him to act as foremen. To be fair, he hadn't had much experience in excavating a site like this one, only a single short season with Reisner the year before. But his work must have been satisfactory, or Reisner wouldn't have asked him back . . .

Ramses shifted impatiently and stifled a yawn. He had dreamed about Nefret – a dream so vivid and intimate he hadn't been able to get back to sleep afterward. He had been in love with her for years. Only recently had he discovered what an uphill battle he had to wage if he hoped to win her. She loved him too – as a brother and best friend. Sometimes he thought he'd stand a better chance if she regarded him with indifference or even dislike. His own instincts, as well as the advice he had been given from an unlikely but incontrovertible source, told him that his best course was patience. It was hard, though, when every fiber of his body and mind ached for her. Being away from her helped a little. He had accepted Reisner's offer in part because it was an excuse to be away from England all summer.

He squinted up at the sun. Reisner was taking his own sweet time. The waiting workmen had squatted and lit cigarettes; listening with half an ear to their low-voiced conversation, Ramses wondered whether one of them was the stone-thrower. The boy with the soft brown eyes, whose beard had barely begun to grow? The bent old graybeard, who wielded a pickax with a young man's strength? Like his parents, he had always made a point of getting to know the men who worked for them – asking about their families, making certain they got medical attention when it was needed. His mother had earned the title of Lady Doctor, and some of the men preferred her treatments to those of Nefret, who had been medically trained. In his mother's case, it was probably sheer force of will that made her so successful. You wouldn't dare die if the Sitt Hakim told you you would live.

With a workforce of more than four hundred men, as was the case here, it was impossible to learn much about the workers, but Ramses had managed to establish friendly relations with several of the men in his own gang. From one of them came a polite cough and a soft inquiry.

'Do we still wait, Brother of Demons? I have no more cigarettes.'

A murmur of mingled disapproval and amusement arose from the other men, but Mitab, the questioner, only smiled guilelessly. Ramses realized that the supervisors Reisner had brought with him from Egypt must have told the locals about his Arabic sobriquet. There was a sort of unwritten rule about the use of these names; they were usually employed in direct address only when they were flattering, like Nefret's Nur Misur, Light of Egypt, and his mother's Sitt Hakim. He had earned his appellation because of his purported control of supernatural forces. It might have been meant as a compliment, but Ramses had made it clear that he didn't much appreciate the distinction. Mitab was not, to put it nicely, the most intelligent of the men. He hadn't meant to offend.

Ramses smiled and tossed down a tin of cigarettes. He had brought an ample supply, knowing they made small but welcome gifts. 'Here is Ali now, bringing the word of the Mudir.'

The word wasn't what Ramses had expected: 'The Mudir wishes you to come to him.'

Ali spoke the idiomatic Arabic of Cairo, which was as familiar to Ramses as his native English. 'Now?' Ramses asked in surprise. 'I have been waiting for him to tell the men how to go on from here. I think we've found a floor level.'

Ali cast an expert eye over the area Ramses had indicated. 'You are right, I think. But the Mudir said come now.'

He didn't have to add: When the Mudir says now he means now. Ramses nodded. He picked up the coat he had removed when the sun rose higher and began picking his way across the uneven surface of the summit, where their excavations had exposed structures dating back to pre-Roman eras. As he approached the western slope, where Reisner was working, he saw a group of people near one of the large circular towers that had been part of a defensive wall.

Ramses swore under his breath. They were frequently interrupted by visitors. Sebaste was off the beaten track for the usual pilgrims, whose standard tours of the Holy Land allowed little time for anything except Jerusalem and the nearby biblical sites, but a few of the diehards (fanatics, as Reisner had once been heard to remark) made it there. As the youngest and least important member of the staff, Ramses was the one appointed to show visitors around and keep them out of Reisner's way. The tomb of John the Baptist was the chief attraction, with a massive door said to be that of his prison. There *was* a tomb, or at least a dome covering something, in the courtyard of what had been a

Crusader church before it was turned into a mosque. The remains of the church had some points of interest, but not for Ramses, who had seen them too many times. He had also heard more than he wanted to hear about King Ahab, whose bloodstained chariot had been washed in a pool by the gate of Samaria. There *was* a gate, but the existing structure was Roman, built some eight hundred years after Ahab had ruled at Samaria. He had learned it was a waste of time to mention this to the pilgrims or to point out that according to the historian Josephus, John the Baptist had been beheaded at a castle on the Dead Sea.

They didn't look like pilgrims. Two of them appeared to be part of an official escort, dressed in shabby uniforms trimmed with an excess of tarnished gold braid. A third man wore a white robe and the green turban restricted to descendants of the Prophet. He was an impressive figure, taller than most, with the sculptured features of a Bedouin, but Ramses's attention was held by the woman who was the center of the group.

Her costume was, to say the least, unusual: riding boots and trousers, topped by a knee-length garment of vivid emerald-green. A cloak of gray homespun hung from her slim shoulders; her fair hair had been wound into a coronet around her head. Her hands were covered with gauntlets of supple leather. One held a riding crop.

Seeing Ramses, Reisner broke off his lecture with unconcealed relief. 'Madame von Eine, may I present my colleague, Ramses Emerson. He will be happy to show you around the acropolis.'

A light, uncomfortable shock ran through Ramses when her eyes focused on him. They were an unusual shade of pale blue-gray, but in their depths he saw a spark of light, like a flame under clouded glass. Her gaze moved from his face to his feet and back again, with the cool appraisal of a potential buyer inspecting a piece of merchandise.

'Ramses,' she repeated. 'What an extraordinary name.'

Ramses could not have said what prompted him to reply in German. Her slight accent had suggested she was of that nationality, but it was in part a response to her condescending tone. 'It is a *Kosename,* madam, used by my friends and family.'

'*Aber natürlich.* You must be Walter P. Emerson, who wrote that pleasant little book on Egyptian grammar.'

'I am flattered,' Ramses said mendaciously.

'Mme von Eine is a specialist in Hittite remains,' Reisner said, cutting the amenities short. 'We have found nothing of that period, madame, but Ramses will show you the Herodian forum area and the Israelite levels if you like.'

'Thank you.' She nodded graciously, a noble lady acknowledging the courtesy of an inferior. 'I won't take any more of your time, Mr. Reisner. You are anxious, I know, to get on with your work.'

'Not at all, not at all,' Reisner muttered.

Without waiting for Ramses to lead the way, she started up the slope, her attendants following. Ramses had to take long strides in order to catch her up. He hadn't realized how tall she was until he stood next to her.

'The terrain is a bit uneven,' he said, offering his hand.

After an almost imperceptible hesitation she put a slim gloved hand in his. When they reached the summit she withdrew her hand and looked expectantly at Ramses. Ramses launched into his lecture.

'After the death of Solomon, his realm broke up into two separate kingdoms – Israel in the north and Judah in the south. Samaria was the capital of the northern kingdom, whose most famous rulers were Omri and Ahab. It was Omri –'

Seeing her expression, he broke off in some confusion. 'I'm sorry. I'm afraid I slipped into the standard lecture. You know all that, of course.'

'Of course.' She moved to one side and looked down at the stretches of wall just below. 'Seleucid,' she said.

'Quite. Dated to approximately 125 B.C. by means of coins found above and below the floors.'

He went on with his lecture as they moved forward, getting no response except an occasional nod, until she interrupted in the midst of a description of the Greek and Babylonian remains.

'And the so-called Israelite structures?'

'It's a little hard to make them out,' Ramses said. 'As you can see, the site is very complex. But stratigraphically the walls lie below the Greek and Babylonian structures, and since we know from Second Kings that Omri built his palace here –'

'That is your evidence?' The slight curl of her lip indicated what she thought of the evidence.

Loyalty to Reisner made Ramses resent the implied criticism, even though he had certain reservations of his own. 'One can't help but be influenced by the biblical account,' he said stiffly. 'It offers such a neat written chronology – the only such chronology we have in this part of the world, until we start to get references in Assyrian and Babylonian records. But I assure you neither Mr. Reisner nor I would follow it blindly. The remains we have found so far indicate a structure of considerable size. It could be a palace, and it seems to have been the first structure on the site. And' – he had saved the best for last – 'this season we discovered a number of documents written in Hebrew.'

'Documents.' She turned those remarkable eyes on him. 'Scrolls? Archival tablets?'

'Nothing so impressive,' Ramses admitted. 'They appear to be dockets recording the receipt of various goods such as wine and oil.'

'So you read ancient Hebrew?'

'I'm no expert, but I'm copying the dockets and hope to work on them after I get home. The form of the script seems to indicate a date in the eighth century, which agrees with the archaeological evidence.'

'I see.' Turning to the man who stood close by her side, she spoke briefly in Arabic. Her voice was so soft he understood only the word 'nothing.'

'Is your dragoman interested in archaeology?' Ramses asked. 'I can continue in Arabic or Turkish, if you like.'

'Mansur is not my dragoman. One might describe him as a fellow traveler.'

The man's deep-set dark eyes met those of Ramses. He inclined his head slightly. It was not a bow to a superior but rather a courteous acknowledgment of an equal.

'We must go now. Lady?' He spoke Arabic, with an accent Ramses was unable to identify. Mme von Eine took his extended hand and turned away, leaving Ramses to trail after them. He was beginning to resent Mme von Eine. She hadn't been openly discourteous, but one small jab after another mounted up. If Mansur wasn't a servant, why hadn't she introduced him? And what the hell did that ambiguous term 'fellow traveler' mean?

He decided he was entitled to a few small jabs of his own. Catching up with the pair, he said, 'I apologize for not being familiar with your work. Was it at Boghazkoy or Carcemish that you excavated?'

'There is no reason why you should be familiar with it' was her cool reply. 'Hittite culture is not your specialty.'

She hadn't answered his question. He persisted. 'Carcemish is by way of being a British concession, and no one has worked there for more than twenty years. Winckler was at Boghazkoy a few years ago. Were you by chance present when he came upon the Hittite royal archives?'

'Unfortunately, no.'

Not present at that time, or not ever at Boghazkoy? Why wouldn't the woman give a direct answer?

'It was, by all accounts, an extremely inept excavation,' he persisted. 'Some of the tablets were lost or stolen.'

He reached for her as she stumbled, but Mansur, on her other side, was quicker. 'Take care, lady,' he said softly, his hand closing over her arm.

Increasingly intrigued by the odd pair, Ramses said, 'I can show you an easier way, a little longer, but not so difficult. Where is your camp located? Or are you staying in the village?'

Mme von Eine's lips parted in a smile. It gave her face a warmth that was very attractive – and, because Ramses was his mother's son, suspicious. Apparently he had passed some sort of test. Or had he failed one, in a way that gave her satisfaction?

'Not in the village, but nearby,' she said.

'This way, then. Mind your footing.'

She turned and addressed a sharp rebuke to the two uniformed men, who were slouching along behind, kicking at scraps of rubble.

'I should have told them to stay below,' she remarked through tight lips. 'They and their fellows are a nuisance, but the authorities insisted I take them with me. For protection, they said.'

'This part of the region is safe enough,' Ramses said. 'But some of the tribes to the north and west can be unruly at times.'

She ducked that implied question too, confining her answer to a brief, 'So I have heard. We mustn't keep you from your work any longer. I know the way from here.'

'It's no trouble at all,' Ramses said truthfully.

Like Emerson, I did believe for a moment that Major Morley was in German pay. The Germans were obviously attempting to extend their influence in the region, but I doubted they were desperate enough to employ such a dullard. However, our agreement to investigate the major provided Emerson with an excuse to do what he wanted to do, as well as a means of accomplishing that aim. Getting permission to work anywhere in the Ottoman Empire was a tedious, frustrating procedure, which could take months and necessitate a personal visit to Istanbul. Emerson had been assured that this problem would be dealt with. Furthermore, working in Palestine would solve the problem of where we were to excavate that winter and would give Emerson an excuse to 'drop in on' Reisner and criticize his procedures.

As a loyal Englishwoman I felt obliged to respond to a personal appeal from the sovereign. (To be sure, the appeal had not been to me, but Emerson and I are as one.) However, my own motives were also mixed. Nefret had been correct about Ramses; if he could get in trouble, he would, and we had not heard from him for some time. The area was unfamiliar to me, and fraught with interest. I shared Emerson's skepticism about the historical validity of some events described in the Old Testament, but by the time of Christ a plethora of documentary evidence verified the accounts of the Evangelists. To a devout Christian like myself, the idea of walking the streets the Saviour had walked, viewing the Mount of Olives and the site of Golgatha, the Church of the Holy Sepulchre and other sacred spots, had an irresistible appeal.

The arrangements were not quickly concluded. In the course of the week following Morley's visit, Emerson was back and forth to London several times. I occupied the time refreshing my knowledge of Scripture. Since in my opinion a rational approach to the Bible is at best confusing and at worst impossible, I had never approached it from the point of view of a historian concerned only with verifiable facts. My research confirmed this opinion.

When Emerson returned from his final visit to London I was in the library. The weather was damp and dreary and I was on the verge of dozing off when the door burst open. I had not expected him back so early. He shook himself like a large damp dog and seated himself behind his desk.

'It is all settled,' he announced. 'We will leave for Jaffa in two weeks.'

'We?' I repeated, raising my eyebrows. 'You and your humble followers, you mean?'

Emerson fingered the cleft in his chin. 'Now see here, Peabody, you know I didn't mean –'

'Yes, you did. Really, Emerson, you ought to know better than to try those tactics on me. They have never succeeded and they never will.'

'But I enjoy seeing your eyes flash and your lip curl,' said Emerson. 'Come now, Peabody, you knew perfectly well how this would work out. You are making lists.'

'And if I have?'

'May I see them?'

'If you will show me yours.'

'Bah,' said Emerson. 'I never make lists, and I keep my notes in my head. I intended to confide fully in you as soon as the arrangements were complete. What did you do with your damned lists? They weren't in your desk, or under the mattress, or –'

'I keep them with me at all times,' I replied, removing a few folded papers from my pocket. 'And the next time you search my desk, please don't make such a mess.'

Grinning, Emerson held out a large calloused hand.

After perusing my lists, he pursed his lips and nodded. 'As I expected, you seem to have matters well in hand. Are you certain you have taken into account the fact that we will be going directly to Jaffa?'

'Naturally. I assumed that we would, since it is the major port for Palestine. Until I know how many of us there will be, I cannot calculate quantities properly,' I went on.

'I assumed you would already have settled that. You and I – You are allowing me to accompany you, I trust?'

'There is no need to be rude, Emerson. I presume you mean to take a crew of our trained men to act as supervisors, but the decision as to which and how many is yours. Selim, of course, and Daoud and . . . As I said, the decision is yours.'

Emerson's well-cut lips twitched, whether from amusement or (more likely) the effort to repress a swearword, I could not determine.

'Selim and Daoud will suffice,' he said. 'With you and me and Nefret and –'

'You propose to take a young, attractive woman into what you yourself have described as a dangerously unsettled region?'

'Come now, Peabody, you are only trying to make difficulties. It is no more unsettled than the Lost Oasis or more dangerous than the western desert.'

'I was unable to prevent her from joining us in that expedition, Emerson. She was determined –'

'And still is. She is of age, my dear. You can't prevent her this time either. Anyhow, I will need her.'

Insofar as Emerson was concerned, that was that. He had no fears for Nefret's safety; would he not be present to protect her from any danger that might arise?

Well, I would also be present. And Nefret was no spoiled miss of English aristocracy. She could use a knife with cold-blooded efficiency if the need arose. I was reasonably certain that if we did not allow her to accompany us, she would set out for Samaria by herself – and get there, too.

'Ramses, of course,' Emerson went on. 'We will take him with us when we leave Samaria.'

'Have you informed Mr. Reisner that we will be visiting him, or do you intend to appear in a burst of glory, heralded, perhaps, by angelic trumpets?'

Emerson pursed his lips and appeared to ponder. 'We could hire a troupe of local musicians to precede us. Drums instead of trumpets, dancing girls –'

'I was joking, Emerson.'

'No, you were being sarcastic. I admit,' said Emerson, baring his teeth, 'it was not a bad effort. As a matter of fact, I have written Reisner. Yesterday.'

So had I. Ten days earlier.

'But, Emerson, suppose Mr. Reisner has not finished his season and doesn't want Ramses to leave?'

'Reisner can hardly refuse my personal request,' said Emerson complacently. 'We will need David too. A skilled artist and draftsman will be essential. Well! I believe we have settled the important points.' He pushed his chair back from the desk and made as if to rise.

Thus far I had succeeded in speaking quietly and rationally. The look of smug complacency on Emerson's face caused my temper to snap. 'We have barely begun,' I cried indignantly. 'Where in Palestine do you intend to excavate? If, as I assume, that is our ostensible purpose, we will have to settle on a specific site. We cannot go wandering around the countryside like a party of pilgrims; nobody who knows you would believe for an instant that you have suddenly become a convert. You have kept me in the dark for days, Emerson, and I insist on answers to all my questions.' My breath control is admirable, but it has its limits; I was forced to pause at that point to inhale, and Emerson let his breath out in a roar.

'Hell and damnation, Amelia! How dare you imply –'

Fortunately for him, a knock at the door stopped him before he said something I would cause him to regret.

'Come in, curse it,' Emerson shouted, at the same decibel level as before.

The door opened just enough to allow Gargery to put his head in.

'There is a person,' he began.

Emerson let out another, even more emphatic, oath. 'I told you we were not to be disturbed. Send him away.'

'I beg your pardon, sir, but the person was somewhat insistent.'

Emerson leaped up from his chair. 'Insistent, was he? I will teach him not to –'

'Just a minute, Emerson,' I said. 'Who is this person, Gargery?'

'A police person, madam.'

From Manuscript H

Ramses had assumed that the accommodations available in villages like Sebaste would not be good enough for a lady of fastidious taste, but he was unprepared for the extravagance of her caravan. The camp was located on the bank of a little stream pleasantly shaded by locust and mulberry trees. In addition to a dozen or more Turkish soldiers, a small army of workmen was present, unloading packing cases and various articles of furniture from the wooden donkey carts. The largest of the tents – her personal quarters, no doubt – had already been set up; porters were carrying in rolled rugs, a mahogany table, and a number of large wooden crates. Did the lady insist that her table be laid with crystal and linen and fine china, like the British traveler Gertrude Bell? He had heard his mother's biting commentary on Miss Bell's aristocratic habits and activities. (At the time she had been scrubbing the walls of a house in Luxor with carbolic.)

Apparently the work wasn't proceeding as rapidly as Madame had expected. She frowned and issued a curt order in Turkish to one of the uniformed guards. The man broke into a run, shouting in the same language. The porters quickened their pace imperceptibly. They were a motley lot, their attire as diversified as their complexions. Their slowness and sour looks gave the impression that this was not a happy group of people.

He was about to speak when she turned and held out a gloved hand. 'Good-bye. Thank you for your company.'

Ramses took her hand, wondering whether he was supposed to kiss it. He settled for bowing over it.

'It has been a pleasure, madam. Are you sure there is nothing more I can do to –'

'Thank you, no. Please give my regards to your distinguished parents.'

She left him standing with his mouth open and his extended hand empty. She had controlled the conversation, neatly ignoring the gambits he had tossed out in the hope of learning something about her travels, past and future. Why should she be so reluctant to admit she had visited Carcemish, or anyplace else, for that matter? If this was a professional pilgrimage, from one archaeological site to another, why had she avoided talking about them?

Obviously her caravan had only just arrived. She might have arrived before it – he could see several horses tethered near the stream – but she had gone straight to the tell, without stopping to rest or freshen up. Why the hurry? Why come at all, for that matter?

His mother claimed that idle curiosity was his besetting sin. She'd be right in this case; it was none of his business what the lady and her party were doing, or why. But he stood watching while a pair of veiled women emerged from her tent to greet her with bowed heads and hands raised in a gesture of respect. They must be her personal servants. A well-bred lady wouldn't travel without them.

When he turned to go back, he saw a crumpled shape of pristine white on the ground just behind him. It was a handkerchief unadorned by lace or embroidery, but it certainly wasn't one of his – too small, too clean, of fine linen fabric. Looking back, he was in time to see the tent flap close.

With a shrug, Ramses put the handkerchief into his pocket.

He went back by way of the village. As he passed the mosque he saw a tall white-clad form slip into the door. None of the villagers was that tall. The man was Mme von Eine's taciturn fellow traveler. He must have slipped away while Ramses was spying on the lady.

Stop looking for mysteries, Ramses told himself. Why shouldn't the fellow take advantage of the opportunity for formal prayers? It was almost midday, and Madame obviously had no intention of moving on that day.

The thin voice of the muezzin came to his ears as he reached the tower. The men had been dismissed and Reisner and Fisher were seated in the shade, eating a frugal lunch. It was the same every day, unleavened bread, cheese, grapes and figs and olives.

'Did you get rid of the lady?' Reisner asked, offering the basket of food.

'I walked her back to her camp. What the devil was she doing here?'

'Damned if I know,' Reisner said placidly. 'People do drop in for a variety of inexplicable reasons.'

'Is she really an archaeologist?'

'Damned if I know.'

'Her name is familiar,' Fisher said, digging into the basket. 'One of the Germans mentioned it, I think – Winckler or Schumacher.'

The name of his predecessor at Samaria brought a scowl to Reisner's face. He had been horrified at Schumacher's sloppy excavation methods, and his vehement criticism had led to Schumacher's dismissal from the site.

'She did seem to be interested in the Hebrew ostraca,' Ramses offered.

'Maybe she's a philologist,' Fisher said.

'Modesty prevents me from mentioning that if that were her field I would have recognized her name,' Ramses said.

'Forget the damned woman,' Reisner said irritably. 'I couldn't care less who or what she is; we'll never set eyes on her again.

Unless,' he added, with a sidelong look at Ramses, 'she invited you to call on her?'

'Why should she?'

Reisner chuckled. 'That little byplay, pretending not to recognize you? She knew, all right. She asked for you.'

'You're joking.'

'Well, not by name. But she asked if my "youthful assistant" could show her around. How would she know I had one if she didn't know who it was?'

'Don't distinguished archaeologists always have youthful assistants hanging about?' Ramses inquired.

'Hmm. Well, back to work. You can start the men on that next section.'

Ramses went back to the dig in a thoughtful mood. Reisner had enjoyed teasing him, but his syllogism made a certain amount of sense. And Madame had known who his parents were.

Later that afternoon, Ramses took a short stroll toward the stream. He didn't venture close to the camp, but from what he could see from a distance there was no indication that a move next day was contemplated. There was no sign of the lady. The tent flap was still closed.

The sun was setting as he went back. Passing the mosque on his way to the village, he was moved by a sudden impulse. He stopped and looked into the courtyard. It was almost time for evening prayers, but the number of worshippers who were assembling was larger than the usual crowd. As far as he could remember, this was not a particular holy day; it wasn't even Friday.

When he reached the dig house he found the others already there. He expected a reprimand – he'd been ordered not to wander off alone – but Reisner greeted him with a cheerful announcement. 'The mail's just come. Several for you.'

The arrival of mail was a cause for celebration, since its delivery was spasmodic at best. After arriving at Jaffa, the nearest port, it sat around until someone, for reasons known only to himself, decided to send it on. Ramses's pleasure was muted by the recollection that he hadn't responded to the last batch of letters. In fact, he couldn't even remember what he had done with them. Anticipating a forcible rebuke, he was about to open the first of several from Nefret when Reisner let out a loud groan. The envelope he had just ripped open was directed in a hand with which Ramses was only too familiar.

'What's the matter?' he asked, expecting the worst.

'He wants,' Reisner said in hollow tones. 'He says . . .'

His voice faded out. Wordlessly he handed over the piece of paper.

As Ramses had expected, his father didn't waste words. 'Will arrive Sebaste shortly to take Ramses with me to assist my forthcoming excavations in Jerusalem. Regards, R. Emerson.'

'It can't be true,' Ramses gasped. 'What excavations, where? Are there any others letters from him?'

He began looking through his own accumulation. A few frenzied moments later they had managed to sort the letters into sequence. Finally Reisner let out a gusty sigh of relief. 'This one from your mother seems to be the most recent. She says instead of coming here to collect you, they want you to meet them in Jaffa on . . . Good Lord, that's less than a week away.'

'She's written the same to me,' Ramses said. 'At least she had the decency to apologize, and gave us more information than Father deigned to do. Have you ever heard of this fellow Morley?'

'No, but he wouldn't be the first to follow some biblical will-o'-the-wisp and rip an archaeological site to shreds,' Reisner replied. 'Your father will make certain that doesn't happen, at any rate.'

He had resorted to his pipe early in the procedure, jaws clenched on the stem. Now he leaned back in his chair and gave Ramses a friendly grin. 'You'd better start getting your gear together.'

Ramses finished reading Nefret's latest – it wasn't so much reproachful as threatening – and handed it to Fisher, who had been collecting them. 'I won't simply walk out on you, sir. They have no right to expect it.'

'That's quite all right,' Reisner said, looking off into space.

'You mean you want me to go?'

'I don't want you to go. But if you don't . . .' Had he only imagined it, Ramses wondered, or had Reisner's tanned countenance paled? 'If you don't, they'll come here.'

Gargery is secretly thrilled at the prospect of 'another of our criminal investigations,' as he deems them, but he feels it his duty as our butler to be offended by the presence of vulgar policemen in our home. (I would not like to imply that we frequently entertain police officers, vulgar or otherwise, but it has occurred on a number of occasions.) In this case his snobbishness was particularly obnoxious, since the police person in question turned out to be our local constable, George Goodbody. Gargery had left him standing in the hall, and one would never have supposed from Gargery's frozen stare that he and George often enjoyed a convivial glass of ale in the bar of the White Boar. Observing poor George's hurt expression, I put myself out to be agreeable.

'How nice to see you, Constable. I trust your family is well?'

George whipped off his helmet and clasped it to his large breast, like a mother cradling a baby. 'Yes, ma'am, thank you. Them pills you gave Mariah for her catarrh worked just fine.'

'Good Gad,' Emerson burst out. 'Have you been dosing the local population, Peabody? You might at least confine your dubious medical experiments to Egypt.'

'They worked just fine, sir,' George insisted. 'Mariah said –'

'Never mind, never mind.' Emerson waved a dismissive hand. 'What do you want, Goodbody?'

Emerson makes George very nervous. (He has that effect on most people.) The constable maintained a convulsive grip on his helmet, and began to stutter. 'Well, sir, it's a peculiar sort of thing, to tell the truth, and I am sorry, sir, indeed, to bother you, but I couldn't see what else to do, since there was nothing on the body except your –'

'Body!' Emerson and Gargery cried in an unmelodious duet. Emerson's tone was one of outrage, Gargery's of delight.

'Stop it at once,' I said, observing that George was about to lose his grip on his helmet. 'Let him speak. Or rather, let me direct the course of the discussion. Just answer my questions, Constable. Is it a dead body of which you speak? A corpse?'

'Well, as it turned out, ma'am –'

'Yes or no?'

'No. Uh . . . as it turned out. But we thought at first –'

It required considerable skill to extract the requisite information, so I will spare the reader Goodbody's ramblings. To summarize: the unconscious body of an unknown individual had been found in a bedchamber of our local inn (the aforementioned White Boar). He had arrived the night before. When the chambermaid brought his morning tea, she found him stiff and stark (I quote Goodbody) on his bed. He was fully dressed except for his coat, which was hanging over a chair. Goodbody, summoned by the agitated owner, had sent for Dr. Membrane, our local medical man, who had examined the body and declared the individual was alive. He had applied a few obvious methods of resuscitation without result and had then taken himself off, remarking that the victim had probably suffered a seizure and that there was nothing he could do. (This diagnosis came after a hasty search of the unknown's garments and luggage had failed to find any money except a few crumpled pound notes.) Nor was there any means of identification except . . .

'This bit of paper,' said Goodbody, extracting it from his breast pocket. 'All crumpled and pushed down in one of his trouser pockets, sir. With your name on it, sir.'

Emerson snatched the scrap from him. 'Curse it,' he remarked.

'So we thought . . .' Goodbody resumed.

'Yes, quite,' I said. 'Very sensible. We will go round at once.'

It is only a short walk from the gates of the estate to the village and the White Boar. I took advantage of the time to point out to Emerson facts he knew quite well but was too irritated to admit. 'It is our duty to inquire into this matter, Emerson; we are obliged, by custom and by our position in this little community, to assume responsibility. Surely it struck you as highly suspicious that there should be no identification on the fellow, not even a pocketbook. Someone must have removed that identification after drugging or attempting to poison –'

Stamping along beside me, Emerson let out a growl like that of an angry bear. I knew what he was about to say, so I raised my voice and went on.

'It is an assumption, I know, but one that fits the known facts. The man was robbed and left for dead. Dr. Membrane would not recognize a case of arsenical poisoning unless the victim held a sign with the word "arsenic" on it. Once he learned the fellow had no means of payment, he left.'

'So now,' said Emerson resignedly, 'we have progressed from poisoning in general to a specific poison. I despair of you, Peabody. I refuse to discuss the situation further until you – er – we have examined the individual.'

The village of Camberwell St. Anne's Underhill consists of a few houses, a forge, a small general store and post office, and the White Boar. It is a picturesque edifice whose main fabric dates from the fifteenth century. Additions and renovations over the years have given it a sprawling look, and the original building has sagged so that the half-timbering slants and the roof appear to be in imminent peril of collapse. However, it is a comfortable hostelry and the bar is the social center for many residents of the area.

Mrs. Finney, the proprietress, was waiting for us at the door, bouncing up and down and wringing her hands. The moment we appeared she burst into agitated speech. Nothing like this had ever happened in the White Boar. (Most unlikely, in my opinion, since the inn had seen the Wars of the Roses and the Civil War, to mention only a few.) What was she to do with the poor gentleman? She could not keep him here. He required nursing. She would not dare go in the room for fear of finding he had passed on. Perhaps he was an escaped murderer! What other sort of person would travel without papers or money?

She fixed trusting brown eyes upon me. Mrs. Finney is shaped like a cottage loaf, very tight around the middle and very full above and below. I patted her shoulder.

'Leave it to me, Mrs. Finney.'

'She will, she will,' muttered Emerson. 'Curse it.'

'Tell me – did not the gentleman sign the register last night?'

'Oh, yes, Mrs. Emerson, ma'am. I will show you.'

The signature was a scrawl, totally unreadable except for an initial letter that might have been a *B*. Or a *P*.

'So much for that means of identification,' I said, returning the register. 'Very well, let us go upstairs.'

The unknown had a small chamber at the back, on the second floor, where the ceiling slanted down at a steep angle. The furnishings were simple but adequate: a blue-and-white-braided rug, a wardrobe, a narrow brass bed, and a set of the usual china necessities, painted with bright red roses. Some of the paint had chipped off.

Emerson came to a halt in the center of the room, the only place where he could stand without hitting his head on a beam, folded his arms, and stared fixedly at the individual lying on the bed.

Someone, presumably the doctor, had loosened his cravat and opened his shirt. The rise and fall of his breast was so slight as to be almost imperceptible. His countenance was pale, but not deathly white, and his lips were curved in a faint enigmatic smile. Beard and hair framed his face like a fallen halo.

'Damnation,' said Emerson.

I had, of course, anticipated that it would be he.

The reverend's heartbeat was faint but steady, his respiration slow but regular. His temperature was normal. There were no needle marks on his arms. When I delicately raised one eyelid, I found myself staring into a placid blue orb, the pupil neither dilated nor shrunken. He lay limp and acquiescent as a stuffed doll as I moved him about.

Mrs. Finney watched the proceedings in pleasurable horror. No doubt she hoped for a convulsion or a death rattle. Two of the maids peeked in through the door, which I had left ajar.

'No smell of prussic acid?' inquired Emerson. 'No gaping wounds? Broken bones? Pools of blood?'

I had proceeded to the next stage of the examination. 'Not a pool,' I said, withdrawing the hand I had inserted between the pillow and the back of the reverend's skull. 'I doubt there was much blood to begin with, and it will have dried by now. Emerson, stop swearing – there are ladies present – and help me turn his head. Carefully, if you please.'

The injury was on the side of the head, above and behind the right ear. Mrs. Finney clapped her hands to her mouth when she saw the small stain on the pillow. 'Cold water and lemon juice,' I said over my shoulder and then addressed Emerson. 'There appears to be no damage to the skull and only a small abrasion. The blow was hard enough to have resulted in a concussion, but the symptoms are not –'

'He may have fallen,' said Emerson desperately. 'Hit his head and –'

'Hit it on what, while he was doing what? Banging his head against the mantel, which is made of wood? Washing his hands in a china basin which is at waist height? There is nothing in the room hard enough or blunt enough to have caused such trauma.'

'Curse it,' said Emerson.

'Oh dear, oh dear,' lamented Mrs. Finney.

In my opinion we had no choice but to remove Papagopolous to Amarna House. Emerson did not share in this opinion but gave in, simmering silently, when I pointed out that we could not leave him on Mrs. Finney's hands, and that the nearest hospital was a good twenty miles distant. I also wanted Nefret's opinion, for though my experience is extensive, her training was more up-to-date. While we awaited the arrival of the makeshift ambulance, I questioned the good landlady and made a thorough search of the room, announcing my deductions aloud and countering Emerson's objections as he made them. (I have found this saves time in the long run.)

According to Mrs. Finney, the gentleman had arrived at six the previous night. He had refused her offer of refreshment and asked not to be disturbed until morning. Therefore the assailant had not waited for darkness, which was not complete until approximately ten o'clock, before entering the room . . .

(Emerson: 'Jumping to conclusions again, Peabody.' Myself: 'He had not unpacked nor prepared to retire. What was he doing for three or four hours?' Emerson: 'Taking a nap, praying, scratching his . . .' Myself: 'Never mind, Emerson.')

The attacker must have entered through the door, since the room was on the second floor and the window was inaccessible from below.

(Emerson: 'Ladder.' Myself: 'How would he know where to find one? How could he ascend without being observed, or climb in through a window without arousing the suspicions of his victim?' Emerson: 'Hmph.')

It would not have been difficult for the assassin to gain entry to the room. He had only to wait until Mrs. Finney left the desk to attend to her other duties, inspect the register to determine Papagopolous's room number, and knock at the appropriate door. Papagopolous would probably have assumed it was the maid. Turning to flee when he recognized his enemy, he had been struck down by a blunt instrument.

(Emerson: 'What blunt instrument?' Myself: 'For pity's sake, Emerson, will you stop making irrelevant objections? A pistol butt, a rock, a stocking filled with sand.')

'Damnation,' said Emerson morosely. 'Very well, Peabody, let us not drag this discussion out. I have not the slightest hope of winning it anyhow. Your hypothetical assailant then removed all means of identification, overlooking only the scrap of paper naming me, and put the body onto the bed in the hope that a cursory examination would conclude Panalopagus – Panepororous – curse it, I cannot be expected to remember such a ridiculous name – that he had suffered a stroke or heart attack?'

'Well done, Emerson.'

'It is good of you to say so. Have you concluded your investigations?'

'Almost.' I had searched the reverend's small valise, which contained only toilet articles, a change of clothing, nightclothes, and a well-thumbed Bible. Turning back to the bed in order to make another examination, I was surprised – and, of course, relieved – to find that my patient's breathing had strengthened and that some color had returned to his face.

'He appears to be regaining consciousness,' I exclaimed, and removed the bottle of sal volatile from my medical bag. Waving it under his nose, I was rewarded by a sneeze so violent that Panagopolous's lower limbs jerked up and his head jerked forward. His eyes opened.

'Excellent,' I exclaimed. 'How do you feel?'

'Feel,' the reverend repeated dreamily. 'I feel, therefore I am. But who, kind lady, am I? Who are you? And who is this Panagopolous to whom you refer?'

'Hell and damnation!' cried Emerson. Hands clapped to her ears, Mrs. Finney fled.

The reverend's physical condition being sufficiently improved, we called for our own carriage and dismissed the ambulance (a nice hay wagon belonging to Mrs. Finney's cousin). He came with us willingly, having concluded – as he informed us – that I must be a dear acquaintance from one of his former lives. Emerson's attempts to correct this misapprehension were met with a shake of the head and an amiable smile. 'Perhaps it was in Athens, when I was preaching to the heathen,' he mused. '"Whom therefore ye ignorantly worship, him declare I unto you . . ." They mocked me, but some believed . . . Were you by chance the woman Damaris?"

'I doubt that very much,' I said gently but firmly. To Emerson I remarked, 'Apparently in that life he was the apostle Paul. Do not argue with him, Emerson, I feel sure his amnesia is temporary and that he will come out of it in due time and with the proper treatment.'

'One of the kindly women in Bordeaux who sewed the crosses on our surplices when I proclaimed the great crusade?'

'Peter the Hermit?' asked Emerson, increasingly intrigued. 'He doesn't suffer from excessive humility, does he?'

Panagopolous ignored this as he had ignored our other comments, and I said, 'People who believe they have lived past lives were seldom anonymous commoners in those lives. Napoleon is a favorite, I believe, and so is Ramses the Second.'

'I must admit,' said Emerson, over the mumbling of Panagopolous, 'that the fellow is rather entertaining. I give you three days, Peabody. If you haven't got him back to 1910 by then, I will inform Captain Morley and request he remove his demented friend from our premises.'

Nefret had returned from her ride during our absence and, having been informed of our mission by Gargery, was waiting impatiently to hear what had ensued. She agreed with me that the reverend should rest, so we handed him over to John, our large and dependable footman, who helped him to his room and into bed. I told Rose to ask Cook to make chicken soup. Panagopolous submitted to Nefret's examination without protest; indeed he seemed quite pleased to be with us, though he was still trying to decide who we were. When he saw Horus, who had pushed his way into the room in pursuit of Nefret, his face flushed with pleasure. 'One of the sacred cats of Bastet,' he exclaimed. 'Her worship was proscribed after I brought Pharaoh Akhenaton to the knowledge of the One God, but do you know, I missed having the cats about.'

After he had eaten a hot bowl of chicken soup, Panagopolous declared he would sleep awhile. Once outside the room, I asked Nefret for her diagnosis. It agreed, of course, with mine. Temporary loss of memory is not uncommon following such a blow on the head. It is usually only a matter of time. Panagopolous's belief in reincarnation probably would not pass off, but I doubted there was anything I could do about it.

Emerson was mightily entertained by the reverend's comments about the so-called heretic pharaoh. 'So he was Moses, was he? Who will be next? I wonder. Abraham? Pope Leo?'

'He knows his history, at any rate,' I replied thoughtfully. 'Few people are familiar with the short-lived religious revolution of

Akhenaton, or the theory that he learned of the sole god from Hebrews dwelling in Egypt.'

'Far-fetched theory, you mean,' said Emerson.

Panagopolous's recovery was slow but sure. On the following day he remembered my name, and the day after, his own – his present name, that is to say. His vital signs were normal and his appetite was excellent. On the third day I deemed him well enough to join us for tea, and the plate of chocolate-iced biscuits proved, as I had hoped, the catalyst.

'I have been here before,' he exclaimed (taking a biscuit). 'Or have I been here all along? What has happened?'

'We were hoping you could tell us,' I replied. I proceeded to recount the circumstances that had led to his present whereabouts. 'Do you remember arriving at the inn?'

Stimulated by my questions (and the consumption of a number of biscuits) Panagopolous was able to recall his arrival, and being shown to a room. He was engaged in prayer (Emerson smirked at me) when a knock at the door interrupted him. Here he paused, his brow furrowed.

'Who was it at the door?' I asked.

Panagopolous shook his head. 'I remember nothing more.'

'Don't distress yourself,' Nefret said, patting his hand. 'It doesn't matter.'

'The devil it doesn't,' said Emerson. 'Well, well. Of equal importance, sir, is the question of what you were doing at the inn. Were you coming to see us? And if so, for what reason?'

'You,' Panagopolous repeated. The lines across his brow were perfectly parallel, like those of a musical staff. In mounting excitement he went on, 'For what reason? Why, to show you the scroll. To give it into your keeping. Is it safe? Is it secret? You must not let him have it!'

The news that no scroll had been found – blurted out by Emerson before I could stop him – brought the reverend to his feet in a fit of incoherent agitation. We put him back to bed and after Nefret had administered a sedative we returned to the parlor for a council of war.

'All is now made clear,' I said. 'Someone was after the famous scroll, the manuscript that describes the location of the treasure. And he found it.'

'Clear as a foggy day,' said Emerson. 'We have no proof that any such scroll exists. This may be a plot designed to convince us that Morley's project is worth supporting.'

'Forgive me, sir, but that is rather far-fetched,' Nefret exclaimed. 'His injury was genuine. Would he go to such an extreme to persuade you?'

'Hmph,' said Emerson, rubbing his chin.

'Neither have we proof that such a manuscript did not exist,' I said. 'When the reverend is coherent again, we can ask him whether he has reason to suspect that any particular individuals wished to gain possession of the scroll.'

'It all depends on his word,' Emerson protested. 'The word of a man who is not in full possession of his senses.'

'Not entirely,' I said. 'Emerson, did you ever bother to look at that brochure Major Morley brought with him?'

'Why should I have done so? It was pure fiction.'

'What did you do with it?'

After excavating in the pile of papers on his desk, Emerson located the pamphlet. We perused it together. A good deal of it did sound like pure fiction – for instance, Morley's grandiose claim that he knew the precise location, within ten feet, of the temple treasure.

'Why ten feet, I wonder?' I said.

'It is a good round random number,' said Emerson, with a curl of his lip. 'He does not supply precise information.'

'One could hardly expect him to disclose the location,' I said fairly.

'You are leaning over backward to be reasonable, Peabody. Look at this photograph, which purports to be that of the notorious scroll. It looks to me like a large knockwurst which has been chewed by mice.'

'The photograph is somewhat unfocused,' I admitted.

'And here,' said Emerson, reading on, 'are the comments of the so-called experts Morley mentioned. Do you recognize any of the names or organizations?'

'They all appear to be foreign. "Le Société Biblique, Marseilles . . ."'

'He made them up,' said Emerson. 'They might impress possible donors who are unfamiliar with the field and who wouldn't bother investigating them. Good Gad, the gullibility of the human race never ceases to astound me. Look at some of the names on this list of contributors. Hardheaded businessmen, some of them, who ought to know better.'

'When emotion supersedes reason, my dear, gullibility must follow. The subject is dear to the hearts of many true believers.'

'Bah,' said Emerson, dismissing the subject. 'What are we going to do about Papapagopolous?'

'Our obvious course is to communicate with Major Morley. In my opinion we ought to have done so before this.'

At my suggestion we dispatched telegrams both to his flat in Mayfair and his club. Not until the next day did we receive a reply from the latter source. 'Major Morley sailed on Tuesday last. Forwarding address, the Augusta Victoria Hospice, Jerusalem.'

Chapter Three

Pacing up and down the drawing room, waving the telegram, Emerson ranted and cursed until I interrupted his tirade with a timely reminder.

'Why should the War Office inform you of Morley's departure? They would have no excuse for detaining him, and you had already informed them that he was not a German agent.'

'I had also informed them that I was prepared to follow the bastard to Palestine, sacrificing my own plans –'

'What plans? You didn't have any.'

Emerson's response was to snatch up his coat and dash out of the room, leaving the door ajar. Seconds later I heard the front door slam.

I knew where he was going – straight up to London by the first train – and why he had departed so precipitately – in order to prevent me from accompanying him. I could only hope that by the time he arrived he would have calmed down enough to be sensible.

I would not have wished to go in any case. Shouting at General Spencer would be a waste of time and breath, and I had too many other things to think about.

We hadn't heard a word from Ramses, though I had sent a series of letters to him and Reisner, each more emphatic than the last. I tried to tell myself that my son's dilatory habits and the uncertain state of postal delivery in the region were probably responsible for his silence, but in my heart of hearts, doubt lingered. I knew my son only too well.

The reverend was an additional source of concern. What were we to do with him? He appeared to be quite happy to remain with us; when I asked, in my tactful fashion, if his family and friends might not be worrying about him, he had replied he had no family, few friends, and no plans whatsoever. I felt about him as I might feel about a friendly, dimwitted stray dog that had decided to move in with us. He could not be cast out onto the street, but he was shedding all over the furniture. (I speak metaphorically.) I found an ally in Nefret, who had taken him under her wing, as she might have done with any other stray.

We had been unable to settle on final plans for our forthcoming expedition (forthcoming, that is, unless Emerson infuriated the War Office into canceling its support altogether). I wanted to arrange for our men to meet us in Jaffa instead of 'stopping off in Egypt to pick them up,' as Emerson had nonchalantly suggested. I had managed to persuade him that going out of our way to remove Ramses in person from the dig at Samaria would be an additional waste of time. He too could meet us in Jaffa. Emerson put up a stiff fight about that, since he had been looking forward to inspecting Reisner's excavations and telling him what he had done wrong, but eventually I prevailed – as I generally do. I had taken the precaution of writing to Reisner myself, putting the matter as a request instead of an order, as Emerson would have done. I felt sure Reisner would oblige me, especially since the alternative would have been to have Emerson descend upon him.

Another little matter Emerson had blandly refused to discuss was the question of additional staff. What we lacked, in my opinion, was an individual acquainted with pottery. To an untrained eye there is nothing more boring than undecorated, broken pieces of pottery. I am inclined to share this view, since I have seen too many of the cursed things. Unlike most of his predecessors, who were primarily interested in impressive architectural features and attractive grave goods, Emerson considered that every scrap of material from a site had potential value and must be noted and preserved. When inscriptional material was lacking, the comparative development of pottery types was sometimes the only way a tomb or occupation level could be dated. I could not argue with this principle, but since I was generally the one in charge of sifting the debris and finding such fragments, my feelings about them were less than enthusiastic. I did not look forward to continuing that labor in an area where the pottery was likely to be even less interesting than in Egypt. However, my inquiries (made without Emerson's knowledge) failed to locate a suitable person. Our staff, therefore, consisted of Nefret, David, and Ramses in addition to our two selves.

Well, we had managed with as few persons before, particularly since our primary purpose was not excavation but preventing Morley from doing the same. The site we had fixed on was on a rocky slope south of the Old City of Jerusalem. The modern name of the village there was Silwan, and there was general agreement that it derived from the biblical Siloam. According to Second Chronicles, King Hezekiah, anticipating an attack by the Assyrians, had dug a tunnel from a spring outside the walls in order to bring its waters directly into the city. The actual tunnel had been found in 1838, thereby confirming the accuracy of the biblical account, and thirty years later a British engineer named Robinson had traversed its entire length, despite the silt that had accumulated over the years. I hoped we would have an opportunity to explore the tunnel, since Robinson's description of crawling on his stomach through its dark, dank, constricted length was quite intriguing. When I mentioned this possibility to Emerson, his response was so profane that I decided not to pursue the matter . . . For the present.

Emerson returned in time for tea, his arrival heralded by his usual slam of the front door and his hearty halloo: 'Peabody, where are you? I am back. Peabody!' I was reading in the drawing room, but I had no difficulty in hearing him.

'Well!' I said, returning his friendly embrace. 'You are in a much better frame of mind than you were when you left. I take it all went well at the War Office?'

'I cannot imagine why you should assume otherwise.' Emerson removed his coat and tossed it in Gargery's general direction. 'Why isn't tea ready, Gargery? I am famished.'

'I suppose you didn't take time to eat lunch,' I said, after Gargery had stalked off and Emerson and I had returned to the drawing room.

'Lunch? Oh.' Emerson pondered. 'No, I can't recall having done so. That bastard Spencer kept me cooling my heels for a good half hour, and then persisted in arguing with me.'

'What about?'

'It was more or less along the lines you had suggested,' Emerson admitted. He took a seat next to me on the sofa and put his arm round my shoulders. 'The bloody idiot said that since we had already agreed we would follow Morley to Jerusalem, he couldn't see that it made any difference when we went, so long as we were there in good time. So I told him –'

'That he was a bloody idiot?'

'More or less. He took it quite well,' Emerson said in mild surprise.

'He was trying to get you out of his office, I expect. Did you ask about the firman?'

'It hasn't arrived yet, but he promised we would have it by the time we reach Jaffa. Ah, there you are, Nefret. And – er –

Papadalopous. He follows her about like a puppy,' he added, in what he probably believed to be a whisper.

'He has been telling me about the fall of Jericho,' Nefret said, giving Emerson a reproachful look.

'Ah,' said Emerson, perking up. 'He was Joshua?'

'He explained that it didn't happen quite as the Bible describes it,' Nefret said.

'It didn't happen at all,' said Emerson, his mood improving even more at the prospect of argumentation, and the sound of the tea cart rattling along the hall. 'The excavators of 1907 concluded that the latest remains dated from 1800 B.C., a thousand years, give or take a century, before your apocryphal Joshua.'

The reverend paid no attention to any of this. His attention was fixed on the tea cakes which Gargery placed on the table.

'I wouldn't mind taking a crack at Jericho myself,' Emerson went on. 'But the Germans still hold the concession, and we must be nearer Jerusalem.'

Panagopolous looked up. 'When shall we depart?'

By dint of Herculean efforts on my part we were ready to depart in less than a week. I was busy from morning till night telegraphing Selim, sending final orders to Ramses, purchasing supplies, packing, and of course making lists. Emerson offered to make our travel arrangements, which I accepted because I didn't suppose he could locate a disreputable old friend in London who happened to own a steamer. He had perpetrated that indignity several times before, but that was in Egypt and the Sudan, where Emerson had only too many disreputable old friends. I took comfort in the fact that he could not have many old friends in Palestine.

The reverend had come to us with only the contents of a single valise, so another of my chores was to outfit him for a prolonged stay in the Middle East. My inquiries as to where he had left the rest of his luggage were met with a blank stare and a murmured reference to the House of David. Sometimes I got quite impatient with him, but Nefret always leaped to his defense. Amnesia was unpredictable. An individual's memory might return, or it might not. Certain parts of it might be lost forever.

Emerson's continual mispronunciation of his surname didn't seem to bother Panagopolous, but Nefret began to find it unacceptable. 'It suggests you don't care enough about him to remember his name,' she complained to Emerson.

'I don't,' said Emerson, surprised that she should have thought otherwise.

'Call him "Reverend,"' I suggested.

'If he is a reverend of any recognized church, I am Attila the Hun,' said Emerson. 'I refuse to give him a title to which he is not – er – entitled.'

'Use his first name, then,' said Nefret, losing patience. 'He wouldn't mind.'

Emerson shook his head. 'How can I contemplate that vacant countenance and address it by the name of one of the greatest of the Greeks? Impossible.'

'It strikes me as an excellent solution,' I said.

Emerson, of course, dismissed this solution with a few ill-chosen words and from then on tried to avoid addressing Mr. Plato directly. However, he accepted Plato's accompanying us with more grace than I had expected. He had managed to have a talk with him, and found him 'uncharacteristically coherent,' to quote Emerson himself. 'He claims to have memorized the information on the notorious scroll,' Emerson explained. 'Not that I believe for a moment that it has any value, but the fellow does seem to be familiar with the former excavations near the Temple Mount, including those of Warren and Bliss.'

'Doesn't that indicate that there is some basis for his claims?'

'Are you determined to provoke me, Peabody?' Emerson inquired with perfect good humor. 'It indicates that he took the trouble to read up on the subject, as any clever charlatan would do. However, I don't see that we have any choice in the matter. We can't expect Gargery and Rose to be responsible for him, and if we abandoned him on a street corner in London, he would only find his way back here.'

So Mr. Plato was at the rail with us the day we set sail from London. Our family had come to see us off, as they always did. The weather was fine, and the sun, only slightly dimmed by the perpetual haze of smoke, illumined the beloved faces: Emerson's brother Walter and his wife, my dear friend Evelyn; their eldest son Raddie; and their daughter, my namesake. Lia's pretty face was set in a forced smile as she blew kisses to David, who stood next to me at the rail of the steamer. His expression was scarcely more cheerful, though he strove as valiantly to smile.

They had been engaged for two years. Her parents had been opposed to the match initially. Their objections were based solely on prejudice of a nature that is unfortunately only too common in our society, for David was the grandson of our late and greatly lamented foreman Abdullah. He was also a fine young man and a talented artist. I had pointed out the illogic and injustice of their position to Walter and Evelyn, and naturally my arguments had prevailed. The young people had several more years to wait, since Lia was only just nineteen and David was determined to establish himself in his career before marrying. This brief interruption of that career, as Emerson insisted, would not be a serious impediment, since archaeological copying was one of David's specialties, and we were certain – said Emerson – to make important discoveries. I had serious doubts about this. We weren't likely to discover exquisitely painted tombs like those in Egypt, or monumental temples covered with carved reliefs. Nothing of the sort had ever been found in Palestine.

There had been no letter from Ramses. I could only hope that he had received ours, and that he would act upon our instructions.

From Manuscript H

Ramses wasn't surprised that Reisner wanted to be rid of him as quickly as possible. Not only did he face the dire alternative of Emerson's critical presence, but the rock-throwing incidents had never been explained. There had been no further attacks, but that might be accounted for by the fact that Ramses had obeyed orders and avoided nocturnal strolls. Mme von Eine's visit might be regarded as another untoward occurrence. Reisner didn't like untoward occurrences interrupting his work, and Ramses really couldn't blame him for suspecting his assistant was somehow responsible for all of them.

However, he was damned if he was going to sneak away before he had tried to find explanations for certain questions, or at least made an attempt to do so. He knew better than to mention this to Reisner; instead he pointed out that he could reach Jaffa in a day and that he would feel less guilty if he could finish his work.

A few furtive forays over the following twenty-four hours told him that Madame was still encamped, with no signs of imminent departure. She kept to her tent, at least during the times when he was watching. On his third trip he narrowly escaped discovery by one of the Turkish guards, who had taken to prowling the perimeter armed with rifles.

Though he was increasingly curious as to what the lady found so fascinating about Samaria, he was just as curious about the nocturnal attacks. They made no sense. He hadn't responded to the languishing glances of certain village maidens, or failed to respect the hours of prayer. As for old enemies, anyone who was really after his blood would have been more persistent.

There was one obvious way of proceeding, and it was something his father would have done long before: Confront someone in authority, and demand an explanation. Sebaste boasted a mayor, of sorts; he was Turkish, and when he wasn't lounging around his ramshackle villa he was extorting extra taxes from the locals. A more likely source was the imam. Ramses had encountered him a number of times but had never spoken at length with him.

The following day was Friday, the weekly day of rest for the men. After lunch, while his superiors were at work on the incessant record keeping, he announced his intention of visiting the bazaar to buy a present for his mother, and got out of the house before Reisner could think of a good reason why he shouldn't. Ramses had learned that the mere mention of his mother had an unnerving effect on his superior.

As he made his way through the narrow streets he wished he had taken the time to look for ancient building materials. His father would certainly quiz him about them. In Egypt it wasn't unusual to find Fourth Dynasty column drums used as steps and limestone blocks from three-thousand-year-old temples forming parts of the foundations of houses. Such was the case here, but the visible remains were scanty enough: columns and Corinthian capitals built into the walls, none of them earlier than the first century. The only structure of interest was the former Crusader Church, now the mosque; thanks to his visits there with pilgrim groups he knew the place well enough to satisfy any inquiries Emerson might make. His father's interest in the twelfth century of the Christian era could only be described as indifferent.

At first glance the open court of the mosque was deserted. Then the sound of snoring led him to a quiet corner, where the imam lay curled up like a cat, enjoying his afternoon nap.

It was the first time he had got a really good look at the man. He was younger than Ramses had realized, now that the cleric's face was relaxed in sleep. His cheeks were pockmarked above his neatly trimmed black beard. Ramses hesitated, reluctant to disturb him, and then reminded himself that he was supposed to be acting as his father would have. He nudged the recumbent form gently with his toe.

The imam opened drowsy eyes. They widened in alarm when he saw who had waked him. He pulled himself to a sitting position and wriggled back until he was pressed against the wall. Ramses begged pardon for disturbing him in his most formal Arabic. 'I am leaving Sebaste soon, reverend sir, and wanted to speak with you before that.'

'Ah, so it is true.' The imam scratched his side and gave Ramses a wary look. Ramses squatted next to the imam, so that their heads were on the same level.

'Yes, it is true. You had heard?'

Ramses wasn't surprised, although his imminent departure had not been officially announced. He knew how quickly news spreads in rural villages. Gossip was one of the chief sources of entertainment and eavesdropping was considered a perfectly legitimate activity.

The imam nodded dumbly. He looked terrified. Since it was obvious that he wasn't going to be invited in for a glass of tea or a cup of coffee, Ramses decided to go straight to the point.

'A few days ago I was walking through the olive grove when someone threw a large stone at me. It had happened once before. Have I been guilty of some unwitting offense?'

His conciliatory tone was beginning to have an effect. The young man relaxed a little, and pondered the question briefly before replying.

'It was a mistake. It will not happen again.'

'A mistake? So you know who was responsible?'

Wrong question, Ramses thought, seeing the fellow's eyes shift. 'I do not ask in order to take revenge or demand punishment,' he said. 'I only want to know the reason. If I have committed an offense, I want to correct it.'

'It was a mistake.' The bearded lips set stubbornly.

'You say it will not happen again? Why not?'

'I must prepare for evening prayers.'

The imam started to get to his feet, still avoiding Ramses's eyes. Ramses put a hand on his shoulder and held him down.

'It is too early for evening prayers. I will not leave until I have an answer, reverend sir.'

'Because . . .' The imam moistened his lips. The words came out in a rush. 'It will not happen again because you are the Brother of Demons, the son of the Father of Curses. We have been told of him. Why should we risk his displeasure, when soon you will all . . .'

He didn't bother to finish the sentence. The mention of his father's name – the last thing he had expected – made Ramses's grip relax. The imam squirmed out from under his hand and fled into the mosque.

Pursuit would have been useless and possibly counter-productive. He had got all he was going to get from that source, and the conversation had given him a new perspective and a potential lead.

That last uncompleted sentence had been illuminating. It wasn't difficult to guess how it would have ended: '. . . when soon you will all . . .' Be gone? Be dead? One or the other, surely. The attacks had not been personal. He was part of a group, 'you' plural.

He went out of the mosque and walked aimlessly along the street, pondering. 'They' had been told about his father, no doubt by one of the Egyptian foremen. Egyptians reveled in tall tales about Emerson; his fame encompassed the entire country, from Cairo to Aswan and out into the Nubian deserts. Stories about Emerson's feats of strength and his imposing presence were accurate enough to require no exaggeration, and many Egyptians regarded him as possessing supernatural powers. It was a reputation Emerson took some pains to encourage. No one who had watched him perform one of his famous exorcisms would ever forget it, for Emerson threw himself heart and soul into his performances. When he cursed an enemy, that enemy was likely to meet an unpleasant end. If fate didn't see to that, Emerson did.

It was a tenuous lead, but the only one he had.

He didn't know where Mitab lived, but everybody in Sebaste knew everybody else, and his description of the man he wanted eventually led him to a house on the outskirts of town. It was a little larger and in better condition than the majority of dwellings; Reisner paid good wages. In many cases the money supported an extended family, which appeared to be the case here. The door opened as he approached, and a mob of children spilled out into the street, yelling and laughing and shoving at one another. The boy leading the group, a bright-eyed ragged urchin of about ten, came to a sudden stop when he saw Ramses. Ramses recognized him as one of the basket boys on the dig.

The other children fell silent, staring. Ramses fished in his pocket and brought out a handful of coins – an irresistible offering in this impoverished part of the world. Jingling them in his hand, he said, 'I have come to see Mitab. Please tell him I am here.'

The boy had heard the stories too. His eyes widened until the whites showed all round the pupils, and for a moment Ramses thought he would bolt. Ramses spoke gently, as he would have done to a nervous animal. 'I only want to talk to him. I mean him no harm. I will wait for him here. Take this, as a gift.'

The word was 'baksheesh.' It was regarded, not as payment for services actual or potential, but as a present from one equal to another. The dignity of the recipient demanded a return present, though in a good many cases the present consisted solely of thanks or freedom from harassment.

It took additional reassurance and the handing over of several more coins before the boy nodded. He went back into the house. Ramses prepared himself for a long wait, but it was only a few minutes later when the boy reappeared and held the door open. Ramses dropped a few more coins into his outstretched hand as he entered.

Cooking smells and the reek of charcoal fires mingled with the stench of too many bodies, animal and human, occupying too small a space. Ramses thought he caught a whiff of hashish too. At first glance he believed the room was unoccupied. Then the curtains covering a door at the back of the room stirred. A worried face peered out.

'I came to ask you a question,' Ramses said. 'One question only, one truthful answer, and then I will go.'

The curtain parted and Mitab edged into the room.

'Only one?'

'Yes. The answer will be locked in my heart, no one else will hear it.'

'You swear?'

'By God and the Prophet, may his name be blessed, I swear.'

'I meant no harm. It was a warning.'

'It was you who threw the stones, then?'

'I meant no harm.'

'Did someone tell you to throw them?'

'They said you must all go. All the unbelievers. Yusuf and I meant you no harm. It was a warning, that you must go before greater harm came to you.'

'Who are "they"?'

Mitab gave him a blank stare. Ramses took out his tin of cigarettes and offered it. 'Take it,' he said. 'Smoke, be at ease. Who are they?'

Mitab accepted the offering with a childish smile of pleasure. 'They are the Those Who Come Before,' he said simply. 'One of them spoke to us in the mosque and told us of the time when we must rise up against the infidels who want to steal our land.'

'When was that?'

Mitab counted on his fingers. Notions of exact time were too difficult; he said simply, 'Two . . . three times – and again . . . I do not know.' He accepted the box of matches Ramses handed him, lit up, and drew the smoke into his lungs. A blue fog of expelled smoke veiled his face. 'But he was angry when he heard what Yusuf and I had done, and we had heard of the great and powerful magician who is your father, and Yusuf and I did not want his wrath to fall on our heads.'

You were in trouble enough already, poor devil, Ramses thought.

Aloud he said, 'I promise you I will appease his wrath. You meant no harm, you will take no harm from him or from me. I will tell the one in the mosque the same, if you –'

'Will you? Will you?' In his excitement Mitab dropped the cigarette. 'I saw that you spoke with him that day on the tell, when he was there with the lady. You know him, you have power over him. I will pray for you at the mosque today, Brother of Demons.'

He picked up the stub of the cigarette from the filthy floor before he vanished behind the curtain.

Ramses hurried back to the dig house. He'd been gone longer than he had anticipated. For once, Reisner wasn't working. Pipe clenched in his teeth, feet on a packing case, he was reading a book whose lurid cover depicted a body with a knife protruding from its chest, lying in a pool of blood – one of his favorite mystery novels. He had decided to take part of the day off too. Looking up, he asked, 'Did you find a suitable gift?'

Wrapped in thought, Ramses had forgotten his purported errand. 'No,' he said.

'The local bazaar doesn't have much of interest. But there's one fellow, a wood-carver, who does some excellent work.'

73

'I didn't see him there today.' His mother would have approved the statement; it was the literal truth.

'I understand our visitor hasn't left yet,' Reisner said.

'Yes. I mean, no, she hasn't.' He had been trying to think of an excuse to leave the house so that he could visit the camp. Now it occurred to him that it might be prudent to inform someone of his destination, if not his purpose. As his mother had once been heard to remark, 'If a good lie won't serve, try telling the truth.' He was wearing the same coat he had worn the day before. After some fishing about he extracted von Eine's handkerchief. 'She dropped this the other day. It would be only courteous to return it, don't you think?'

Reisner inspected the now grubby item and burst out laughing. 'She dropped her handkerchief? I thought women quit doing that fifty years ago. Fisher, what do you think of this? The lady dropped her handkerchief. Didn't I tell you she had her eye on Ramses?'

Fisher had emerged from his room, yawning. He found the handkerchief as amusing as Reisner had; the two of them teased Ramses until he left.

As he made his way toward the camp, Ramses began to have second thoughts about carrying out his plan. Even supposing he was admitted to the lady's quarters, the tactics he had employed with innocent Mitab and the imam, a combination of intimidation and persuasion, were unlikely to succeed with the lady and her enigmatic companion. He pictured himself demanding answers to his questions, and imagined their reactions: a contemptuous smile from the lady, a dismissive shrug from the other.

On the other hand, what did he have to lose? Humiliation was a small price to pay for the chance of satisfying his curiosity.

He came close to paying a higher price when he stepped into view from among the trees and found himself face-to-face with a guard who was pointing a gun at him. Ramses raised his hands and said quickly, 'Is this how you greet visitors? I have come to see the lady. Take me to her.'

He had spoken Turkish. That, as much as the self-confident words, had the effect he had hoped for. The guard lowered the gun. It was only a slight improvement, since his finger was still on the trigger and the gun was now pointing at Ramses's knees. He resisted the impulse to step back out of the line of fire, folded his arms, and fixed the guard with a stern stare.

'Take me to her,' he repeated.

The fellow raised a hand to caress his luxuriant mustache. 'She said to keep everyone away . . . Wait here. I will ask.'

Ramses stood waiting, loftily ignoring the dozens of pairs of eyes focused on him. He didn't have to wait long. The guard was back almost at once.

'The lady is seeing no one. Leave now.'

Arguing with an underling would lower his prestige. Retreating with as much dignity as he could command, he found a spot among the trees where he could see without being seen, and sat down to consider what to do. Didn't she ever leave the tent? Behind him the sun was setting, casting long lingering fingers of light across the shaded landscape. As the shadows deepened the canvas walls of Madame's tent glowed yellow with lamplight; he saw indistinct silhouettes move about inside, too vague to be identifiable. The tent flap opened, and two women came out carrying an object Ramses couldn't identify at first. They tipped it up and water poured out; watching in fascination, he decided it must be a portable bathtub, made of canvas and collapsible. Porters and guards gathered round newly lighted campfires. The smell of food reached his nostrils and reminded him he was getting hungry.

So far his investigations had only raised more questions. Mitab wasn't the most reliable of informants, but Ramses believed he had told the truth – as he saw it. He had identified Frau von Eine's 'fellow traveler' as one of Those Who Come Before – not once, but a number of times – and if poor Mitab's interpretation of their purpose was accurate, they were stirring up antagonism toward infidels and foreigners. From what he had observed so far, it appeared to be a fairly ineffectual operation, but he would like to have found out more about the plan and what part, if any, the lady played in it.

It was now so dark that venturing closer might get him shot, and there were too many people about. He started to get to his feet.

There was no warning, not even the snap of a twig or an indrawn breath. He fell flat under the impact of a heavy body. A hand clamped over his mouth and a voice hissed in his ear.

'For God's sake don't make a noise or you'll get us both scragged!'

The voice had spoken English. Unaccented, idiomatic English.

Ramses forced his taut muscles to relax. After a few seconds the hand over his mouth lifted.

'Who –'

'Ssssh! Let's get farther away. Someone may have heard you fall.'

It struck Ramses as excellent advice. He followed the crawling figure as it made its way rapidly but silently through the grove. When they were some fifty yards away from the camp the other man stood up. Ramses couldn't make out his features, only the general outline of someone wearing a loose dark garment and headcloth. The large leaves of the fig tree against which his back was pressed provided deep shade.

'Well done,' said the unknown, in the same barely audible murmur. 'We should be all right now. But keep your voice down.'

'Who the devil are you?'

After a moment of hesitation the other man said resignedly, 'I'll have to come clean, I suppose, although it's against regulations.

Name's Macomber. We met at Oxford two years ago. Hogarth's rooms at Magdalen.'

Macomber's name meant nothing to Ramses, but Hogarth's did. Distinguished scholar, experienced archaeologist, rabid imperialist, Hogarth despised 'men in the lump' and believed in the God-given superiority of the white 'races' – particularly the British. He gathered round him young men whom he inspired to share his vision, who asked nothing more than to serve their country in the great game of empire, without recognition or reward. Ramses had been invited to join the select circle because of his long years of experience in the Middle East, but he had only attended one of the meetings: he had found Hogarth's beliefs and air of certitude thoroughly offensive. He remembered Macomber now – a pale young man with a shock of yellow hair and eyes that glowed with adolescent fervor as he listened to his mentor hold forth. Officially Hogarth had no connection with any of the intelligence organizations, but Ramses wasn't the only one who suspected he recommended worthy acolytes for recruitment.

'Regulations,' he repeated. 'Which lot are you working for?'

'Never mind that, just listen. I spotted you when you came here with her the first time, been trying to speak with you ever since, but you were always with someone, and I wasn't allowed to leave camp except once or twice to go to the mosque, and –' A rustle of leaves nearby brought him up sharp. He wasn't as cool as he had tried to appear. Ramses was getting uneasy too. If they were found together they would both be in trouble.

'Get to the point,' he said. 'Why is MO2 interested in Mme von Eine?'

'She's high up with the German government. They are trying to move into the Middle East, preparing for war eventually –'

'I know. Be specific. Why her, why here, why now?'

'She's after something. Some talisman, some document, some . . . I don't know what, but she and that fellow Mansur consider it vital in their plot to unify Islam against us. I overheard them talk about other places to look – Jericho, Jerusalem –' He glanced over his shoulder. 'I've got to get back before I'm missed. I'm telling you this so you can pass the word on if something happens to me.'

'Why do you think it might? Has something gone wrong?'

Macomber swallowed noisily. 'Mansur caught me listening outside her tent the other night. He's been watching me ever since. Tell them they were right about von Eine, she's a major player; tell them about the talisman and about Mansur – I don't know who he is or what his particular game is, but they can –'

'Tell them yourself,' Ramses said. The sixth sense his mother often spoke of, the feeling of being watched, was raising the hairs on the back of his neck. He put his hand on the other man's shoulder. 'Come with me now. I can supply you with clothes, you'll be a friend from university on a walking tour.'

'I have to finish the job.' The muscles under his hand stiffened.

Ramses bit back a blistering expletive. 'You've done the job. The chance of your finding out anything more is negligible, especially since you are now under suspicion.'

'One more thing. I overheard them mention the Sons of Abraham. I don't know what it means, but it sounded important.'

To Ramses's heightened senses the night seemed to be alive with movement and sound. 'Don't go back there,' he said urgently.

'I'll be all right.' Ramses's face was so close to Macomber's he saw his teeth flash in a smile. 'I was getting a little . . . Well, you know. It's helped, talking to you.'

He moved quickly, slipping out from under Ramses's restraining hand, and was gone into the night before Ramses could stop him.

Ramses stood listening for several minutes before he dared hope Macomber had slipped back without being spotted. There had been no outcry, no gunfire. His skin was still prickling, though, and he concentrated on moving with exaggerated caution, slipping from shadow to shadow and tree to tree, making use of every bit of cover. It wasn't until he had reached the outskirts of the village that he was able to relax a bit and consider the implications of that extraordinary encounter.

Macomber had not answered him when he asked who had sent him on his mission. Some section of MO2, probably; the Ottoman Empire was under its jurisdiction. Whoever they were, they had no business sending a novice like Macomber out into the field. He could get in deep trouble just for being what he was: a lone Englishman trying to pass as a native of the area, for purposes unknown and therefore threatening. It was a miracle he had pulled it off as long as he had. The knowledge necessary to pass as a member of a completely different culture couldn't be drilled into someone, like cramming for an examination. It took years of living the life, learning the language fluently and idiomatically, and a thousand little things that could mean the difference between success and failure – or life and death.

He could only hope that Macomber had got carried away by the thrill of a secret mission and let his imagination run away with him. What had he actually learned, after all, that could put him in danger? Germany's aspirations in the Middle East were a matter of public knowledge. Vague references to conspiracies and amulets, mysterious phrases . . . It sounded like the plot of a spy novel, and there hadn't been a single hard fact in that rambling narrative. As for the Sons of Abraham, it was the sort of romantic name that might have been selected by a religious cult or one of those strange American fraternal organizations.

He had to put up with more teasing when he returned. 'You've been gone quite a long time,' Fisher said, with a sidelong glance at Reisner. 'Enjoy yourself?'

'I wasn't admitted to the presence,' Ramses said. 'They kept me waiting awhile. I'll just go finish copying the ostraca now.'

'That's right, you're leaving tomorrow,' Reisner said.

Don't you wish, Ramses thought. 'Day after tomorrow,' he corrected. 'If that's all right with you.'

'If you think that gives you enough time. You wouldn't want to be late meeting them.'

'Plenty of time.' Enough, not only to finish tracing the ostraca but to give Macomber a chance to reconsider his offer.

The others set off for the dig early next morning, leaving Ramses bent industriously over his work. As soon as they were out of sight, Ramses headed for the camp.

But when he reached the spot, the camp was gone. Only the blackened scars of campfires and a stretch of trampled earth littered with animal droppings and miscellaneous trash showed where it had been.

He walked slowly across the area where Frau von Eine's tent had stood, on the unlikely chance that something of interest had been overlooked among the scraps of packing material and other debris. He picked up a crumpled paper and smoothed it out. It seemed to be a page torn from a diary or notebook, bearing only a few words in German – the beginning of a letter to *Mein lieber Freund*. A disfiguring blot on the last word showed why it had been discarded. The only other unusual item was a scrap of baked clay, so close in color to the earth on which it lay that he almost missed it. Roughly triangular, it bore a few marks that might have been the wedge-shaped cuneiform script that had been used in the Middle East for international correspondence and diplomatic documents during the second millennium B.C. Could this have been broken off one of the clay tablets employed for such letters? If so, it would explain why Madame had reacted to his casual statement about tablets missing from Boghazkoy, and why she had been so wary of admitting where else her travels had taken her.

All this, inspection and theorizing, was only postponing the discovery he hoped he wouldn't make. He put the scrap in his pocket and moved on. The ashes of the fires were cold. They must have left before dawn, not lingering to cook breakfast or make coffee. It would have taken a long time to break camp, pack the lady's furniture and belongings, and load the carts, so they must have started not long after . . . The sky was clear and the sun was bright, but a shiver ran through him.

He searched the area, walking in widening circles, his eyes on the ground. He didn't know what he was looking for until he found it – a rectangle of recently disturbed soil, on the edge of the encampment. The dirt had been trampled down, but it was still loose. He dug with his bare hands. He'd only got down a few feet when his fingers touched something hard. Hard and cold. He scraped away enough of the soil to expose a pair of bare feet.

It was all he needed for identification. Some of the brown dye had worn off and the soles, though calloused, lacked the thick integument acquired by years of going without shoes or sandals. He sat back on his heels, swallowing strenuously. He should have made Macomber come back with him, by force if necessary. He should have realized that the faint sounds he had attributed to birds or wind meant that they were being watched.

Squatting there in a blue funk, struggling with guilt, wasn't doing any good. He tried to remember what his mother had said about rigor mortis. The bare feet were ice-cold but flexible. Did that mean rigor had set in and was starting to pass, beginning with the extremities? If so, Macomber had been dead for approximately twelve hours, give or take an hour. He had been killed shortly after he had left Ramses.

He didn't want to do it, but he forced himself to dig at the other end of the rectangle. There was no doubt in his mind that Macomber had been murdered, but there were other things he needed to know.

He had dealt with a number of dead bodies, not all of them mummified. His parents had a way of attracting 'fresh-dead people,' as their reis Abdullah had called them. He had thought himself fairly hardened, but when he drew aside the dirty cloth that covered the face and saw Macomber's empty brown eyes looking up at him, he had to draw several long breaths before he could go on.

The cause of death was only too obvious. Macomber's throat had been cut. His tattered robe was drenched with blood. Ramses wondered why they had bothered to pull a fold of cloth up over his face before they dumped the dirt on him. Perhaps even a murderer preferred not to look at the eyes of the man he had killed.

He forced himself to dig out the torso, looking for other injuries. He found nothing that would indicate Macomber had been tortured before he was killed. That didn't necessarily mean they hadn't questioned him. Some methods of causing pain left few marks.

He drew the cloth back over the dead face, replaced the dirt and stamped it down. Removing the body to a more seemly place would necessitate explanations he couldn't give, and delay he could no longer afford. The only thing he could do for Macomber was get to Jaffa as quickly as possible and pass on the information he had been given – information whose importance and accuracy had been verified in the worst possible way.

If he could get to Jaffa.

The conveyance was the fastest the village had to offer, a once-elegant carriage drawn by horses instead of donkeys. The proud owner also hired out riding horses and operated a delivery service of sorts between Sebaste and Nablus, the capital of the district. A hazy sunrise lit the clouds to the east as Ramses finished loading his gear into the carriage. Abdul Hamid had turned up before dawn, but anxious as he was to be off, Ramses preferred not to be on the road during the hours of darkness. A firm handshake and a clap on the back from Reisner, a hearty 'Have a good trip' from Fisher; he swung himself up onto the seat beside Abdul Hamid.

The road descended and climbed again; the carriage rattled alarmingly as the horses broke into a trot. Ramses had forbidden the use of the whip, to the openmouthed astonishment of Abdul Hamid. 'You told me we must be in Jaffa before nightfall,' he protested. 'We can go faster, much faster.'

'Not on this road.' Ramses caught hold of the seat as the carriage swung wildly around a flock of goats. Traffic wasn't heavy, but there were enough pedestrians, donkey riders, and varied animal life to bring out the best – or worst – in his driver. Abdul Hamid stopped for neither man nor beast, and the carriage had long since lost any springs it might once have possessed.

The carriage rounded a curve. Straight ahead Ramses saw the houses of a small village and the minaret of a mosque. He saw something else – a line of uniformed men drawn up across the road where it narrowed to enter the village.

Abdul Hamid let out a strangled bleat and yanked on the reins. Ramses had approximately thirty seconds to decide what to do. Luckily the options were too limited to require prolonged thought. The country on either side was open and the soldiers carried rifles. They were stopping every vehicle. Flight and concealment were both impractical.

Abdul Hamid had stopped ten yards from the roadblock. He looked wildly from side to side. Turkish soldiers meant trouble, even for the innocent.

His hands tightened on the reins, and as the soldiers approached them, Ramses said softly, 'Don't try it. Let me do the talking.'

He sat still, looking down his nose at the officer in charge. 'Why are you stopping us?' he asked in his best Turkish.

'You are the one we are looking for. Get down and come with me.'

He could have tried bluster: 'I am a British citizen and you have no right to detain me.' That would almost certainly be the wrong tack. He had recognized two of the men. They were Turkish army, all right, but they were also part of Frau von Eine's personal guard.

He reached in his pocket and pulled out a handful of the miscellaneous currencies used in the area. 'Perhaps we can come to an agreement.'

The initial effect was encouraging – an exchange of interested glances and a moment of hesitation by the officer. Only a moment, though.

'You will come with me,' he repeated, and reached for Ramses's arm. Ramses pushed his hand away and descended with dignity, taking his time. He was several inches taller than the officer, including that worthy's fancy fez, and he took full advantage, looming as best he could, his lip curling.

'Take me to your superior,' he snapped. 'At once.' To Abdul Hamid he said curtly, 'Wait for me.'

'Oh, he will wait,' said the officer. 'You may be sure of that.'

Three of them, including the officer, trotted along with him as he strode into the village. The other soldiers remained with the carriage. The street was typical of such villages, narrow and littered, walled in by the facades of the houses that lined it. It was a gloomy, tunnel-like stretch, made even gloomier by the clouds that were gathering. They passed one or two slitlike side passages and Ramses fought the urge to dart into one of them. Common sense told him it would be jumping from the frying pan into the fire – being trapped in a cul-de-sac or dead end. Anyhow, he couldn't run out on Abdul Hamid. He'd brought the poor devil into this and in the unlikely event that he could get away Abdul Hamid would be in for it.

Their destination was a house next to the mosque. It was a trifle more pretentious than the others they had passed, with barred windows and a heavy ironbound door. The door opened as they approached. The man who had opened it was Frau von Eine's companion.

Mansur stood back and gestured to Ramses to enter. The soldiers crowded in after him and took up positions on either side of the door. Another gesture to Ramses indicated the divan against one wall. There wasn't much else in the room, only a few cushions, a low wooden table next to the divan, and a brazier that gave off an acrid-smelling smoke and just enough light to make out Mansur's features.

Ramses didn't even think of trying to make a break for it. Nor would bluster serve him here. He took the seat indicated and waited for the other man to speak first.

Mansur clapped his hands. A servant entered through a curtained doorway, carrying a tray which he put on the table. He was neatly dressed in a brightly embroidered vest over a brown galabeeyah, with red slippers on his feet. He gave Ramses a quick sidelong glance before salaaming profoundly to Mansur and backing out of the room.

'Would you care for tea?' Mansur asked, indicating the glasses on the tray.

It was the first time Ramses had heard him utter more than a muttered word or two. His voice was low and melodious, a deep baritone. Even more surprising was the fact that he spoke educated English, with only the faint trace of an accent.

'Oxford?' Ramses inquired, taking one of the glasses.

'Cambridge.'

'And before that?'

Mansur's eyes narrowed, and Ramses explained disingenuously, 'What I meant to say was that your English is excellent.'

'How kind of you to say so.'

'To speak a language so well, most people require years of study, starting at an early age.'

Mansur took a seat beside Ramses and helped himself to tea.

'We can go on fencing, if you like, but it would save time if we went straight to the point. What do you want to know?'

Ramses raised his eyebrows. 'You want *me* to ask *you* questions? I expected it would be the other way round.'

The other man's thin lips curved in a smile. With the turban low on his brow and his beard hiding the outline of chin and jaw, and those deep-set, hooded eyes, his face was to all intents and purposes masked, no feature that might have expressed his feelings exposed. 'Still fencing. I don't have to question you. Last night you met a man who was a British spy. He told you a number of things he was not supposed to know. Please don't bother to equivocate. I let him leave the area so that I could follow him.'

'You couldn't have overheard what he said to me,' Ramses said.

'I heard enough. He had only suspicions, no proof, but if those suspicions were passed on, an investigation might interfere with our work.'

'So you killed him. Was it you who cut his throat?'

'Why should you think that? These vagabonds one hires are a quarrelsome lot.'

And by the time someone went looking for the grave, the body would no longer be there.

Mansur finished his tea and put the glass onto the tray. 'In any case,' he continued, 'his disappearance won't be discovered for some time. By then we will have finished our work and be . . . elsewhere.'

'And how do you propose to prevent me from reporting his death? If you kill me –'

'My dear chap!' Another fleeting, sardonic smile. 'I wouldn't do anything so foolish, even if my civilized instincts did not forbid it. Your disappearance would be known immediately, and your devoted family would move heaven and earth to find out what had become of you. I spent some time in Egypt and I know your father's reputation – and that of your mother. They would learn that you had had encounters with our group, and that we don't want. No, my young friend, you will have to accept our hospitality for a brief period.'

Ramses sipped his tea. His mouth was dry, but he was beginning to entertain a faint, cowardly hope that he might survive a little longer. He didn't believe in Mansur's 'civilized instincts,' but his reasoning made sense. There was one large flaw in his plans, though. Ramses debated with himself as to whether he should point it out.

He might have known his wily adversary had anticipated that too. 'The same problem will arise if you don't turn up in Jaffa at the appointed time. Oh, yes, we know all about that. We have allies in the village. They listen to your conversations, they read your letters. Therefore you must write to your parents and make some excuse for not meeting them. We will see it is delivered.'

'What excuse? I can't think of one they would accept.'

'A secret mission?' Mansur suggested, eyebrows elevated. 'You have a reputation, I believe, for independent action. The less specific your excuse, the better. Perhaps the best thing would be for you to say something like, "Have been delayed. Will explain when I see you. Go on to Jerusalem."'

So even the contents of his parents' letters were known. How many villagers could read English that well? Maybe the letters had been 'borrowed' and shown to Mansur or Madame. Their temporary absence might not have been noticed.

'They won't buy that,' Ramses said, knowing that they probably would. For some reason his parents had a low opinion of his common sense.

'Are you trying to persuade me to kill you?' Mansur inquired. 'I won't do that, for the reasons I have explained. But I can make life very unpleasant for you while you are in my custody if you refuse to cooperate.'

'Civilized men don't torture prisoners,' Ramses pointed out.

'I don't believe in torture. It is ineffective. A man in pain will say whatever he believes his questioner wants to hear. Come now, be sensible.' He leaned forward, his deep-set eyes intent. 'As I said, you have no proof of wrongdoing on our part. Our mission is secret, but it poses no threat to anyone. In fact, if our plans succeed, many people will be helped. One day soon I will be able to tell you about it and it may well be that you will find yourself in sympathy with our aims.'

'Then why not tell me now?'

'I have taken a vow of silence.'

Can't argue with that, Ramses thought. Nor with any of the other vague hints Mansur had dropped. He remained silent, and Mansur went on, 'You will not be harmed and you will have the usual comforts. And –' This time the smile was broader. 'Who knows, you may find a means of escape.'

'There is that,' Ramses agreed. Against all his inclinations he was inclined to believe the other man's assurance that he would not be harmed. Anyhow, what choice had he? Assuming he could overpower Mansur and three men carrying rifles, which was not so much unlikely as impossible, where would he go?

'I'll write the letter,' he said. 'Have you paper and pen?'

'No. But I expect you have, in your luggage if not on your person. Shall I have your suitcases brought in?'

'No need.' Ramses reached in his pocket, where he carried a small notepad and pen. He'd never got over the habit of cramming his pockets with various objects picked up during his daily activities. After removing a fragment of stone with a carved leaf – which he had forgotten to leave at the dig – a handful of figs, a coiled length of string, and the clay fragment he had found, he located the notepad. When he took it out, something else came with it – a crumpled piece of white linen.

'You may as well return this to Frau von Eine,' he said, handing it over. 'She dropped it the other day. Or will I have the opportunity to do so myself?'

Mansur stared at the motley objects on the table. After a moment Ramses rephrased his question. 'Will I be encountering Frau von Eine in the near future?'

'I cannot say.'

'You mean you will not say, or that her future activities are not known to you?'

'Write,' Mansur said. He picked up the handkerchief and slipped it into the breast of his robe.

Ramses wrote as Mansur dictated, almost word for word, the same message he had suggested earlier, tore the page from the notepad, and handed it over.

'Now what?' he asked.

'You accompany us to . . . where we are going.'

'What about Abdul Hamid?'

'Who? Oh, your driver. He will return to Sebaste tomorrow, having left you, at your request, with a group of pilgrims whom you encountered in Nablus and who were planning to travel to Jaffa next day.'

'That should muddy the trail nicely,' Ramses said with grudging admiration. 'I presume Abdul Hamid will be well bribed.'

'A combination of greed and fear will convince him to stick to his story.' He rose to his full impressive height. 'We must be on our way.'

In the enclosed courtyard behind the house were a wooden cart, into which his suitcases had already been loaded, and a yaila, one of the traveling conveyances more common in Syria than here. Drawn by a pair of horses, it was shaped like a tube, in which the passenger lay at full length on his bedding. At the back was a platform for a servant, who supplied the traveler with food and drink. Substitute guard for servant, and the enclosed conveyance was admirably suited for transporting a prisoner. There were plenty of guards available – at least a dozen muscular men in local garb, as well as the three soldiers.

Ramses looked inquiringly at his companion. The yailas had room enough for two, if they were very friendly, but he didn't suppose Mansur would be careless enough to let him travel without restraints of some kind. So far he had proved himself a thorough sort of fellow.

'I apologize for the blindfold,' Mansur said, beckoning one of the guards. 'If you will give me your word as an Englishman that you will not attempt to remove it or try to escape . . .'

He left the sentence incomplete.

'That wouldn't be playing the game, would it?' Ramses inquired.

From Mansur's expression, or lack thereof, he realized Mansur hadn't understood he was being ironic. That was one of the problems with humor. Sometimes it didn't translate well.

He submitted to being blindfolded and having his hands tied behind him. Mansur himself helped him stretch out on the mattress that had been provided.

'I can give you something to make you sleep,' he said, for all the world like a conscientious physician to a patient. 'The time will pass more quickly.'

'No, thank you.' There was always a chance he would overhear something that would give him a clue as to their destination or their real purpose.

And the possibility of getting back at Mansur for his infuriating condescension.

Chapter Four

I had landed at Port Said and at Alexandria and thought myself prepared for the mingling of races and the general lack of organization that characterizes ports in that part of the world; but I had never seen anything quite so disorganized as the port of Jaffa. It is the great pilgrim port for the Holy Land. Earnest American Protestants, Bibles in hand, mingle with turbaned Moslems, Orthodox Jews, bearded Greek Orthodox priests robed in black. The city, ringed in by crumbling walls, clings to the slopes of the hill rising from the harbor. On the brow of the hill, a hundred feet above the harbor, stands the oldest part of the ancient city. An ancient city indeed, for it was already flourishing when Thutmose III conquered it in the fourteenth century before Christ. It has had a rich and bloodstained history. (Alas, the two are often the same.) Phoenicians and Philistines were followed in turn by the Assyrians, the Greeks, and the Romans; it was a Christian bishopric until conquered by the Arabs in the eighth century. Crusaders succeeded the followers of Mohammed, and Saracens succeeded Crusaders; eventually the Ottoman sultans reduced the city to ashes and, as was their normal habit, put the inhabitants to the sword.

The harbor was not deep enough to allow large steamers to dock, so we were taken ashore in little boats – a somewhat unnerving procedure, since the boats bobbed up and down and the crewmen thereof lowered passengers and luggage alike with more haste than care. As our boat approached the shore I beheld a familiar face towering above the crowd.

'There is Daoud,' I cried, waving. 'And yes – Selim too.'

'You sound surprised,' said Emerson, sounding surprised. 'You told them to be here, didn't you?'

Daoud was something of a dandy, but I had never seen him so magnificently dressed as now, his elegant robes of the finest saffron wool, his sash of striped silk with a fringe a foot long. His intricately wound turban sported an ornament six inches across that sparkled with crimson gems.

'Goodness gracious, Daoud,' I exclaimed somewhat breathlessly, as he lifted me clean off my feet in a hearty embrace. 'How splendid did you look!'

'It is in your honor,' Daoud explained proudly, embracing the rest of us in turn. Emerson submitted with a resigned roll of his eyes; he had learned it was useless to resist Daoud's demonstrations of affection. Having greeted Nefret and David, Daoud inspected Mr. Plato with amiable curiosity. Nefret introduced them, adding that the reverend was a friend and a member of our group, whereupon Daoud embraced him as well, to Mr. Plato's obvious alarm.

'Where has Selim got to?' I asked, straightening my hat.

'He is coming. With the porters.'

The sight of Selim wrung a mild expletive from Emerson. If Daoud had dazzled our eyes, Selim blinded them. His turban pin was larger and more sparkly than Daoud's, his robes consisted of several layers of silk, each finer and more colorful than the next. Through his sash had been thrust an ornately decorated sword, the hilt ablaze with gems. The gems were – at least I hoped they were – glass, but they made an impressive show.

Another round of embraces followed. 'What the devil is this?' Emerson demanded, indicating the silk, the gems, and the sword.

Selim grinned. He was a handsome fellow, closely resembling his nephew David except for the beard he had grown so that his men would respect him more. 'You will see, Father of Curses. Will you come now? Daoud!'

'Yes, yes,' said Daoud, beaming. He raised his voice in a shout. 'Make way for the Father of Curses and his wife the Sitt Hakim and for Nur Misur, the Light of Egypt!'

He made sure everyone would make way by preceding us, moving with the ponderous inevitability of an avalanche and gently but firmly moving aside anyone in his path.

One face I had hoped to see was conspicuous by its absence. Turning to Selim, I said, 'Where is Ramses? I ordered him to meet us here and gave him our date of arrival.'

'He has not come, Sitt Hakim.'

'Nor any message from him?'

'Not to me, Sitt. But it may be that there is a message waiting for you at your hotel. We came here from Kantara on the train two days ago, and I made certain that your rooms would be ready for you.'

'Aren't you and Daoud staying there?'

'No, Sitt. The hotel is for Americans and Europeans only.'

Observing my frown, Selim said tactfully, 'Excuse me, Sitt, I must look after the porters. They are not honest people.'

I expected that we would have some little delay passing through customs. In Egypt we are well known; the mere sight of Emerson is enough to inspire instant obedience from officials, and shouts of welcome from those who recognize him. We had a great deal of luggage, some of which was bound to arouse the suspicion or the cupidity of the inspectors: cameras and photographic plates, tents and sleeping equipment, notebooks and painting materials, medical supplies and what would probably strike the customs officials as an unnecessarily large quantity of soap. But when we approached the counters with their long lines of waiting passengers, I understood the import of our friends' attire.

Shouting – and sparkling – Daoud led us past the staring tourists. 'Make way for the Father of Curses and his lady, the Sitt Hakim. Make way for Nur Misur, the Light of Egypt, and for the great and powerful Brother of Demons!'

David, walking beside me, let out a strangled exclamation. 'That's not me!'

'That is not I,' I corrected. 'Perhaps Selim was unable to think of an appropriately impressive sobriquet for you.'

'But that's what they call Ramses,' David protested.

'No one here knows that,' I said. 'And it seems to have made quite an impression.'

People were staring and whispering. I turned my head to look at Emerson, who was escorting Nefret and Mr. Plato. As I had expected, he was bowing from side to side, and raising one hand in a gesture of regal condescension. Behind him trotted a long line of loaded porters, with Selim bringing up the rear. I couldn't see much of Selim; I wondered if he was brandishing his sword.

We swept past the crowd of lesser beings and out of the customs shed, the throngs and even the guards at the door parting before Daoud like the waters of the Red Sea.

'Keep moving,' said Emerson, taking his place at my side and gesturing to David to fall back with Nefret.

'Carriages – carts,' I gasped, for our pace had quickened.

'Just follow Daoud.' Emerson gave me his arm. 'No doubt the officials have been well bribed and thoroughly intimidated, but if we stop they may have second thoughts.'

From the quayside we climbed the hill into the old town, and I understood the need for so many porters. Carts and carriages would have had a difficult time passing along the narrow and winding streets. Evidently donkeys did pass through them, for the evidence of their presence littered the street, along with rotting fruit and other signs of habitation.

We emerged from the old town into a rather pleasant open square, with (as I was later to learn) army barracks on one side and the residence of the kaimakam (governor) on another. Our hotel was just off the square. Leaving the porters to wait outside, we entered the lobby. Everything in the place was brown – a drab olive carpet on the floor, weak-coffee-brown paint on walls and ceiling, rusty brown upholstery on the chairs and single sofa, a few pathetic potted plants whose leaves had not a trace of green. They were, in short, brown. The walls were hung with notices announcing the hours of meals (no seating after the designated time), the availability of dragomen and porters (arrangements must be made through the manager), a pointed request for payment in British pounds or American dollars, and so on. The most conspicuous notice proclaimed proudly that this was a Temperance Hotel. Behind the registration desk stood a man wearing a morning coat and a supercilious sneer. He could only be British. The sneer faded when Emerson stamped up to the desk and addressed him in a peremptory basso.

'The rooms of Professor and Mrs. Emerson and their party.'

'You are Professor Emerson?'

'Who else would I be? Who the devil are you?'

'Er – the manager of this hotel, to be sure. My name is Boniface. Mr. Boniface.'

He held out his hand. Emerson stared at it as if he had never seen such an object before. 'Come, man, don't stand there gaping like a fish; Mrs. Emerson is not accustomed to being kept waiting. Show us to our rooms at once.'

Visibly unnerved, the manager emerged from behind the desk and led the way to our rooms. Emerson, who takes pleasure in annoying pompous persons, followed close on his heels, so that the manager was almost running when we arrived at our destination. The accommodations consisted of three sleeping chambers on the first floor. The furnishings of the room assigned to Emerson and me were a remarkable combination of European and local wares: a purple plush sofa, toilet articles of porcelain behind an ornately carved wooden screen, and a hideous brass bedstead covered with a spread of woven fabric. Gloomy sepia photographs of Jerusalem and Nazareth were interspersed with even gloomier copies of religious paintings. The one hanging over the bed was a particularly realistic rendition of the Crucifixion.

Accustomed as I was to the elegance of Shepheard's and the Winter Palace, I spoke only the truth when I remarked, 'If this is the best you can offer, I suppose it will have to do.'

Nefret's room, next to ours, had a green plush sofa and a hand-tinted depiction of Saint Veronica wiping the face of Jesus as he knelt beneath the weight of the cross on the Via Dolorosa. Quite a lot of red paint had been employed.

We left Nefret studying this work of art with pursed lips, and inspected the third room, which contained two beds and very little else.

'The two – er – gentlemen will share?' said the manager, eyeing David askance.

'I booked four rooms,' I said. 'We are expecting our son, who will share with Mr. Todros. Are you certain he is not here or that there is no message from him?'

'What name?' Boniface asked nervously.

'Emerson, of course,' said my husband. 'Good Gad, Peabody, the fellow appears to be lacking in his wits.' Thrusting his face close to that of the manager, he articulated slowly and loudly, as he might have spoken to a person whose hearing was deficient. 'Send. Porters. With luggage. Now.'

'Stop that, Emerson,' I said, tiring of the game. 'Mr. Boniface, send our – our attendants here as well, and please look to see whether there are any messages for us. Until our son arrives, these two gentlemen will occupy the third room.'

Boniface fled, mopping his brow, and we all returned to the room assigned to Emerson and me, which was the largest. Emerson's first act was to remove the painting of the Crucifixion and put it at the back of the wardrobe.

By the time the porters had delivered our bundles and we had unpacked our suitcases, we were all ready for a spot of luncheon. The hotel boasted a dining room, but we were in full agreement with Emerson when he refused to patronize it.

'The food will be the worst of bad British cooking – boiled beef and brown soup – and that pompous ass of a manager probably won't admit Selim and Daoud. Nor will we be able to get a beer or a glass of wine. Confounded temperance! There must be a decent place to eat in the bazaar.'

The manager's coat-tails whisked out of sight as we passed through the lobby. 'I can't understand why we haven't heard from Ramses,' I said uneasily. 'Could a message have been mislaid?'

'The pompous ass swore he hadn't mislaid any messages,' said Emerson, taking my arm. 'I am inclined to believe him.'

So was I. Emerson had reduced Mr. Boniface to such a state, he would have written a note himself if he believed it would satisfy us.

'The boy will turn up,' Emerson went on. 'If he doesn't, we'll go after him. You know how uncertain the mails are in this part of the world. He may never have received your letters.'

The square was crowded with strollers enjoying the balmy air and the pretty flower gardens. Led by Selim, we headed for the old town where, he assured us, there were several adequate establishments – though not, of course, as good as those in Cairo and Luxor.

'I never knew you were such a snob, Selim,' Nefret said, taking his arm. As the pair strolled on, several passersby stared, frowning, and one female said in a strident American accent, 'She's holding his arm, Hiram, just as if he was a white man.'

I did not hear Hiram's response. Letting Emerson go on ahead, I had stopped to admire a particularly attractive bed of marigolds when someone jostled me and I felt a hand press against me. Springing instinctively into defensive mode, I spun round and raised my parasol.

'What is it, Peabody?' Emerson asked, hastening to my side.

Gazing about, I was unable to determine which of the other pedestrians had touched me. No one hastened away; no one looked guiltily in my direction. Soldiers wearing Turkish uniforms, sober pilgrims in shades of black and gray, a Greek patriarch, local residents in a variety of headdresses . . . Surely none of them would have accosted me so rudely or attempted to pick my pocket. My walking costume had several of them, two set into the seams of my skirt and one on either side of my coat. All my valuables were in my handbag; the pockets of my coat contained only a handkerchief and a guidebook.

'I must have been mistaken,' I began. And then my exploratory fingers contradicted the statement. Nothing had been taken from my coat pockets. Something had been added. Quickly I disengaged it from the fold of my handkerchief.

It was a small packet, less than two inches square and not very thick, wrapped in white fabric and tied with a bit of string.

The others gathered round, gazing curiously at the object and asking questions. I began plucking at the string, which was tightly knotted. Emerson snatched the packet from my hand.

'Come over here,' he said, and led the way to a shady spot under an orange tree.

'Someone slipped it into my pocket,' I replied, in answer to Nefret. 'Just now. Emerson, be careful. It may contain a sharp blade, or a poisonous insect, or –'

'Balderdash,' said Emerson. Opening his pocketknife, he cut

through the string, which he handed to David. After returning the knife to his trouser pocket, he unwrapped the folds of cloth, his big brown hands moving with the delicacy he employed with fragile artifacts. At last the contents lay exposed.

'It appears to be a piece of paper,' said Emerson. 'Folded and refolded.'

'A message,' Nefret exclaimed, reaching for it. 'Perhaps it's from Ramses.'

Emerson pushed her hand away. 'Be careful. It may contain a sharp blade or poisonous insect.'

'Oh, for pity's sake, open it,' I said irritably.

We crowded round Emerson, heads together, as he unfolded the paper. I recognized the handwriting at once. Since Ramses's handwriting is virtually indecipherable, it took us some time to make out all the words.

'Have been delayed. Will explain when I see you. Proceed to Jerusalem and sit tight. Will meet you there.'

'Confound the boy,' I exclaimed. 'What is he up to now?'

Emerson refolded the note and put it in his pocket, along with the length of string and piece of cloth.

'Let us go on,' he said. 'We need to discuss this.'

The eating establishment Selim had found was on the outskirts of the bazaar. Emerson was pleased to learn that alcoholic beverages were available, since as Selim informed us, the place was patronized not only by locals but by the more adventuresome brand of tourists. There weren't many of the latter, only a young couple in one corner bent over a guidebook. The proprietor greeted us in person, bowing repeatedly, and showed us to a table.

After Emerson had ordered a glass of beer and we had been proudly presented with actual written menus, Nefret burst out, 'Let me see that again, Professor.'

We passed the note round. 'Perhaps,' said David, 'it is not from Ramses.'

'It is his handwriting,' I said. 'And the paper appears to be a page torn from one of his notebooks.'

Emerson took out his pipe. 'He wrote it. But he may have been under duress. Curse it,' he added, 'we need more light. It is dark in here.'

A blue haze of smoke filled the low-ceilinged room. Upon being summoned, the proprietor produced a candle which he placed in the center of the table. It didn't help a great deal, nor did the smoke from Emerson's pipe, at which he was puffing furiously.

'If he was a prisoner,' David said, in response to Emerson's comment, 'he gives no indication of it.' He held the paper close to the candle flame. 'No cryptic hieroglyphs, no code message.'

'He could hardly do that if the person who dictated the note was standing over him,' I said. 'But let us not wander off into wild avenues of theory. We have no reason to believe he was under duress when he wrote this. It is not unlike Ramses to do something so thoughtless and inconsiderate.'

'If he is a prisoner,' said Daoud, who had been thinking it over, 'we must find him.'

'Very good, Daoud,' said Selim, giving his uncle a kindly look. 'Where shall we start looking?'

'Oh dear,' I said with a sigh. 'Let us consider this matter logically. There are two possibilities. Either Ramses is a prisoner and wrote this at the dictation of his captor, or he has come across something that roused his insatiable curiosity and is pursuing the matter. If we assume that the first alternative is correct, our obvious course is to go to Samaria. He was last seen there, or rather, that is the place where he was last known to be.'

'Hmph,' said Emerson, chewing on the stem of his pipe. 'I can't see that we have any choice, Peabody. We must go to Samaria, interrogate – er – question Reisner, and trace Ramses's subsequent movements.'

'I see several objections to that plan,' I said.

'I am not at all surprised that you do. Well?'

'Tracing his movements might mean delaying our arrival in Jerusalem for a considerable period of time, in which case Morley may already have made mischief. Furthermore, if Ramses is off on some quest of his own, our attempts to find him could endanger him or the quest itself. He says – let me see the note again – yes, he says, "Sit tight." Does that not imply he wants to be left to his own devices?'

'That wouldn't be out of character,' David admitted. 'But what could he possibly have found to set him off? An illegal excavation? Rumors of a remarkable discovery he wants to investigate?'

'I must admit I can't think of anything that would be so enticing he would ignore MY express orders,' I replied. 'Unless . . .'

'Unless what?' Emerson demanded.

'Nothing.' I had been seized by a hideous foreboding, of the sort that often seizes me. Emerson had strictly forbidden me to mention them, since he does not believe in forebodings of any variety.

The others – except for Daoud, who only spoke when he had something sensible to say – had not remained silent. Speculation ranged from 'He broke a leg doing something idiotic and is afraid to admit it,' to 'Mr. Reisner has come across a find so important he needs Ramses to stay.'

'Then why didn't Reisner write and tell me so?' Emerson demanded.

The answer to that was obvious, but I was the only one who had the fortitude to state it aloud. 'Because he doesn't want you dashing off to Samaria and interfering with his work.'

'Bah,' said Emerson indignantly. 'I never interfere.'

'This is a waste of time,' Nefret said. 'Professor, please let me see the bit of string and the cloth.'

Emerson handed them over. 'I regret to inform you, Nefret, that the string is nothing out of the ordinary and the knot is not a unique variety only employed by members of a single, unusual profession. As for the cloth –'

Nefret smoothed it out on the table, pushing aside a platter of bread and a dish of hummus. It was a small square, approximately six inches on a side.

'What do you see?' Selim asked excitedly. 'Is there writing? Is that a bloodstain?'

'No.' Nefret continued to stare at the cloth. 'Just dirt. But there is one interesting thing about it.'

'I don't see anything,' Emerson said.

'It's a woman's handkerchief.' Nefret handed it to me. 'Does that suggest a possible reason for Ramses's being delayed?'

I had heard of blazing eyes but had always believed that was a literary metaphor. Perhaps it was only the reflection of the candleflame in her blue orbs.

From Manuscript H

They had only been traveling a short time before Ramses was inclined to regret he had not accepted the offer of a sleeping potion. The equipage was going at a good clip, and although the bedding cushioned him to some extent, he was being thrown from side to side. At least he had been left alone. He braced his feet against the side of the yaila, squirmed into a slightly more comfortable position, and forced himself to go over that extraordinary conversation in minute detail.

He had a fairly good idea now who Mansur was – or rather, what he was. He had heard that particular accent before, from a pair of Indian students he had met at university when he spent a term brushing up on his classical Greek. Languages were his chief interest and his specialty; he had cultivated the two young men in the hope of learning something of their native tongue. Most

Indians were Hindus, but there was a sizable Moslem population too, particularly in the northwest provinces. It really didn't matter whether Mansur had been born Moslem or had converted. What mattered was that the plot, whatever the hell it was, might extend beyond the Ottoman territories. India was the jewel in the crown, the pride of the empire. If there was even a slight possibility of an uprising in India, the War Office would go off its collective head. Memories of the Mutiny of 1857, when thousands of British and Europeans were slaughtered, still haunted the nightmares of government officials. That catastrophe had been kindled by a stupid, unnecessary affront to the religious sensibilities of the Indian troops.

If Mansur was from India, it would explain his manner toward his prisoner – an odd mixture of kindness and contempt. Ramses had observed how his Indian friends at Oxford were treated by many students and some of the dons. The derogatory names, the veiled sneers, and – perhaps hardest of all for a proud man to bear – the kindly condescension. He had seen the same thing in Egypt and he knew how bitterly it was resented.

It would also explain why the attacks at Samaria had been directed at him rather than Reisner and Fisher. Americans had never established a political foothold in the Middle East. They were regarded as guests, sometimes annoying but not threatening. England bestrode the region like a colossus – one foot in India, one in Egypt, its influence stretching into large parts of Africa. England imposed her own laws and controlled every aspect of government, from education to trade. Imperialists like Hogarth would claim that it was Britain's duty to civilize the lesser breeds; but it was an unfortunate fact that people resented being told how to live their lives by outsiders, no matter how kindly their intentions.

It made a perfectly reasonable theory, but, Ramses had to admit, it was a little too reminiscent of his mother's thinking processes. She was perfectly capable of proposing an interesting hypothesis and claiming it was fact. His father would have sneered. 'All very interesting, my boy, but what does it have to do with your present dilemma?'

How was he going to get out of this mess? Escape was impossible as long as they were on the road. The driver was at one end of the conveyance, and a guard on the platform at the back. He'd have to wait until they reached their destination and he could reappraise the situation. Mansur had taken pains to keep him from knowing where they were going. That could imply that they would end up in some town or city that was familiar to him.

Or it might mean nothing at all.

Sheer boredom finally sent him into a restless slumber, shot through with fleeting dream images. Usually it was Nefret's face that haunted his sleep. This time the images were less pleasant. Hilda von Eine, poised on the staircase of the tell, looking down at him with hissing snakes instead of hair crowning her head; the face of Macomber stained with the ugly colors of corruption, the pebble-dull eyes sunken. Then the eyes were no longer dull but shining with a reddish glow, the mouth opened, and instead of a tongue –

He woke up with a jerk, sweating and shaking. The blindfold made it worse, he couldn't replace the dream images with a sight of reality. Then he realized the vehicle was no longer moving.

Someone crawled into the tube next to him. A hand touched his shoulder.

'Are you awake?'

'Yes.' He'd had time to steady his voice. 'Do you intend to feed me anytime soon?'

'My apologies.' Mansur untied his hands. 'I saw a storm was coming and wanted to make as much time as possible before it hit.'

Ramses snatched the blindfold off. He had never realized what a subtle form of torture it was to be cut off from the world of sight, dependent on the goodwill of others even to move safely in a dark, unfamiliar world . . .

With Mansur's help he slid, feetfirst, out of the vehicle. It had pulled into an open courtyard. He could see very little; the sky overhead was dark as night and rain was falling heavily. Stiff and stumbling, he let his guide lead him to a door.

A lamp on a table in the room gave limited light, but it dazzled his eyes after the long darkness. Tenderly Mansur led him in and lowered him onto a seat. As his eyes adjusted, Ramses saw that the small room was like most rooms in the houses of the region, its only furnishings the usual divan, a few tables, tattered rugs on the floor.

After being escorted by Mansur himself to a primitive latrine, he was led back into the house and served food and tea by the same servant he had seen before. Mansur left him to eat alone, exiting through a door on the wall to the left. The food restored him considerably, and he got up and examined the room. A second door, presumably to the street, was locked. The windows were high on the wall and barred. The only thing in the room that could conceivably be used as a weapon was the lamp; he had been given nothing except a spoon with which to eat the stewed vegetables.

Mansur came in, followed by his servant carrying a tray. 'Coffee?' he inquired genially. 'I will join you if I may.'

Ramses bit back a rude response. He was damned if he'd let the man goad him into losing his temper.

'Delighted,' he said. 'We can chat about university and the architecture of Christ Church. Did you take your degree –'

Smoothly Mansur cut in. 'You were at Oxford, I believe.'

'Only to attend a few lectures.' The coffee was excellent. 'My father didn't believe in a public school education.'

'A remarkable man, your father.'

'Quite. How long were you in Egypt?'

'One doesn't have to remain long before learning of the famous Father of Curses.'

Another thrust neatly parried, Ramses thought. Only once in his life had he encountered an adversary who anticipated his every move and who was as good at verbal combat: his family's nemesis, the Master Criminal, as his mother insisted on calling the fellow.

It wasn't the first time he had wondered if Mansur could possibly be Sethos. The man was a genius at disguise; Ramses had learned a number of useful tricks from that source. Middle Eastern garb was a godsend to a man who wanted to assume another identity. A turban could add a few inches to one's actual height, the loose robe concealed a man's real build, and there was nothing like a beard to blur the shapes of mouth and chin. Ramses leaned forward, trying to make out Mansur's features more clearly. Sethos's one distinguishing characteristic was the color of his eyes, an ambiguous shade between gray and brown. Unfortunately it was also a characteristic that could be altered by the judicious use of cosmetics that darkened lashes and lids, and even drugs that enlarged the pupils. Mansur's heavy brows overshadowed his deep-set eye sockets, and his trick of squinting . . .

Mansur rose to his feet. 'We will be spending the night here. The road is too muddy for travel in the dark. I hope you will find the divan comfortable. If you will excuse me, I have a few matters to settle before retiring. I will return shortly to – how shall I put it –'

'Tuck me in?' Ramses suggested.

Mansur turned on his heel and went out the front door. Ramses stretched out on the divan, hands clasped under his head. Mansur seemed to be a little short-tempered. He can't be Sethos, Ramses told himself. Sethos wouldn't bother with a bizarre scheme like this one. Profit, and lots of it, was his only interest.

What if there was profit to be earned, though? Macomber had talked of a talisman. Islam didn't go in much for relics, actual or fabled. Christians collected the bones of saints, bits of the True

Cross, nails from the Cross – the list went on and on. They were always in the market for a new relic. Jews lived in hopes of finding the lost Ark, or even any unmistakable, datable remains of the First Temple of Solomon. So far nothing from that period had been found. What object could have such importance to Moslems?

The sound of the rain had grown louder. A river in the sky, as an Egyptian pharaoh had called the frequent rainfall of those foreign lands that were, during most of the fourteenth century B.C., under Egyptian dominance. Akhenaton's all-loving god had thoughtfully provided rain for the regions that lacked the ever-present, predictable Nile flooding.

Ramses sat up. No wonder the rain sounded louder. Mansur had neglected to latch the door. The wind must have blown it open a few inches.

He approached the door with the caution of a cat investigating a new smell. The darkness outside was total, not a glimmer of light anywhere. The drumbeat of the rain muffled sound. He knew, as certainly as if he had been told, that if he went out that door he would find it unguarded.

Smiling, he went back to the divan. Mansur wouldn't have forgotten to close the door tightly or dispense with guards. This was a test, and come to think of it, a kind of insult. Did the man think he was fool enough to plunge out into the pouring rain and the blackness, not knowing where he was or where he was going? He wouldn't get far. He'd be dragged back, soaked to the skin, a dripping, miserable figure – another means of humiliating him, or rather, allowing him to humiliate himself.

When Mansur came back, Ramses was lying full-length, hands folded peacefully on his chest, and snoring.

The reverend had not joined in the discussion. One would have supposed he was off in some happy dream of his own –

remembering his life as the emperor Constantine, for example – if one had not become accustomed to his habit of plunging headfirst into a conversation to which he had not seemed to pay attention.

In the silence that followed Nefret's pointed question, he declared, 'We must go immediately to Jerusalem.'

'Oh, must we?' said Emerson, that being his automatic response to anything that sounded like an order. He had been visibly taken aback by Nefret's implicit accusation.

Naturally the same thought had occurred to me even before she spoke. Before the others could come to grips with the idea and join in an interminable, unprofitable, discussion, I said, 'We must come to a decision sooner rather than later. By sooner, I mean today. I want to be ready to leave tomorrow morning.'

'Very good, very good,' said the reverend, scraping up the last of the hummus with the last of the bread.

'Leave for where?' David asked. There was a certain set to his jaw that told me he had already decided where he was going. David was a gentle soul, not given to controversy, but once he made up his mind he could be as stubborn as Ramses.

'That is what we must decide,' I said. 'Emerson, I suggest you go immediately to the British consular agent.'

'Is there one?' inquired my annoying husband.

'There must be some official of our government here in Jaffa, Emerson, or at the very least a telegraph office. Find out if there are any messages for you, and whether anything is known of Major Morley. He must have landed here.'

'Hmph,' said Emerson unhelpfully.

'Take Selim with you. He can assist with your inquiries.'

Selim bounded to his feet, exuding his willingness to assist. Emerson rose more slowly. 'What about you, Peabody?'

'We will wait for you at the hotel.'

Which I had every intention of doing . . . Unless another idea occurred to me.

We did not linger in the souk. When we reached the square with its charming gardens, the sun was sinking into a bank of clouds, rimming their purple gray with gold.

'Let us sit here awhile,' I said, taking Nefret firmly by the arm.

'I believe I will go to my room,' David said. 'I want to . . . I must . . .'

Find a map and figure out the quickest route to Samaria. Ah, well, it would keep him occupied, and he would have some little difficulty finding a means of transportation, unaccustomed as he was to the city.

'Take the reverend and Daoud with you,' I said.

The reverend, who had been in the process of joining Nefret and me on the bench, obediently straightened himself. Daoud folded his arms and shook his head.

'I will not leave you and Nur Misur alone.'

'What on earth do you suppose could happen to us?' I demanded.

'Anything,' said Daoud darkly.

'Oh, very well. Stand over there by the tree and keep watch.'

Daoud duly took up his position, glancing suspiciously at every passerby, and the others went toward the hotel.

Nefret was prepared for a lecture. She sat with head bowed and chin protruding and refused to meet my eyes.

'I presume you have had time to reconsider your assumption,' I said, arranging my skirts neatly.

'Perhaps I was unjust.' Her voice was so low I could barely hear it.

'Not necessarily unjust. Ramses has got beyond my control these past few years and I would not be surprised to discover he had formed an attachment to some female person. What would surprise me would be to discover he would announce the fact in such a direct fashion.'

'It might be regarded as a request for discretion on our part.'

'Oh, come, Nefret. Ramses knows me – us, that is – well enough to realize I will cast discretion to the four winds before I will allow him to fail in his duty to me – to us, I mean to say. It is not unlike him to go off on some hare-brained scheme of his own, but he is certainly capable of inventing a more believable excuse than – er – dalliance.'

'Then . . . then the message did not come from Ramses.'

'The note was almost certainly written by him. I do not believe he was responsible for its delivery.'

Nefret turned to face me. 'Then he is in trouble!'

'Nefret, I can think offhand of at least two other explanations for that message. We must keep our heads and not go jumping to conclusions. I need you to keep calm and help persuade Emerson that we must not try to find Ramses. At least not immediately.'

'What can we do, then?' Nefret demanded. 'We must do something!'

'He might not thank you for interfering, Nefret.' In fact, I was reasonably certain he would not. Like many young persons of that age, Ramses was convinced he could manage quite well without the assistance of his loving family. Like other young persons of that age, he was mistaken, but only painful experience would teach him the truth. I went on, 'What we must do is go on to Jerusalem and, as he put it, "sit tight." Ramses knows where to find us. We can get to Samaria as easily from Jerusalem as from here, and if we don't hear from him in, let us say, a week, we will reconsider the situation.'

My firm but kindly manner did not have the effect I had hoped. 'How can you be so calm?' Nefret asked passionately. 'An entire week? He could be –' Her voice caught.

'I doubt that,' I said, suppressing my own qualms. Perhaps I was reassuring myself as well as Nefret when I continued, 'In any case, he is in no more danger of . . . of that now than he was at the time the message was written. And if . . . that . . . were intended, our intervention would almost certainly come too late. We might even bring on the result we dread by dashing wildly in pursuit.'

Reason, however sound, does not convince loving hearts. Nefret remained silent, her furrowed brow and out-thrust chin expressing her resistance. I did not – could not – tell her my own theory. I felt certain that my hideous forebodings were, as usual, accurate. Ramses had, heaven knows how, got himself involved with some secret service operation. MO2 was concerned about German influence in Syria-Palestine. Ramses spoke German, Arabic, and Turkish like a native, and archaeologists, as Emerson had pointed out, made admirable agents. Either the War Office had recruited Ramses – in which case I would have General Spencer's head on a platter – or Ramses had come across something that, in his opinion, merited investigation. My – our, that is – demand that he meet us in Jaffa had given him an excuse to leave Reisner's dig. I was reasonably certain that if we did inquire we would find he had taken his departure in the normal fashion. What had happened to him thereafter was a matter of speculation. I am never guilty of idle speculation, so I kept an open mind on that. Except that once I caught up with him, I would have Ramses's head on another platter.

The sky overhead was dark gray and the first drops of rain were falling. 'Let us get inside,' I said, rising. 'It looks as if we are in for a storm. A Nile in the sky, as Pharaoh Akhenaton once poetically expressed it. Come, Daoud.'

The three of us were rather damp by the time we reached the hotel. The manager tried to duck behind the counter when he saw me. 'Twas of no avail, as I could have told him. Leaning over the counter, I ordered tea to be brought up and asked him to look again for messages. After fumbling about, he handed me two envelopes. One was an impressive document, covered with seals and official stamps. The other appeared to have been delivered by hand.

'When did these arrive?' I asked.

'Today. Today. This afternoon. The post in this country is extremely –'

'In future,' I said sternly, 'make sure all messages and letters are delivered to us at once.'

'Open them,' Nefret urged, trying to get a look at the envelopes. 'Perhaps Ramses –'

'I can't do that, Nefret, both are addressed to Emerson. The handwriting is not that of Ramses.'

We went straight upstairs to my room, and I asked Daoud to tell David to join us for tea. It was early, but the skies were so dark and the rain was falling so heavily, I felt the familiar ritual would cheer us.

It certainly cheered the reverend, who, of course, accompanied David. Watching him tuck into biscuits and scones, I wondered how he could eat so much and retain his willowy figure.

I had intended to steam the letters open, but the others came too soon and Nefret ignored my hints that she change her damp clothing. Under other circumstances I might have opened them anyhow and braved Emerson's loud complaints; however, I had a difficult task ahead of me persuading him to go along with my plans. A further source of aggravation might render him even more recalcitrant.

A considerable noise in the corridor finally betokened the arrival of Selim and Emerson. Emerson's primary source of complaint appeared to be the weather. Flinging the door open, he continued without interruption: '. . . ridiculous for this time of year. The rains do not come on until November.'

'God works in mysterious ways.' Plato piped up.

Emerson gave him an awful look. He and Selim were both drenched. Emerson had, naturally, insisted on walking the entire way instead of searching for a covered conveyance or waiting until the heaviest of the rain stopped. Nefret hurried to him and helped him out of his coat. She hung it over the back of a chair, where it continued to drip distractingly for the next hour.

David took Selim off to his room and persuaded him to change into one of his dressing gowns; Emerson divested himself of his boots and wrung out the bottoms of his trousers, which he declined to change. I knew he would not catch cold. He never did. I rang for more tea. The arrival of the genial beverage and a further supply of bread-and-butter sandwiches put Emerson in a better frame of mind.

Comparatively better, that is. Fixing me with a critical look, he declared, 'Selim and I will probably catch pneumonia, Peabody, and all for nothing.'

It had occurred to me, after I sent them off, that it probably would be for nothing. The War Office would not risk sending information by telegraph. It had also occurred to me that Emerson must have worked out some covert means of communication with MO2. He certainly had not bothered to mention it to ME. Why hadn't I sat him down and interrogated him? I ought to have made one of my little lists. The answer was now plain to me, and I realized I ought to have anticipated it. Emerson would never of his own free will have selected a temperance hotel.

Controlling my understandable vexation, I replied in moderate tones. 'The message came here, to the hotel, Emerson. May I ask why you did not tell me that was the arrangement?'

I held out the envelope.

Emerson snatched it and inspected it carefully. 'I didn't tell you because it was none of . . . Er, hmmm. Well, where else could it have been sent, to be certain of delivery?'

He gave me another look, reminding me that the others were still in the dark about our connection with the War Office, and it was obviously preferable that it should stay that way.

'Were you expecting a particular message?' Nefret asked, stressing the adjective.

Emerson rose nobly to the occasion. 'I have been expecting the firman – our permission from the Sublime Porte to excavate at Siloam.' He ripped open the envelope and withdrew a document even more impressive than its container, edged in gold and covered with blobs of red sealing wax. 'And here it is,' he concluded triumphantly.

'Emerson,' I said, forestalling further questions, 'you really must change out of those damp trousers. Will the rest of you please excuse us?'

'We haven't decided what we are going to do tomorrow,' Nefret protested.

'We will discuss it later, when we meet for dinner. Now run along.'

I got them all out the door, closed it, and leaned against it, sighing. Keeping the lot of them under control had begun to tax even my powers.

'What are we going to do tomorrow?' Emerson inquired.

'We may find the answer here.' I took the second envelope from my pocket. I felt sure Nefret had not forgotten about it, but my dictatorial manner had prevented her from pursuing the subject. She was certain to bring it up again, however, and we had to have a plausible reply ready.

'Hmph,' said Emerson, taking the envelope. 'Hand-delivered. I wonder who –'

'Open it!'

The envelope contained a single sheet of paper. The message had been printed in block letters. I read it over Emerson's shoulder.

'Send pomegranates Glasgow. Humboldt seeking Siberian lettuce v.I.'

'Code,' I said.

'What did you expect? "Morley is a German spy, we told you so, now find proof"?'

'Is that what it says?'

'I rather doubt it,' said Emerson, holding the paper close to the lamp.

'You do have the key, don't you?' With an effort I kept my voice calm.

'Certainly. It is a simple substitution code, almost impossible to decipher without the key, since the substitutions are arbitrary and not susceptible to the –'

'Where is it?'

'What? Oh,' said Emerson, recognizing in my measured tone signs that an explosion might be imminent. 'In my head, of course. They made me memorize it before I left the office. One doesn't carry such –'

'Do you remember it?'

'Um,' said Emerson, squinting at the paper. 'Er. Most of it.'

'Oh, bah,' I cried. 'If that isn't just like a man! Men, I should say – you and that pompous fool General Spencer. He believes no mere female should be trusted with classified information, and you – don't tell me, you gave your word to remain silent, didn't you?' In my agitation I jumped up and began pacing back and forth across the room. 'It is my own fault,' I said bitterly. 'I ought to have questioned you. But I trusted you, Emerson, I trusted you to confide in me.'

Emerson intercepted me and caught me in a close embrace. 'Peabody, my love, you are right to reproach me. I was a fool. It will never happen again, I promise.'

It is unusual to see Emerson in a penitent mood. I find him much more persuasive when he is in one of his rages, sapphirine eyes narrowed, heavy brows drawn together, teeth bared. However, I did not suppose his conciliatory mood would last, and his embraces have a softening effect, even when, as in this case, he was squeezing the breath out of me. I indicated with a gesture that such was the case, and Emerson relaxed his grip.

'My love,' he began.

'I accept your apology, Emerson. Now let us see how much you remember of the code.'

Emerson has what I believe is called a selective memory. He can recall minute details of particular excavations but is likely to forget where he left his hat. Since he was scarcely more interested in codes and ciphers and spies than he was in the location of his hat, I did not suppose he had made much of an effort to remember the key. However, with the proper prodding, he might be prevailed upon to dredge up enough detail to interpret this particular message.

It was not really a very ingenious code. Perhaps in order to make it easier to remember, the inventor had used proper names for other proper names and verbs for other verbs. Once Emerson had recollected that 'send' stood for 'proceed' and 'seeking' for 'made contact' it was childishly easy to interpret the gist of the message. 'Glasgow' had to be 'Jerusalem'; that was our agreed-upon destination, after all. Prodded by me, Emerson admitted that 'Siberian' was a not too clever substitution for 'German.'

'So "lettuce,"' I said, 'must stand for "spy" or "agent."'

'That is right,' Emerson exclaimed. 'I remember now. How did you know?'

'Because the War Office is obsessed with German spies. Humboldt, of course, is Morley. Why Humboldt, I wonder? Really, one could almost anticipate their instructions without any written orders at all. We are left with only two unknowns. I would hazard a guess that "pomegranates" is an adverb – "immediately" or "posthaste." What about "v.I."?'

'Any ideas?' Emerson inquired hopefully.

'Nothing occurs to you?'

Emerson fingered the dimple, or cleft, in his chin. 'Honestly, Peabody, it strikes no chord whatsoever. Thanks to your intelligent reminders I now recall a good many other words – Dutch for British, Norwegian for French, Julius for Wilhelm –'

'Caesar for Kaiser,' I said contemptuously. 'Why on earth would Kaiser Wilhelm need to be mentioned?'

'Well, one never knows what the old buzzard will be up to next,' said Emerson. He proceeded to reel off several dozen other words and their code equivalents, which I immediately committed to memory, knowing that Emerson would probably have forgotten them the next day. However, try as he might, he was unable to interpret the final, unknown word.

'It could mean anything,' I said. 'A place name in Jerusalem, a day of the week. In any case, the instructions are clear. We are to proceed immediately to Jerusalem because Morley has been in contact with someone the War Office believes to be a German agent – although precisely what they expect us to do about it I cannot imagine. If this rain lets up we should be able to leave tomorrow.'

'You mean, then, to abandon our son?' Emerson's manly tones were tremulous with reproach.

I repeated the arguments I had used with Nefret. The one that finally convinced Emerson was the last – that we might endanger Ramses by going openly in search of him.

'We cannot be certain that he is held prisoner,' I concluded. 'Ramses may have had some obscure motive for using a woman's handkerchief – his motives are often obscure – or someone may have added it without his knowledge.'

'For equally obscure motives,' Emerson grumbled.

'I can think of at least two that are not obscure to me.'

'That does not surprise me in the least.' After a moment, Emerson added, 'What are they?'

'Time is getting on,' I said, rising. 'Nefret will be pounding on the door before long, demanding to know what we intend to do. Are you and I agreed? We must present a united front, since I expect protests from both Nefret and David.'

'I suppose so,' said Emerson glumly.

'I think we have time for a little sip of whiskey,' I suggested. 'It was clever of you, my dear, to think of bringing several bottles.'

A little compliment, I always say, smooths over small disagreements. (The whiskey was no deterrent either.) Emerson cheered up and even agreed to change his trousers before Nefret, as I had predicted, knocked emphatically at our door.

'You haven't changed for dinner,' I said.

'Neither have you.' She settled herself into a chair and gave me a challenging look. 'Is that whiskey? May I have some?'

Except for wine and sherry before dinner, Nefret seldom touched alcoholic beverages. On this occasion I saw no reason to deny her request. It might put her in a more pliable mood.

The others soon joined us and we returned to the café where we had lunched. The rain had stopped and the air smelled clean and fresh. Once we were seated I made my announcements, since I believe in taking the bull by the horns – or, as Emerson had once expressed it, riding roughshod over objections.

'We are leaving for Jerusalem first thing tomorrow morning. I will make arrangements for travel this evening. There is a good carriage road, but if anyone would prefer to ride we can hire horses. Selim, I am sure you would rather do that. In fact, I would appreciate it if you would take charge of selecting the beasts. Nefret, what about you?'

'I too would prefer to ride,' Nefret said quietly.

'And I,' said David.

'And you, Mr. Plato?' I asked, expecting I would have to explain what I was talking about.

'I have not bestrode a beast since that memorable day on the road to Damascus,' Plato replied. 'It was not a horse, of course. A dear little donkey.'

Emerson decided he too would ride if he could find a steed up to his weight, so after we had returned to the hotel I left the others to make the necessary arrangements and went to my room to pack.

The sun was setting and lingering clouds darkened the west; even after I had lighted the lamps the room was gloomy and dismal. It had to have been the War Office that had selected this particular hotel; it could not have been recommended by any fastidious traveler.

Another idea came to me then, and I let out a little expletive of annoyance. Why hadn't I thought of it before? I had had a good deal on my mind, but that was no excuse. I usually have a great deal on my mind.

Picking up my handbag and my parasol, I hurried back to the lobby. Mr. Boniface was not behind the desk. Under interrogation the clerk on duty admitted he was in his office and indicated the door to that room.

I did not knock. Boniface had his feet on his desk, a cigar in one hand and a glass of amber liquid in the other. My unexpected appearance caused him to drop the cigar and spill a considerable quantity of the liquid onto his shirtfront.

'What a hypocrite you are,' I said. 'Swilling liquor in your office while refusing to supply it in this temperance hotel of yours. Are you also an agent of the British government?'

The question made his eyes widen even more. His mustache vibrated with agitation. 'Good God,' he gasped. 'Mrs. Emerson – please . . . don't say such things! Not with the door standing open!'

I closed the door and took a chair. 'Confess, Mr. Boniface. What are you afraid of? We are on the same side, I believe. If I am correct, and I am certain I am, your hotel is a communication center for agents working in this region. Really,' I added vexedly, as Boniface continued to gape stupidly at me, 'this cursed obsession with secrecy is a confounded nuisance. The time may come when I will need to use that system of communication. Who gave you the code message you passed on to me today?'

Boniface took out his handkerchief and mopped his brow. 'You've got it all wrong, Mrs. Emerson. That is . . . Yes, I do

119

receive and pass on messages. But that is all I do! I don't know names. I don't want to know them. That is the truth, I swear.'

'You didn't know the man who delivered that message?'

'Never saw him before in my life. Dressed like a pilgrim – spectacles, dark suit, clerical collar. But he gave me the sign, so I knew he was –'

'Sign? What sign?'

Solemnly Boniface pinched the tip of his nose between thumb and forefinger and wriggled it back and forth. He looked perfectly ridiculous, with his bulging eyes and perspiring brow.

'Ah,' I said. 'That could come in useful. Though it seems to me a rather unsafe signal. It might be made by chance.'

'It's the number of times that matters,' Boniface said. He seemed almost relieved to have unburdened himself. 'Back and forth, back and forth. Twice, no more.'

'I see. Thank you, Mr. Boniface, for your cooperation. I believe you know we are leaving in the morning. I may or may not see you again.'

I deduced, from Boniface's expression, he hoped the second alternative was the correct one.

I had almost finished my (and Emerson's) packing when he returned to announce that the arrangements had been made.

'According to Selim, the horses are a poor lot, but Nefret says they are healthy enough.'

'Selim's standards are high,' I remarked. 'And he prefers to believe nothing in this country is the equal of what Egypt can provide. I trust the others have gone to their rooms to pack?'

'Yes.' Emerson flung himself into an armchair and took out his pipe and tobacco pouch. Then he burst out, 'I am worried about Nefret.'

'What has she done?'

'Nothing! That is what worries me. I expected her to complain, protest, object. It's unnatural, Peabody.'

'Not at all, my dear. You know my methods. Once again they have proved to be effective. She has seen reason and will not try to run off by herself.'

My judgment was correct. When we gathered in the gray light of dawn, Nefret was present. David was not.

Chapter Five

David was never late.

Turning on Mr. Plato, I cried, 'Where is he? Was he still in your room when you left it?'

The reverend took a step back. 'What is the matter, Mrs. Emerson?'

I had not the patience to deal with him then. I hastened up the stairs, with Emerson close on my heels.

The room David and the reverend had shared was unoccupied. Both beds were unmade; David's two suitcases stood against the wall. It was Emerson who saw the piece of paper pinned to the pillow of his bed.

'I beg you will refrain from mentioning hideous forebodings, Peabody,' he remarked.

Wringing my hands, I cried, 'I had none, Emerson. Would that I had! I ought to have had! Let me see that.'

Emerson held it away from me. 'I will read it to you. Sit down and get a grip on yourself.'

Characteristically, the note began with an apology.

'"Forgive me for going against your expressed wishes and neglecting the duty I owe you, but there is another duty that must come first. I do not believe Ramses would neglect his responsibilities so cavalierly. He is in trouble, and I must find him. I think I have found a way to do that without endangering him. I am the only one who can.'"

'Is that all?' I demanded.

'It is quite enough, I believe.' Emerson folded the note and put it in his coat pocket.

Regretting my temporary loss of calm, I made a hasty inspection of David's suitcases. The wardrobe was empty; he had packed all his belongings, ready for us to take with us. So far as I could tell, he had taken only a small valise, toilet articles, and a change of clothing with him.

Emerson carried the suitcases downstairs and handed them to Daoud, instructing him to place them with the rest of our luggage. Daoud obeyed without comment, his broad brow furrowed.

The reverend broke off his sotto voce rendition of what sounded like a hymn. 'Shall we have breakfast now?' he asked.

I was tempted to take him by the collar and shake him, but I refrained. 'When did David leave?' I asked.

'David? Oh.' The reverend pondered. 'I don't know. He was not there when I was wakened by the servant. So I came down at once, because you said last night –'

I waved him to silence and looked at Nefret. She made a pretty picture, in her riding costume of tan soldier's cloth. The coat was cut à la militaire, with many useful pockets, and the skirt could be unbuttoned to form trousers. She looked down and began unfastening the buttons. Why had I not realized that her seeming acquiescence was an ominous sign? It was only one of many I had missed.

'You and David planned this,' I said. 'You knew he meant to go after Ramses.'

She stopped fiddling with the buttons and met my gaze squarely. 'If he hadn't, I would have. I am sorry, Aunt Amelia.'

I studied her more closely and saw that her eyes were shadowed and her face rather pale, as was usually the case when she had slept poorly. No doubt guilt and shame had been responsible.

Accusations and recriminations would have been a waste of time. 'What is he planning to do?'

'He wouldn't tell me. But he said he was the only one who could carry it off, and only if he were alone.' Her moods were as variable as spring weather. Defiance gave way to remorse; tears flooded her blue eyes. 'I didn't want to deceive you, truly I didn't, but –'

'Don't try that trick on me, young lady,' I said sharply. 'I am not moved by womanly tears.'

She knew that. The tears were not meant for me, they were aimed at Emerson, who had been talking with Selim.

For once they failed to have the desired effect. Emerson was too full of the news he had heard from Selim. 'David came downstairs several hours ago. The grooms can't say precisely when; they do not carry pocket watches. He told them he was going on ahead, mounted the beast he had selected, and rode off. They had no reason to stop him, since they had seen him last evening and knew he was one of our party.'

'They can't be blamed,' I agreed. 'Did any of them see which way he went?'

Emerson pointed, and then shook his head. 'That's no help. The main roads to Gaza, Nablus, and Jerusalem are in that direction.'

'It doesn't matter,' I said grimly. 'I know where he is going. Samaria.'

From Manuscript H

The rain had stopped the next morning, but the roads were still waterlogged, as Ramses discovered after he had been wedged back into the vehicle, blindfolded and bound. He found himself unpleasant company, since Mansur had denied his request that he be allowed to bathe and change his clothes. He was also developing a bristly growth of beard.

The artificially imposed blindness was beginning to take its toll. He knew the blindfold and Mansur's oh-so-polite refusal to give him so much as a basin of water and a bar of soap was part of a deliberate process, a slow and subtle method of reducing a prisoner to something less than a human being. Being spotlessly clean at all times had never been one of his major preoccupations; when he and David had prowled the back alleys of Cairo, their disguises had often necessitated filthy rags and a rancid odor. But that had been a matter of choice, and of self-imposed limits. Now a stranger and an enemy controlled even that basic aspect of his existence. For an arrogant Englishman, the control itself was intolerable. At least that's how Mansur would reason – and he'd be right. I wonder what he'll come up with next? Ramses thought. His imagination, enriched by knowledge of his own inner weaknesses and fears, supplied a variety of ugly possibilities. He knew what Mansur wanted – to reduce him to such a state of misery that he would beg for even a small comfort. In many ways it was a more intolerable form of torture than physical pain.

He wasn't able to sleep, since the vehicle kept sinking into water-filled ruts. The only advantage to sightlessness was that his other senses were keener. He could hear water sloshing around as the men grunted and shoved to lift the cart, and smell the tobacco smoke whenever the man perched on the apron at the back of the cart lit a cigarette. There was always someone there, discernible by the smell of tobacco and the small noises he made shifting position, coughing, clearing his throat. Ramses had tried speaking to him, but he never got an answer.

After an interminable interval he was allowed out, still blindfolded, to relieve himself and eat. He couldn't see the man who kept a firm grip on his arm throughout – and who let go his grip once, so that Ramses stumbled and fell flat in the mud. He wasn't even allowed to wipe the muck off his face; his silent attendant did it with a rough cloth, like a nursemaid cleaning a grubby child.

The man's brisk face-scrubbing had had one positive effect. The lower edge of the blindfold had been pushed up, over the bridge of his nose, so that a thin strip of light was visible. He managed to worry it up a little more by rubbing his face against the side of the vehicle. He couldn't see anything except the inside of the vehicle, but even that small window into the world of sight lifted his spirits.

Sometime later the worst of the jolting stopped and their progress became more even. They must have turned onto a larger highway, after traversing less-traveled back tracks. He pricked his ears. Yes; there were other travelers, he could hear snatches of conversation and laughter, hoofbeats, the creak and rumble of wheeled vehicles, and an occasional burst of profanity directed by one driver at another who had got in his way. A well-traveled highway, then. There weren't that many roads fit for all-weather travel. One to Nablus and on to Jerusalem, another to Jaffa; unless they had headed north, toward Haifa, or west, toward Damascus. Too many possibilities, and no clue.

Their pace slowed till it was hardly faster than a walk. Mansur was in no hurry. Was he early for a rendezvous, or waiting until after dark to reach his destination? Probably the latter, Ramses thought, as the light faded and their speed began to increase. They were entering a town, a town of some size; the sounds of traffic were louder and he saw flashes of light, from lanterns or torches, under the blindfold.

When the vehicle finally stopped, he was yanked out of it, not too gently, and assisted to stand. It was not Mansur's hand that guided him; he had learned to recognize that touch.

The surface underfoot was stone, but the place must be open to the sky. A brisk breeze cooled his face and ruffled his hair. He was led through a door, along a corridor, and up a flight of stairs. Another length of corridor, another open door; this was no peasant dwelling, but a house of some size. The man gave him a shove that brought him to his knees. Then his bonds were untied, and the door closed with a reverberant slam.

His first instinctive act was to pull the blindfold up over his head. Blinking in the light, still on his knees, he took in his surroundings.

The light came from an ornate brass chandelier high overhead. Only half the candles had been lighted; the flames flickered in a chilly draft. The room was large, furnished with tawdry elegance – silk- and velvet-covered cushions scattered about the marble floor, ivory-inlaid tables, a long divan whose covering shimmered like cloth of gold. Ramses got slowly to his feet. It was definitely an improvement on his former quarters, but knowing Mansur as he had come to do, he was not reassured. Cautiously he moved around the room, staying close to the walls. The draft of air came from windows on a side wall. They were closed by elaborately carved wooden screens, the apertures too small to allow the occupant of the room to see out. Peering into dark corners, Ramses continued his search. He had almost decided he was alone when he came face-to-face with an apparition that wrung a muffled cry from him – a tall figure with staring eyes and a face horribly mottled with green and brown stains, a tangle of black hair crowning its head. His nerves were in such a state that it was several seconds before he realized the monster was his own reflection in a floor-to-ceiling mirror, distorted by the crackling of the glass.

He got his breathing under control and moved on. The door through which he had entered the room was a massive affair, heavy wood bound with iron. It was, as he had expected, locked or bolted.

A closer examination of the room and its furnishings told him what sort of room it was. Mashrabiya screens, ornate mirrors, velvet cushions – a harem chamber, probably the ka'ah, or main salon. But the fringe on the cushions was unraveling, the mirror was speckled, and a thin film of dust covered the flat surfaces. The Turkish official who owned the house hadn't kept his women here for some time.

The rattle of hardware at the door made him spin around.

Two of the guards entered, carrying, of all things, his suitcases. They dropped them and took up positions on either side of the open door, standing at attention.

Mansur looked as if he had just come from a long hot bath. His caftan was spotless, his beard oiled, his feet encased in elegant red leather slippers. Ramses knew only too well what he looked like. He had to fight the temptation to duck his head or raise his hands to hide his horrible face. The contrast between their appearances couldn't have been sharper.

Suddenly, unpredictably, his sense of humor came to his rescue. This was a farce, the sort of nasty but harmless joke one schoolboy might play on another. Ramses raised his hand to his brow in ironic salute.

'How neat and tidy you are,' he said approvingly. 'What's the occasion?'

Mansur looked him over, from disheveled head to mud-caked boots, and back again. His deep-set eyes narrowed.

'I apologize for the discomfort you have endured the past few days,' he said.

Ramses smiled and shrugged. He hoped Mansur hadn't observed him shriek and recoil from his image in the mirror. Rooms of a harem were fitted out with listening devices and hidden spy holes, so that the owner could keep an eye, and ear, on his property.

Mansur gestured him out of the room and preceded him along a narrow corridor. He himself opened a door. 'I hope this will make amends,' he said.

It was a bath chamber, lined with mirrors, with a sunken tub large enough to hold a pasha and several of his ladies. The marble was chipped and stained, the mirrors cracked, but the sight was glorious. Steam rose from the water that filled the tub. On a ledge next to the bath, toilet articles and a change of clothing had been neatly laid out. They were his own.

He wanted nothing more than to strip and plunge into the tub but he didn't want to appear too eager – or appear before Mansur naked. It was a form of humiliation he had been spared so far. He raised an inquiring eyebrow and stood waiting.

'Someone will come for you in a quarter of an hour,' Mansur said. The door closed behind him. Ramses didn't waste time trying it. Either it would be bolted or there would be a guard. But he took his time about undressing, inspecting the amenities – a bar of highly scented soap, several large but rather threadbare towels, a loofah. He lowered himself into the tub with a groan of pleasure. There were probably peepholes in these walls too, but at that point he didn't give a damn.

Since he had no way of measuring time, he couldn't allow himself the indulgence of soaking his stiffened muscles, but he felt a thousand percent better after he had toweled himself off. As it turned out he could have wallowed longer. He was fully dressed and had been pacing the room for what seemed much longer than a quarter of an hour before Mansur returned. He was alone.

'Back to your room,' he said curtly. 'Quickly.'

He followed close on Ramses's heels but instead of opening the door to the harem chamber he put a hard hand on Ramses's arm and turned him so that they were eyeball to eyeball.

'You are the son of the Father of Curses. The one they call Ramses.'

Wondering what this was all about, Ramses nodded.

With a dramatic gesture Mansur flung the door wide.

'Then who is this?'

One of his men stood over a recumbent form. His face was hidden in the crook of his arm, but Ramses recognized him instantly. His stomach sank down into his boots.

What man or woman will ever forget the moment when he (or she) stood gazing for the first time on the thrice-holy city, its minarets and steeples and its great golden dome swimming in the purple haze of evening?

Emerson, perhaps. His first words were, 'What a jumble!'

Conquering my own emotion, I replied, 'It is a very ancient city, my dear. Let us pause for a moment here, and reflect upon the centuries, nay, millennia that have passed since David first established –'

'If you can believe the Old Testament, which I don't, the city was Jebusite before the Israelites took it.'

I looked up at the imposing figure of my spouse. Emerson is always imposing; when on horseback he is no less than magnificent. We had at my direction stopped our little caravan at the top of the last hill. The road was excellent, and although our open carriage was somewhat deficient in springs, that did not detract from the comfort of the journey. Nefret and Selim had also halted their steeds. Her expression was courteously indifferent; but Selim sat gazing in awe at the dome of the Noble Sanctuary, ablaze in the light of the declining sun. Jerusalem was the third most holy city for Moslems; and some might have thought it ironic that the symbol of Islam now dominated the city which had been sacred to Judaism and Christianity before it.

The reverend, seated beside me, had been silent most of the time. Now he stirred and began muttering.

'We entered through the tunnel under the city where the water flowed. We crept in silence, man behind man, obedient to my will.'

'Now what is he babbling about?' Emerson demanded.

'Hmmm. Let me think. Ah – I believe he is responding to your statement about the conquest of the Jebusite city. That means he is now Joab.'

'Who?' Emerson's brow furrowed. 'Oh, yes; the Israelite commander who led troops into the city by way of the old tunnels. Something of a comedown for the reverend, isn't it – a mere commander?'

'The tunnels are there,' Mr. Plato said.

'Hmph,' said Emerson. 'Well, my dear Peabody, have you indulged your romantic fantasies long enough? We still have a way to go.'

He had done his best to destroy my 'romantic' mood. He was correct, however; we had yet to enter the city and locate our hotel.

'Yes, let us go on,' I said. 'Is Daoud all right?'

Selim looked back at the second carriage, where Daoud was sitting surrounded by boxes and bales and baggage. He had insisted on occupying that position, 'to keep the heathen from stealing our things.' I had explained to him that most of the local inhabitants were not heathens, but coreligionists of his. The argument made no impression on our friend; by his definition heathens were foreigners and foreigners were heathens.

'He waves to say all is well,' Selim reported. 'He is hungry, I think.'

It was a safe assumption. Daoud was a very large man and required frequent meals.

Traffic was brisk, as people sought the city before the fall of night. Camel trains, shepherds and their flocks, the innumerable and omnipresent little donkeys kicked up clouds of dust. I did not doubt the pilgrims found them very picturesque. There were several other carriages like ours on the road, and other riders, including a few females uncomfortably encased in woolen habits riding sidesaddle. They looked absolutely miserable.

The road led us down a slope and back up toward the heights on which the ancient city had been built. From my reading I knew it was not a plateau but separate hills which had once been divided by a deep valley, now partially filled in by the accumulated debris of centuries. Other valleys bounded the city on two sides, the Kidron on the east and the Hinnon on the west. The descent on both sides was steep, and Emerson's rude description had some justice to it; an untidy jumble of structures clung to the slopes as if they had slid over the edge and stuck partway down.

The Old City itself was girded by the magnificent wall built by Suleiman the Great in the twelfth century. We entered through the Jaffa Gate, one of seven, and found ourselves in a commercial district of comparatively recent date, with shops and banks and hotels. After we had passed several of the latter I began to suspect that the hostelry selected by Emerson and the confounded War Office would be neither new nor convenient.

Before long the modern streets were succeeded by the narrow winding lanes of a typical mideastern city. Fortunately our drivers knew the way; guidebook in hand, I attempted to follow our route but lost track within a few minutes. My attempts to locate sights of interest – the Ecce Homo Arch, the Church of the Holy Sepulchre, and so on – were frustrated by increasing darkness and the inadequacy of the map in the book. The Dome of the Rock was hidden by the houses and small shops that closed in the street, so even that landmark was no longer visible. I gave it up, and addressed Mr. Plato, who was peering interestedly out the window of the carriage.

'Do you know where we are?' I asked. 'You have been here before, haven't you? You must know the city well.'

'It has changed a great deal since my day,' was the reply.

From anyone else I would have interpreted that as evasion. From Mr. Plato it sounded like a casual reference to a visit he had made in the first or second century B.C.

'What was it like in your day?' I asked.

The carriage turned a rather sharp corner, swayed, and stopped abruptly. The impediment appeared to be a camel, whose hindquarters were visible just ahead. Our driver rose, brandished his whip, and began shouting at the beast and its driver. The effect, as he must have known it would be, was negligible. The camel didn't even look round. Its rider made gestures of an indeterminate but probably rude nature at our driver, who responded with another flow of invective. I poked him with my parasol.

'Be patient,' I said in Arabic. 'Our future is in the hands of Allah.'

Realizing that I had understood his curses, the driver turned an embarrassed face toward me. 'We are almost there, lady,' he stammered.

The camel proceeded calmly on its way. It did clear a path for us; donkeys and pedestrians were forced to one side, since a camel yields to no one. It was not long before we entered a newer section of the city. The streets were wider and straighter. I was conscious of mounting fatigue, for we had started early that morning, and I was considerably relieved when the carriage stopped before a modern structure.

Emerson had decided we would not stay at the same hotel as Morley. His was on the Mount of Olives, not in the city itself, and '. . . we don't want the fellow to think we are trailing him.' This was, in my opinion, an absurd argument. We *were* trailing him, and he would soon know that. It was, I deduced, Emerson's little way of forestalling any complaints I might make about our own hotel.

In fact, it was not nearly as bad as I had feared, and a distinct improvement over the one in Jaffa. Jewish and Christian pilgrims,

Ottoman dignitaries in fezzes like crimson flowerpots, and turbaned Arabs mingled in the comfortably furnished lobby and the dining room, and an efficient young Egyptian assistant manager saw us to our rooms. They were among the best in the establishment, consisting of a sitting room and a number of sleeping chambers. An adequate if primitive bath chamber was just down the hall.

Accompanied by Mr. Fazah, I personally inspected the arrangements and approved them. He was about to take his leave when I asked him to wait a moment. Raising thumb and forefinger daintily to the tip of my nose, I wriggled it back and forth.

He appeared somewhat taken aback. 'Was there anything else, madam?' he asked, averting his eyes.

I had assumed that this establishment, like the one in Jaffa, had connections with the secret service. If so, the assistant manager was not the connection. It was of course possible that Boniface had deliberately deceived me. To picture me making that absurd gesture to one bewildered person after another might have been his notion of a joke.

I dismissed the young man with appropriate thanks, and in a somewhat thoughtful mood returned to the sitting room, where I found Emerson pouring the whiskey.

'You had better not be so liberal with it,' I remarked, taking the glass he handed me. 'I don't know whether it is easily obtainable here. Moslems don't indulge, nor the stricter Christian sects; is the same true of Orthodox Jews?'

'It probably depends on the particular sect. Fear not, Peabody. Anything is obtainable in this country for a price.'

'I believe the same is true of most countries, Emerson. Even dear old England.'

'True.' Emerson took a long refreshing sip. 'We both know places in London where one can hire an assassin or a – er –

companion, or purchase any variety of deadly drugs. You aren't drinking, my dear. Is something wrong?'

'Yes. No. Oh, Emerson, I am having second thoughts about our decision to come on here. Are we doing the right thing?'

'Well, my dear, you rather railroaded us into it,' Emerson remarked. 'It is unlike you to question your own decisions.'

His jesting remarks were intended to stir me up, but my mood was too somber. With nothing else to do during the long carriage ride, I had had all day to rethink my decision – for it had been mine, and I had not allowed dissent or discussion.

'But now we have lost both boys,' I murmured. 'What if –'

'No what-ifs, Peabody. Bear in mind they are not boys but young men who have had a good deal of experience in unusual situations. Give them a few more days.' He patted my hand. 'Now cheer up and drink your whiskey like a lady.'

From Manuscript H

'What have you done to him?' Ramses pulled away from Mansur and knelt beside David. There was blood on his face, but he was breathing evenly.

'He brought it on himself.' Mansur sounded somewhat rattled. 'He should not have resisted. I must – I have another matter to attend to.'

The guard had backed off a few feet, his weapon raised. Ramses gave him an ingratiating smile, and prodded David.

'I know you're awake. Sit up very, very slowly and tell me what the hell you're doing here.'

'Looking for you.' David opened one eye and then the other. Ramses braced his shoulders as he raised himself, very very slowly, to a sitting position. 'I went to Samaria and –'

'You needn't explain what you did.' The same idea might have occurred to him if their positions had been reversed. David had shown himself at or near Samaria, dressed like Ramses and imitating his mannerisms and speech as only David could do, in the hope that word would get back to the kidnappers that there was a second Ramses Emerson on the loose. It was a wild, crazy scheme, but obviously it had worked. Up to this point. He and David did look enough alike that a verbal description would have matched both: six feet tall, black hair and eyes, thin faces and prominent features, brown skin. But no one seeing them together could mistake one for the other.

'Why did you put up a fight when they caught up with you?'

'I felt it advisable to live up to your reputation for bellicosity.' David raised a hand to his head and winced. 'It may not have been such a clever idea.'

Worry made Ramses's voice sharper than it should have been. 'Not that I don't appreciate your good intentions, but I can't see that they have improved the situation. Unless you have a pistol or two tucked into your trouser pockets.'

''Fraid not. They searched me quite thoroughly. But it was worth it. At least now I know you're alive.'

Touched, terrified, and furious, Ramses found it difficult to speak for a moment.

'Talk fast,' he said urgently. 'The guard doesn't understand much English, but Mansur won't leave us alone together for long. What made you believe I was a prisoner when I wrote that note?'

'It was enclosed in a woman's handkerchief. Your mother was the first to point out that if you had done something so uncharacteristic as run off with a woman, you wouldn't have advertised it. But she said she could think of several innocent reasons why someone else –'

'Yes, she would.' For once Mansur had been a little too clever. And it had led to this.

'Who are these people?' David asked. 'And what do they want?'

'Good question.' He wondered what was delaying Mansur. Was it David's unexpected advent that had thrown him off balance, or was something else going on? Well, they would find out soon enough. No use crying over spilled milk, as a lady of his acquaintance might have said. Take the bull by the horns and time by the fetlock, put your shoulder to the wheel, and figure out what to do now.

'Their aim is to expel foreigners, especially Englishmen, from this part of the Ottoman Empire. It may come to jihad one day, but at present they are preparing the ground and spreading the word. Mansur is one of the leaders; the other is a woman, a German.'

David started to speak. Ramses raised a hand for silence and went on rapidly: 'Her motives may not be the same as Mansur's, but they have formed an alliance because their goal is the same. They murdered a British agent who was with their group in disguise. He told me several things before they caught him. They are searching for some sort of talisman to inspire the faithful. It could be an artifact, a manuscript, even a man. If – when – you get out of here you must take that information back to Father. He'll know what to do with it.'

'When *we* get out of here,' David said, in that gentle inflexible voice.

Ramses shook his head vehemently. 'I must stay with them. I haven't made any attempt to escape – probably couldn't have pulled it off anyhow, but I didn't try because I need to know what they're after. And stop them if I can.'

'Why you?'

It was a reasonable question, and one he couldn't answer. Not patriotism, not love of country, not duty; they were catchwords that could be used for good or ill. Certainly not a fanatical dedication to the ideal of empire, which had inspired so many young idiots like Macomber. Because a lot of innocent people will be killed if they bring this off? That made better sense, but it wasn't the only reason. And one of those reasons did him no credit. He wanted to get back at Mansur. It had become a personal duel.

He was trying to think what to say when the door opened, to admit not only Mansur but a group of servants carrying loaded trays. They moved efficiently around the room, moving two of the small tables together and spreading them with cloths, setting them with silverware, crystal, and even linen napkins. Ramses's empty stomach reacted embarrassingly to the savory odors wafting from various dishes. He hadn't had anything to eat or drink for hours.

Mansur stood looking on with folded arms, then dismissed most of the servants with a lordly wave of his hand. The few that remained, including Mansur's servant and a veiled female, took up their positions behind the chairs that had been placed at the tables. Four chairs.

She swept into the room with the assurance of a queen, head high and step firm. She wore a long gown of some pale blue floating stuff, and little jeweled slippers; her fair hair was wound round her head in a braided coronet.

David leaped to his feet, eyes widening. The image he had formed in his mind of the unnamed German female obviously didn't match the reality.

She inspected him with cool detachment and then glanced at Ramses.

'Can there be any doubt?' she inquired of Mansur.

'No. No, lady.'

'Then why is he here?' She gestured dismissively at David.

'Those who brought him had not seen the other. They heard him spoken of by name.'

'And there is a certain resemblance,' she agreed. 'Perhaps they are not wholly to blame. But it does present a difficulty.'

'One that is easily solved, lady.'

They had spoken English. Ramses felt sure the choice of language was deliberate; they wanted him and David to understand the half-veiled threat. He managed to refrain from question or comment. She was watching him as if through a microscope, alert to every change of expression.

Then a smile curved her lips. 'Of course, Mansur. We will dine together, like reasonable beings, and find a way out of our difficulty.'

The china was Bavarian, the glasses crystal, the silverware heavy and ornate. Frau von Eine had done Gertrude Bell one better; she had brought along the family silver, complete with crest.

The veiled woman waited on her mistress and Mansur's servant on him. The latter avoided looking at Ramses or David, but the woman stole glances at them from time to time. She had big, soft brown eyes outlined with kohl, and the veil was thin enough to outline a neat little nose and rounded chin. Once Ramses caught her eye and smiled. Madame saw the smile. She didn't miss much. It seemed to amuse her.

The other servants were competent enough, though not so well trained as the personal attendants of their host and hostess. The food was excellent: lamb prepared with spices and vegetables, fresh-baked bread, bowls heaped high with fruit.

'I trust you find yourselves comfortable here?' was Madame's opening gambit.

'We are hardly in a position to complain,' Ramses said.

'You are our guests. You must tell Mansur if there is anything you require.'

Ramses realized he was no longer hungry. With the exception of Mansur, they had been served wine, a dark red beverage that was a little too sweet to accompany the lamb. He picked up his glass and raised it in an ironic salute. 'We require only our freedom, Madame. Since both of us were brought here by force, the word "guests" is hardly accurate.'

The lady acknowledged his salute with an inclination of her head. 'I regret the necessity.'

'Then explain the necessity.' Ramses felt his temper giving way. He had been able to control it – barely – when he was the only prisoner, but David's safety – his very survival, perhaps – was at stake now. He went on with mounting heat. 'I'm tired of lies and equivocation. Just tell me what the hell you want from me, and perhaps we can come to a sensible agreement. I've become bored with the childish games Mansur has been playing.'

Mansur, who hadn't spoken a word or looked directly at Ramses, turned toward him with bared teeth and a raised fist – the first crack in that impenetrable facade Ramses had seen. 'We want nothing from you. You are not a danger to us, only an inconvenience, and if we decide the inconvenience is too great –'

'Mansur!' Madame's voice cracked like a whip.

Mansur's sleeve had fallen back. On the inside of his forearm, just below the elbow, Ramses saw a crimson mark, too regular to be an accidental disfigurement. He was trying to make it out when Mansur lowered his arm and sat back.

'I ask your pardon,' he said.

'Granted,' Ramses said, though he was sure the apology hadn't been directed at him. 'Why don't you try telling me the truth?' he suggested. 'Mansur implied I might sympathize with your aims if they were explained to me. What harm can it do, so long as we are closely guarded . . . guests? If those aims are, as I suspect, freedom and independence for the Arab people, I'm on your side, so long as your methods aren't violent.'

She pondered the question, propping her chin on one slim hand. 'A reasonable suggestion,' she said after a moment. 'But it grows late, and you are no doubt weary. Rest well, and tomorrow we will talk again.'

The waiting servant girl pulled Madame's chair back as she rose. The men got to their feet. What else would a gentleman do in the presence of a lady? Ramses wondered if she had stood watching while someone cut Macomber's throat.

The sun rose behind me as I climbed the steep slope from Deir el Bahri to the top of the cliff and the path that led to the Valley of the Kings. I knew what I would see when I reached the summit, and my heart beat fast with anticipation. Sure enough, he was there, walking toward me with the long free stride of a man in the prime of life. Abdullah's beard had been white when he died in my arms after giving his life to save mine. In these dreams beard and hair were black and his handsome, hawklike face was unlined.

I turned so that we stood side by side, in silence, watching the scarlet orb of the sun lift above the eastern cliffs, banishing the darkness with the life-giving rays of Re Harakhte.

'Or perhaps it is Amon Re, or Aton, Akhenaton's sole god,' I mused aloud.

'The One has many names,' Abdullah replied in sonorous tones. 'Do you intend to waste the time we are allotted in meaningless chatter?'

'That sounds more like my old friend,' I said, laughing. 'First and most important – I am glad to see you. Why has it been so long?'

'You had no need of me.'

'It was not that I did not think often of you,' I said, answering the implicit reproach. 'If I had no other cause, I would remember you whenever I see David or speak with Selim. He has taken on his responsibilities as reis admirably.'

'As he should. He is my son. Now, Sitt, let us speak of other things. Why must you leave your homeland to wander in dangerous and uncivilized places?'

By homeland he meant Egypt. And he was correct; I knew that if I did return after death to a place I loved, it would be this place – looking down on the Valley of the Nile and the scene of my happiest years. This was an old complaint of Abdullah's; no traveler he, he could never understand why any sane person would want to be anywhere else.

'It was Emerson's idea,' I said disingenuously. 'Should I not follow my husband wherever he leads?'

'Ha,' said Abdullah, condensing a paragraph of sarcasm into a single syllable.

I did not defend myself, although in this particular case my statement was true. Abdullah would only go on and on about 'taking foolish chances' and not being careful.

'What about giving me some practical advice for a change?' I inquired. 'Or a hint of dangers to be avoided?'

'Rather,' said Abdullah, folding his arms and looking stern, 'I will tell you what I think of your latest foolish action. My grandson has bared his throat to the knives of your enemies. Why did you let him go?'

'I forbade him to go. He has never disobeyed me before. But I should have done more, I should have . . . Oh, Abdullah, don't scold me, I am too miserable and too worried.'

I hid my face in my hands. For a moment I imagined I felt a touch, fleeting as the flutter of a bird's wing, against my cheek. When Abdullah spoke, his voice was very gentle.

'Ramses is his friend, close as a brother. How could David do otherwise and keep his honor?'

'That is just like a man,' I said bitterly. 'I don't give a curse about his honor, or that of Ramses. I want them back, safe and sound. And soon. What shall I do?'

'Wait,' said Abdullah.

I turned on him, so abruptly that he stepped back a pace. He had been standing very close. I had known, instinctively, that I must not try to touch him in these visions.

'I know that is advice you do not like,' Abdullah said. 'But I cannot tell you the future, Sitt. Until it becomes the present, it exists as one possibility out of many. You are not the one who determines what will come to pass.'

'Yes, yes, I know. It is in the hands of God,' I said.

'In the end. But He works through human agents and you are only one of them. A powerful agent to be sure,' he added, and I saw that he was smiling.

'Tell me, at least, that they are both alive. Please, Abdullah. I can wait – if I must – for a while – if I know that.'

'The allotted time has passed, Sitt.'

There were rules in this strange other world, and my question had violated one of them. Sunk in despair, I watched him walk slowly away, along the path that would lead him across the plateau to the royal valley. Slowly and more slowly he went . . . And turned, and spoke a single word.

And I woke with my face wet with tears and my heart filled with joy.

Emerson was still sound asleep, so I lay quiet beside him, watching the gray light brighten at the window. Morning brought the inevitable reaction to my moments of happiness. Doubt and – yes, I admit it – irritation. Those visions of my dear old friend comforted me for his loss and I never doubted the truth of what he told me. But it was an infuriatingly limited truth. Why hadn't I phrased that final question differently? It was not enough to know that the boys were still alive. I wanted a glimpse into the future and advice on what to do.

Emerson let out a grunt and turned over. His outflung arm landed heavily on my diaphragm, but being accustomed to this maneuver I was prepared for it. I had no intention of mentioning my dream to Emerson. He would not have found it as meaningful as I, since he did not believe in the reality of those visions. Once he had made the mistake of referring to them as products of my unconscious mind. I had of course reminded him that he did not believe in the unconscious mind either.

By the time Emerson began muttering and thrashing about, in his habitual prelude to waking up, I had come to a decision. Abdullah had given me one piece of advice. 'Wait.' It went against the grain, no doubt of it, but it did accord with my preliminary plan: to give the boys a few more days and in the meantime carry out our initial purpose, or at least make a good beginning.

I arranged for breakfast to be served in our room, since I knew Emerson was incapable of reasoned discourse until he had had several cups of coffee. When the servant arrived he brought with him two messages. Emerson was splashing about in the washbasin at the time, so I hastily inspected them. None bore the writing I had hoped to see, so I handed them over to Emerson unopened and waited impatiently until he had imbibed a sufficient amount of caffeine.

'Well, well,' he remarked, perusing the first. 'Our arrival, it seems, has become known. Furman Ward of the American Palestine Organization begs the favor of a meeting at our earliest convenience.'

'I am not familiar with that organization, Emerson.'

'It is, I believe, of fairly recent date. This,' he continued, 'is from Ward's British counterpart. He would be happy to call on us as soon as is possible.'

He handed the notes to me. 'There is a certain air of urgency about them,' I commented. 'I believe I can hazard a guess as to what – or rather, who – has prompted it.'

'More than a random guess, Peabody. Morley has been here for several weeks, long enough to stir up the local archaeological community. Suppose we call on these gentlemen this morning? They can tell us what the bastard has been up to.'

We dispatched messages to the individuals in question. I could only hope that they would be able to receive us, for Emerson refused to wait for a reply. He never made appointments; he simply turned up and carried on with extreme indignation if the person he wanted was not there. Ah, well, I told myself philosophically, we would at least enjoy a stroll through the hallowed streets of the world's holiest city.

The others were finishing their breakfast when we joined them. Nefret's eyes were shadowed, as if she had not slept well. Daoud was his usual placid self but Selim seemed a trifle on edge. He kept looking at a group on the far side of the room. Heads bowed, Bibles in their hands, they were intent upon a peroration delivered by one of their number. Garbed all in black, he resembled a bird of prey, with a nose like a beak, and thin, clawlike fingers. His eyes were raised to heaven (the ceiling of the dining salon, to be precise) and his voice was remarkably penetrating; I could hear him clear across the room.

'"Beautiful for situation, the joy of the earth, is Mount Zion." How true the words of the Psalmist, O my beloved brothers and sisters! If her beautiful situation charms us now, what will it be in that day when the true king returns, when that psalm will have its perfect fulfillment?'

'Good Gad,' said Emerson, over a chorus of rapturous 'amen's.' 'Why is that fellow making such a racket? He needs to be reminded of his manners. This is not a cursed church.'

'If you have all finished breakfast, we must be on our way,' I said, slipping my arm through that of Emerson before he could explain his notion of good manners to the speaker. I was just in time. The speaker started on another psalm, at an even higher pitch than before.

Nefret had scarcely spoken, except for a murmured 'Good

morning.' Now she asked, 'Where are you and the Professor off to?'

I explained our mission, adding, 'We are all going. You will enjoy meeting the gentlemen, I am sure. We will go on foot, enabling you to photograph the sights of the city.'

'Very well. I will just run up and get the camera and my hat.'

'Dear me,' I said. 'I seem to have forgotten mine as well. And my parasol.'

'I'll get them,' Nefret said. 'There is no need for both of us to go. May I have the key to your room?'

She gave me a winning smile and met my eyes with a candid gaze that aroused certain suspicions. I am a firm believer in the old adage that says 'Never trust a man who looks you straight in the eye.'

Or words to that effect. I couldn't think what mischief Nefret could get up to in ten minutes, but after David's defection I was taking no chances. With a winning smile of my own I said I would accompany her, since I hadn't made up my mind which hat to wear. (The hat I selected was my traveling hat, of fine straw with ribbons that tied under the chin and topped with a tasteful arrangement of dried flowers.) She came out of her room before I could knock at the door, hat and camera in hand. So perhaps the offer had been genuine. Perhaps I was becoming too suspicious.

The men had scattered in all directions, which men are inclined to do when women leave them to their own devices for any length of time. I believe they are easily bored. Selim and Daoud had gone back to the dining room for a last bite, and Emerson was arguing with a bewildered man, whom I deduced to be a Protestant minister. I collected them, to the relief of the clerical gentleman, and then looked round.

'Now where has Mr. Plato got to?'

'Perhaps he is waiting outside,' Selim suggested.

However, he was nowhere to be seen. 'Confound the man,' I exclaimed. 'He has wandered off. We will never locate him now.'

'The devil with him,' said Emerson, consulting his pocket watch. 'He will find his way back, or he won't. I'll wager he will turn up when he gets hungry – within an hour or two, at most.'

The British Society for the Exploration of Palestine was housed at that time in a lovely old Arab building in the center of the Old City. It took us a while to get there. None of the persons we asked for directions had ever heard of the place. So we wandered, quite happily on my part, quite otherwise on the part of Emerson, along tortuously winding streets, under ornamented arches, up and down steps as narrow and as steep as staircases. The Babel of tongues, the cries of street vendors, the variety of costumes, the elegance of carved fountains and elaborate doorways – all added to the pleasure of the stroll. But when Emerson's complaints rose to a thunderous grumble I returned my attention to our errand. Stopping a picturesquely garbed individual towing a goat, I asked where the mosque of Sheikh Abu al Mahmud was to be found. The Society offices, as I had taken pains to ascertain from the clerk at the desk, was nearby.

Following the directions provided by the amiable goatherd, we were soon at our destination.

'We are late,' said Emerson, beating a tattoo on the door with the massive iron knocker. 'Why didn't you ask for the mosque before?'

I never lie unless it is absolutely necessary, so I did not reply. The time elapsed from our leaving the hotel meant that we had arrived at a respectable hour in midmorning, instead of turning up at 8:00 A.M.

From the enthusiastic welcome we received I realized we might have come at almost any hour. The director, Mr. Samuel Page, was a lean individual almost as tall as Emerson, and only half his bulk. His shoulders had the characteristic scholarly stoop, and his hair had vanished except for a thin gray tonsure. His office was a pleasant room lined with bookshelves and carpeted with several fine old oriental rugs. Peering at us through gold-rimmed eyeglasses, he shook hands with everyone except Selim and Daoud, whom he acknowledged with a polite inclination of his head.

'You have brought your own reis and assistant with you, I see. An excellent thought. What other staff have you?'

Settling himself with a thud into the chair Mr. Page had indicated, Emerson replied, 'Mrs. Emerson and myself, Miss Forth, and – and . . .' He cleared his throat loudly and looked to me for help.

'My son and his friend, the artist of our group,' I finished. 'They have been delayed but will soon join us.'

'Quite right,' said Emerson, overcoming his moment of weakness.

'Will that be sufficient? I may be able to introduce you to a few qualified persons who are familiar with this region.'

'As a matter of fact,' I began.

'It will be sufficient,' Emerson said loudly. 'Our excavations will be limited in time and extent.'

'Then . . . then dare I hope that your primary intent is otherwise? That you are here in response to the protests we have been sending to our colleagues in England and America regarding a certain – er –'

'Major Morley,' said Emerson.

'Then you are aware of the situation. Thank heaven! All of us here feel helpless to stop him. He has been enthusiastically welcomed by the governor of Jerusalem, Azmi Bey Pasha, and has official permission from Constantinople. Professor Emerson, so far as we can determine, the fellow has absolutely no professional training. No one seems to know who he is, or what he is after, though there are distressing rumors that this is purely a treasure-hunting expedition. We cannot –'

Emerson raised a magisterial hand. 'Calm yourself, sir.'

'I do beg your pardon.' Mr. Page took out a handkerchief and mopped a forehead now liberally bedewed with drops of perturbation. 'When we heard of your arrival it gave us fresh hope. Your reputation is well known, Professor, not only for professional integrity, but for . . . er . . . how shall I put it?'

'Cutting through red tape?' I suggested.

Emerson, who had been expecting a more emphatic metaphor, nodded graciously at me. 'What's he doing now?'

'He has just begun his so-called excavations on the Hill of Ophel.'

'Well, well.' Emerson fondled the cleft in his prominent chin. 'By a strange coincidence, my own excavation is nearby.'

'The whole area is surrounded by guards and soldiers. No one has been able to get near it,' Page said.

If Emerson had entertained doubts as to how to proceed, that challenge would have ended them. His sapphirine-blue eyes shone with anticipatory pleasure. 'We will see,' he said.

Belatedly remembering his manners, Mr. Page offered us refreshment. Emerson declined with thanks. 'I want to inspect the site this afternoon,' he explained.

'We promised to call on Dr. Ward this morning,' I reminded him.

'No time for that, no time for that,' said Emerson. 'I presume Page here is speaking for the entire archaeological community of Jerusalem. Reassure your associates, sir. Mrs. Emerson and I are on the job.'

We returned to the hotel for luncheon. Emerson considered this a frightful waste of time and said so, at length. I had got him to agree by pointing out that Nefret and I were not dressed for scrambling up and down the hills of Jerusalem. I was also anxious to know whether Mr. Plato had returned. He was becoming an infernal nuisance, but we had assumed responsibility for him and I do not abandon responsibilities lightly.

As Emerson had predicted, we found him already at luncheon. He greeted us with a vague smile and asked whether we had had a nice morning. Emerson asked him where the devil he had got to, and he explained, 'I wished to be alone when I refreshed my memory of the Holy City.'

'We were worried about you,' Nefret said. 'Please don't go off again without telling us.'

Plato ducked his head and looked a trifle abashed. 'You mustn't worry about me, my dear.'

'But I do.' The warmth of her smile and voice brought a faint flush to the reverential cheek. 'You are a friend, and I care about my friends.'

'Yes, yes,' said Emerson. He does not approve of public displays of affection, especially when they are directed at someone of whom he does not approve. 'Hurry up and change, ladies. We must be on our way soon.'

'Where are we going?' Plato asked brightly.

Emerson's mouth opened, but I got in ahead of him. 'The day is half gone, Emerson. I propose we wait until tomorrow morning before visiting the site.'

'You deliberately delayed us!' Emerson exclaimed. 'See here, Peabody –'

'Furthermore,' I continued in a somewhat louder voice, 'Daoud and Selim have not yet seen the Haram al-Sharif. They must be anxious to do so, as am I, though for different reasons. Would you deprive our friends of the opportunity to visit the third-holiest shrine of their faith?'

Selim began, 'Sitt Hakim –'

'Do not protest, Selim, I know you are always willing to subvert your own desires to those of Emerson, but I cannot allow such self-sacrifice. I know you are desirous of visiting the Noble Sanctuary, Daoud.'

Douad's mouth was full. He nodded vigorously, his face alight.

'Curse it,' said Emerson inappropriately.

It was impossible to miss our destination. It dominated the city from all directions. We entered the sacred enclosure by way of a covered street called the Bab el-Kattan. It was an impressive entrance, with its high-vaulted roof, if one ignored the occasional donkey or heap of rubbish.

Opening my guidebook, I read aloud. 'It was probably here that Christ turned out the moneylenders and Ezra gathered –'

'Bah,' said Emerson.

Emerging from the tunnel, we found ourselves in an open space shaded by cypresses and fig trees and adorned with fountains and shrines. A flight of steps led up to the platform where the magnificent structure stands. We were walking in that direction when we received an unexpected check in the form of a turbaned attendant, who informed us that Christians could only be admitted when accompanied by a kavass from the consulate of the nation to which they belonged, and by a Turkish soldier.

'I am no Christian,' Emerson said forcibly.

'He is the Father of Curses,' Daoud declared. He went on, in rolling tones, to identify the rest of us by our sobriquets. The attendant, a wizened little man whose face was dwarfed by his imposing turban, opened his eyes very wide. It would have been difficult to say whether he was impressed or simply bewildered. I suspected the latter. We left him scratching his head and contemplating with satisfaction the baksheesh Emerson had handed over.

'Such nonsense,' said Emerson, bounding up the stairs.

Leaving our shoes at the door, we entered. The light was dim and the aspect one of peaceful reverence. In the center, in stark contrast to the intricate designs that decorate the interior of the dome, was a large unhewn rock surrounded by a screen of wrought iron.

'It was upon this rock,' I said in appropriately soft tones, 'that Abraham was prepared to sacrifice his beloved son.'

Before Emerson could voice his opinion of a God who would put a faithful servant to such a test, I went on, 'And from which Mohammed ascended into heaven.'

'Very interesting, Aunt Amelia,' Nefret said politely.

Our friends joined the worshippers who were at prayer (all of them men) and we passed the time admiring the exquisite workmanship of the mosaics and inlays of gold and marble that adorn the interior. I noticed that Nefret had Plato firmly by the arm, and that he was muttering to himself.

Emerson waited till Selim and Daoud had finished their prayers and then announced we must be going. 'There is a great deal we haven't seen,' I protested. 'The Al-Aksa Mosque, the stables of Solomon –'

Emerson's response, as I expected, was an emphatic 'Solomon, balderdash. We will come back another day.'

Since Emerson seldom pays attention to where he is going, I was able to arrange our return route in such a way as to view another of the famous sights of the city. Selim and Daoud were perfectly agreeable to visiting the Church of the Holy Sepulchre; Jesus, whom they call Issa, is a venerated prophet to Moslems. It was surrounded by Turkish soldiers, who were there – I regret to say – in order to keep the peace among the various Christian sects. Despite the relatively late hour, the edifice was full of people, some pilgrims, some clerics going through various rites at various altars. The smell of incense was strong and the noise level high. A group of pilgrims, weeping and praying, had gathered around the Stone of Unction, where the Saviour's body was anointed after being taken down from the cross.

'If someone isn't keeping an eye on them,' said Emerson, doing so, 'they'll chip chunks off for souvenirs until there's nothing left of the stone. Not that it matters, since –'

'Hush,' I said.

The Tomb itself was completely encased in marble and illumined by dozens of lamps. Emerson, who had relieved me of my guidebook, read aloud:

'"Of the lamps in the outer chapel, five belong to the Greek Orthodox, five to the Latin Church, four to the Armenians, and one to the Copts." The whole bloody church –'

'Emerson!'

'. . . is divided among the various sects. If one intrudes on the space of another, a – er – sanguinary battle may ensue. Orthodox priests battering at their Latin brothers with incense burners, Armenians trying to throttle Copts . . .'

At one end of the vast chamber was a wooden structure covering the Hill of Calvary. Upon request, a panel in the box was lifted. Underneath was a rock.

Emerson, who was by now thoroughly enjoying himself, remarked, 'How very convenient that the Tomb was within a few hundred yards of the place of the crucifixion, and that both were within the city.'

'Emerson, if you cannot speak politely, do not speak at all.'

In duty bound, we visited the various chapels, though I was beginning to get a headache from the close air, the babble of voices, and – since I must be candid – the garish ornamentation that covered every available surface. Emerson trailed after me, reading aloud from the guidebook and bumping into people. A chorus of complaints followed our little group. I caught Daoud, who was beside me, in the middle of a gigantic yawn, and informed my companions that it was time to leave.

'Not yet,' said Emerson, turning pages. 'We have yet to view the Chapel of the Derision, and the chapel where

Adam was buried, and there must be another thousand icons we haven't –'

Turning on my heel, I led the way to the entrance. Emerson followed, chuckling.

Chapter Six

From Manuscript H

'Well?' Ramses asked. 'What do you think?'

After the conclusion of the banquet, they had been shown to a smaller chamber behind the haremlik. It was part of a suite that had probably belonged to a favorite wife, consisting of a small bathroom and a sleeping room decorated in the same shabbily elaborate style as the main salon. The only light came from two oil lamps of pierced brass. Their hosts had also left a jug of water and a basket of oranges and figs.

Stretched out on the divan, David said sleepily, 'I can't complain about the accommodations or the food. Have you always been treated so well?'

Squatting at the head of the divan, his face on a level with David's, Ramses said softly, 'Tonight was the first time I've been allowed to bathe or change clothes for three days, and the amenities have improved considerably. It's part of Mansur's strategy – insignificant annoyances, but the sort that mount up. The question is, what is the lady's strategy?'

David said in the same low murmur, 'I assume we are being watched?'

'Or overheard, or both. Keep your voice down. It's a safe assumption.' He went on in the schoolboy Latin he and David had sometimes used when they didn't want to be understood. 'Where are we?'

'You not know? I know not. I was a – uh – from Nablus when they . . . damn!'

This wasn't working too well. David had forgotten most of his Latin. Ramses switched to the Cairene dialect of Arabic and spoke rapidly. 'We need to get away. I don't like the way this is going.'

'What do you mean?'

It would have taken too long to explain, even if he had been able to find the right words. He had assumed that Frau von Eine was the one giving the orders. Mansur's petty tricks might have been his own idea; none of them would have violated a general order that Ramses not be physically abused. But watching the pair during that bizarre dinner party had left him with the distinct feeling that their relationship had changed – or that he had been mistaken about the nature of that relationship. Open conflict between the two could leave him and David uncomfortably in the middle, subject to the whims of whichever party was on top. And neither party had their best interests in mind.

Instincts weren't evidence, but there was another, even stronger reason for his decision. David's arrival had caught them by surprise; perhaps they hadn't had time to arrange separate accommodations for him. Wily Mansur wouldn't allow that to last. He must know that neither would try to escape without the other. This might be their last, best chance.

'Later. Is there anything in your pack that could be useful? A knife, even a torch?'

'I had an extra knife, but I doubt it is there now. They wouldn't have given us our luggage if –'

'Look,' Ramses snapped.

David sat up with a grunt. 'I ate too much,' he said in more audible tones. 'Do you have anything to settle one's stomach?'

Ramses suppressed a smile. David hadn't lost his touch.

One of the lamps flickered and went out. The other was burning low. They dragged their luggage closer to the light and began sorting through the contents. The wind must be rising. The carved mashrabiya screens rattled and squeaked. A draft of air rustled the tattered hangings.

'Here's the medical kit Mother gave me before I left,' Ramses said. 'There may be something there. If I know Mother, there will be. She thinks of everything.'

'You haven't looked?'

'Reisner had his own medical supplies.'

Silently David shoved the open box under his nose. Under layers of rolled bandages, compresses, cotton wool, and tightly packed, neatly labeled containers of aspirin, iodine, stomach powders, and alcohol was a small leather folder that contained a set of surgical instruments.

Ramses breathed out a word that would certainly have won him a scolding if his mother had been there. David's response was less profane but equally admiring. 'Amazing! Er – the stomach powders. Just what I need.'

He uncapped the bottle and reached for the jug of water. Ramses took a closer look at the bottle labeled 'Alcohol.' He couldn't see the contents, since the glass was dark brown, but he didn't doubt the label was accurate. His mother favored brandy as a general antiseptic, since it could also be drunk.

Their search turned up several other items that could be useful, including all the money Ramses had been carrying. Ramses put it aside, with the medical kit. Honest fellow, Mansur, he thought. Either it hadn't occurred to him that a large sum of cash could be the equivalent of a key to a locked door, or he believed his people were too fanatical or too intimidated to be bribed.

They were methodically going through the pockets of coats and trousers when a stronger gust of air extinguished the lamp. It came, not from the windows but from the door. A slit of light appeared and widened.

Ramses sprang to his feet, gesturing David to stay where he was, and took up a position next to the opening door. If this was another of Mansur's games, allowing them to find items that gave them a faint hope of escape and then confiscating them, he'd have to take them by force.

The light came from an electric torch. Its beam focused on David, kneeling by the suitcase. He was trying to look ineffectual, his mouth ajar and his eyes squinting – but he had tossed a few items of clothing over the medical box. The beam moved away from him, darting round the room as if in search of something. Ramses had averted his eyes as soon as the light was switched on; now he made out a dark shape in the doorway. He plunged through the opening and caught hold of it. Before he could get a solid grip or whisper an order for silence, he knew who it was.

It had been, I admitted to myself, a grave error to take Emerson to the holiest site in Christendom. If anything could have reinforced his negative opinion of organized religion, the garish, unsuitable adornments and the quarreling of the followers of the gentle Prince of Peace would have had that effect. However, he had the sense to let the matter lie, and we spent a quiet evening going over our lists and planning our schedule for the following day.

I had learned enough about the terrain we would have to cover to conclude that stout boots and trousers were de rigueur. It was a pleasure once again to assume my working costume, with its many pockets and belt of useful accoutrements. I selected the stoutest of my parasols, made to my specifications with a heavy steel shaft and somewhat pointed tip, and proceeded to the dining salon, where I found that Emerson had ordered for me and was already halfway through his meal. He paced up and down (to the annoyance of patrons coming and going), talking to himself while I took my time about eating. The rapid consumption of food is detrimental to the digestive processes.

Having finished, I persuaded my impatient spouse to sit down and addressed our little group. 'You all know where we are going today.'

Plato looked up from his plate. 'Where?'

'Do we have to take him with us?' Emerson addressed the table at large. It was obvious from Daoud's and Selim's dour expressions that they were against the idea, but, as always with Emerson, Nefret's emphatic 'Certainly' won out. Emerson sighed.

'Very well. See here – er – it is time you made yourself useful. We are going to Siloam, where I intend to begin excavations. You claim to be well acquainted with the earlier archaeological excavations there. I will wish to discuss the current situation with you after we return, so stay on the qui vive and don't go wandering off again. And if I find you have nothing useful to contribute . . .'

He left the sentence unfinished, perhaps because he couldn't think of an appropriate threat. I certainly could not.

Selim had offered to arrange for donkeys, but we all declined except Mr. Plato, whom I overruled. Given the narrow streets and abundance of obstructions, animal and human, we could cover the ground more quickly on foot. Emerson and Daoud led the way, clearing a path through the crowded streets. It was still early morning when we stood on the Hill of Ophel looking down on the site of our future labors.

Behind us, high on its platform, the great golden dome of the Noble Sanctuary rose against the azure vault. The steepening slope before us was a jumble of broken walls, natural crevices, and gaping pits that might once have been tombs. The houses of the small village of Silwan spilled down the southern slope.

'There it is,' said Emerson, pointing. 'The pool of Siloam. It is fed by a spring carried here through the ancient water tunnel.'

'Where is the entrance to the tunnel?' I asked, shading my eyes with my hand. 'Emerson, I would like very much to explore it. I remember reading the description of the gentleman who was the first to explore it thoroughly – Mr. Warren, I believe – when it was silted up almost to the roof and the explorers had to slide through on their stomachs carrying candles in their mouths!'

'I am not at all surprised that you should find the idea attractive, Peabody,' said my husband. 'Given your penchant for crawling through the bat-infested substructures of pyramids. However, you will have to postpone that pleasure. It seems that Morley has got there first.'

People swarmed like ants around the pool and its environs. A number of them were filling waterskins and climbing back up the hill toward the city, for the pure spring water was reputed to have healing qualities. More to the point for us, one end of the area was closed off by ropes and barricades, and surrounded by armed men.

'Is that his aim, then?' I asked, as we descended. 'To excavate the tunnel?'

'It may come to that,' said Emerson, taking my arm. 'Where would the temple treasure be hidden but under the Haram, which is on top of Herod's temple, which is supposed to be on top of the temple of Solomon? Morley won't be allowed to dig at the base of the Haram, so he will try to come at it from below, like earlier explorers. They sank shafts deep into the ground and then drove tunnels horizontally toward the base of the Mount.'

One of the guards came running toward us, waving his rifle and shouting. He stopped short at a burst of extremely bad language from Emerson. My spouse's command of Egyptian insults is as

160

remarkable as the power of his voice. A rain of small pebbles rattled down the slope. As the guard stared, eyes wide, Daoud, towering over the rest of us, added his comments. 'Do you know to whom you speak, son of a camel? This is the mighty Father of Curses, and his chief wife the Sitt Hakim, who brings the dead back to life, and his daughter the Light of Egypt. Beg his forgiveness lest he strike you blind and deaf.'

The guard had been joined by another, equally unkempt, individual, who appeared to be in command of the squad. He also appeared to have better sense than his subordinate, for he addressed Emerson politely. 'You must have permission to be here, effendi. By order of the governor, Azmi Bey Pasha.'

Emerson took the firman from his coat pocket and held it up. 'I have permission. By order of the Sublime Porte.' He didn't give the guard time to read the document, supposing he had been able to do so, but put it back in his pocket. 'You may tell your Mudir that Emerson Effendi is here and will return.'

He turned his back on the guards and took my arm. We walked on together, and Emerson said, 'My tentative plan, Peabody, is to begin work at the other side of the hill, just there, where you see the foundations of what looks like a wall. The first step is to lay out a grid system.'

'The first step,' I corrected, 'is to find a house. We cannot carry our supplies back and forth every day. The terrain is too difficult.'

'What about those confounded tents you dragged all the way from England?'

'Where do you propose we set them up? The whole area is swarming with people. We wouldn't have a moment of privacy.'

'Not like Egypt, is it?' I could see that I had already lost his attention; his eyes were fixed, with greedy intensity, on the stretch of uneven tumbled stones that, in my humble opinion, looked nothing like a wall. 'By all means, Peabody. I leave the domestic arrangements up to you.'

We had already collected a little crowd of followers, mostly men and half-naked children. The local costume was simple, if not becoming: a shirt belted at the waist with a leather pouch attached to the belt, an abba (loose robe) over that, and a white tight-fitting cap wound round with a colored scarf to form a sort of turban. Leather slippers completed the ensemble. Some of the men were hoping for work; they had recognized us as archaeologists. The others had been drawn by pure inquisitiveness – a basic human trait. Turning, I addressed the gathering. 'We wish to hire a house. If any man knows of a good place, let him come here and talk to me.'

An animated babble of conversation ensued among the members of the audience. I seated myself upon a rock – there were plenty of them around – with an expression of gracious amiability, but for a while no one seemed brave enough to approach closer. Selim and Plato had gone on with Emerson, leaving Nefret and Daoud with me. 'Step back a bit,' I said to Daoud. 'I believe you make them uneasy.'

'They must show proper respect,' Daoud rumbled.

'They do, they are, they will. Back off, Daoud, and stop scowling. They are simple, friendly people who mean us no harm.'

It was at that moment that a large muscular man, waving a pistol, with a large knife and even larger sword stuck through his sash, came sliding down the slope straight at me.

From Manuscript H

She freed herself from his grasp and pushed past him, closing the door behind her. 'Don't be a fool,' she said quietly. 'I am here to help you.'

The torch had gone out when he took hold of her. She switched it on again, shielding it with her hand.

'Why?' Ramses asked.

'Why do I offer to help you? Because I need your help.' Completely composed, she seated herself on the divan and gestured him to join her. She was wearing a loose dark robe, her hair covered with a scarf of black lace. 'You need not fear being overheard,' she went on. 'Mansur is asleep – I made sure he would sleep soundly – and the man at the listening post understands very little English.'

'So we are being watched,' Ramses said.

'There are spy holes in every room of this place. An old Turkish custom.'

'Are there guards at the door?' Ramses asked.

'They are mine.'

'So it's yours and his, is it?'

'It has come to that. Listen now, you and your friend. He is trustworthy?'

David had settled onto the floor, legs crossed, next to the box that held their only weapons. 'We are brothers,' he said briefly.

'If you expect us to help you carry out your mission,' Ramses began.

'And you believe you know what that mission is?'

'Why don't you tell us?' Ramses said.

Her eyes reflected the dim light with a pale glow. 'I did not set out on this journey to foment rebellion and violence. My wish was simply to visit the archaeological sites where I have worked in the past and others where I would like to work in the future. I am looking for relics, if you like; I would call them artifacts, objects that will tell us more about the history of this region. I visited Samaria because the site has many possibilities; if Mr. Reisner gives up his concession, I may ask for the firman.'

She paused, reaching for the water jug. David jumped to his feet and poured a cup for her. He pointedly avoided looking at Ramses.

He hasn't fallen for it either, Ramses thought. But, by God, she was doing a beautiful job of covering the suspicious points. He didn't doubt she had spoken the truth when she said she was not trying to stir up a rebellion. Not now. It was too soon, Germany wasn't ready. And her claim to be investigating future sites for excavation couldn't be disproved.

'So where does Mansur enter into this?' he asked.

'He came to me before I left Istanbul and offered his services. It was clear to me that he was in the pay of the Sublime Porte and that I had no choice but to accept his offer or be refused permission to travel. The soldiers who accompanied us were under his command. As I learned to know him, I came to admire his intelligence and knowledge of Islam. I found myself increasingly in sympathy with his aspirations, his detestation of Ottoman rule, his hopes of freedom and prosperity for his people.'

A rattle of the screens made her start. She spoke more hurriedly. 'It took me some time to realize that he was not willing to wait for that freedom, that he was spreading messages of hatred and violence. When I charged him with it tonight, he denied it, but now he knows I am no longer in sympathy with his schemes. He will make me stay with him. I am afraid of him.'

'What can we do?' David asked. 'We are prisoners.'

'He hasn't made up his mind what to do with you. He would like to kill you both, but he is familiar, as am I, with Professor Emerson's reputation. If you disappeared, he would move heaven and earth to learn what had befallen you. For the time being you are safe with Mansur – and I will be safe if you are with him. Perhaps together we can come up with a plan. Will you give me your word you will not try to escape without me?'

'Word of an Englishman,' Ramses said solemnly.

'Thank you. I must go now. We will speak again soon.'

She held out her hand. Instead of kissing it, Ramses gave it a firm British shake.

She left them in darkness, and a lingering fragrance of lily.

David let out his breath. 'How does she do it? She's a small woman, with a soft voice –'

'"An excellent thing in woman,"' Ramses quoted.

'– but I feel as if I've been leaning into a gale for the past five minutes.'

'I know what you mean. It's called force of personality.' Ramses slid off the divan and felt his way toward David. The room wasn't totally dark; irregular spots of light danced on the floor under the wind-shaken mashrabiya screens.

'The screens are loose,' he said. 'And cracked. Empty your bag and start packing the things we'll need. We're getting out of here tonight.'

'What about word of an Englishman?'

'It has about the same value as word of a German lady. That was just another gambit, to convince us to submit quietly to captivity. Which leads me to believe we'd better get out of here as soon as we can.'

David's bag was surprisingly and encouragingly full when they finished. The box of medical supplies, the rolls and sacks of cash, a pair of rather gaudy blue-and-white-striped pajamas and two of the galabeeyahs Ramses preferred for sleeping attire. A small adjoining bath chamber contributed several linen towels and a bar of soap. Some of the money went into their pockets, along with a roll of twine, a box of matches, and the scalpels from the surgical kit.

'What if we can't break through the screens?' David asked.

'We'll set fire to them. There's some oil left in the lamp.'

'Are you serious?'

'I want out of here tonight. When Frau von Eine turns soft and timid she's up to no good.'

The only object that might conceivably serve as a lever was the fluted rim of the lamp. While David pried away at one of the sides,

Ramses inserted his fingers into several of the holes and pulled. A small segment broke off, then another. The wood was old and in some places rotten enough to yield to pressure, but progress was slow – too slow for his taste. The small frustrations and torments of the past few days had suddenly become unendurable.

'How's it coming?' he asked.

'Not so good. If I had a proper lever –'

'Why not wish for an ax while you're at it? At the rate I'm going it will take all night to open a large-enough hole. I think the whole damned thing would give way if I hit it hard enough.' He picked a few splinters out of his fingers.

'The fellow at the listening post might take notice of that,' David said drily. 'We haven't made a lot of noise or struck a light, but crashing through the screen would certainly get his attention.'

'I have my doubts about the spy hole. She didn't seem worried about being seen or heard with us, did she? It doesn't matter. I'm willing to take the chance.'

He didn't have to ask David if he was willing. David would go along with any plan he suggested. It was a foolhardy plan, but the alternative might be worse, especially for David. He himself was his father's son and a valuable hostage. If David became a nuisance they might decide he was expendable. They couldn't know that the entire Emerson family would track his killers down with the same ferocity they would have demonstrated for Ramses himself.

'Maybe we had better have a look before we leap,' David said. 'How high up are we?'

It was, like all David's suggestions, eminently sensible. Ramses tried to remember the route they had followed when they brought him into the haremlik. An open stone-paved courtyard, then a long corridor, a flight of stairs, a turn to the right, another corridor. They were on the first floor of the building and toward the back. The main reception rooms were below and at the front. They probably faced, as was customary, onto an enclosed court.

The harem quarters might face another court or even a street. The heavy screens were designed to keep lascivious eyes from ogling the beauties within. The beauties couldn't see out, either, but at least the poor creatures got a bit of air. He applied an eye to the opening, which was roughly eight inches in diameter.

The light came from a glorious full moon. Its rays illumined a narrow street lined with dwellings and shops. The shops were shuttered; there were no lights in any of the houses. The cobblestones of the street were a good twenty feet below. They looked extremely hard.

At the last moment the bandit, for such he appeared to be, veered away from me, toward the spot where Selim and Emerson stood. I cried out a warning. Emerson spun round and assumed a posture of defense as the apparition rushed toward him. Avoiding the blow directed at him, the fellow threw both arms round Emerson, pulled his head down, and planted whiskery kisses on both cheeks.

'It is you!' he cried. 'It is indeed you. We heard you were come to the Holy City but I did not allow myself to believe I would see you so soon. You will come to my house, you will stay with me and make my heart rejoice.'

'Well, well,' said Emerson, freeing his head in time to avoid a second round of kisses. 'If it isn't Abdul Kamir. What are you doing here, you old villain?'

I had of course risen to my feet, parasol at the ready, when it appeared my husband might be in danger of attack. Now I sank back onto the stony seat. Another of Emerson's dear old, disreputable old, friends. Was there no spot on earth free of them?

Upon closer examination Kamir did not look so menacing or so disreputable. His gray beard was neatly trimmed, the robes he had tucked up under his belt in order to run were clean and without holes. A pair of cracked spectacles perched on the end of his nose gave him a whimsical appearance, reinforced by his rotund frame and broad smile.

'An Arabic Father Christmas,' said Nefret, chuckling. 'He looks much jollier than the Professor's old friends usually do. Perhaps he can solve our housing problem.'

'We are certainly not staying with him,' I remarked – but softly, since Emerson was leading Kamir toward us. He presented all of us in turn. It took a while, since Kamir kept interrupting with effusive words of praise and pleasure at having the honor of meeting us.

'Are you then the sheikh of this village?' I asked, when Kamir had run out of compliments. I knew the word could mean any number of things, from an actual position to a generalized title of respect.

'No, no. But I am a man of importance here, with a fine house. You will stay with me, you will be my guests.'

'No, we won't,' said Emerson, who considers courtesy a waste of valuable time. 'We need a house of our own, Kamir. Can you find one for us?'

'Yes, yes. Come, I will show you now, you and your honored wife and your daughter. A light she is indeed, fair as the sun on the –'

'Mrs. Emerson will decide on the house,' Emerson said, shifting restlessly from one foot to the other. He had come upon something that intrigued him and could hardly wait to get back to it.

'But you will come and drink tea?'

As Emerson was well aware, it would have been a serious affront to refuse the invitation. 'Er – yes,' he said resignedly. 'As soon as I . . . er. Go on, go on, Selim and I will be there shortly.'

I asked Daoud to come with me, since I felt certain he would have come anyhow. He had not been favorably impressed by the locals he had met so far, and I had to admit that Kamir's array of weaponry did not inspire confidence. 'You, Daoud,' I went on, 'and . . . Confound it! Where is Mr. Plato? Emerson, was he with you? Do you see him?'

Emerson did not pause or look back. 'He was here a few minutes ago. The devil with him. Proceed, Peabody, proceed.'

'Really,' I said to Nefret, 'the man is impossible. Emerson strictly forbade him to wander off.'

'He is probably close by, Aunt Amelia, examining the terrain as the Professor asked him to do. Shall I try to find him?'

'The devil with him,' I echoed. 'Time is getting on and I want to find a house this morning.'

I had assumed the task of selecting a suitable abode would be mine. In fact I would have insisted upon it, since Emerson's notion of suitable does not agree with mine. Followed by Daoud, Nefret and I made our way toward the village along a steep but manageable path.

'And where did you know the Father of Curses?' I inquired of Kamir, who was walking along next to me.

'In Babylon, Sitt,' said Kamir, referring not to the city of the famed Hanging Gardens but to an area of Cairo. 'I came here to – uh – retire. Is that the word? Yes, retire from my labors. It was many years ago, but who could forget the Father of Curses?'

I did not inquire into the nature of Kamir's 'labors.' They had probably been illegal, and his 'retirement' a hasty departure to avoid arrest.

Our arrival had been heralded by some of the children, dashing ahead to announce the news. In such villages the arrival of strangers is always of consuming interest. Women came to their doorways to stare; some called out greetings and questions. When Nefret and I responded in their language, cries of admiration rewarded us. I noticed that there were no appeals for baksheesh from the children who tagged along at our heels, and that even the village dogs kept their opinions to themselves. Whoever the sheikh might be, he kept good order in his domain.

We inspected two houses. It did not take long. I had seen many such dwellings in Egypt: varying in size and state of repair, but similar in their basic plan. I selected the larger of the two, which had a spacious central room surrounded by bedchambers, one of which would serve as an office. The kitchen, such as it was, was located in a walled courtyard behind the house. It must have been vacant for some time, since there were birds' nests in corners and the floors were littered with a variety of substances, from dust and dirt to petrified orange peels and bird droppings.

As I had surmised, the house belonged to Kamir. He explained disingenuously that he had not rented or sold it because no one had been able to meet the price he deemed proper for such a fine house. I told him it would have to do, since he had nothing better, and haggled over the price – he would have thought less of me if I had not.

We then proceeded to Kamir's house, which was on a higher level. The village was a curious place, almost perpendicular, with houses perched on natural or buttressed ledges, but there was space for gardens and shade trees. Kamir's house had both, surrounding an establishment of some size and, considering that he was one of Emerson's old friends, remarkably clean and tidy.

We were seated in the main salon drinking tea when Emerson finally joined us. After hurrying through the formal greetings – and trying, unsuccessfully, to avoid another affectionate embrace from Kamir – he inquired, 'Everything settled, then?'

'The first step has been taken,' I replied. 'As you ought to know, Emerson, a number of other arrangements must be made before we can move in. I may be able to purchase some furniture in the mercantile establishments in the city, but I would prefer to deal with local carpenters who can construct simple bed frames, tables, and the like. No doubt Kamir can suggest likely persons.'

Kamir assured me that he could. I was not at all surprised. He went on to remark, 'If you have settled on the place where you want to dig, Father of Curses, I will speak to the owner of the land. You can trust me to get the best price for you.'

'Damnation,' said Emerson. 'I confess that particular issue had not occurred to me.'

It ought to have done. This was not Egypt, where we had usually worked in designated archaeological zones under the control of the Antiquities Department. All the land hereabouts was private property, and although the Ottoman government could probably seize anything they wanted, we could not. However, when Emerson is intent on a new excavation he loses sight of minor issues.

After stroking his chin and pondering, Emerson said, 'I will do my own negotiating, Kamir. Have the owner here tomorrow.'

This pitiable effort won a kindly smile from Kamir. One way or another he would get his cut of every transaction, from the carpenter to the servants we would hire, to the food we would purchase.

'How many men and boys will you want for the dig, Father of Curses?' Kamir asked. 'I will find them for you, I know the best workers.'

'And take your cut of their wages?' Emerson gave him a knowing smile. 'None of that, Kamir. I will hire my own workers. Many of them have had experience, I expect.'

Recognizing this for the useless attempt it was, Kamir grinned back at him. 'Oh, yes, and their fathers and grandfathers before them. The infidels have been digging here for many years, looking for sacred relics.'

'They are searching for knowledge,' Emerson corrected. 'Knowledge of the history of your people and theirs.'

'What good is history to a man who cannot feed his children?' Kamir asked rhetorically.

Emerson grunted. 'I refuse to enter into a philosophical discussion with you, you old wretch. And who are you calling an infidel?'

Daoud, who had been following the discussion with wrinkled brows, finally caught up. He let out a grumble of protest.

'I meant no offense,' Kamir said quickly. 'I bear malice toward no man, Moslem, Jew, or Christian. Are we not all sons of Abraham?'

From Manuscript H

No bedsheets, no rope, and no projection sturdy enough to hold a man's weight even if they had a means of descending. Ramses's sense of urgency was mounting. Ignoring David's muttered remonstrance, he drove his fist into the section of screen next to the hole. Wood shattered and fell, some scraps inside, some out. A second blow and the opening was now large enough. He forced his head and shoulders through and looked down.

The cobblestones extended clear up to the base of the wall, with no convenient shrubs or flower beds or heaps of trash to break one's fall. The wall itself was of dressed stone, without ornamentation or breaks, except for a few windows, each covered by a grillwork of curved iron bars set close together. One of them was directly below.

He reported this to David. 'There's a stone lintel about six inches deep, probably to keep rain out. I'll lower you. From there it's only a drop of ten or twelve feet.'

'How are you going to get down?'

'Don't argue, David, just do it.' He sat down and began unlacing his boots.

By leaning out the window as far as he could stretch, he got David down onto the lintel. He swayed unnervingly when Ramses let go his hands but managed to catch himself.

Once David was on the ground Ramses dropped the pack into his lifted hands, tied his boots together by the laces, and tossed them down too. Then Ramses climbed out the window. The uneven edges of the screen dug into his hands as he let himself down, groping for holds with his bare feet. Like the interior of the old villa, the walls were in poor repair, with enough missing mortar and crumbled edges to make the descent easy for someone who had spent years climbing up and down the cliff faces in Luxor, till the soles of his feet were hardened and his toes almost as prehensile as his fingers. But it was a relief when his feet found the solidity of the lintel. He was about to lower himself the rest of the way when a warning hiss from below made him freeze, his body flattened against the facade.

Until now the street had been deserted. The moon had set; in the starlight he made out a dim form coming toward him. David and the pack had disappeared – where, he couldn't imagine. He felt as exposed as a lizard on a wall, but any movement, even the slightest, would draw attention.

The pedestrian moved briskly, his sandals slapping on the stones. He wore a woolen coat over his abba and a scarf wound round his head. Ramses's muscles tensed. If the man looked up and saw him he would have to jump, and hope he could silence the fellow before he cried out.

The man passed out of his line of vision; he was directly below the window now. The regular slap-slap of leather soles didn't stop or pause. A workman, still half asleep, hurrying to be on time for the job.

Ramses let his breath out. He waited until the sound of footsteps had faded. Then he heard David's whisper. 'Come ahead. Quick.'

Once on the ground, Ramses said urgently, 'Let's get away from here.'

David drew him into the shelter of a recessed doorway. It wasn't deep enough to afford adequate shelter for two. 'We've got to get out of these clothes. The early birds will be waking up soon.'

Ramses was twitching with nerves. It had been easy so far – too easy? He remembered a story he had read, about a jailer who let his prisoner get all the way from his cell to the outside of the prison before recapturing him.

It was too late to worry about that. They had to go on, and fast. The next early riser might not be so unobservant, and European clothing would be remembered. He dug into the pack and pulled out the two galabeeyahs. It didn't take long to slip them on over their clothes, or to tie the towels onto their heads with pieces of twine. The result wasn't very convincing, but it might pass if no one examined them closely.

'Which way?' David asked.

Ramses was about to say it didn't matter when it occurred to him that the front entrance to the villa might face a plaza or a main thoroughfare. 'Right,' he said, and led the way into the odorous darkness.

They began to meet other pedestrians and a donkey or two, heavily laden with market produce. The sky had lightened and the cobblestones were slippery with dew. Ramses led the way, turning into one side street after another whenever anyone they met looked closely at them, or seemed about to speak. In the strengthening light their makeshift disguises were sure to arouse curiosity. Sooner or later they would have to find a bolt-hole and make a plan, but his only purpose now was to put as much distance as possible between them and the villa. Their best hope was to get out of the town and into the countryside, where they might find an abandoned shed or convenient ruin.

When the sun rose they were still in the town – it was a town, possibly even a city, not a village. This area was even more wretched and refuse-strewn than the other sections through which they had passed. Most of the houses were hovels, piles of stone held together with crumbling mortar and bits of wood. One or two of the structures on this stretch of street, if it could be called that, were somewhat more pretentious. He knew what they were even before the flimsy door of one house opened and a pair of Turkish soldiers staggered out. Their tunics were unbuttoned, and they were boasting in loud voices of the pleasures they had experienced.

The street cleared as if by magic – men, women, and even the dogs fading back into doorways and behind walls. Ramses had only time enough to drop to the ground, head bowed, hands cupped, and begin the whining litany of the fakir. 'Alms, for the love of Allah, alms for the poor, O beneficent ones!'

The men were dead-drunk – so much for the laws of Islam – and in no state of mind to be observant. One of them burst out laughing. The other called the beggar a filthy name, and kicked him in the side as they swaggered past.

Ramses doubled over with a howl of pain. Cautiously the residents ventured out of hiding. A murmur – a very soft murmur – of sympathy and anger arose. Ramses could have done without the sympathy. At any moment someone would get a closer look at his face and wonder why a beggar would be so young and healthy-looking.

The curtains at the doorway of the house behind him were drawn aside and a woman's voice said, 'Come in, holy one. We have medicines and food.'

It wasn't the sort of bolt-hole he would have chosen, but there really wasn't any choice. Bent over, clutching his side and groaning, Ramses stumbled in.

He had seen a number of brothels in el Wasa, the red-blind district of Cairo. He had never been inside one, not only because fastidiousness had triumphed over curiosity but also because he knew his mother would skin him alive if she found out he had done so – and Nefret would have set fire to the remains. He was pretty sure this was a pathetic specimen of the type: a small grimy room lit by a few cheap brass lamps, its only furnishings a wooden table, a few chairs, and a long divan presently occupied by three underdressed, weary-looking girls. The woman who had invited him in was older, her wrinkled face coated with cosmetics and her fleshy body covered by a loose wrapper. Hands on hips, she studied him through narrowed eyes.

'Honored Sitt,' Ramses began.

Her hand shot out and caught hold of his chin, forcing his head up so that one of the lamps shone full on his face.

'You are no beggar,' she said. 'Who are you? And why are you being hunted by the Turks?'

As we started up the hill Nefret asked, 'Do you intend to leave here without discovering what has become of Mr. Plato?'

Her tone was critical and her look severe.

'I don't give a curse what has become of him,' Emerson growled. 'Stop worrying about him, Nefret. He has done this before and always manages to find his way back to board and lodging. Particularly board.'

However, when we reached the foot of the great wall and the gate called the Dung Gate, whom should we behold but the reverend himself, seated on a boulder and surveying the scene with his usual vague smile.

'There you are,' he said. 'I thought you would come this way, so I waited for you.'

'What happened to you?' Nefret asked. 'That is a nasty bruise. Did you fall?'

Plato raised his hand to his jaw. 'I was met with resistance from the heathen when I preached to them.'

'Oh, for God's sake,' Emerson exclaimed. 'Who is he now, John the Baptist or one of the Apostles, or . . . Take him by the collar and drag him along.'

So we did, metaphorically speaking. Plato came without demur. In fact he seemed livelier than usual; every now and then a pleased little smile quirked his mouth. The rising bruise, which his beard did not wholly conceal, looked to my expert eye as if it had been caused by a fist striking his jaw.

In order to make ensuing events clear to the Reader, I should explain that the city is divided into quarters, Christian, Jewish, Moslem, and Armenian. There are no barriers between these sections, and people pass freely from one to another – not always in harmony but seldom in actual conflict. The famous Wailing Wall, where devout Jews gather to mourn the downfall of the Holy City, is on the eastern side of the Jewish Quarter; the huge stone blocks are, in fact, part of the enormous platform on which the Haram stands. The style of masonry and other archaeological evidence prove beyond a reasonable doubt that the entire platform was built in Herodian, i.e., Roman, times, to serve as the foundation for Herod's temple. Nothing remains, alas, of the temple itself. The entire circumference of the walls is only about two and a half miles; devout pilgrims follow the entire route on foot or on donkeyback, taking in such sights as the supposed tomb of Saint John and the Pillar of Absalom. Even I was willing to abjure this pleasure. Access to the city is provided by seven gates that pierce the great walls. The route we followed led from Siloam to the nearest gate, whose unattractive name I have already reported, and into the Jewish Quarter.

There is not much difference in appearance between this area and the other quarters – narrow winding streets, dilapidated dwellings, feral dogs foraging for scraps of food. The city's synagogues are in this section, as Christian churches tend to congregate in that part of the city. Two of the largest and most recent of the former were used respectively by the Sephardim and Ashkenazim sects. The latter's conspicuous dome was visible from the upper floors of our hotel. I meant to pay a courtesy call there one day – without Emerson.

We were on David Street when it happened. The sky had clouded over and I felt as if I were walking at the bottom of a narrow passageway, walled in by buildings of several stories, and arched over, at intervals, by extensions of dwelling places on one side or another. It was impossible to stay together as a group in the jostling, hurrying throng. Emerson had taken me firmly by the arm and Daoud was looking after Nefret. Should we become separated, I felt sure everyone knew his or her way back to the hotel; we had come that same way earlier. I was not aware of trouble until a penetrating shriek rose over the polyglot babble and the importunities of merchants.

'Stop, Emerson,' I cried, attempting to free my arm. 'Someone is in need of help.'

However, Daoud was the first to respond, since he and Nefret were closest to the cause of the disturbance. Plunging into a tangle of bodies, he lifted from its midst a familiar face framed in floating hair.

From Manuscript H

This was obviously a case in which physical coercion wouldn't work, even supposing he could bring himself to throttle four women. Try to throttle, rather; the proprietress, for all her bulk, had a grip as strong as a man's, and after a long night on the run Ramses was beginning to tire.

'What makes you think we – I – am being hunted?'

She caught the slip. A gleam of amusement brightened her eyes, but she did not refer to it at once. 'They have spread out all over the city searching for you. The two fools you saw leave this house were among the searchers. They were – distracted. And too stupid to see through your clumsy disguise. Are you hungry?'

'I – I do not understand,' Ramses stammered.

A snap of her fingers dismissed the girls. They filed out through a curtained doorway behind the divan, without so much as a backward look.

'Sit down,' the woman said. 'You are weary. I will bring your friend to you if you wish.'

Ramses had given up hope of directing the conversation. She was far ahead of him. 'Yes,' he said. 'Please. Where is he?'

She let out a high-pitched, girlish giggle. 'Just outside. Trying to make himself invisible.' She raised her voice. 'Come in, you there, or make way for others.'

David pushed through the curtains. His eyes went at once to Ramses. 'Are you all right?'

In his relief he spoke English. Ramses replied in Arabic. 'Aywa. Thanks to this noble lady.'

The florid compliment failed to move her. 'So you are the Inglizi,' she breathed. 'I would not have thought it. They said you attacked a lady who was a guest in the house, and that you fled when she cried out for help.'

'It is a lie,' David said vehemently.

'I believe you.' Her eyes narrowed with laughter. 'I think neither of you would have to force himself on a woman. Now come with me, to a more private place.'

'Why are you doing this?' Ramses asked.

She answered with a familiar proverb. 'The enemy of my enemy is my friend. Come.'

They followed her along a passageway lined with curtained doors, to a small closet next to the kitchen. Shelves along one wall held a supply of foodstuffs – bags of flour and meal, lentils and dried fruit. There was barely room on the floor for both of them to stretch out, and no light, but it had the advantage of a solid wooden door. Their hostess handed in a jar of water and a bowl of cold mush, presumably the remains of last night's supper.

'Rest while you can,' she said. 'My name is Majida. No, I do not want to know yours. Make no sound. I will return later.'

The door closed, leaving them in darkness except for a few thin rays of light from cracks in and around the door. 'She's locked us in,' David breathed, hearing the unmistakable drop of a bar into its socket. 'Perhaps they're offering a reward, and she wants to collect it.'

'If so, there's not a damned thing we can do about it.' Ramses was suddenly so tired his knees bent of their own accord. He sank down to a sitting position.

The wretched food revived them, and they used the empty bowl for a drinking vessel.

'I think we can trust her,' Ramses said, after they had stretched out, heads close together. The floor was hard and dirty, but at that point he could have slept on a rock. 'The Turks are hated everywhere in the territories, and for good reason.'

His only answer was a faint snore.

They left the house at dawn the following morning, wearing homespun robes over cotton shirts and loose trousers, and the caps wound round with cloth that were the local headgear of choice. David's valise had been exchanged for a pair of bags with long straps that could be slung over the shoulders. Majida gave them a last inspection as they stood by the door that led out into a narrow rubbish-strewn back street.

'Keep the scarves over your faces,' she instructed. 'Your beards shame you.'

'True,' Ramses agreed. He offered her two gold sovereigns. 'We cannot repay your kindness, but for the clothing –'

'Kindness deserves repayment too,' said Majida, taking the money. 'Go with God.'

'One more thing,' Ramses said, as she turned away. 'Er – where are we?'

She must have been very beautiful once, he thought, seeing her face break into a broad, uninhibited smile and dimples pop out on either cheek. 'You need someone to take you by the hand and lead you like a child. How can it be that you are ignorant of that?'

'It is a long and tedious tale,' Ramses said with a sheepish grin.

'Then you must not tell it.' She reached out and patted his cheek. 'This is Nablus, and you are on the east side. The road to Jerusalem is that way, an hour's walk.'

She pushed them out into the alleyway and closed the door.

They followed the route she had suggested earlier, one which would take them out into the countryside most quickly.

'Nablus,' Ramses said. 'We're only ten miles from Samaria, where I started out! They must have been driving in circles all that time.'

'Same for me,' David agreed. 'I was just outside Nablus when they picked me up. What's the plan now? Back to Samaria? Jaffa?'

'No, the parents will be in Jerusalem by now. If we don't turn up soon they'll come looking for us. Anyhow, I'm ready to admit my inferiority and ask for a council of war. This business is more complicated than I realized. I'll be damned if I can figure out what's going on.'

'What do you mean?'

They squeezed past a donkey loaded with fodder. The houses were thinning out. Ramses waited until there was no one within earshot before he answered.

'David, we've been told three different stories by two people whom we can't believe, and a third, poor Macomber, who may have been deliberately misled. I don't even know who's on whose side now. Did you happen to notice the tattoo on Majida's arm when she reached out to touch my face? It was the same as that peculiar mark on Mansur's forearm.'

Chapter Seven

Once again Plato Panagopolous had wreaked havoc with my schedule. By the time we had taken him back to the hotel and wrung the truth out of him, it was too late to return to our new house and begin a thorough cleaning.

I examined Mr. Plato, despite his insistence that he was unharmed. A bump on his cranium and a few more bruises were the only damage I could see. Daoud had a shallow cut on one arm. As Nefret cleaned and bandaged it, he explained that his arm 'got in the way of a knife one man was holding.'

We were in our sitting room at the time. When Plato referred to the subject of luncheon, I was in complete sympathy with Emerson when he seized the reverend by the collar and addressed him in the ominous growl that is feared by every man in Egypt.

'I have reached the end of my patience. Not a morsel of food shall touch your lips until you have answered all my questions fully and truthfully. Where did you go this morning? Why is a man with a knife after your blood? Who sent him? I would like,' said Emerson, his voice rising, 'to write the fellow a letter of thanks!'

Plato's eyes were bulging and his pale countenance had darkened. I said, 'Loosen your grip, Emerson, and let me conduct the interrogation, if you please. You must ask more direct questions. Mr. Plato, was it Mr. Morley you went to see this morning? There is no sense in lying, for I am fairly certain of the answer. Yes or no?'

Plato inserted a shaking finger into his collar. 'Yes,' he stuttered. 'Yes. Why should I not? I went on your behalf, to persuade him to ask your advice before proceeding with –'

'And he punched you on the jaw?'

Plato hung his head. 'At first he took my suggestion badly. The role of the peacemaker –'

'Did not succeed in this instance,' I said. 'Was it Morley who sent the assassin after you?'

'I cannot believe –'

'Have you other enemies in Jerusalem?'

'No. That is . . .'

I will spare the Reader the rest of his rambling discourse. In the end, between my pointed questions and Emerson's threats, he admitted it had been Morley who robbed and attacked him at the inn in England. He had come to us after he discovered Morley intended to leave him behind when the expedition – based on his discoveries! – left England. Morley had used and then abandoned him, leaving him penniless. But he bore no hatred toward his betrayer, no indeed! He had accompanied us in the hope of bringing Morley to a better understanding. Had he not preached forgiveness?

'Oh, good Gad,' said Emerson. 'Now he claims to have been Jesus. I don't know how much more of this I can stand.'

'His explanation is consistent with what we already knew,' I pointed out. 'We had assumed from the first that Mr. Morley was a conscienceless adventurer, concerned only with profit.'

'Oh, quite,' said Emerson glumly. '"Consistent" is the correct word. Either he is the most consistent liar I have ever met or he is a perfectly consistent fool. Now, then – er – since it is clear Morley has no intention of cooperating with us, we must take steps to control his activities. Here is paper and pen. You claim to recall the text of your famous scroll. Write it down.'

Plato complied readily, explaining that he was giving us only the part of the text that contained directions as to the location of the treasure. It was certainly a curious document. It read in part: 'Now while the workmen were lifting up their picks there was a rift on the right hand, one hundred cubits from the entrance, leading to the place of the treasure, and one hundred cubits was the height of the rock over the heads of the workmen.'

'This is, of course, a translation,' said Emerson, studying the paper. 'You read ancient Hebrew?'

'At one time I did. My memory –'

'Aha,' said Emerson. 'If you are the scholar you claim to be, you ought to be able to reproduce at least part of the original.'

Plato blinked at him. 'Do you understand –'

'Are you hungry?' Emerson replied with a wolfish smile.

Plato picked up the pen.

To my astonishment he proceeded to inscribe several lines of what certainly appeared to be a variety of Hebrew. Emerson's smile vanished. He cannot read the ancient form of the language any more than I can, but he knew enough, as did I, to tell that the text was not a scribble of meaningless symbols.

Nefret spoke for the first time. 'Touché, I believe,' she remarked.

By then the hour was late for luncheon and the dining salon was only half full. Emerson, still in a state of aggravation, directed Plato to a table clear across the room from the one at which we gathered.

'I wish to discuss a number of matters that don't concern him,' he said, in response to Nefret's attempted objection. 'I have yet to make up my mind about the creature.'

'I quite agree,' I said. Selim nodded emphatically.

'Very well, then,' said Nefret, frowning. 'Let us begin with the matter of Ramses and David. You said we should wait a few days. We have waited. I propose one or all of us leave for Samaria tomorrow.'

'If we do that, it will mean postponing our activities here for several days,' I said. 'There is a great deal to do. Setting up the house – a complex chore in itself – keeping watch over Morley, arranging for Emerson's excavations.' Nefret's lips parted, so I hurried on. 'Would you care to explain to us, my dear Emerson, what intrigues you about that particular site?'

The waiter delivered the soup we had ordered, which gave Emerson time to consider his response. It took the form of a lecture.

'Egypt ruled this entire region during the fourteenth century B.C., including Jerusalem, which is mentioned in the Egyptian archives. Yet no artifacts of that period have been found here.'

He paused to have a sip of soup, and I took advantage.

'Don't tell me you have found evidence of remains from that remote period? After a cursory examination of surface material? I understand, my dear, why you would be thrilled to discover Egyptian material here, but surely –'

'You would not sacrifice the safety of your son for such a discovery?' Nefret cut in. The verb is appropriate; her voice was as sharp as a knife blade.

'Certainly not,' Emerson exclaimed. 'You wound me deeply by such a suggestion. However, we have no proof at this time that his or David's safety is at risk.'

'Proof!' Nefret cried. 'What are you waiting for, a ransom note, or . . .' She paused, biting her lip. The image in her mind was as clear to the rest of us as it was to her. There was no putting her off, and to be candid I had come round to share her concerns.

'I will go,' Selim said. 'Daoud and I. To Samaria.'

'A compromise,' I said. 'One more day. If, by the day after tomorrow, we have had no word, we will all go. Are we agreed? Emerson? Nefret? Selim?'

It is the nature of compromise that it pleases none of the parties concerned. The agreement, in the form of nods or mumbles, was not wholehearted, but it was unanimous.

'Good,' I said. 'Next comes the question of Mr. Plato. He sought Morley out today, on our behalf, as he claims, or on his own, as I believe. He came away –'

'Aunt Amelia!' It was not like Nefret to interrupt me. 'Surely he is the least of our concerns just now. He is only –'

'We do not know what he is,' I said, raising my voice just a trifle. 'That is the point, Nefret. Until we are certain of his true motives we cannot assume he is not a danger to us. Do you happen to have a photograph of him?'

She had not expected that question, but she was not stupid. After a moment she said, 'I see what you are getting at. Yes, I think I do. I took a number of photographs.'

'At my request,' I said with a forgiving smile. 'They will be wonderful souvenirs of our visit to Jerusalem. Now if I may go on? Thank you. As I was saying, Plato came away from his encounter with Morley with the belief that they had reached some sort of agreement. The later attack upon him may have proved his assumption was incorrect, or it may have been instigated by another party. We know almost nothing about him. I suggest that we take steps to inquire further into his background, here and through –' I caught myself in time. 'Through – er – other sources.'

'What sources?' Nefret demanded, eyes narrowing.

'Archaeological sources,' I replied smartly. 'Museums and professional organizations. And police records.'

'Excellent idea,' Emerson exclaimed.

'You will see to that, Emerson?'

'What? Oh. Yes, certainly.'

'I will spend this evening and all day tomorrow hiring servants, acquiring the necessary household supplies, and so on. Thus we will be able to set out for Samaria the following morning – assuming, of course, that we have received no word from the boys. Have we all finished eating? Shall we go now?'

A gentle cough stopped me in the act of rising. Turning, I saw a person standing at my elbow. He was young, he had fair hair and a feeble little blond mustache, and that was about all one could say about him, for his form and features were strikingly unremarkable. In his hands he held a cloth Alpine-style hat, which he was twisting nervously.

'I beg your pardon,' he said. 'I waited until I believed you had finished your dinner, but if I am mistaken I will leave and return another time.'

'And interrupt us a second time?' said Emerson. 'Speak up, young man. Who are you and what do you want?'

'Camden – Courtney Camden. I was told by Mr. Page of the British Society that you might be looking for additional staff for your excavation.'

'I distinctly told him we were not. Good day, sir.' Emerson pushed his chair back and rose.

'Just a moment,' I said. 'What do you know about pottery, Mr. Camden?'

Mr. Camden was less intimidated than I had supposed. Though he continued to mangle his hat, he spoke up stoutly.

'It is my specialty, Mrs. Emerson.'

'What experience have you had?'

'I worked at Tel el-Hesi with Mr. Petrie and Mr. Bliss.'

'Nonsense,' Emerson grunted. 'That was twenty years ago. How old were you at the time, twelve?'

'Twenty years of age, sir. I am older than I look.'

'Hmph,' said Emerson, stroking his chin. 'Well, Peabody, you

188

seem to have decided we need a pottery person, so I will leave it to you.'

What Emerson knew, but refused to acknowledge, was that Mr. Petrie had been among the first to study Palestinian pottery and construct a relative chronology of types. Anyone who had worked with him was bound to be knowledgeable, for he was not an easy taskmaster. I studied Mr. Camden critically. He certainly did not look his age. Something about the set of his features struck me as familiar.

'Have we met before?' I asked.

'No, ma'am. I would certainly remember if we had.'

'Very well,' I said. 'If you will meet us here tomorrow morning, Mr. Camden, we will give you a try.'

'Six A.M,' said Emerson.

'Eight,' I corrected.

The young man backed away, bowing to everyone, including Selim and Daoud.

'He has excellent manners,' I said, beckoning the waiter. 'Would anyone else care for a sweet?'

Daoud indicated that he would. Emerson sat in brooding silence until the waiter had come and gone. Then he said, 'I trust you know what you are doing, Peabody. Is it not something of a coincidence that a pottery expert should turn up just when he is wanted?'

'All the more reason for keeping him under observation, Emerson. If he is what he claims to be, he will be extremely useful, for none of us is familiar with the pottery of this region and you are certain to encounter –'

'Yes, yes, Peabody. And if he is not what he claims to be?'

'We will determine his true motive and turn it to our advantage!'

Nefret burst out laughing. 'Of course, Aunt Amelia.'

I was pleased to see she was in a more congenial frame of mind.

My agreement that we should go in search of the boys had satisfied her for the moment – and I must confess, in the pages of this private (for the time being) journal, that I myself had become increasingly uneasy about them. However, stern mental discipline had taught me to concentrate on the task at hand. My first task that afternoon was to shop, and I persuaded Nefret to accompany me. Emerson declined the offer, explaining that he had a few more questions to put to – er – that fellow and that he wanted Selim to be present at the interrogation. With a significant glance at me, he added that he had certain investigations to pursue as well. So Nefret and I set out, with Daoud as our escort.

There were modern shops in that part of the city, so I was able to procure cleaning materials and insect repellent. I ordered a number of other items, including a nice tin bathtub, directing that they be sent to the hotel at once. We were longer than I had meant to be, since I also stopped at the souk to purchase rugs, woven mats, and bolts of fabric for curtains, so when we arrived the others were at dinner. Plato had a rather hangdog look, but it had not affected his appetite. I deduced that Emerson had appointed Selim as Plato's escort, for when we parted after dinner Selim went with him.

'I hope you are not planning to lock Mr. Plato in his room,' I said, as Emerson poured a postprandial libation.

'I was tempted. But it might be dangerous, if not actually illegal. No, Selim and I and Daoud will take it in turn to watch his door tonight.'

I accepted the glass he handed me with a nod of thanks. 'What on earth did you discover about him to inspire such precautions?'

'Nothing definite as yet. It is too soon to expect –'

A soft knock at the door prevented him from completing the sentence. It was Nefret, holding a small sheaf of photographs. Handing them to me, she said, 'These are the only ones in which Mr. Plato appears. Good night.'

And off she went, without another word!

It did not take us long to examine the photographs. Mr. Plato was present in all of them – or to put it more accurately, part of Mr. Plato was present: the back of his head, a face covered by a raised hand, a figure retreating from the camera.

'Hmmm,' said Emerson.

'Hmmm indeed. The images of the rest of us are quite good – except this one, when you were shouting at someone. Is it only a coincidence that we have no identifiable picture of Plato?'

Emerson answered with another question. 'What were you planning to do with it if you had it?'

'Show it to various people. He has been in Jerusalem before, I have no doubt of that. I had hoped we could send a copy to Scotland Yard.'

'It would be weeks before we could expect a response,' Emerson said.

'Quite. I had another possibility in mind. Don't you think it is time you told me which of the persons at this hotel are in the employ of the War Office?'

'I haven't the vaguest idea,' said Emerson. 'Now, Peabody, don't lose your temper. Here, let me refill your glass.'

Having done so, he continued, 'The idiots at the War Office have already come up empty on the subject of – er – that person. Their investigation seems to have been superficial in the extreme. I sent off telegrams to Jacobsen at the British Museum, Frankfort in Berlin, and a few others, as well as to Scotland Yard. Cursed expensive it was, too, since I gave them not only his current name but a description as well. I mean to make the same inquiries here in Jerusalem, but there wasn't time yesterday.'

Determined to stick to the point, I said, 'You haven't answered my initial question. Do you deny that the War Office sent us to this hotel, just as they did in Jaffa?'

'No,' said Emerson. 'That is, yes. That is –'

'Then they must have told you how to communicate with their local representative in case of trouble.'

'Yes,' said Emerson, resentment replacing his initial confusion. 'Curse it, Peabody, just give me a chance to speak. I was told that I would be approached by their agent here. He was to give a particular signal when –'

'Aha,' I cried. 'This particular signal?'

Taking the tip of my nose daintily between thumb and forefinger, I wriggled it twice.

Emerson stared at me, his mouth ajar. Then he burst out laughing.

From Manuscript H

Dust billowed up around their feet as they trudged along the path. Sheep grazed on the yellowing grass and oxen dragged primitive plows across the fields. The scene was peaceful and pastoral, the valley framed by mountains north and south of the city.

'How far is it to Jerusalem?' David asked, shifting his bag from one shoulder to the other.

'As I remember, it's only thirty or forty miles in what passes in these parts for a straight line. But it's easy to get lost if you don't know the country.'

'Should we take a chance on the main road, then?'

Ramses had been wondering the same thing. One part of him – the part his mother had tried to eradicate – was tempted to make a run for it, risking recapture or worse. Another, more sensible part, told him that although their disguises were good from a distance, they might not hold up under close inspection. He wished he knew how far Mansur would go to get them back – or to keep them from passing on what they had learned. If he was desperate enough he might have ordered they be shot down rather than let them escape. An unfortunate accident, the soldier had mistaken them for wanted criminals, perfectly understandable considering that they were in disguise . . . But what if conceit had made him rate his and David's importance too high? It could take them days to reach Jerusalem, skulking around the countryside, while his family worried and nobody else, including Mansur, gave a damn about them.

'My mind's going round in circles,' he said in disgust. 'I think we'll try to avoid the road for a while longer.'

As the sun rose higher, he began to wonder if he had made the right decision. The narrow paths, some of them no more than goat tracks, wound round small fields, vineyards, groves of trees. The terrain became increasingly difficult as they climbed out of the valley into a region of rolling hills, with higher peaks visible to the west. After a few hours Ramses had no idea where they were, except for the fact that they were headed generally south, and that they were east of the main road.

'How far have we come?' David asked.

'Damned if I know. We've been walking in circles part of the time, trying to stay away from villages and houses. I suggest we climb higher and try to get an overall view of the countryside.'

'You sound uncharacteristically tentative,' David remarked.

'If you have a better suggestion, kindly make it,' Ramses snapped. They hadn't seen or heard anything suspicious for hours, but his sense of uneasiness was growing. Having David with him was a great comfort, but knowing David wouldn't be there but for him was an equally great burden.

They made their way up a steep ridge, past dark openings that might have been ancient tombs. Crowning a hilltop ahead was a structure that stopped both of them in their tracks. It might have been the ruin of a Norman castle, magically transported from England to this improbable location. The massive walls were still eight or ten feet high in some places, with flanking towers at intervals and the remains of a keep visible beyond the walls.

'What on earth is that?' David asked. 'Not biblical, surely?'

Ramses eased the pack off his shoulder and stretched. 'It must be a Crusader fortress. Eleventh century – A.D., that is. There are a number of them in Syria-Palestine.'

'Crusader,' David repeated. 'Oh, yes – that lot who wanted to save the Holy Land from the infidels. They built to last, didn't they?'

'They built to hold off a good many people who hated them and their religion. And the builders didn't last. The Kingdom of Jerusalem endured for two hundred years, off and on, spawning seven or eight bloody Crusades, costing countless lives, and in the end they were forced to give up and go home.'

'You certainly are a repository of useless information. How do you know all that?' David asked, with more amusement than admiration.

'I have a mind like a magpie's, easily distracted by interesting odds and ends,' Ramses admitted. 'Actually I learned about the Crusades from a young fellow I met at Oxford. He had chosen Crusader castles as his special subject.'

'I don't suppose you know which one that is, or precisely *where* it is.'

Ramses was too discouraged to resent the implicit criticism. 'There are too many damned ruins in this country,' he said gloomily. He turned slowly, shading his eyes against the sun. 'There's another one down in that valley – could be a derelict church. I can't see . . . Wait a minute. Isn't that Nablus, that darkish blur across the plain, north and slightly west?'

David let out a heartfelt groan. 'We've only come that far?'

Ramses sat down, crossing his legs. 'Let's take a rest and see what Majida has given us for luncheon.'

It was the usual fare – flat bread and goat cheese, a handful of figs, plus a flask of thin, sour beer. Ramses wolfed his half down, and then realized David hadn't eaten more than a few bites.

'Are you feeling all right?' he asked.

'I'm fine. Just a little thirsty.' He raised the flask to his lips and took a long drink. 'Horrible stuff.'

'We'll have to find water soon,' Ramses said, watching him. 'And there's not enough food for another day.'

'Water shouldn't be a problem. There must be wells and springs.'

'Plenty of both, I should think. We've been avoiding villages and people, but I don't see any need for continuing to do so.'

'All right.' David got to his feet. 'Let's go.'

They had passed a number of small settlements earlier, but now that they were looking for habitation, they failed at first to find it. Ramses kept an unobtrusive eye on his companion. David kept up the pace, but he was unusually silent, as if every ounce of energy he possessed was focused on walking. The path had virtually disappeared and the hilly terrain was tiring: down into a valley and back up again, over and over. Ramses was about to suggest they stop for a rest when he spotted a moving form heading straight for them.

David made an abortive movement, as if to turn. Ramses caught his arm. 'Keep walking. It's all right. He's not wearing a uniform.'

The man's sheepskin cap and loose garment were those of a local, and he moved with the assurance of someone who was used to the terrain, using a stout staff to steady his steps on the slope. As he came closer Ramses saw a dark, weather-beaten face marked by heavy gray brows and framed by a grizzled beard. Hoping his own pathetic beard would pass muster, Ramses was about to voice a greeting when the man spoke first.

'You are the ones they are looking for.'

It was at that critical moment that David buckled at the knees and collapsed.

Ramses's only weapons were his hands and feet. The bag he carried was too light to inflict an injury. He gathered himself together; the other man, reading his intention, jumped back and raised his staff.

'No! I am a friend, I come to warn you. See!' He pushed his sleeve up. 'I am a Son of Abraham.'

The sun was low in the west when they reached the ruined castle and passed through a narrow gate flanked by massive towers.

'They will not find you here,' their newfound ally said. 'There are many places to hide. Stay until someone comes for you.'

Ramses had had no choice but to trust him. He had set a pace that left both of them too out of breath for conversation or questions. David had to be supported most of the way and actually carried the last difficult fifty feet; he was barely conscious when they lowered him to the ground.

'It is the fever,' their guide said, putting a calloused hand on David's forehead. 'It will pass in time . . . Or not. He is young and strong, it is likely he will live.'

'Wait,' Ramses said. 'How did you know who we were? Why are you helping us? What is your name?'

'It is better you do not know my name. The word went out, we were told to watch for you. I will pass the word now to the others. There are Turks' – he spat neatly on the ground – 'along the road all the way to Jerusalem. I must return, there are those in the villages who would sell you if they could. Take this.'

He handed Ramses the bag he carried, and then he was gone.

The bag contained a goatskin of water, a single piece of bread, and a bunch of grapes – possibly the remains of the man's midday meal. Ramses made David as comfortable as he could, and got him to drink a little water. The shadows inside the high walls were deepening, and he wanted to explore the place before dark.

It was still a formidable fortress. There were two enclosing walls, with narrow gates flanked by towers; inside the inner wall was a larger tower or keep, the last place of defense. The ground was littered with stones of various sizes, from pebbles to fragmented building blocks, and with animal spoor. There was no sign of human habitation; Ramses wondered if the place was considered haunted or demon-ridden. There were certainly ample hiding places; the rooms in the lower floors of the keep were still intact.

He went back to David, who was deep in troubled sleep and burning with fever. It was impossible to know what variety of fever. There were too many sources of infection, from the water to insect bites. One thing was sure: they wouldn't be going anywhere for a while.

He rummaged in his bag and located the box of medical supplies, lighting one of their few remaining matches to inspect the contents. The only thing he found that might be helpful was a bottle of aspirin. Wasn't that supposed to lower fevers? He wished he had paid more attention to his mother's lectures. He decided it couldn't do any harm, and managed to get David to swallow one, with a sip of water. It was pitch-dark by then and he decided it would be too dangerous to move David farther into the fortress. Working by feel, he took out the galabeeyahs and spread them around and under David. It was the only covering he could provide; they had left their European clothing with Majida.

Lying on his back staring up at a sky brilliant with stars, he knew he wouldn't be able to get the sleep he needed. Owls hooted mournfully. The cooling temperature produced weird creaks and snapping sounds. Small nocturnal animals began to prowl. At least they were small, to judge by the patter of their feet. He tried to remember whether there were still wolves in the region.

Every now and then he dozed off, to be jarred awake by a movement or muttered word from David. The fever hadn't broken. That meant, if he remembered correctly, that it wasn't malaria. Which left only a dozen unknown possibilities. He felt so damned helpless. If David wasn't better by morning, he would have to go for help, that's all there was to it. Better to risk recapture than have his best friend die for lack of care. His anonymous guide had spoken of villages. He had observed several of them along the way.

Exhaustion, physical and emotional, finally sent him into deeper slumber. He was jarred out of it by a sound that was different from the ones he had grown used to – the crunch of stone under the foot of a heavier creature than a rat or a fox. The air was moist with dew; it smelled of dawn. He lay perfectly still, listening and hoping. Soldiers would not have moved so quietly. His guide had promised someone would come . . .

Another footstep and then another. Ramses decided to risk it.

'The Sons of Abraham,' he said softly, and repeated the words in Arabic.

He heard a sharp intake of breath and then a long exhalation, like a sigh of relief. Ramses got slowly to his feet. He could see a little now, make out a darker form in the darkness. The voice that answered him was that of a man, still young to judge by its pitch and very nervous, to judge by its unsteadiness.

'Friend, yes. I bring food.'

Ramses came out of the shadow of the buttress. 'Water?' he asked. 'My friend is –'

'Sick, yes. I bring medicine.'

In the first flush of light Ramses made out the fellow's features. He was young, his beard hardly more developed than that of Ramses, his dark eyes wide.

'You speak good English,' Ramses said, taking the woven basket he was offered.

'A little.' The boy bent over David, who lay still, breathing heavily. 'It is the fever, yes. The healer says to put this in water and let him drink.'

He took a bundle of dried plants from the basket. Ramses rubbed a pinch between thumb and forefinger and smelled, then tasted it. It was an herb of some sort, strongly scented. The taste was sharp but not unpleasantly so.

'He not go on today,' the boy said. 'Write. I take it.'

'What?' Ramses asked. 'I don't understand. Write?'

As the light strengthened, the boy's uneasiness increased. He threw up his hands in an unmistakable gesture of frustration. 'Write a message, to those who await you. Tell them to come for you. I will see that it reaches them.'

He had spoken Hebrew.

We were rudely awakened next morning by persistent knocking. Leaving Emerson cursing and flailing about, I hastily assumed dressing gown and slippers and went to the door. The room was gray with predawn light; it was still very early. It was obvious to me that something of a serious nature had occurred. A variety of hideous images flooded my mind, many of them having to do with my son. I flung the door open.

The manager stood on the threshold. He was in a state of great agitation and barely coherent. 'I beg your pardon, Mrs. Emerson, but there are persons who insist on speaking with your husband. Something of a serious nature has occurred!'

'Damnation!' shouted Emerson from the bed. 'What sort of hotel is this, when a man cannot –'

'Do stop shouting, Emerson. Something of a serious nature has occurred. I will ascertain its precise nature, but I suggest you rise at once.'

Hastily assuming proper garments and directing that coffee be served immediately to Emerson, I went down to speak with the individuals in question. They turned out to be Mr. Samuel Page of the British Society and a stranger, round-faced and portly, who introduced himself as Edmund Glazebrook, the British consul. I apologized for not having paid him a courtesy call before this, to which he replied that he readily forgave me, since he had enough to do dealing with complaints from our compatriots.

'May we see Professor Emerson?' he went on. 'It is urgent, ma'am, very urgent.'

When I had explained the situation they agreed that I should be the bearer of the bad news – never a comfortable position and, in the case of Emerson at this stage in his arousal, potentially dangerous.

'There is a riot brewing at the Temple Mount,' Glazebrook explained. 'The authorities are attempting to control the mob, but I must say –'

'Get to the point, please,' I said impatiently.

'Er. It was Mr. Page who persuaded me to come here. For some reason he believes Professor Emerson may be able to intervene to better effect. Though I must say –'

I left him and hastened at once to Emerson. As I had expected of him, he rose nobly to the occasion, finishing his coffee as – with my assistance – he dressed. We were ready in ten minutes or less, and went down to join the others.

Pale sunlight strove to penetrate the morning mist as we hastened along the street. 'Now then,' said Emerson to the consul, 'what is this all about? Be succinct, I beg.'

Glazebrook was forced to be succinct, since, like Hamlet, he was fat and scant of breath, and he had to trot to keep up with Emerson. Apparently early worshippers had discovered a party of foreigners at the base of the Mount, attempting, as they believed, to begin engineering activity at that most sacred spot.

'The first ones on the spot were Moslems,' the consul panted. 'But the news was quick to spread and they were soon joined by

A River in the Sky

Jews coming to defend the Wailing Wall. At last report both groups were hurling stones and threats at the foreigners . . .'

His breath gave out and Emerson said coolly, 'And eventually at each other, if they haven't already begun to do so. Hmph. Well, let us see what can be done.'

We heard the riot before we saw it. The roar of an angry crowd is one of the most terrifying sounds in the world. Most of them were clotted round the base of the great wall, so that when we came out onto the square we were some hundred yards from the scene of action. At first it was difficult to make out precisely who was hitting whom. There were, thank God, no firearms; but stones flew through the air and clubs were brandished. Thuds and screams of pain and screams of fury made a horrible din. At the farthest point, up against the wall itself, stood a ragged row of Turkish soldiers. They appeared to be armed with rifles, but they must have been ordered not to fire into the crowd. Using the weapons as clubs, they were trying to fend off the attackers from a small group huddled against the stones. Presumably these were the foreigners whose appearance had started the trouble, but I could not make out their features owing to my lack of inches.

Emerson, who suffered from no such disadvantage, said, 'Ha! As I expected. Stay here, Peabody. Gentlemen, kindly make certain she does.'

Whereupon he plunged into the crowd.

In fact there was only one gentleman left, for Mr. Page had taken one look at the turmoil and beaten a hasty departure. I did not blame him; he was a scholar, not a man of action. Glazebrook, to do him credit, stuck close to my side.

The consul notwithstanding, I would have followed Emerson had I not known my presence would distract him from his primary aim. His progress was marked by a sort of eddy of bodies, as he swept combatants aside by the sheer strength of his arms. I verily believe the only thing that saved him from serious harm was the

201

fact that the fighters were taken so by surprise and pushed aside so suddenly that they failed to realize what had happened to them.

Frantic to observe, ready to plunge into the melee should my valiant spouse be in need of my assistance, I scrambled up onto a projecting ledge in time to see Emerson triumphant. His catlike quickness, which he could summon at need, saved him this time; one of the soldiers, understandably confused as to his purpose, pointed a rifle at him. Emerson snatched it from his hand and turned to face the mob. His stentorian voice rose over all lesser sounds.

'Salaam! Shalom! Peace!'

The hubbub died, not as yet into complete silence, but to such an extent that Emerson's additional remarks rang out across the square. 'Go to your homes at once. Leave the foreigners to me – me, the Father of Curses! I will punish them as they deserve. Go now, or face my wrath and the wrath of God.'

Perhaps the fact that he was brandishing the rifle as he spoke had an additional effect, but in my opinion the major factor was the charismatic presence of Emerson. The sound faded to a sullen murmur, and people began to sidle away. The trickle became a flood, and before long the square was empty except for scattered bodies. Some lay unmoving; others writhed in pain, their garments bloodstained. Much as I yearned to assist the fallen, my first duty was to my husband. When I reached his side I saw that he had not escaped entirely unscathed; a lump was rising on the side of his head and his sleeve had been slashed by a sharp instrument. However, righteous fury raised him above these minor inconveniences. Addressing the officer in command of the soldiers, he bellowed, 'Are you in charge here? You confounded idiot, why did you fail to disperse the mob?'

(I translate from the original Arabic, substituting a less vulgar epithet than the one actually employed.)

'We were told not to shoot,' the officer stuttered. 'There were not enough of us to –'

'Bah,' said Emerson. 'Go away, all of you, you are of no use whatsoever. Ah, Peabody, there you are. You remember our acquaintance, Mr. Morley, I presume?'

I was not surprised to see that Morley was the cause of the disturbance, though at first glance I would not have recognized the sleek dapper individual who had taken tea in our parlor. His expensive tweed coat was wrinkled and dusty and his face pale. His pith helmet had been knocked off by a well-aimed stone; it lay on the ground next to him. Two other men, unknown to me, were with him. All three were trying to look as if they had not been in fear of their lives, but not succeeding.

'What the devil did you think you were doing?' Emerson demanded.

'Taking measurements,' Morley stammered, indicating the instruments strewn about. 'Nothing more. We had no intention –'

'Your intentions don't matter a damn,' said Emerson. 'You ought to have known that any activity this close to the Haram would lead to trouble. In fact, I believe you were strictly forbidden to come here.'

'I have the permission of –'

'You haven't mine,' said Emerson, baring his teeth in a manner no one could have mistaken for a smile. 'From now on, Morley, you are not to make a move without informing me. You are in disfavor with the local British authorities for starting a riot, and with the international archaeological community for excavating without professional supervision. Henceforth I am that supervisor.'

Foreseeing a certain amount of meaningless discussion (for Emerson was certain to prevail in the end), I went to see if I could assist the wounded. A few poor souls had returned to search for friends or kinfolk. A woman swathed all in black knelt keening by the body of a fiercely bearded man. Observing that his eyes were closed, his breathing regular, and that there was no blood on face or clothing, I pushed her gently aside and addressed him in soothing tones, while loosening his upper garment. His recovery was instantaneous. I had expected it would be. Aghast at finding himself tended by a strange female, he rose up and fled, followed by the woman in black.

Nearby lay a twisted form, whose bloodstained garment and staring eyes told me the sad truth even before I knelt at his side. Long curling sidelocks proclaimed him to be of the Jewish faith. I closed his eyes and bowed my head. Not knowing what words might be deemed appropriate, I decided that the Twenty-third Psalm ought to be safe. 'The Lord is my shepherd, I shall not want . . .' I broke off midway when I realized that by my side stood a tall dignified figure robed in black and crowned with a broad-brimmed hat of the same somber hue.

'That was a well-meant gesture, Mrs. Emerson,' he said in heavily accented English. 'But you can leave him and the others of our faith to us now. I am Rabbi Ben Yehuda.'

'How do you know my name?' I asked.

'Your name is well known in this city, as is that of your distinguished husband.'

Emerson advanced upon us. I did not blame the rabbi for staring, since Emerson did not in the least resemble a distinguished scholar. Black hair wildly windblown, garments torn, face streaked with blood, he announced in stentorian tones, 'That takes care of that bastard Morley. The soldiers have escorted him to safety, and . . . Who the devil is this?'

I introduced the rabbi. 'Hmph,' said Emerson, fixing him with a critical stare. 'Where were you, sir, while your coreligionists were trying to slaughter fellow human beings on this sacred ground?'

The rabbi was at least six inches shorter than Emerson, but he met the latter's eyes with an equally hostile gaze. 'It was not we, sir, who began the fighting.'

'Oh, I feel certain everyone pitched in,' Emerson agreed. 'I will have the same question to ask the sheikh of the mosque. And will, I do not doubt, receive the same evasive answer. Once hostilities had begun it was your duty, and his, to stop them. Instead you left it to an infidel like myself to speak the word "peace."'

'It was another of your kind whose actions broke the peace,' was the angry response.

'Ha,' said Emerson, eyes sparkling at the prospect of argumentation. 'See here, sir –'

'Now, Emerson, we have no time for this sort of thing,' I said firmly.

The rabbi signified his agreement by turning on his heel and walking away. There were still a few bodies lying about, but I concluded that, given the reception my assistance had hitherto received, I could be of no further use. I was about to allow Emerson to lead me away when a very small gentleman sidled toward us. I concluded from his dress that he was also a rabbi, though his attire was not as elegant as that of Ben Yehuda. His robe was patched, his wide-brimmed hat worn down to the nap, and his graying beard was wildly disheveled, as if he had been clawing at it.

'I wish to thank,' he said in halting English. 'For helping.'

'He has better manners than the other one,' Emerson remarked to me.

'Hush, Emerson. Your thanks are unnecessary, reverend sir. Is that the correct mode of address?'

The little rabbi looked bewildered, so I rephrased the question. 'What should I call you?'

'Ah. Rabbi Ben Ezra you should call me. I live on David Street, all know me. Come to me when you want help.'

He drew himself up to his full height, which was approximately the same as mine, and nodded emphatically. The offer was ludicrous but made with such obvious goodwill that Emerson managed to keep his face straight. 'Thank you,' he said with equal gravity.

'Thanks are unnecessary. Are we not all sons of Abraham?'

'As a matter of fact,' Emerson began.

I raised my voice. 'We must go, Emerson. Good day, Rabbi Ben Ezra.'

'Why must you always start an argument,' I hissed, drawing Emerson away. 'The poor fellow was trying to be friendly.'

'Well, but you are not a son of Abraham, being female,' said Emerson. 'And I am not because no such person existed. Hmph. Where have I heard those words before?'

I stepped carefully over a pool of blood. 'From your dear old villainous friend Kamir, the other morning.'

'Hmmm, yes. Doesn't it strike you as odd that two such disparate persons should use the same phrase?'

'Not at all, Emerson. If you had actually read Genesis, instead of pretending you had, you would know that the sons of Abraham were Isaac, the progenitor of the Jewish people, and Ishmael, the father of the Arab race.'

'I did read it,' Emerson said indignantly. 'And a fine moral tale that one was. For a man to cast his firstborn son and that son's mother into the desert to die because his jealous wife told him to –'

He was forced to leave off because we were accosted by Mr. Glazebrook (the British consul), who came hurrying toward us.

'Good Gad, sir,' he exclaimed. 'That was – I must say, sir – you are a credit to the British nation! Our prestige in this city must increase as a result of your heroic action. Though I must say –'

'I would prefer you did not,' said Emerson. 'Come, Peabody. We have already wasted too much time on this business.'

We got rid of Mr. Glazebrook by walking so briskly he could not keep up, and returned to the hotel. Our three friends were waiting in the lobby in a state of some agitation. When we failed to appear for breakfast they had questioned the person at the desk and learned that we had gone out to join in a riot. As Daoud explained, this had seemed reasonable enough to him, but Nur Misur had thought otherwise, and Selim had considered it unlikely that I would do so, though it was not unlikely that Emerson would. Rumors of death and destruction had spread with the speed of light, and by the time we arrived the entire place was abuzz and some of the more timid pilgrims were fluttering about like chickens that had seen a hawk, not knowing whether to hide or flee.

Once again Emerson's formidable presence calmed the storm.

'The disturbance has ended,' he announced in the loudest possible voice. 'There is no danger. Go about your business. What about breakfast, eh?'

This last to me. I acquiesced, for the morning's activity had left me quite peckish, and we all proceeded into the dining salon. In response to our friends' questions, I explained what had occurred.

'But, Professor,' Nefret exclaimed. 'You are injured. Come upstairs and let me –'

'Just a bump on the head,' said Emerson, shoveling in eggs and toast. 'Hurry and finish, all of you. We must be on our way. Where is that fellow – er –'

'Hiding in his room, I think,' said Selim, who fully agreed with Emerson's refusal to mention Plato's name.

'Go and roust him out,' Emerson ordered. 'From now on I want him under my eye.'

I persuaded Emerson to allow me to examine his injuries, which were, as I had realized, superficial. He had an impressive lump on his cranium, but as he pointed out with perfect equanimity, that portion of his anatomy had frequently suffered in such a manner. We returned to the lobby, where I arranged for porters to carry the supplies I had purchased the night before. Selim had Plato firmly by the arm; Nefret and Daoud were waiting; and so was a slim young man with a little blond mustache. He was still twisting his hat.

I had completely forgotten about him. Emerson would have said so and was, I believe, about to do just that when I bade Mr. Camden a courteous good-morning.

'I was here at eight,' he hastened to remark. 'But no one seemed to know where you had gone, and then you went to breakfast, and I did not like –'

'Most considerate, 'pon my word,' said Emerson. 'Well, well, let us be off.'

We made an imposing procession, proceeding two by two like the animals entering the Ark, Emerson and I in the lead, Nefret behind us with Selim, and Daoud towing Mr. Plato. The latter had protested making one of the party, claiming that his throat was sore, his head ached, and his feet hurt. Needless to say, his complaints had no effect on Emerson, nor on Daoud. Mr. Camden trailed along behind, followed by a string of porters carrying my purchases.

'That was something else I neglected to do,' said Emerson in a low voice. (Low for Emerson, that is.) 'Ask Page about that chap Camden.'

'No doubt you will be able to test his knowledge yourself, Emerson. You are proceeding directly to the site you have chosen to excavate, I presume?'

'Too damn many things to do first,' Emerson grumbled. 'I will get you settled at our new house, and talk to Kamir about leasing the land. This is the last time I try to work in this benighted country, Peabody. Things are much simpler in Egypt, and not so dangerous.'

Remembering our frequent encounters with violent criminals thirsting for our blood, I smiled a little. I understood what he meant, however. Ordinary villains are one thing; religious rioters and spies of various nationalities are less predictable.

'Then,' Emerson continued, 'I intend to reinforce what I told Morley yesterday by inspecting his excavation. It is a sacrifice, but one I am obliged to make.'

'In fact, you are dying to find out what he's up to,' I remarked.

Emerson's scowl became a broad grin. 'Quite right, my dear. As a reward for your insight, I will allow you to accompany me.'

Our arrival was announced in advance by the usual idlers who had nothing better to do than lounge around waiting for something interesting to happen. As we neared the house I had selected, we were met by Kamir himself, beaming and bowing.

'What is this?' he demanded, surveying our porters with scorn. 'You need nothing, I have made all ready for you. Come and see, come and see.'

To give him credit, which I must do, he had accomplished quite a good deal. The worst of the dust had been removed and several pieces of furniture supplied – chairs and tables and several bedsteads. The best one could say for the furniture was that it was very sturdy.

Waiting for us in an adjoining room were three potential servants. All three were unveiled; they had expected to see only other females, but Daoud, who had not realized what we were about to do, had followed Nefret, still towing Plato. The women shrieked and readjusted their veils. Plato pulled away from Daoud and fled, and poor Daoud, horribly embarrassed at his breach of manners, backed out of the room mumbling apologies.

Once the men had left, two of the women were persuaded to lower their veils. Stout females of middle age, both pressed their cases vehemently, promising to work their fingers to the bone (the Arabic equivalent). One claimed to be an experienced cook, adding proudly, 'I can make the English dishes too. Bistek, butter toast, egg.'

The other woman had retreated to a corner, where she stood with bowed head. 'And you?' I said. 'Do you also wish to work for us?'

She raised her head and I saw a smooth, fine-skinned brow and two big brown eyes, rimmed with kohl, under delicately curved brows. 'I can, I wish to . . .' She faltered.

'Speak up,' I said, not unkindly. 'Can you clean? Carry water from the pool?'

'No, Sitt. I wash clothes, I wash them very clean, I work at my house, I bring them all back next day, I cannot be here because I . . . because . . .'

'She has a child.' The self-proclaimed cook, who had told me her name was Yumna, spoke up loudly. 'A child who has no father.'

There was no particular malice in her voice, she was simply stating a fact; but the girl shrank back and bowed her head. Nefret, her sympathy immediately engaged, said gently, 'How old is the child, and who watches over it when you are not at home?'

We hired the girl, of course. Nefret told her she must bring the baby, which was a girl a little over a year old, with her when she came to us, since the old woman who looked after her did not sound reliable.

'I wish you had consulted me before you said that, Nefret,' I remarked in English. 'What are we supposed to do with an infant underfoot?'

'It won't be underfoot, or on the premises for long at a time, Aunt Amelia.'

Her protruding chin and firm mouth told me argument would be futile. She would probably take not only the baby but its youthful mother under her wing. I knew I could expect no support from Emerson. He is hopelessly sentimental about unprotected young women and infants. (He suffers from the delusion that no one knows this.) I am not wholly hard-hearted myself. I gave in with no more than a sigh.

After unpacking the supplies I had brought, I gave the two older women a lecture on cleaning methods, warning them in the strictest possible terms about the danger of inhaling or consuming ammonia, carbolic, Keating's powder, and other dangerous materials. 'If I find you have done so,' I said sternly, 'I will dismiss you.'

In fact, doing what I had forbidden might well have 'dismissed' them permanently; but I had made that point as firmly as I could, and felt an additional inducement to sensible behavior would do no harm. After I had demonstrated the proper method of scrubbing floors and walls, I decided I could leave them to it.

'Finished?' Emerson inquired when I joined him. 'Finally! Women do make such a fuss about these things.'

He would be the one to make a fuss if he were made to sleep on the floor or do without his morning coffee. Remembering our comfortable, well-furnished house in Luxor and my excellent housekeeper Fatima, I too had begun to regret agreeing to this expedition, if for no other reason (and there were other reasons) than that I would have to start all over again here. And, thanks to my son's thoughtless behavior, I would not be present for the next few days in order to supervise the work.

'Have you come to an arrangement with the owner of the property where you intend to excavate?' I asked.

A grunt from Emerson and a pleased smile from Kamir acknowledged that arrangements had been made, to the satisfaction of the latter at least.

'Now for Mr. Morley,' I said.

'He will be at luncheon,' said Emerson scornfully.

A slight movement from Daoud indicated that he too wished he were, but Emerson was in no mood to brook delay. He led the way down the hill and off to the right, stopping at last at the base of a steep slope of rock. It was not very high, only about twenty feet, but it was almost sheer and devoid of vegetation except for thorny shrubs and an occasional cactus. How he found the right

211

spot I do not know, for the place looked no different from the terrain on either side – stony and barren, strewn with stretches of what might once have been walls or terraces – or random heaps of stone.

Several men of the village had followed us, offering their services as diggers. Their importunities wrung a mild 'Curse it' from Emerson. 'I want this area roped off,' he said to Selim. 'Ask Kamir for the necessary materials, I feel sure he can supply them – at a price.'

'What about him?' Selim asked, indicating Plato.

'Nefret will make sure he doesn't wander off.'

'Of course.' She took Plato by the arm. 'Are you feeling quite well, Mr. Plato?'

Plato lowered the scarf he had wound round his neck and coughed hollowly. 'Better, my dear, better. A trifle faint from lack of nourishment, that is all.'

'We may as well have a spot of lunch while we wait for Selim,' I suggested.

Daoud was happy to go in search of nourishment. He came back with bread and cheese, dates and figs. We had not quite finished when Selim returned, with a coil of rope over his shoulder and an armful of stout stakes. Emerson paced off the area he wanted enclosed, and then addressed our audience.

'In two days' time I will return and hire workers. Until then no one is to dig in this place or pass behind the ropes. If you disobey I will know and my curse will fall upon you. Your eyes will go dark and your ears will wither and fall off, and so will your –'

It was this last threat – which propriety prevents me from recording – that carried the greatest conviction. A chorus of protestations arose, and as Emerson waved his arms in mystic gestures, some of the men retreated to a safe distance.

I handed Emerson the last piece of cheese, plucking it out from under Plato's hand. 'Well done, my dear. Have we finished here? Obviously you cannot begin work today.'

'No,' Emerson admitted reluctantly. 'We haven't the necessary tools or the cameras, or . . . Camden, did Petrie teach you anything about opening a new site? How would you begin here?'

'Well, uh . . . As you said, sir, photographs . . . Laying out a grid . . .' He looked helplessly at the unprepossessing slope. 'This isn't at all like an ordinary tell.'

'Hmph,' said Emerson, rubbing his chin. 'Very well, that will be all for today. We won't begin here for several days. How can we reach you?'

'I am at the King David Hotel, sir. Good day to you all.'

And off he went, at a pace that suggested he was relieved to have been relieved.

'He may know a great deal about pottery, Emerson,' I said, interpreting Emerson's frown.

'He doesn't seem to know much else, Peabody. What I wouldn't give to have . . .' He broke off with a catch of breath. 'Well, well. Let us see what we can do with Morley.'

We retraced our steps, back toward the pool and the area guarded by Morley's men. I decided to improve Emerson's state of mind by giving him a chance to lecture. He always enjoys that.

'I confess, Emerson, that I am somewhat confused about what Mr. Morley is doing. Is it Warren's shaft he is exploring?'

Emerson took my arm and said in a pleased voice, 'I don't wonder that you find the situation confusing, my dear. This area is a warren of tunnels and sewers and cisterns, some ancient, some modern. In ancient times two passages were dug to ensure that a source of water would be available to the city in case of siege. The first, constructed by the Jebusites, was a shaft from inside the walls down to a point where jugs could be lowered into a pool below. That's the one your friend Joab' – he jerked a thumb back at Plato – 'is supposed to have used to lead the forces of David into Jerusalem. There is, of course, no evidence whatever for this. Eh, Joab?'

'It was a hard climb,' Plato droned. 'The stone was slippery with damp and some fell, down, down into the pool.'

'At any rate,' said Emerson, 'the next water tunnel was constructed by Hezekiah on the eve of the Assyrian attack.' He gave me a challenging look, which dared me to remind him that he had denied the historicity of the entire Old Testament. There was no denying this fact; the inscription found in the tunnel had been dated to that period.

'It ran,' Emerson went on, 'from the Gihon spring to the present pool of Siloam and is still extant today.' He whirled on Plato, so abruptly that the latter let out a little scream. 'Is that the tunnel referred to in your famous scroll?'

'I believe so.'

'Don't you know?'

Plato raised his eyes to heaven. 'It has been many centuries since I led the Israelites into the city. Since then Assyrians and Babylonians, Greeks and Romans –'

'Never mind the rest of them,' Emerson growled. 'Confound it! That bastard Morley has gone on with his excavation despite my warning.'

We had reached the barricades, which were guarded by a few men in uniform. Some little distance beyond we could see a line of men carrying heavy baskets. They were stripped of most of their clothing and so coated with grayish dust, they resembled ambulatory mummies.

'They have been working underground,' said Emerson. 'The tunnel must be badly silted up. Here, you – where is the Englishman?'

The man addressed had obviously been told about Emerson. He lowered the barrier and stepped back, gesturing. We found Morley seated under a shelter of canvas that resembled a tent whose sides have been raised. He was not at luncheon. He was taking tea. Seated next to him at the table was a woman whose fair hair was confined by a scarf of emerald-green silk and whose costume was an interesting mixture of East and West – tailored trousers and leather boots partially covered by a flowing silken tunic that matched the scarf.

'Typical,' Emerson muttered. 'Dallying with a woman instead of supervising his workmen.'

She did not look the sort of woman with whom a man dallies. Her attire was exotic but not provocative; her features were strong, and her pale blue eyes studied me with steady self-assurance.

'Will you join –' Morley began.

'No,' said Emerson. 'Devil take it, Morley, I told you not to go on with your work without a professional supervisor.'

'I have complied with your demand, Professor, though I still question your right to make it.' Morley's cheeks rounded in a smug smile. 'May I present my professional colleague, Frau Hilda von Eine, a noted excavator of Hittite and Babylonian ruins.'

Chapter Eight

Morley could not have planned his strategy better. Not only had he acquired a professional archaeologist, but that professional was a female. Emerson enjoys intimidating other men, but the chivalrous part of his nature makes it virtually impossible for him to bully a woman. This can be a cursed inconvenience at times. However, I am perfectly capable of dealing with it.

Seeing that Emerson was taken aback (quite understandably) by Morley's announcement, I stepped into the breach.

'How do you do,' I said, offering the lady my hand. 'I am Mrs. Amelia P. Emerson.'

'You are unmistakable, Mrs. Emerson,' was the reply, in a soft gentle voice. 'I have been looking forward to meeting you.'

I went on to present my companions, beginning, as was proper, with Nefret. The lady – properly – acknowledged each with a smile and an inclination of her head. Reminded of his manners, Morley rose belatedly to his feet. Reminded of *his* manners, Emerson confined his response to a wordless mumble.

'How long have you been in Jerusalem, Frau von . . .' I began.

The lady took my catch of breath for a failure of memory and courteously repeated her name.

'Yes, of course,' I said, recovering myself with my customary aplomb. 'Something caught in my throat. Hem. Well, we must not keep you from your tea. I hope you will do us the honor of calling on us one day.'

'Tomorrow, perhaps?' Frau von Eine suggested.

Nefret, who had not spoken a word until then, said, 'Unfortunately, we are leaving Jerusalem tomorrow and may be gone for several days.'

It was too late to poke her with my parasol.

'Are you considering another site, then?' the lady asked. 'Tell el Nasbeh and Jericho, for instance, have great possibilities.'

'Thank you for the suggestion,' I said. 'I look forward to a meeting at a later time. Good day to you. Good day, Mr. Morley.'

Nefret was the first to turn away, followed by Selim and Daoud. Still staggered by the realization that had struck me, I did not notice at first that Plato had disappeared again. Interrogation produced the information that he had informed Nefret he intended to remain with Morley for a short time; she had seen no reason to forbid it.

'No reason!' I burst out.

'We cannot keep him a virtual prisoner indefinitely,' Nefret said. 'What harm can he do us, after all? You weren't proposing to take him with us tomorrow, were you?'

'Speaking of that,' I began.

'I hope you don't mean to go back on your word,' Nefret said, fixing me with an icy blue stare.

'Just a bloody minute,' exclaimed Emerson, coming to a dead stop. 'Why did you drag me away, Peabody? I had a number of questions to ask that bastard, and – er – the lady.'

'You were singularly inarticulate at the time,' I replied somewhat sharply. 'This new development necessitates thought and consultation. In private, Emerson.'

After passing out through the barrier, we had collected the usual followers, half-naked children and idle men, some asking for baksheesh, some simply curious to see what we would do next. They had stopped when we stopped and were watching us interestedly.

'Aunt Amelia,' Nefret said.

'*In private,* Nefret.'

Never had the walk back seemed so long and arduous; never had I so regretted not having nearby accommodations. I accepted the help of Emerson's strong arm as we climbed the slope. Always (almost always) sensitive to my state of mind, sensing my agitation, he towed me along with such vigor that my feet seldom touched the ground. Our followers abandoned us when we reached the Dung Gate. Wending our way past donkeys and carts, stepping over the money changers and letter writers who had set up shop along the narrow streets, we were passing David Street, the main thoroughfare, when we were intercepted.

'Honored lady! Mrs. Emerson! Hear me, please. Talk.'

The rabbi's gray beard was in wild disarray, his speech even more disjointed. His hands on my arm held me fast.

'Here now,' said Emerson, pulling me away. 'What do you think you are doing? Mrs. Emerson is not to be manhandled by strange men, even if they are rabbis.'

'He only took my arm, Emerson. I don't believe he understands what you are saying. Curse it, I wish one of us could speak Hebrew.'

One of us could. But he was not here.

'Curse it,' Emerson echoed. 'We haven't time for a chat about religion. Tell him so. Politely.'

Addressing the rabbi, who continued to pluck at my sleeve, I said slowly, shaking my head, 'Not now. Good-bye.'

'That was very polite,' Emerson said approvingly. 'Good-bye, adieu, auf Wiedersehen, God be with you.'

Continuing to shout words of farewell in various languages, he led me away.

By the time we reached the hotel I had decided how best to deal with the situation. It had changed dramatically, and not for the better.

'Let us all meet in our sitting room in one and a half hour's time,' I said. 'Nefret, you will want to bathe and change. Daoud, do go and have a little something to eat. Selim, go with him. Emerson, ask at the desk whether there have been any messages for us. Don't be too long.'

I left at once, without giving anyone a chance to protest. In fact, I did want to change my dusty, crumpled garments; I have found one thinks more clearly when one is clean and tidy. The bath chamber was occupied, so I had to content myself with the jug and basin at the washstand. I was engaged in this process when Emerson came in. His scowl changed to a pleased smile.

'In private, you said?' he inquired, advancing toward me with outstretched arms.

'Emerson, how can you be so frivolous at a time like this?'

I slid out of his grasp and adjusted the shoulder straps of my combinations.

'A time like what? Something is worrying you, I can see that, but I fail to understand why it should –'

'Get out the whiskey, Emerson. And lock the door.'

It was not necessary for me to say more. Brows furrowed, Emerson at once complied. Seating myself on the sofa, I motioned him to take a place at my side.

'We must discuss this before Nefret comes, Emerson. I take it there were no messages from the boys?'

'I would have told you at once,' Emerson said reproachfully. 'What have you to say that Nefret must not hear? You haven't changed your mind about –'

'No, no, it has nothing to do with that. Or at least I hope it has not. It concerns Frau von Eine.'

'She does seem to be a legitimate scholar,' Emerson admitted. 'I remember hearing her name. She worked at Boghazkoy with –'

Had it not been for the soothing effect of the genial beverage, I might have shouted at him. Instead I interrupted in almost my normal tone.

'Have you forgot the code message and the one word – phrase, rather – we could not interpret?' Knowing he had, and would start making excuses for having done so, I hurried on. 'It was a lower-case *v*, followed by a stop, and a capital *I*. Or so I thought. It is a number, Emerson, the number one. And the number one in German is ein, or eins. Frau von Eine is a German spy!'

I am sorry to say that Emerson's first thought was of himself.

'But – but that must mean that Morley is in German pay! Hell and damnation! Do you mean to say that the confounded War Office was right, and I was wrong?'

'We were both wrong, Emerson. Apparently.'

My willingness to share the blame failed to console my husband. 'What do you mean, apparently? The message can only be interpreted as referring to –'

'What it said was that Morley had been in contact with v.I. That contact may have been for what seemed to him harmless purposes. He may not know that she is in the employ of the German government. In fact,' I went on, seeing Emerson's face brighten, 'we don't know for certain that she is. The War Office is obsessed with espionage. She may be just what she claims to be, an archaeologist visiting Palestinian sites.'

'Do you believe that, Peabody?'

In point of fact, I did not. I preferred not to explain my reasons to Emerson, lest I be accused of 'jumping to conclusions, as usual, Peabody.' My instincts, which have seldom been wrong, told me that Frau von Eine was not what she seemed. That steady stare had felt as if it were boring into my brain, trying to read my thoughts.

Other facts might have seemed equally inconclusive to Emerson, but Emerson has absolutely no grasp of the social conventions. It had been out of character for a well-bred lady to propose a definite time for what had been an indefinite invitation. She had followed this by mentioning two specific places, one to the north and one to the west of Jerusalem. A subtle attempt to discover where we meant to go? It would have been natural, had our purpose been innocent, for us to answer yes or no. I wished even more that Nefret had not told her we planned to leave the city.

I was saved from replying by a peremptory knock at the door. The half hour was up.

'Let her in, Emerson,' I said, reaching for my dressing gown.

It was Nefret, of course, her faithful shadow Daoud behind her.

'I took the liberty,' said Nefret, 'of making arrangements for us to leave tomorrow. Selim is selecting the horses now.'

'That was very thoughtful of you, my dear,' I said. 'What about our baggage?'

'All taken care of,' said Nefret. 'I have already packed a small valise and my medical supplies. You can ride in the carriage with the luggage, Aunt Amelia, if you prefer. Or stay here.'

'Thank you,' I replied.

Her frozen expression melted. 'I didn't mean –'

'Never mind, Nefret.'

'It's just that I –'

'Quite,' I said. 'Has Mr. Plato turned up?'

'I don't know. Shall I go and see?'

'If you will, please. I must change for dinner. We will meet you in the dining salon.'

Nefret took her departure looking subdued but not repentant. She closed the door very softly.

'You were rather hard on her, weren't you?' Emerson asked.

'She is taking too much on herself, Emerson. I approve of independent young women, but in recent days she has made decisions without consulting ME, and some of them may have unpleasant consequences. For instance, her mentioning to Frau von Eine that we were leaving Jerusalem. If the woman is a German spy and if we are the ones she is after –'

'Too many ifs, Peabody, even for you. Why should she give a curse about us?'

'If the War Office has discovered her true mission, Emerson, German Imperial Intelligence may have discovered ours.'

I could see that this eminently logical deduction shook Emerson, but he was in no mood to admit it. 'More ifs,' he grumbled. 'I still think you were unkind to Nefret.'

'I understand her worry, but not this sudden urgency.' I slipped into my evening frock of black-beaded silk georgette and turned so that Emerson could deal with the buttons. I was becoming very tired of the frock, and of black in general. Too many people – Moslem ladies, Christian pilgrims, and Orthodox Jews – seemed to favor that dismal shade.

'Well, curse it, Peabody, I am worried too. We ought to have heard something from the boys by now.'

'We ought to have heard something from someone,' I agreed, running a brush over my hair and twisting it into a neat coil. 'Emerson, are you sure you were not told how to reach the Jerusalem representative of MO2? After all their fuss and bother, they have left us dangling. And you laughed at me the other day when I gave you the signal.'

Emerson tried not to grin but failed. 'My dear, someone was teasing you. Whoever heard of one hardened spy making that absurd gesture to another of the same?'

From Manuscript H

After the boy had gone, with Ramses's note tucked carefully into his belt pouch, Ramses decided he could chance making a small fire. The herb, whatever it might be, would be easier to take and probably more effective if it was brewed, like tea. He had eaten a small quantity himself; so far, no ill effects. Anyhow, why should the village healer take the trouble of poisoning them when all he had to do was call in the Turks?

Ramses was able to collect enough dry twigs and branches to get a fire going. Waiting for the water to boil, he thought over the latest encounter with the Sons of Abraham. He had assumed the name referred only to Arabs, the descendants of Ishmael, but apparently the membership included both Jews and Moslems. The boy spoke a little Arabic, but he was more at home in what must be his native tongue. Ramses's Hebrew had been good enough to understand him and to ask questions. However, he hadn't got much useful information. The boy had been in a hurry to get away, explaining that his absence would be noted if he wasn't in his usual place on time. No, he would not carry the message himself; it would be passed on, from one hand to another, until it reached its destination. When, he could not say. With luck, today. If not, tomorrow. Ramses had written his father's name in all three languages. 'I don't know where they are staying,' he explained. 'The last messenger will have to inquire at the major hotels –'

The boy had cut him short. 'We have our own ways. Now write the same again.'

Complying, Ramses thought to himself that someone in the group had a good head on his shoulders. Two messengers stood a greater chance of getting through than one.

The water was boiling. He stirred in the rest of the dried herb. Waiting for it to cool, he wiped David's hot face with a wet towel.

David stirred slightly; his forehead wrinkled, and then his eyes opened. They focused on Ramses's face and then moved slowly from side to side.

'Where –' he croaked.

'Someplace safe. How do you feel?'

David tried to moisten his dry lips. 'Thirsty.'

Ramses lifted his head and helped him drink. 'Better,' David said, lips cracking in a smile.

He did seem better, his temperature a few degrees lower, but Ramses didn't dare hope too much. Some fevers behaved this way, lower in the morning, climbing as the day went on.

'I've got some medicine for you,' he said, testing the water with a forefinger. 'Drink it down like a good boy.'

David managed a few sips, and Ramses decided to save the rest for a second dose. 'Can you eat something?' he asked. 'We've got food. Cheese, grapes . . .'

'Not hungry. Tell me where –'

'Lie still and rest while I talk. Nothing new about that, is there?'

He brought David up-to-date, starting from the moment when he had collapsed. 'So you see,' he concluded, 'things are looking up. My note is on its way to the parents and we have friends hereabouts.'

'That's nice.' David's eyes were half closed. 'So damn sleepy . . . Sorry, can't . . .'

His voice trailed off into a snore. The medicine must be a soporific as well as a febrifuge. Ramses wished he had kept a sample of the herb. Nefret would want to test it.

It was the first time he had dared think about her for several days. David had told him he had had a hard time talking her out of coming with him. Only his assurance that he alone could carry out the plan had won her over.

He put out the fire and went to the gate. It was a beautiful morning. A few white clouds moved overhead, like sheep in a blue pasture. High above, a hawk balanced on a current of air, and from the ruined heights of the keep a chorus of birdsong arose. In the valley below he saw neat little patches of green and gold, vineyards and fields of ripened grain. This was a peaceful land, fertile enough to support a small industrious population. It was hard to imagine the crops ablaze and the hillside strewn with the bodies of the dead; yet it must have happened many times, not only during the Crusades but for centuries before and centuries after.

This was the first time he had had a chance to find out exactly where they were. He had been too preoccupied with getting David up the hillside and then with exploring the inside of the castle before night fell. He was higher up than he had expected. The hill was almost a miniature mountain, its slopes steep and rocky. If there were people working the fields below, they were surely too far distant to see him, but he moved cautiously, close to the base of the wall. The view was spectacular from that height; the city they had left was hidden by the hills, but to the east he could see as far as the coastal plain. He moved on, picking his way around spiny shrubs and gnarled trees that had struck their roots down into the subsoil, till he reached the south side of the castle. The slope wasn't as steep there; goats grazed on the coarse patches of weeds, and several groups of small flat-roofed houses were visible below, some marked by the minaret of a mosque.

Shadows hid him from anyone who might look in that direction, but he decided he had better get back to David. Another truncated tower stood at the southeast corner. The sun was directly in his eyes when he got round it. What he saw when his vision adjusted made him draw back into the angle between tower and wall: a stretch of road hugging the curve of the hill below. It could only be the main road to Jerusalem, and it was less than half a mile from the castle height – close enough for him to make out the shapes of moving vehicles and the forms of animals and people. One group was distinguishable by their vivid red headgear – the fezzes worn by Turkish soldiers.

He went back the way he had come as fast as he dared. David was awake and trying to sit up. 'Thank God,' he said weakly. 'I didn't see you. I thought . . .'

'Sorry.' Ramses braced his shoulders and reached for the water skin. 'I went out to reconnoiter.'

'Anything new?'

'No.' He helped himself to a drink after David had finished. 'But I think we had better move farther inside. We're too exposed here. Do you feel up to it?'

'I'll crawl if I have to. I was just thinking that I was in plain view to anyone who walked through that gate and past the tower.'

'You won't have to crawl.' Ramses began gathering their scanty supplies together. 'Here, finish the medicine. I'll go ahead and find a good spot, and come back for you.'

Ramses felt a little easier after he had got David through the gate in the inner wall. David managed to stay on his feet but he didn't argue when Ramses suggested they rest awhile before going on. If Ramses hadn't known it was impossible, he would have thought David had lost a stone or more in the past twenty-four hours. His cheeks were hollow and his eyes sunken. He hadn't lost his nerve, though. Looking round at the wilderness of tumbled stone and stunted trees and brambly shrubs, with the dark mass of the keep rising in its midst, he let out a low whistle.

'All the comforts of home. Plenty of hiding places, wood for a fire . . . Those can't be fig trees, surely.'

'They say olives and figs can grow out of solid rock,' Ramses said somewhat absently.

'Pity there isn't a spring.'

He was making idle conversation in order to hide the fact that he needed to catch his breath, but the comment got Ramses's attention.

'One would think there would be, wouldn't one? A place like this wouldn't be defensible for long without a source of water. I'll have a look round later.'

Brambles tugged at their clothes as they went on. David kept stubbing his toes on chunks of stone hidden by the rampant weeds and leaning more heavily on Ramses's arm. He was weakening fast, or perhaps the medication had begun to take effect. Ramses got him inside the keep and lowered him onto the ground. He was out of breath himself. David looked as if he had lost weight, but he didn't feel as if he had.

'Cozy, isn't it?' he wheezed.

'Forbidding' would have been a better word. The walls of the lower floor of the keep were intact except for the gap through which they had entered. There had never been a door on this level; invaders would have to climb a steep narrow flight of stairs, under constant fire from the defenders, in order to reach the entrance. The stairs had slumped into a steep uneven ramp. The stairs inside remained, though Ramses hoped they would not have to use them; they circled the inner wall, but after seven centuries, give or take a decade, he would not have wanted to trust his weight to them. There were no windows on this level either. The only light came from above, through sections of the ceiling that had fallen in. The floor was littered with scattered stones, possibly the remains of partition walls, with bird droppings and straggling weeds, and with a grisly collection of bones. The bones, those of small animals like hares, were dry and brittle; he could only hope this was an indication that the predator had taken up residence elsewhere.

He cleared away bones, weeds, and rocks from a space behind a pile of stones and persuaded David to lie down, with one of the galabeeyahs under his head for a pillow. 'Can you eat something?' he asked.

David made a wry face. 'I'm not hungry, but I suppose I had better. What have we got?'

The answer was, nothing to tempt an invalid's appetite; the bread was hard, the cheese pungent, and the grapes were withering. David forced down some of the grapes and bread soaked in water to make a tasteless gruel. 'What time is it?' he asked.

'I forgot to wind my watch,' Ramses admitted. 'Getting on for midday, at a guess. My message has been on its way for several hours. With luck we could be out of this place tonight.'

His attempt at encouragement was a dismal failure. 'Not bloody likely,' David said. 'Don't treat me as if I were a child, Ramses. I may be sick, but I'm not stupid.'

'You must feel better,' Ramses said, smiling. 'Or you wouldn't talk back to me. You're right, of course. At best the messengers will take at least a day to reach Jerusalem. They won't risk the main road, because it's being patrolled by Turkish soldiers. Then they'll have to track down the parents, who are notoriously unpredictable; God only knows where they've got to by now. It may take even Mother a while to figure out exactly where we are, my directions were necessarily vague, and even if they receive the message tonight, they won't be stupid enough to start out in the dark. That's the truth of the matter. I hope you like it.'

'You only left out one uncomfortable fact. The messengers may not get through at all.'

'That's a possibility.'

'Then we had better get ready to move on our own,' David said coolly.

Ramses gave David's shoulder a quick, awkward squeeze. 'Thanks.'

'What for?'

'For not suggesting I leave you here and go to get help.'

'It would have been a waste of breath. You never listen to sensible suggestions.' He yawned. 'Is there any more of that vile medicine left? It makes me sleepy, but it does seem to have lowered the fever.'

'Just the dregs.' He had put the cup, with its contents, into his belt pouch along with all the other evidence of their presence. He took it out and inspected what remained of the herbs. 'I'll try adding some boiling water, let it steep awhile. Go back to sleep, there's nothing else to do.'

'Wake me in a few hours. Take it in turn to keep watch . . .'

His voice faded out and his eyes closed.

Ramses went back to the entrance and began gathering twigs and dried leaves for a fire. The thin smoke dissipated in the breeze, but he was afraid to let it burn too long; as soon as the water began to steam he stamped out the fire, taking care that no sparks reached the patches of dried grass. The water was running low, and had a distinct taste of goat. He'd seen a gleam of running water farther down the slope, on the side of the villages, but he was afraid to risk a sortie in case he might fall and break a limb. That would leave David alone and helpless.

When the brew was steeping he sat down, his back against the trunk of a fig tree. Keeping watch was definitely a sensible idea. They were too close to the road for comfort and the man who had brought them here had said not all in the villages were trustworthy. Did that mean that some of the villagers were not members of the Sons of Abraham, whoever those ambiguous individuals might be? They had done well by him and David so far. But Mansur had the same identifying mark, and if he was a member of the group, they couldn't all be as well-intentioned. Or were they? Had Mansur been playing a double game all along? Their escape had been a little too easy, some of the items left in their luggage a little too useful. The word of their escape had spread with remarkable speed. Thinking back on that morning, Ramses began to wonder if they hadn't been driven like cattle, headed off into byways that would lead them eventually to a safe refuge.

He hadn't felt so stupid and ineffectual since he was ten years old, when the girl he was trying desperately to impress had had to save him from the grasp of an abductor. He had fallen on his head and rolled into a ditch, a figure of shame and ridicule. And here he sat, waiting for her and his parents to rescue him again . . .

The sound of a voice jerked him awake. He had fallen into heavy slumber, sitting there. Hazy with sleepiness and berating himself for his failure as a lookout, he hurried in to see if it was David who had called him. David was sound asleep; he didn't stir even when Ramses spoke his name.

He made his way back to the entrance and peered out. There was no one in sight, and no further sounds – except the faintest of noises that might have been bare feet picking a path over pebble-strewn ground. The sounds faded into silence as he listened, and then he realized something was there, just inside the gate, something that hadn't been there before. The shadows were thickening; the object was an amorphous shape whose outlines were hard to make out.

He waited for another five minutes, counting off the seconds. The object didn't stir, and the sounds of movement had stopped. It wasn't curiosity that brought him out into the open, but need. Their water was running low and their food was gone. If this was, as he dared hope, another contribution of supplies from allies in the village, it would get them through the night and he wouldn't have to risk looking for a spring or a well. Still, it was with a long breath of relief that he recognized the object as a water skin and, behind it, a smaller cloth bag.

When he got back to the entrance, David was there. He looked terrible – sunken eyes peering out of a tangle of beard and hair, and he was leaning against the wall as if he couldn't stand without that support. He was holding a rock.

'Why didn't you wake me before you went gamboling out into the open?' he demanded. 'There might be a whole damned troop of Turkish soldiers lying in wait for you to show yourself.'

'You'd have been a great help with that pathetic rock,' Ramses said. He lowered his burden to the ground and reached out a supportive arm. 'Sit down before you fall down and let's open our presents. One of the Sons of Abraham has paid us a visit.'

'Just like Christmas, isn't it?' David said, after a long drink of fresh water. He passed the skin to Ramses and rummaged around in the bag. 'Cheese, bread, grapes . . . What's this?'

'It looks like more of the herbal medicine. I'll brew up a fresh batch. You look better, but a few more doses wouldn't do you any harm.'

'It makes me too sleepy.'

He was eating grapes with more relish than he had yet shown for food. Ramses watched him with an affection he would never have displayed in words or actions. It was amazing what a difference that humble gesture of goodwill had made; the mellow evening light seemed rich and comforting, the hoary old walls protective rather than forbidding. The small fire he had started burned clean and bright.

'I think we can sleep without worry tonight,' he said gently. 'People are looking after us.'

As we made our way toward the dining salon I pondered an idea that had only recently occurred to me. We had been contacted by the War Office a day or two after we arrived in Jaffa, yet there had been no communication from them here. For all I knew, Jerusalem could be swarming with spies of all nations, including our own; certainly one would expect that MO2 would be on the trail of Frau von Eine and would notify us of her presence in the city. The more I thought about it, the more convinced I became that a message had gone astray, so when I saw Mr. Fazah behind the desk I told Emerson to go on ahead and I approached the assistant manager.

I was tempted to wriggle my nose at him again, in case he had had some reason for ignoring the first signal, but he was watching me so warily I decided it might alarm him. If my newfound theory was correct, he was not the contact I wanted. When I asked to speak to the manager he stiffened. Underlings always expect the worst when one asks for the manager.

'If madam has a complaint,' he began.

'No, not at all. Seeing you always on duty, and performing so well, I wanted to pass on my commendation to your superior.'

His face brightened. 'Thank you, madam. If you would care to write a message to that effect, it would be most kind.'

Subtlety had not availed me. I took a more direct approach. 'Is there some reason why I can't speak to him in person?'

It took some persistence to get it out of him. The manager was at home, ill with the fever. He didn't want the word to get out for fear patrons would think they might be in danger of catching the same illness. Mr. Fazah assured me earnestly that there was no danger of infection, that such fevers were common, debilitating but not life-threatening; that all food and drink served in the hotel were perfectly safe. I promised him I would keep the matter under my hat, regretting that I was unable to demonstrate the meaning of the phrase since I was not wearing that article of apparel.

As if to indicate his dedication to duty, Mr. Fazah informed me that although there had been no written messages for us, several persons had come round to see us. One had been Mr. Page, earlier that afternoon. The other, 'a queer shabby sort of little old Jewish person,' had been there within the past hour. 'I was forced to ask him to leave,' said Mr. Fazah, nose in the air, 'since he began waving his arms and shouting.'

The description, unkind though it was, left no doubt as to the identity of our most recent visitor. The poor man was determined to help us, whether we wanted help or not – and I could not imagine any way in which he might be of use. However, simple civility dictated that I give him a few minutes of my time.

'I will send him away if he returns,' Mr. Fazah offered.

'No, no. Notify me unless the hour is unreasonably late.'

The unexpected absence of the manager might explain why we had not received any word from MO2, if such messages were only to be delivered to him in person. The process seemed haphazard and potentially dangerous. But after all, I reminded myself, the War Office was run by men.

I found the others, including Mr. Plato, in the dining salon.

'Did you have a fruitful encounter with your friend Major Morley?' I inquired of the latter.

'I rejoice to say that we are again in amity,' was the reply, accompanied by a soulful look.

'In that case,' I said, 'you will, I expect, prefer to take up your living quarters with him.'

Plato gave me a startled look. 'But, Mrs. Emerson –'

'What precisely was the nature of your original agreement with him?' I asked.

Planting his elbows on the table, Emerson regarded me with approval. 'See if you can winkle it out of him, Peabody. When I tried, all I got was vague biblical references.'

Unfortunately the waiter turned up to take our orders, which gave Plato time to organize his thoughts – or, as Emerson would have said, think up a convincing lie. I immediately resumed my interrogation.

'You supplied the information contained in the scroll,' I said. 'He supplied the funds and financial support. Were you to divide the proceeds?'

'No such mercenary object was in my mind,' Plato said with a show of dignity. 'I only wished to see the Holy Scriptures confirmed, the truth shown to the world.'

'Who paid your living expenses while you were in England?'

'We were as brothers, united in our burning faith.'

'Oh, yes, I can see Morley burning with faith,' said Emerson. He added, 'If he mentions David and Jonathan I will send him to his room without his supper.'

'In other words,' I said sternly, 'you lived off the money Morley brought in from his subscribers. Since you are now in amity again, he can go back to supporting you. I will arrange for a carriage to collect you and your luggage first thing tomorrow morning.'

No one had the temerity to protest. Nefret looked down at her plate, lips compressed, ignoring the pitiful looks Plato shot at her. Her tender heart was at war with her keen intelligence, and finally, it appeared, intelligence was in the ascendancy.

Plato ate his way through the soup course, the fish course, and all the other courses as if he expected it would be his last meal – which for all I knew might well be the case. When we retired to the lounge for coffee, he trailed after us. Since we needed to discuss our plans for the morrow, I told him to go to his room and begin packing. Thus far he had not got wind of our intentions, and I wanted it to remain that way.

I had reason, shortly thereafter, to be thankful I had sent him away. Scarcely had we taken our seats than Mr. Fazah came toward us. 'That person,' he began. He did not finish; the little rabbi pushed past him and ran to me.

'God be thanked,' he panted. 'You are here.'

'Oh, good Gad,' said Emerson. 'Tell him we do not need his help and get rid of him. Be polite, of course.'

The rabbi reached into the breast of his robe and took out a folded piece of paper, which he thrust at me. 'Help,' he said. 'Help.'

I cannot say what I expected; but one glance at the crumpled paper dispelled any doubts as to the rabbi's intentions. I recognized the paper as a page from my son's notebook, and the handwriting as that of Ramses.

'It appears to be addressed to you, Emerson,' I said. 'In Arabic, Hebrew, and English. Rabbi, how did you –'

'For pity's sake, Aunt Amelia, open it!' cried Nefret. Seated next to me, she had also identified the handwriting. In her agitation she actually snatched the note from my hand and unfolded the paper. The flush of health faded from her cheeks as she read.

'What?' shouted Emerson. 'What?'

'Sssh,' I said. 'Let us not draw attention to ourselves. Read it aloud, Nefret. Quietly.'

In fact quite a number of other patrons were looking in our direction. A gathering of pilgrims, the same ones we had observed in the dining salon, turned to stare, and a Turkish dignitary edged closer.

Looking over Nefret's shoulder, I saw that Ramses's handwriting was even more irregular than usual, but she read it off without hesitating. It began abruptly, with no salutation. '"A friend is bringing this message. We were prisoners but got away. We are holed up in Crusader castle approx. ten m. south of Nablus, e. of the main road. David ill. Would appreciate assistance but please be careful, think we are being pursued."'

'We must go at once,' Selim exclaimed. 'Where is this place?'

'We will find it,' Nefret said quietly. 'But, Selim, we cannot leave this moment.'

I looked at her with surprise and admiration, for I had been about to make that point myself. As was so often the case, she could control her fiery temper when the occasion was desperate. The color had rushed back into her cheeks; they glowed as if with fever.

'Quite right,' I said. 'We cannot set out in darkness, particularly when we don't know the precise location of the place. Rabbi, how did you come by this message?'

But when I turned to address him, he was gone.

*

I doubt that any of us slept well that night. Emerson certainly did not; he kept tossing and turning and muttering to himself. We were all afire to be gone, but as I had pointed out, it would be folly to charge blindly ahead, risking an accident or missing the place in the dark. Paging patiently through my guidebook – whose index had no entry for 'castles' – I had finally found a reference to a place that must be the one Ramses had referred to. Known as Tal'at-ed-dam, or 'Hill of Blood,' it was described as the ruins of a Crusader castle, and I did not doubt that in its heyday the name had been only too appropriate. Under other circumstances I would have considered it a most interesting side trip.

The only other thing we could do before retiring was to make certain our means of transportation would be available on time. There was now no need to pack changes of clothing and other nonessentials, but we decided to retain the carriage in case David was not able to ride. Despite the press of new arrangements, I found time to inform Mr. Fazah that we would no longer be responsible for Plato's hotel bills.

Lying awake beside my restless spouse, I addressed a little prayer of thanks to Him who watches over us – and also to the governesses and nannies who had instilled in me their notions of proper behavior. (My esteemed father had taught me languages but not manners; his own left a good deal to be desired.) Had I not had the courtesy to listen to the little rabbi, we might have set out on a fruitless quest, never knowing our dear ones were so close, and in mortal danger. I did not minimize that danger, despite Ramses's offhand request for assistance. He hated asking for help, but I wished he had gone straight to the point and mentioned details such as the time and date. As it was, we had no idea how long the message had taken to reach us; it might have been days.

He and David must have been on their way to Jerusalem when David fell ill. The illness must be severe enough to prevent David from going on. I had packed every variety of medicine I had with me, and I knew Nefret had done the same. If only Ramses had had the decency to add a few more words that would give us a clue as to what ailed the boy, and how serious it was!

The friend who had offered to carry a message could not have been the rabbi; he was not the sort of person to go tramping in the hills. Grubby and tattered as the paper was, it might have passed through several hands before reaching its destination – and that destination was the rabbi. The final messenger had delivered it to him instead of doing the rounds of the Jerusalem hotels.

What did it all mean? I was unable to concentrate on any single issue, my mind kept wandering off into irrelevant byways. I had just convinced myself I would not get a wink of sleep when I was awakened by a knock at the door and a voice calling my name.

All the worries of the night came flooding back. I sprang out of bed, instantly alert, and fell over Emerson's boots, which I had placed near the door in preparation for the morrow.

'Are you all right, Aunt Amelia?' Nefret asked.

'Yes, yes, and wide awake.' I rose, rubbing my shin. The room was pitch-dark – the utter darkness before the dawn, as some poet or other has put it.

Nefret had obviously been up for some time. She had rousted out (her phrase) the cook and had carried to our door, with her own hands, the beverage essential to Emerson's arousal. On this occasion he was much easier to manage; like myself, he had been awake half the night, itching to be on our way. When we assembled on the steps of the hotel the sky was still black, but my watch, which I never neglect to wind, assured me dawn was not far distant. I beheld not a single star. The morning fog had moved in, mixing with the varied and noxious effluvia of the city.

I had expected we would be the only early risers, but I had overlooked the dedication (or zealotry) of religious persons. The group of pilgrims that had made such a memorable impression must have a distant holy destination on their agenda for the day;

they were assembled in the dining salon. Daoud cast a longing glance in that direction; observing it, Nefret assured him she had asked that picnic baskets be ready.

Selim was waiting with the drivers and mounts we had ordered. Nefret was the first in the saddle. To his disgust, Daoud was relegated to the carriage, which was drawn by two sturdy horses. Selim had been unable to find a horse that was up to his weight. The one assigned to me was almost as small as a pony, which was reassuring; but when I approached the creature it shied back, showing the whites of its eyes.

'That damned belt of tools is spooking the horse, Peabody,' said Emerson, already mounted. 'Take it off.'

'I cannot proceed without my accoutrements, Emerson. They jangle a bit, to be sure, but we may need one or all of them before the day is over.'

'Then get in the carriage with Daoud,' said Emerson shortly.

I did so, not without a certain feeling of relief. I am not an accomplished horsewoman and the pony had obviously taken a dislike to me.

The carriage driver, hunched over and well wrapped up against the chill of the morning, cracked his whip, and we were off, with Emerson, Nefret, and Selim in the lead. Someone, probably Nefret, had ascertained the quickest route out of the city. With a minimum of delay, for the streets were comparatively empty at that hour, we reached the Damascus Gate and left the city proper. The population had spilled out beyond the walls; we passed several fine villas and groups of houses. The sun peeped over the horizon. The recently completed road allowed for reasonable speed, but I was pleased to see that Emerson, now in the lead, kept a moderate pace. We must not be separated, I had told him.

We had been on our way for slightly more than an hour when we rounded a curve and saw ahead a barricade guarded by a group of Turkish soldiers. Observing Emerson, who was hard to miss, the officer stepped forward and held up his hand.

I saw no other vehicles or individuals waiting. It was as I had feared. Someone had anticipated our intentions – and I thought I could guess who. I gripped my parasol tightly, prepared for combat if it became necessary. We dared not risk delay.

I should not have doubted my admirable spouse. Instead of stopping, he urged the horse into a gallop and burst through the barricade, shattering the flimsy wooden structure into splinters. The soldiers scattered in panic as Nefret and Selim thundered down on them. I poked my driver with my parasol. 'Faster,' I cried. 'Yallah, yallah, do not stop.'

He may have thought it was a knife at his back (as I believe I have mentioned, my parasols have extremely sharp points) or he may have been carried away by the general stampede. Emitting a loud cry, he brandished his whip. Stony dust and a rain of small pebbles flew up from below the horses' hooves as they dashed forward. We met with no impediment; the riders ahead of us had removed them.

Gripping the side of the carriage, which was swaying and bouncing, I looked back. No one appeared to have been seriously injured; the soldiers were slowly getting to their feet and the officer was expostulating (to judge by his impassioned gestures) with a person on horseback.

Emerson kept up the pace for another mile before he slowed his horse to a trot. Waving Nefret and Selim on, he fell back beside the carriage.

'All right, are you, Peabody?' he inquired. 'Daoud?'

Daoud nodded. He was a trifle green and he was clutching the side of the carriage with both hands. I said, 'Well done, my dear. Did you anticipate the roadblock?'

'I thought some such contingency might arise. I ought to have warned you, as I did Nefret and Selim, but I felt certain that you would rise to the occasion.'

'Our driver deserves commendation as well,' I said. Leaning forward, I said in Arabic, 'Good work, my friend. You have earned much baksheesh.'

A wordless mumble was the only response.

'He may be one of those who believe it improper to look upon the face of an unveiled woman,' said Emerson. 'Damn-fool notion, but no more idiotic than a good many of the –'

'I am familiar with your views on that subject, my dear,' I said. 'Should we not press on with all possible speed?'

'How much farther, do you suppose?'

'We must be fairly close. If the guidebook is accurate, the place should be visible from –' I broke off with a cry of excitement and pointed with my parasol. A short distance ahead, on the left-hand side of the road, rose a steep hill crowned with uneven stones like jagged teeth. From it rose a thick column of smoke.

From Manuscript H

Despite David's objections Ramses managed to persuade him to take another dose of the herbal brew. He couldn't be sure it was doing any good – the fever might have run its course naturally – but it wouldn't hurt David to have a solid night's sleep. David badgered him into taking a few sips himself. The keen eye of a friend hadn't missed the signs Ramses was unwilling to admit even to himself. They weren't severe and might have been the result of fatigue and worry – loss of appetite, moments of unsteadiness. He told himself he could stick it out for another day. Things were looking up, there was even a chance of rescue soon, but he wasn't willing to risk the possibility that an enemy might catch both of them dead to the world – which they would be, literally. He spat out the last mouthful of medicine when David wasn't looking at him.

Even then, his slumber was heavier than he would have wished. It might have been a birdcall or animal sound that woke him – or that sixth sense his mother called the sleeping sentinel. It sent the adrenaline flooding into his veins, and he stiffened, listening intently. A dim light filtered into the keep through the broken entrance where he lay. Night was ending. Dawn was not far off. He pulled himself to his feet and looked out into a gray morning and the shapes of moving shadows.

He couldn't tell how many of them there were, but one or more was already inside the gate. He drew back, wishing, not for the first time, that he had a weapon, even a club. He had tried to break off a tree limb, but the tough old branches resisted his best efforts. He picked up a rock and waited.

The voice spoke again, closer now, but not close enough for him to make out the words. Mansur stepped into view. His hands were raised. Neither held a weapon. He took a few steps forward, and Ramses saw he was not alone. Immediately behind him was his manservant, the one who had waited on him during the banquet. Several other men crowded through the gate. They were dressed in the same rough garments his first guide had worn, and each had a long knife thrust through his belt.

'Come out. We know you are there. Resistance is useless.'

The words were English, but the voice wasn't the one he had expected. Mansur's lips had not moved.

The speaker had to be Mansur's servant. It could be a trick to get him out in the open. What would be the point, though? There were at least six of them, all armed. He couldn't hold them off. If he gave himself up they might not bother looking for David. He could tell them David had got away.

He moistened his dry lips and spoke. 'Who are you?'

'The enemies of your enemy. Come out, we mean you no harm.'

They all moved forward, step by step, like hunters trying not to startle a timid animal. The rising sun shone full on them now, and

Ramses saw that Mansur's face was streaked with blood and that the man behind him held a knife at his back, and that the other men had boxed him in on three sides, their knives drawn.

His mind seemed to be working at half-speed. Not until Mansur's servant pushed his sleeve back and showed his bare forearm did he put the clues together. Cautiously he came out into the open.

'The Sons of Abraham,' he said. 'Then you are – you are . . .'

He couldn't think of the right word. The fellow didn't look like a commander or a spiritual leader; he was as unremarkable as ever, short-statured and slender, his beard scarcely touched with gray. His eyes ought to have been glowing with intelligence, his pose one of pride and dignity. The eyes were a muddy brown, and his narrow shoulders were hunched.

'You may call me Ismail,' he said, giving the name its Arabic pronunciation. 'Or Ishmael, if you prefer.'

Ramses rubbed his aching forehead. 'I don't understand. Why did you bring him here?'

'We did not bring him. He brought us. When he ordered me to come with him to the Hill of Blood and bring those who would assist him, I knew your presence had been betrayed. So I did as he asked. Except that the men I chose were my men, not his.' He looked around at the grim walls and desolate ground. 'This place is fitting. Prepare him.'

Ramses watched in disbelief while two of the men stripped Mansur of his robe and laid him down across one of the larger blocks, his bare arms extended, his wrists held tightly. For the first time Ramses had a good look at the mark on his forearm. It was the same as the others he had seen, a strange cryptogram that might have been the Hebrew letter aleph crossed by another symbol. Mansur was passive in their grasp, his face as wooden as ever. To judge by the blood on his face, he had put up a fight initially, but he was now resigned to whatever fate awaited him.

He didn't look at Ramses, not even when Ismail stood over him with a drawn knife. The tableau was horribly reminiscent of scenes from Aztec tombs depicting a priest cutting the heart from a living sacrifice.

'No,' Ramses exclaimed. 'No. You mustn't.'

'Who will stop me? You?'

'If I can.' He twisted away from the first man who would have taken hold of him and kicked out at a second. His foot missed its target, delivering a blow on the thigh that didn't even stagger the fellow. Then they were both on him, and after a brief, ineffectual struggle, they held him fast.

Ismail hadn't moved. He studied Ramses with mild curiosity. 'You would fight for him? He would have taken your life.'

Ramses was aware of Mansur's dark, sardonic eyes watching him. He's waiting for me to spout a string of public-school clichés, he thought. 'I would fight him, on equal grounds, and kill him, if it were the only way of saving my own life. I am no saintly martyr. I cannot stand by while you murder a helpless man.'

'You do. In your prisons and execution chambers. In war.'

'I deplore both. But the prisoner has had a fair trial and the soldier is armed.'

The other man's lips parted in a smile. 'That is not always true. You reason like a philosopher; if I had time I would enjoy debating with you. Will your conscience be at ease if I tell you that he has been tried, by his peers, and condemned?'

'No. What is his crime?'

'That is not your concern. Where is your friend?'

There hadn't been a sound from David. Ramses hoped he was still sleeping, or that if he wasn't, he had sense enough to remain silent and out of sight. 'Gone,' he said curtly.

'So long as he does not try to interfere.'

The men who held Ramses tightened their grip. The knife blade

243

caught the light, once, twice, in flashing movements. Blood spurted up in the cuts, obscuring the design on Mansur's arm.

Ismail stepped back, wiped the knife on his robe, and then sheathed it.

'He is yours now,' he said. 'Do as you will with him.'

The men restraining Ramses let go their hold. With Ismail in the lead, the entire group started back toward the gate.

'Wait!' Ramses shouted. 'Come back. I want . . . Oh, dammit.'

He had a choice between catching Ismail up and demanding answers to various vital questions, and letting Mansur lose a vital amount of blood. Ripping a strip from the hem of his shirt, he hurried to the recumbent man and whipped a makeshift tourniquet around his upper arm.

The injury wasn't as bad as it had appeared. The knife had nicked a small artery, but most of the blood came from one of the large veins. Still, it required attention, and Mansur wasn't doing a damn thing to help himself. He remained motionless, staring up at the sky.

'Hold on to this,' Ramses snapped. 'I've got antiseptic and bandages in my pack.'

He tumbled the contents of his pack onto the ground and hurried back with his mother's medical kit, pausing only long enough to look in on David. His slumber was so profound that Ramses began to wonder whether the most recent packet of herbs hadn't been stronger than the first. Mansur didn't speak until Ramses had finished disinfecting and bandaging the wound.

'You expect thanks, I presume,' he said.

'No. A few answers would be nice, though.'

'For example?'

'Who are the Sons of Abraham?'

'You would call them a cult, I expect.' Mansur sat up and reached for his robe. 'Is there water?'

Ramses fetched the skin and waited impatiently while Mansur drank long and deeply. 'Go on,' he said.

Mansur wiped his mouth on his sleeve. 'They prefer to call themselves a faith. They are very old, many centuries old. They believe in the brotherhood of Jew and Arab, of all those who have lived in this land and become part of it. They work peacefully and patiently for freedom and independence.'

'And they let you join?'

Mansur's lips curved in a tight smile. 'Their goals are mine. However, after a time I realized that they were willing to wait for many more centuries rather than take the action that would win them what they want. They would lose, because the pacifists and idealists always lose.'

He paused. Ramses waited for a few moments and then prompted him. 'You used the prestige you gained from being a member of this old and respected organization to instigate a revolution. You betrayed their principles. It took them a while to catch up with you, though.'

Mansur glanced up at the sky. The sun was visible over the top of the wall. 'Matters did not go quite as I planned,' he admitted. 'Have you a cigarette?'

Ramses had been hoarding them and the few remaining matches, but he wanted Mansur to go on talking. He handed them over, with a wary eye on the other man's hands. Mansur wasn't armed, and although Ramses wasn't at his best, he was pretty certain he could take a wounded man.

That wasn't what Mansur had in mind. He lit his cigarette and tossed the match aside. It landed in an inconspicuous pile of dried grass. Small flames licked up. Mansur leaped to his feet and kicked the spreading fire into a patch of weedy branches.

It had to be a signal. Ramses sprang toward it. Mansur kicked him in the ankle and he fell flat. When he pulled himself to a sitting position he saw Mansur standing over him with a sizable stone in his right hand.

'This is what you should have done to me,' he said, and brought the stone down on Ramses's head.

Chapter Nine

'There! Do you see?' I shrieked, gesturing with my parasol. 'Hurry, Emerson, hurry; they are being immolated!'

Emerson let out a string of oaths in a variety of languages and urged his steed to a gallop. I did not need to prod my driver; with a wordless whoop he cracked his whip, and our equipage thundered away in pursuit of Emerson.

If I had been thinking clearly instead of allowing the anxious heart of a parent to guide my tongue, I would have realized the verb was probably exaggerated. It was just as likely that the smoke was a signal from Ramses himself, to guide us. Still, haste was of the essence – all the more so because coming toward us, though still some distance away, was a sizable body of men wearing Turkish uniforms.

We would have missed the path if we had not been looking for it. Hardly more than a rutted track, it cut off to the left between two rugged banks. Still in the lead, since she had never slackened pace, Nefret swerved abruptly and disappeared into the cleft. Selim was close behind her and Emerson was not far behind Selim. I was on my feet, shouting encouragement and instructions to the driver, when we reached the spot. He made the turn so abruptly that I would have fallen had it not been for my firm grip on the rail and Daoud's big hands holding me. The path was scarcely wide enough for a carriage – if it were carefully driven. Ours struck the side and came to a shuddering stop. Held erect only by Daoud's grasp, I watched in stunned surprise as the driver leaped from his perch and cut both horses loose. Uttering equine noises of alarm, they trotted on up the path.

Daoud jumped down and caught the driver by the throat. 'He turned purposely into the bank, Sitt Hakim. He is one of the enemy! But I will not let him harm you. I have him fast.'

The last sentence was certainly true. The driver's headcloth had slipped down over his eyes and his scarf was twisted tightly round his neck. Clawing at it, he strove to speak but could only gurgle. Conceive of my astonishment, dear Reader, when he took the end of his nose between thumb and forefinger and wriggled it – twice!

The entire incident had transpired so quickly that the wheels of the carriage, two of them off the ground, were still spinning. I climbed out of the vehicle and approached the driver, remarking as I did so, 'You had better release him, Daoud. Go on, I will catch you up.'

Daoud cast an agonized glance over his shoulder. Sounds indicative of combat floated down to us from above, echoed by running footsteps from below, at the entrance to the path. Whipping my little pistol from my pocket, I fired several shots toward the approaching soldiers. Since I had not actually hit anyone, I doubted it would deter them for long, but it might give them pause, in both senses of the phrase.

'Go on,' I said again. 'That is an order, Daoud.'

Daoud was torn between his need to protect me and his desire to aid his friends, but his faith in me was unquestioned. He dropped the driver and ran. I pushed the fellow's headcloth up and looked into a pair of bulging pale blue eyes.

'Ah,' I said. 'Mr. Courtney Camden. Why did you not inform me of your true identity, and why did you wreck the carriage? Be succinct, I beg.'

Mr. Camden, being still short of breath, gesticulated frantically. 'Block the entrance,' he gasped. 'Turks. Do you . . . go on. I will –'

'We will go on together. Though I yearn to be at the side of my valiant allies and, if my prayers have been answered, my errant son, I am confident that they have already got the situation well in hand, and that my assistance is not –'

Mr. Camden emitted a loud growling sound, caught hold of my hand, and proceeded on up the path, pulling me with him.

The path twisted and turned, seeking the easiest ascent, but it was steep enough. Thanks to Mr. Camden and my trusty parasol, which served as a walking stick, I had no difficulty. At last we emerged onto a plateau some ten acres in extent, with the walls of a ruined yet imposing fortress directly ahead. A number of horses, including the two from the carriage, were ambling about nibbling at the rank grass and shrubs that covered the ground. The sounds of combat had subsided, which was reassuring or the reverse, depending on one's anticipations.

'Go slowly,' I urged. 'If our friends have been overcome we will take the enemy by surprise.'

'And hit them with your parasol? Oh, confound it, you are right. Slowly it is.'

The great gateway, flanked by towers, was before us. As we passed through, each of us trying to get ahead of the other, I saw movement out of the corner of my eye and turned my head in time to behold the hindquarters of one of the horses heading (if that term is appropriate) down the path to the road.

After some casting about we located the gate in the inner wall. Mr. Camden would have held me back; I flung off his hand.

'All is well,' I said. 'I can hear Emerson swearing at Ramses.'

To be accurate, he was not swearing at Ramses but swearing in general, interspersing his oaths with such phrases as 'All right, are you, my boy?' and 'We are on the job, lie still!' This was reasonably good proof that Ramses was still alive, and it was with a mind relieved that I entered the inner area.

My first impression was one of utter chaos. Wisps of smoke arose from smoldering patches of brush, which Selim and Daoud were methodically stamping out. The drifting gray shapes lent a spectral look to the scene, with its rubble-strewn ground and the looming shape of the inner keep. Naturally my eyes went first to the touching tableau with David and Ramses at its center. At least I assumed the tatterdemalion, filthy forms were theirs. Their faces were unrecognizable, the lower half covered with straggling beards, the upper half with mops of hair that had not seen a comb or brush for days. However, Ramses's nose was unmistakable. He lay on his back, his head in Nefret's lap. David sat cross-legged on the ground nearby and Emerson paced up and down, rubbing his chin and of course still swearing. Upon observing me he swung round and demanded, 'What took you so long?'

'We were delayed by a slight accident,' I replied. 'It seems you did not require my assistance, however.'

'We could have used a bit of help,' Emerson admitted. 'What with four – or was it five? – villains trying to make off with Ramses, and David staggering after them waving a broken branch, and Nefret –'

'You can continue your spirited narrative later, Emerson.'

I knelt by Ramses and brushed the hair away from his forehead. What I could see of his skin was flushed and red. 'Gracious,' I said, 'he is burning with fever.'

'It's the same illness I had,' David said. 'I'm much better, but he caught it from me.'

'He also has a nasty lump on his head,' Nefret said.

'Concussion?' I inquired, probing the area she indicated with expert fingers.

Before she could answer, Ramses opened his eyes. 'Good morning, Mother. I thought I recognized your touch.'

It took a while to sort things out. Everyone had a tale to tell and everyone wanted to tell it at once, and I had to forbid further discussion until we had dealt with the most important matter, namely, getting the boys safely home and being cared for. A slight diversion, in the shape of half a dozen Turkish soldiers erupting into the courtyard, was quickly dealt with by Emerson, who fired several shots from a pistol I had not known he possessed over their heads and sent them scampering for safety. David gathered their few possessions, and Emerson wanted to carry Ramses, who turned an even brighter red with indignation at the idea, but he was not unwilling to be guided along by Daoud. As they made their way to the gate I took a final look round. 'Are they dead?' I inquired of Emerson, indicating several recumbent forms – another group of soldiers, to judge by their attire.

Emerson chuckled. 'Playing possum, as Vandergelt would say. They are waiting for us to leave so they can skulk away.' He added negligently, 'I got the distinct impression that their hearts were not in this fight. When we went after them they either ran or fell flat.'

Supported by Daoud and David, Ramses suddenly planted his feet and pulled away from them. 'Ran. Who . . . Dammit, Daoud, let me go. I have to see . . .'

His eyes moved slowly round, from one motionless body to another. 'Where is he?' he asked vaguely. 'I don't see him.'

'Who?' I asked. 'We are all here, my dear. Selim and Daoud and –'

'No, no. Mansur. He was here, he . . .'

The name meant nothing to any of us except David. Knowing Ramses would stay on his feet talking until he got an answer, David said, 'He got away, Ramses. Don't think about that now. We'll catch up with him.'

Ramses said distinctly, 'God damn it all to hell,' and fell into Daoud's arms.

Several of the horses were still lazing about the outer entrance; we found the rest along the path, and standing by the overturned carriage, which blocked further progress.

The carriage was undamaged except for a few dents, and Selim was able to repair the harness with some of the bits of wire he always carried with him, so we were soon on our way. I took my seat on the box next to the driver, explaining – truthfully – that the carriage was somewhat cramped with three additional passengers. Neither of the boys was fit to ride. Nefret, promptly and without comment, took her place between them.

Mr. Camden, as I must continue to call him, had retreated into his driver persona as soon as he realized his active assistance was not required. No one paid him the least notice (except for Emerson, who delivered a hearty slap on the back and a loud 'Good chap!'). It seemed to me an excellent opportunity for a private chat, since the ambient noises made it impossible for us to be overheard. I therefore requested he explain himself.

'I can keep nothing from you, Mrs. Emerson,' he said morosely.

'That is correct.'

'You have probably guessed – deduced, rather – a good deal of it. I am the representative of MO2 in Jerusalem. I owe the position to my brother, George Tushingham, whom I believe you met in London.'

'Aha!' I exclaimed. 'Mr. Tushingham, the botanist. I knew you looked familiar. I would have made the connection eventually. So your real name is Tushingham.'

'I beg you will continue to call me by the name the others know. I was told of your mission before you arrived, and my assignment was to assist you in any way possible, without revealing my true identity.'

'Typical male stupidity,' I remarked. 'The obsession with secrecy and the refusal of different parts of the bureaucracy to communicate with one another can only lead to –'

'In any case,' said Mr. Camden, raising his voice slightly, 'it was some time before I realized our contact at the hotel was out of commission and that my message had probably never reached you.'

'Another example of masculine incompetence. To rely on a single link –'

'Quite, Mrs. Emerson. I was therefore forced to approach you directly, with no means of establishing my bona fides should that become necessary.'

The carriage hit a rut; I caught hold of my hat with one hand and Mr. Camden with the other. 'But the signal you gave me –'

This time Mr. Camden's interruption came in the form of a fit of coughing. I slapped him on the back, rather more forcibly than was necessary, since the truth had begun to dawn on me.

'Speak up,' I exclaimed. 'The truth, the whole truth, and nothing but the truth!'

'Well – um – you see . . . I'm afraid that was one of Mr. Boniface's little jokes. He told me of it when I saw him in Jaffa a few days ago.'

'Jokes,' I repeated.

'He laughed quite heartily about it. He had taken a bit too much to drink, I believe.' Glancing uneasily at me, Mr. Camden went on, 'Naturally I reprimanded him severely. However, it served us well in the end, did it not? I couldn't think what else to do when your large friend was throttling me.'

After a few moments of cogitation, I said very calmly, 'So it would seem. I will have a few words to say to Mr. Boniface when next I encounter him. Was there anything in the missing message I ought to know?'

'It concerned Mme – er –'

'There you go again with your confounded secrecy. No one can hear us. Mme von Eine, yes. I deduced her identity without your assistance.'

The great gate of the Holy City came into view; Camden urged the horses to a quicker pace. He was not enjoying our conversation. I had one more important point to make, however, and I proceeded to make it.

'Since your normal means of communication is still inoperative, I think it best that you should be available at all times. Be at the hotel tomorrow morning at eight. We will be proceeding to Siloam. I expect to have the house ready for occupancy within the next day or two. That will put us on the spot while Morley's excavations are progressing and will enable us to find out what the lady is up to. Have you any questions?'

'No, ma'am,' said Mr. Camden meekly. 'Yes, ma'am. I will be there.'

It was late afternoon when we entered the city, having encountered no difficulty. The few Turkish soldiers we met ignored us, and the roadblock was gone except for scattered bits of wood. We were the cynosure of all eyes when we entered the lobby; seldom had such a motley crew arrived at that sedate hostelry. We were all dusty and disheveled, but none of us approached the degree of social unacceptability of David and Ramses. My first act was to whisk them upstairs and order hot baths for them.

I must say, in all modesty, that in slightly more than an hour I had matters under control. All of us were neat and tidy; I had examined both boys, with Nefret's assistance, and applied what remedies seemed appropriate. In my professional opinion David required only rest and nourishment to make a full recovery.

Ramses refused to go to bed, though that was obviously the best place for him. It was during this argument – which I lost, as I might have expected – that David produced a small bundle of dried herbage from his bag.

'This was given us by the village healer,' he explained. 'I took it for several days.'

I examined the herbage. 'I have no idea what it can be,' I admitted. 'Nefret?'

She crumbled a bit, smelled it, and tasted it. 'Some variety of mint? I don't like the idea of giving an unknown substance to either of you.'

'It didn't do me any harm,' David insisted. 'I think it lowered the fever.'

'And put you to sleep for hours,' Ramses said, his jaw set stubbornly. 'I can't sleep yet, I have to warn you about Mansur.'

Much as I yearned to see my afflicted child get the rest he needed, I knew he was right. None of us could afford the luxury of relaxation when there were so many things we needed to know, and without delay.

So we retired to my sitting room, where we found the others assembled and the tea I had ordered set out. Feeling the teapot, I was pleased to find it was just off the boil (I had had occasion earlier to speak to the cook about this). I tipped a teaspoon or so of the herbal mixture into a cup and filled it.

'Mother,' Ramses began.

'I will allow you to tell your tale, Ramses, if you promise that when you have finished you will take your medicine and go to bed.'

A scowl and a nod indicated reluctant agreement. I continued, 'First I would like to make a few remarks.'

Ignoring the slight ripple of amusement that ran through the audience, I cleared my throat . . . And found, to my utter astonishment that I was unable to speak. I suppose I had not fully realized how alarmed I had been – how filled with forebodings I dared not admit even to myself – until I saw all my loved ones gathered together again: Nefret, her golden hair glowing in the lamplight; Emerson, his sapphire-blue eyes fixed on his son with an expression of benevolent affection; Selim stroking his beard and smiling; Daoud amiably contemplating the plate of sandwiches; and my two boys – for boys they will always be to me – returned against all odds from as yet unknown perils. David was too thin and Ramses's cheeks were flushed with fever (or possibly aggravation), but they were there, safe and sound, and that was all that mattered.

They were all looking at me, waiting for me to begin. It was Emerson, as always, who understood my emotion and relieved it, in his own inimitable fashion. 'If you are inclined to say a prayer, Peabody, kindly make it brief.'

I returned his smile. '"But thou, when thou prayest, enter into thy closet, and when thou hast shut thy door, pray to thy Father which is in secret."'

'Excellent advice,' said Emerson. 'We are all waiting for our tea, Peabody. I beg you will pour and allow Ramses to get on with his story. Start from the beginning, my boy. There will be no interruptions.'

This was directed at me, of course; but indeed I had no desire to interrupt a tale that held us all spellbound. Once I had dispensed the genial beverage (I refer in this instance to tea), I took out paper and pencil and began one of my little lists. As I expected, everyone burst out talking at once when Ramses finished. Emerson's shout rose over the rest. 'Damnation! The confounded woman is a spy!'

'And a murderess, in intent if not actuality.' Ramses leaned forward and spoke with febrile intensity. 'Father, you must tell MO2 about Macomber. The body may have been moved, but surely there would be evidence remaining.'

'Yes, yes, my boy,' Emerson said, watching him uneasily. 'I promise it will be done. Peabody, shouldn't he be in bed?'

The medicinal brew was a nasty greenish brown in color. Had it not been for David's urging, I would have hesitated about administering it; but he was now completely free of fever and Ramses radiated heat like a stove. With Nefret's help I got a few sips of the medicine into him and – after he had decidedly refused to accept our further assistance – David led him off to their room.

'Well!' I said. 'We have a great deal to discuss. I have made a few notes.'

Without a word Emerson rose and got out the bottle of whiskey.

After a few refreshing sips, I continued. 'The first order of business is to locate that fellow Mansur.'

'No,' said Emerson. 'The first order of business is to keep my promise to Ramses. I will wire the War Office at once about that unfortunate young man Macomber.'

'Most ill-advised, in my opinion, Emerson. Leave that to me, if you please.'

I ticked off one of the items on my list. Brows forming an emphatic black line across his brow, Emerson said with ominous calm, 'Peabody, are you telling me you are in touch with the local agent here?'

'That is correct, Emerson. I will explain later.'

Nefret rose with quiet dignity. 'Never mind, Aunt Amelia. I have suspected for some time that you and the Professor were under orders from some cursed government bureau. Frankly, I don't give a damn about that, or about them. They were of no help whatsoever when it came to locating the boys, and I doubt they will do anything for us we cannot do better by ourselves. I suggest you all go down to dinner now. Daoud has eaten all the sandwiches. I don't want any dinner. I am going to sit with Ramses.'

I made my peace with Nefret at midnight, when I went in to relieve her vigil, admitting (quite handsomely in my opinion) that we had been wrong to keep her in the dark. She melted at once, dear girl, as she always did, and agreed with me that we ought to wake Ramses for another dose of the medicine. He was groggy enough to offer no resistance and fell back asleep at once. So did David, who had wakened instantly when I came in.

Not long after Nefret had left, Emerson crept in. I think I have mentioned that Emerson believes he can tiptoe, but that he is mistaken. He made enough noise to rouse one of the Seven Sleepers. David sat up with a start.

'All is well, my boy,' said Emerson in a penetrating whisper. 'It's just me.'

'Good,' David mumbled. 'Keep watch. Mansur . . .'

'Go to bed, Peabody,' said Emerson. 'I will stand guard till morning.'

I had also made my peace with Emerson earlier, when I told him of Mr. Camden's true identity and explained my plans for the morrow. He had of course agreed that our best hope of catching up with the murderous Mansur was to keep a close eye on Frau von Eine. The precise relationship between the two was still unclear, but it was likely Mansur would try to communicate with her. In the meantime it was essential that we watch over the boys.

'He cannot possibly get at them here,' I said. 'Nefret had the good sense to lock the door and not open it until she heard my voice. I observed that she had her knife.'

'You didn't lock the door,' Emerson said accusingly.

I showed him my little pistol. 'Speaking of that,' I said, while Emerson mumbled to himself, 'where did you get the weapon you carried today?'

'Brought it with me, of course.'

'Do you have it now?'

'Good Gad, no. I only hope the bastard does turn up. I would prefer to tackle him with my bare hands.'

I will not bore the Reader with a detailed account of my activities the following day, though they would certainly be of consuming interest to any female who contemplates setting up an archaeological establishment. Suffice it to say that by evening our house in Siloam was fit for habitation and our newly hired cook was busy preparing dinner.

I had refused Emerson's well-meant offers of assistance, knowing his efforts would be confined to moving the furniture to the wrong places and demanding how much longer the process would take. He had gone happily off to his excavation. The others had pitched in with a will and by late afternoon we were taking a well-deserved rest in the sitting room. I had, at Ramses's request, just finished bringing him and David up-to-date about our recent activities and discoveries when Emerson came in, accompanied by Mr. Camden.

Emerson wrinkled his nose. 'Carbolic,' he said resignedly. 'Well, well, I ought to have expected it. Isn't it teatime?'

'I have not had time to instruct our new cook on the proper procedure,' I said gently. 'You must expect a few minor inconveniences at first.'

'Perhaps a drop of whiskey instead?' Ramses suggested. He started to rise. Emerson pressed him back into his chair.

'No, no, my boy, you must rest. How do you feel?'

'Much better, sir, thank you.'

'That mysterious herb is amazingly effective,' Nefret said. Perched on a low stool, clasped hands round her bent knees, she looked very pretty, despite – or perhaps because of – the smudges that marked her nose and chin and the loosened locks of hair curling over her brow. 'I must find out what it is.'

259

Following my directions, Emerson had finally located the whiskey and glasses, which were standing in plain sight on the table under the window. 'Your best chance of doing so,' he said, handing me a glass, 'would seem to lie with the Sons of Abraham.'

'I would like to know a great deal more about that organization,' I said. 'They came to Ramses and David's aid on several occasions, and yet their leader went off leaving Mansur alive and capable of doing both of you an injury.'

'They expected you would kill him,' Selim suggested, in a tone that indicated he would have expected the same thing.

Ramses shook his head. 'I don't think so. I had delivered a rather pompous speech about murdering an unarmed prisoner, and Ismail knew I meant it.'

'Well, we know the identity of one of the group,' I said. 'Rabbi Ben Ezra.'

Emerson turned. 'We know two. Our landlord. Has he been round today, Peabody? No? Nor did he turn up at the site of my excavation. Odd, isn't it, considering how ubiquitous he was at first.'

The other servant came in and began to lay the table, as I had taught her. She did quite well, except for mixing up the forks and spoons and forgetting the napkins. I corrected her in a kindly manner and she scuttled out.

'We will pursue that inquiry tomorrow,' I said, suppressing a yawn. 'I believe dinner is almost ready. While we eat, you can tell us what you discovered today, Emerson.'

'I believe we are on the track of something interesting,' said Emerson, as the servant returned with baskets of bread and a steaming pot. 'Ah – that smells good.' He nodded amiably at the woman, who drew her veil tightly across her face and backed out.

'As I was saying,' Emerson went on, 'we managed to get a grid laid out –'

'I am very happy for you,' I said, ladling out the stew. 'But when I mentioned a discovery, I was referring to our primary reason for being here. What is Major Morley doing? Was Frau von Eine with him? Did you see anything of Mr. Plato? You had better let the food cool a bit, Emerson, you will burn your tongue.'

He had already done so. 'Try a sip of water,' I said, over his mumbled swearwords. 'Nefret made sure it was boiled. Now, you were about to tell us about Major Morley.'

'Hmph,' said Emerson. 'Well, in a nutshell, Morley never appeared. He's there, the guards admitted as much, but insisted he was deep down in his damned tunnel and couldn't be disturbed.'

'How do you know he never appeared if you spent most of the day at your dig?' I enquired.

Emerson took a cautious bite and chewed. He looked at me, at Nefret, at Ramses, and at Mr. Camden, who looked off into space.

'You sent him to watch Morley,' I said. 'Well, that makes sense. We have had enough nonsensical secrecy, Emerson. If the rest of you do not know Mr. Camden is really Mr. Tushingham and a British agent, it is high time you did.'

'Who?' said Emerson.

'Speaking of secrecy,' Ramses said, fixing me with a hard stare, 'you told me this morning that Macomber's death had been reported, but refused to say how. Am I to assume that Camden here was the means?'

'I had not yet determined that it was necessary for you to know that,' I explained.

'And now you have? May I ask why?'

His tone was decidedly critical. Since I could not explain what had prompted my change of mind – it had to do with my infallible instincts – I ignored the questions.

'The Sons of Abraham will have to wait,' I said. 'Mr. Tushingham, please make your report.'

'Who?' said Emerson, looking round.

'Camden,' I said with a sigh. 'Emerson, please pay attention.'

'Yes, ma'am,' said Mr. Camden, as I must continue to call him.

'Well, after the Professor left me I hung about for several hours, mingling with the pilgrims and the water carriers. Once I tried to pass the guards, claiming I was a friend of Morley's, but I was summarily dismissed. So I retreated into a clump of cacti and squatted there with my binoculars fixed on the entrance to the excavation. At around noontime Morley appeared, covered with dust and looking, I thought, disgruntled. A few minutes later Frau von Eine showed up, on horseback, and joined him for luncheon. I would have given a great deal to have heard what they were saying, but there was no way I could get closer without being discovered. She did most of the talking. After luncheon she remounted and rode off, and Morley went back into the shaft.'

'So much for her supervision,' Emerson exclaimed. 'It was a token gesture, to keep me away.'

'Never mind that now, Emerson,' I said. 'You saw no sign of Mansur?'

'Not unless he was one of the workmen. They were indistinguishable, all half naked and smeared with dirt. I never set eyes on the fellow, you know.'

'What about Mr. Plato? You are familiar with his appearance, and I cannot imagine he would consent to hard manual labor.'

'He'd have been first at the luncheon table,' Emerson agreed.

'Well, he wasn't. He can't have been at the site or I would have spotted him sooner or later.'

'I wonder what has become of him,' I mused. 'Mr. Fazah told me he left the hotel yesterday morning, with his luggage.'

'Which we supplied,' Emerson growled. 'I doubt we've seen the last of him. Mark my words, he'll turn up before long.'

He did turn up. But not in the way any of us expected.

'The servants seem to be working out well,' I said at breakfast. 'How is your coffee, Emerson?'

'Not bad,' grunted Emerson, who was still on his first cup.

'Quite good,' said Nefret, with an encouraging smile at the housemaid. 'Tell the cook, Safika.'

Both female servants were in mortal terror of Emerson, whose reputation had preceded him (via Kamir) and whose gestures of friendliness only alarmed them. But they had fallen in love with Nefret, who had taken the trouble to learn their names and compliment them on every achievement. Safika's eyes narrowed in a smile. The eyes were all we could see of her face, for of course she remained veiled when the men were present. She murmured something to Nefret, who rose at once.

'Ghada is here with our washing, Aunt Amelia. She wants us to inspect it to be sure it is satisfactory.'

Rising in my turn, I said approvingly, 'She certainly is prompt. I gave her quite a large load only yesterday.'

The girl was waiting for us in Nefret's bedchamber. She had spread the laundry out across the bed – shirts, undergarments, nightgowns, and so on.

'Where is your little girl?' Nefret asked in Arabic.

'I did not know . . .' The big brown eyes were worried.

'That I meant what I said? I did. Bring her next time. Now you must get back quickly. Wait a moment, I will get your money.'

She ran back into the sitting room. The girl said anxiously, 'Is it right, Sitt Hakim?'

The garments had been scrubbed until they were in danger of fraying, and everything had been ironed, including Emerson's stockings. 'Very good,' I said. 'Very, very good.'

Nefret popped in and began counting out coins into the girl's outstretched hand. They were of different sizes and values, for as I believe I have said, the currency in the Ottoman territories was not standardized; from Ghada's reaction it was clear that Nefret hadn't bothered to add them up.

'You give me too much,' she protested.

That was a complaint one seldom heard in this part of the world. I shook my head and Nefret said, 'No. You must have worked very hard. Now go back to your baby.'

'Come tomorrow,' I added. 'I will have more washing.'

'And bring the baby,' said Nefret.

Emerson was on his feet and fidgeting when we returned to the breakfast table. 'Time we were off,' he announced.

Mr. Camden immediately leaped up, leaving his plate half full. I gestured to him to resume his seat, and informed Emerson that most of us had not finished eating.

'Where are we going?' Ramses asked.

'To my excavation, of course,' his father replied. 'I want you to –'

'You are not going anywhere until you have eaten every scrap of your breakfast,' I said to Ramses.

'The fever is gone,' Ramses protested. 'I want to see what Father –'

'You are as thin as a rail. I must fatten you up before Fatima sets eyes on you. You know how she is.'

'I am never fat enough for Fatima,' said Ramses resignedly. But he shoveled the rest of his eggs into his mouth and bit into a piece of bread.

I had a little discussion with Emerson before we left the house. He was determined to show off his cursed excavation and I was determined to continue my investigation of Major Morley. In the end I graciously agreed to a compromise. As Emerson pointed out, we stood a better chance of catching Morley when he sat down to his luncheon. There would be time for a quick visit to the excavation first.

We proceeded on our way. Emerson forged ahead, holding Ramses by the arm and talking animatedly. Mr. Camden walked with me.

'Your husband does not appear too concerned about his son,' said Mr. Camden. 'I mean no disrespect,' he added quickly.

'Oh, that is just Emerson's way. He hasn't the slightest doubt that he can protect Ramses from any possible threat. Which reminds me that I meant to ask whether you agree with me that that threat may be exaggerated. Surely now that Ramses has reported Macomber's murder, Mansur no longer has any reason to silence him.'

'I would not venture an opinion, Mrs. Emerson.' He looked so grave, I continued to press him.

'But you don't agree with me?'

He hesitated for a moment and then said, 'There was a reference, if you recall, to a mission that had to be completed before Mansur and von Eine left Palestine. She is still here. What conclusions may we draw from that?'

At the bottom of the hill Emerson led the way through patches of prickly pears and a few sickly-looking olive trees, till we saw the roped-off enclosure where he had been digging. Cords had been stretched across an area approximately twenty feet square – the grid he had laid out the day before. In one of the squares thus formed, several planks covered a space some ten feet by five.

'What is that?' I inquired of Emerson.

He turned a beaming face toward me. 'The interesting discovery I mentioned. Just wait till you see, Peabody! I covered it as a precaution against . . . Hell and damnation!'

I clapped my hands to my ears. 'Good heavens, Emerson, what is the matter?'

'Someone has been here. See, one of the ropes has been retied so hastily that the knot is loose.' He turned like a tiger on the inevitable assemblage of onlookers. 'Which of you dared brave the curse I laid on this place?'

Before the echoes of his voice died the audience had fled. Shouting anathemas, Emerson ducked under the enclosing rope and ran to the boarded-over square. Removing the planks, he looked down. I alone of the watchers beheld the stiffening of his powerful frame.

'Stay back,' he said very quietly. 'All of you.'

Assuming that this order did not apply to me, I went to his side.

The space below was only a few feet deep, its sides meticulously straight. It was just the right shape for the purpose to which someone had put it.

I am hardened to death in many forms. I had seen worse. He lay on his back, his hands folded and his eyes closed. He might have been sleeping had it not been for the stain, now dark and hardened, that had dyed his white beard a rusty brown.

Emerson put his arm round my waist. 'I told you to stay back.'

'I am hardened to death, Emerson. I have seen worse. We must determine how he died.'

'I believe it is safe to say it was not a heart attack,' said Emerson, tightening his grip. 'You aren't going to determine anything, Peabody. Nor you,' he added, as Nefret came to his side.

'Not here, at any rate,' Nefret said quietly. 'Who could have done this? He was so harmless. I rather liked him.'

'I didn't,' said Emerson. 'And at this moment we cannot be at all certain he was incapable of doing harm. However, I object to murder on principle. Camden, go and notify the authorities. He held British papers, so the consul should be told of this.'

Mr. Camden ran off and Emerson replaced the planks over the hole. 'Selim, stay here and keep everyone away. The rest of you, come with me.'

'And what are you going to do?' I inquired.

'Interrogate the principal suspect. I'll have him out of that hole if I have to go down and drag him out.'

We retraced our steps in some haste. 'It's Major Morley Father suspects, isn't it?' Ramses asked. 'Why? Is – was, I should say – the victim that fellow Plato you told me about?'

'That is right, you never met him,' I said. 'Yes, that is – was – he.'

'But why Morley?' Ramses persisted. 'From the look of it, the fellow's throat was cut. Morley wouldn't dirty his aristocratic hands, would he?'

'He would hire someone to do the job,' I said thoughtfully. 'Perhaps your friend Mansur? We still don't know precisely how they are connected.'

'If they are,' said Ramses, who then relapsed into silence.

I had not been near Morley's excavation for some days. There had been significant changes. Several tents, one large and ornate, now occupied the space beyond the barrier. I wondered why neither Emerson nor Mr. Camden had seen fit to mention this. Or rather, I did not wonder. They were both men. They wouldn't have realized that Morley would not have abandoned his elegant hotel for a tent, however large, without good reason. The obvious explanation was that he had to be on the scene day and night because he was running short of time. Time to do what? Reach the location Plato had designated as the hiding place of the Ark? That would not be as simple as it sounded. According to Emerson and other authorities, the underground regions were a maze of abandoned cisterns, tunnels old and new, deep shafts and ancient burial caves. More than ever I was determined to get into those regions and explore them for myself.

I did not mention this to Ramses.

When we joined Emerson he was talking with one of the guards at the barrier. The fellow was someone I had not seen before, an imposing figure almost as tall and burly as Emerson, distinguished by a black patch over one eye. As we came up to them Emerson turned to me and said, with a deference I had yet to see him display to a Turkish guard, 'My dear, may I present Ali Bey Jarrah, the commandant of the Turkish gendarmerie.'

'And this, of course, is Mrs. Emerson.' Ali Bey made me a polite bow, which I acknowledged with a nod and a smile. His English was excellent, his voice a reverberant baritone, his smile displaying several broken teeth.

Emerson went on to introduce the others. Nefret received an admiring glance, Ramses a courteous acknowledgment, and Daoud an appraising look. I had a feeling that that one eye had measured us and memorized us.

'Ali Bey is also in search of Major Morley,' Emerson explained. 'I was asking him to do us the favor of postponing his errand in light of the sudden emergency that has arisen. As I told you, sir, the body is that of a European, a colleague of Major Morley. I have sent someone to report the discovery, but it is absolutely necessary that I inform Morley at once. I want you to come with me and observe his reaction.'

'Ah.' Ali Bey's one visible eye lit up. 'It is the British police method? You will question him cleverly and determine whether he is the killer?'

'Aywa, yes,' said Emerson. 'With your help.'

'It is well known that the Father of Curses and his lady have brought many criminals to justice. Come, follow me.'

'Daoud has been talking again,' Emerson said to me. 'I really must stop him from spreading those wild stories.'

I thought he looked rather pleased, though.

'Were you formerly acquainted with the commandant?' I asked. 'You seem to be on excellent terms with him.'

'I was not, but I had heard a great deal about him. He lost his eye during a riot at the Church of the Holy Sepulchre when he stepped between an ax-wielding Greek monk and the Franciscan who was the holy man's intended victim.'

I could think of nothing to say to this. So I said nothing.

The commandant led the way to an area some distance behind the tents. The scene reminded me of Doré or some other painter of horrors. A group of half-naked men were gathered around a primitive pulley standing over a black hole in the ground. Grunting and straining, one of the men hauled on a rope stretching down into the hole and brought up a heavy basket, which he unhooked and carried away. Another man took his place; another basket was pulled up and taken off to a dump nearby.

A brusque order from Ali Bey brought the work to a stop. 'Where is the Mudir?' he asked.

'Down there.' One of the workmen gestured.

Before I could stop him, Emerson caught hold of the rope and went down hand over hand.

'Curse it,' I shouted. 'Emerson, come back here at once!'

I reached for the rope and at once found myself in the grasp of four muscular arms. One pair belonged to Ramses, the other to the commandant.

'What the devil do you think you are doing, Mother?'

'The Sitt must not go down there!' cried Ali Bey, just as emphatically.

'It was, perhaps, ill-advised,' I admitted. 'I acted instinctively. You may let me go, gentlemen.'

I leaned over the hole, while Ramses maintained a tight grip on me. There was no sign of Emerson, but far below I could see the glow of torches. I called Emerson's name; after a somewhat nerve-racking minute or two I received a reply.

'Found him,' Emerson shouted, his voice weirdly distorted by echoes.

He ascended as he had descended, and climbed up onto the edge of the hole. 'Lower the harness,' he said to the workmen, and to me, in English, 'The fat fool can't even climb a rope.'

The harness was a wooden seat with ropes on both sides, like a child's swing. The men lowered it and then bent to the windlass, their stringy muscles straining. Emerson's description of Morley as fat was exaggerated. He was only out of condition, but he was certainly no lightweight.

The commandant said reproachfully, 'You said I should watch while you questioned him, Father of Curses.'

'You shall. I have not told him the news.'

'What is the meaning of this?' Morley's haughty manner did not come off so well as he sat with his feet dangling and his gloved hands clutching the ropes. He was coated with dirt and perspiration. 'I did as you required, I hired an archaeologist to assist –'

'Where is she, then? Never mind her, Morley, I have news for you. Plato Panagopolous is dead. Murdered. Why did you kill him?'

Under the grime on his face Morley turned pale. He sputtered wordlessly for a few moments and then gasped, 'Murdered? Killed? Where? Why?'

Emerson turned to Ali Bey. 'What do you think?'

'Hmmm. I see surprise, yes, and fear on his face, and I hear it in his voice. Was it at the news of Pana . . . Papa – the man's death, or of alarm that you have accused him?'

'That may have been an error,' Emerson admitted, looking chagrined.

'Emerson,' I said. 'Perhaps you had better leave the interrogation to ME.'

Morley had recovered himself. 'Interrogation? What right do you have to question me?'

I would have told him, but he hurried on, now flushed with anger instead of deathly pale. 'Why would I want to harm Panagopolous? We had come to an amicable agreement, after a – er – slight misunderstanding.'

'Stemming,' I said, 'from your attempt to cheat him of his share of the profits of this expedition. You took the scroll and left him penniless. Believing, as proved to be the case, that we would be following you to Palestine, he came to us with a cock-and-bull story. You did not attack him; you had already left the country. He inflicted the injury upon himself in order to win our sympathy. Once here, he blackmailed you into taking him back into partnership by threatening to expose the falsity of his famous scroll. He cheated you, and you cheated him. A pretty pair, I must say.'

If Morley had been flushed before, he was now reddish-purple as a beet. 'The scroll is not a fake! It is genuine. It will lead me to the secret passage.'

'He speaks the truth,' Ali Bey said interestedly. 'Or I am no judge of men.'

'He speaks what he believes is the truth,' I said. 'Where is the scroll now, Major Morley?'

His eyes shifted. 'I gave it back to Panagopolous. I have no idea what he did with it.'

'Hid it, I expect,' I said. 'He didn't trust you. With good reason.'

'I don't have to put up with this,' Morley said loudly. 'I didn't kill the old fool and you cannot prove that I did. Now get out.'

'Shall I come with you?' Ali Bey asked Emerson hopefully.

'What about your errand here?'

'It can wait. I wish to observe the English police methods. You may need me if my subordinates are already there.'

'Good Gad!' Emerson shouted. He set out for the barrier at a dead run.

'Come if you like,' I said to the commandant. 'We must hurry, Emerson is in one of his states. Major Morley, you have not seen the last of us.'

'What set the Professor off?' Nefret asked as we hastened away.

'He's afraid someone will get at his precious discovery,' said Ramses, on my other side.

'Do you have any idea what it might be?' I asked.

'I wasn't there,' Ramses reminded me.

Daoud, close behind us, had overheard. 'Something caught his eye, Sitt Hakim, and he ordered us all out of the trench. He trusts no one but himself to deal with unusual objects.'

I suppose Emerson had counted on the usual delays that accompany any official action in Ottoman territory. He had not expected such a prompt reply from the authorities. I myself could only account for it by the fact that Panagopolous held a British passport. At any rate, when we arrived on the scene it was to see poor Plato's body lying beside the open pit, surrounded by a group of policemen, who seemed to be arguing about what should be done next. From the depths of the trench came Emerson's voice, raised in profane lamentation.

'Oh dear,' I said. 'Ali Bey, will you be good enough to take charge of these people? Selim, what has happened to anger Emerson?'

Selim wiped his perspiring face. 'I tried to stop them, Sitt Hakim, but they said they were from the police and they pushed me away, and then they went into the trench and dragged the body out, and –'

'Oh dear,' I said again.

The commandant had taken charge with a vengeance. One of the police persons lay on the ground, nursing a bloody head. Another was in full flight and the others had retreated to a safe distance.

Emerson's head appeared. He was a dreadful sight, his face set in a hideous grimace and his black hair wildly askew. 'Stop that man!' he bellowed, pointing at the fleeing police officer. 'Stop them all! Search them to the skin! It is gone, someone has stolen it!'

With the enthusiastic assistance of Ali Bey, I soon had the situation more or less under control. The uncontrollable part of the situation was Emerson. He insisted on searching each of the police officers so thoroughly that I was forced to turn my back. The one who had fled had made good his escape.

'He's got it!' Emerson shouted, and would have set out in futile pursuit had I not caught hold of him.

'In heaven's name, Emerson, what has he got?'

'I would like to know that too,' said Ali Bey. 'What have we been searching for? A clue to the identity of the murderer?'

'What?' Emerson stared at him. 'No, no, nothing so insignificant.' He passed his hand over his brow, leaving a broad smear of dirt, and groaned aloud.

'An artifact of some sort,' I explained to the officer. 'It is the only thing that sets Emerson off like this. But there is no use trying to get him to make sense just now. We have more imperative matters to settle. Selim, find someone to construct a coffin. He can't be left lying here.'

'What shall we do with him, then?' Selim asked.

'Have him carried to our house,' I said.

As I had expected, this served to distract Emerson. 'Now see here, Peabody –'

'What else can we do, Emerson?'

'Drop him off at Morley's tent. You want to examine the body and look for clues and meddle in matters that ought not concern you.'

'I'm afraid they do concern us, Father,' Ramses said. 'Hasn't it occurred to you that one of us might be under suspicion?'

'Me?' Emerson inquired.

'Your antipathy toward him is well known. He was found in your excavation area.'

Ali Bey was listening with intent interest. 'Motive and opportunity!' he exclaimed. 'It is the British method.'

'Balderdash,' Emerson said.

'What does that mean?' the commandant asked.

'It means,' I explained, 'that other people had even stronger motives for disposing of Panagopolous, and that the body may have been placed here in order to cast suspicion on Emerson. My husband, sir, does not carry a knife and his principles would not allow him to murder a helpless man.'

273

'I'll tell you what,' said Emerson, who – I was sorry to see – had begun to take a perverse pleasure in being a suspect. 'Come up to the house with us and search for bloodstained garments. You can also examine my hands and arms for scratches.'

'You permit?'

'I insist. What is taking Selim so long?'

When Selim came back he was accompanied by Kamir and two fellows carrying planks of wood. The two set to work at once constructing a crude coffin while Kamir stood staring down at Plato's body. He murmured something that might, or might not, have been a prayer and then said, 'Who is he?'

'Don't you recognize him?' I asked. 'He was with us at the house the other day.'

'I did not see him there.' He turned away, as if the sight were distasteful.

The workmen finished nailing the coffin together and were persuaded, by the offer of extra baksheesh, to put the dead man into it. Upon the payment of additional baksheesh they agreed to carry the coffin up the hill to our house. Emerson handed over the money without arguing. His brow was furrowed in thought.

'My dear,' I said, for I believed he was brooding over his lost artifact, 'shall we go?'

'Hmmm? Yes, certainly. Would there,' he asked pathetically, 'be coffee, do you think?'

I made sure there was coffee, enough for all of us, including Ali Bey. Selim and Daoud had been left at the excavation, with strict instructions to allow no one to approach it. We had some difficulty finding a place for the coffin, since none of the servants wanted it anywhere near them. At last we settled on one of the unoccupied rooms, the one I intended to be used as a study.

On the way back to the house I had had a private word with David. 'I am sorry to ask you,' I added, 'but it is absolutely necessary.'

'That's quite all right, Aunt Amelia. I have had worse tasks. I'll get at it right away.'

Ali Bey found our company delightful. He and Ramses got into an animated discussion of the detectival methods of Mr. Sherlock Holmes, and it was not until I reminded him that he had not yet carried out his original errand that he reluctantly rose to his feet.

'May I ask the nature of your errand?' I inquired. 'If you are allowed to speak of it.'

'All the city knows, Sitt. The man Morley is the subject of disquieting rumors, and public anger is rising. They say he is digging in the Haram itself. It cannot be true, but it is my duty to warn him.'

Emerson roused himself enough to mumble a farewell and then relapsed into brooding silence.

'Very well, Emerson,' I said. 'Get it off your chest, metaphorically speaking. Do not brood, but share your loss with us. What was the artifact you found?'

Emerson sighed deeply. 'You won't believe it.' He looked round the room. 'Where is Nefret?'

'She slipped out some time ago,' Ramses said. 'Would you care to guess what she is doing?'

'Examining that confounded corpse, I suppose,' Emerson said.

'Do not speak ill of the dead, Emerson.'

'Bah,' said Emerson. 'I will if I like. Find Nefret, I may as well . . . Ah, there you are, my dear.'

'What did your examination of the body reveal?' I asked.

'Nothing of importance. His throat was cut, but you had already suspected that. There were no other new injuries.'

'And nothing under his fingernails?' I inquired.

'No. I looked, of course.'

'Of course.'

'That would suggest he didn't fight back,' Ramses said.

'Or that he was unable to do so,' I said.

'Of course.'

'Is anyone interested in my discovery?' Emerson said loudly.

The truthful answer was no, not at the moment. However, Emerson was clearly in need of being soothed. 'We are all waiting with bated breath,' I assured him.

'You won't believe it,' said Emerson in sepulchral tones. 'The damned thing is gone, stolen by one of the men who lifted Panopolous out of the pit. I knew it would prove an irresistible temptation. If it hadn't been for that bastard Morley, I would have been there in time to prevent the theft. Selim was no match for –'

'Emerson,' I said. 'Get to the point.'

'You won't . . .' He caught my eye. 'Er, hmph. It was a fragment of gold that might have been part of a cup or vase. It was flattened and crushed, but I was able to make out a few signs. They were Egyptian hieroglyphs.'

Chapter Ten

Regrettably, Emerson's pronouncement did not have the effect he had anticipated. It was very interesting, to be sure, but to most of us it paled by contrast to the murder, riot, and mystery that surrounded us.

The only one who reacted as Emerson had hoped was Ramses. 'Amazing!' he exclaimed, his eyes alight. 'The first actual, physical evidence of Egyptian occupation here. What did the hieroglyphs read, Father?'

'As near as I could make out, they were part of the cartouche of one of the Amenhoteps. I left it in situ, since it had not been photographed or plotted.' He let out another groan. 'So much for proper methodology. I ought to have known . . .'

He jumped up and headed for the door. 'And where do you think you are going?' I demanded. 'Come back here at once, Emerson.'

'There are still several hours of daylight left,' said Emerson. His sapphirine eyes shone with the fearful glow of fanaticism. 'And now, at last, I have my entire crew present. Come, all of you. Bring cameras – tripods – torches – sketching pads – measuring sticks –'

He rushed out, followed by Selim and Daoud. Ramses was about to follow when I stopped him. 'You are a trifle flushed,' I said. 'Are you feeling well?'

'Yes, of course.' He avoided my outstretched hand and ran after his father.

David glanced uncertainly at me. 'Keep a close eye on Ramses,' I said. 'Emerson is the most devoted of fathers, but when he is in this state of mind he wouldn't notice a massacre unless it inconvenienced him.'

'You can count on me, Aunt Amelia.'

'I know I can,' I said affectionately. 'And – er – by the way, there is no need to mention your sketch of – HIM – to anyone else. Tell Emerson Nefret will be along directly with the cameras.'

'No, ma'am. Yes, ma'am.'

Nefret had gone out of the room; I assumed she was looking for the cameras, but when she did not return at once, I went in search of her. I found her in the part of the courtyard we had designated as the kitchen. With her was Ghada, holding a bundle.

'She came for the laundry,' Nefret explained. 'And she has brought the baby! Isn't she sweet?'

The word could have applied to Ghada, whom I saw unveiled for the first time. She had a pretty little face, dominated by those melting brown eyes. I smiled at her; she responded by offering me the bundle. It was meant as a gesture of trust, so I had no choice but to respond. I took the bundle and bounced it experimentally.

There was nothing visible of the baby except a face. A knitted cap covered its head, and layer upon layer of wrappings covered the rest of it. It had its mother's brown eyes and skin several shades lighter than hers; obviously it had seldom if ever been exposed to direct sunlight. After a suspicious look at me it opened its mouth and let out a howl.

'Here,' I said, handing it over to Nefret. She bounced the baby. The aggravating little creature immediately stopped howling and gave her a dimpled grin.

I knew better than to praise the child. Complimentary remarks would bring down the wrath of innumerable demons. I smiled again, nodded, and went to fetch the washing. I had to order Nefret to hand the baby back to its mother, who inserted it into a sling on her back and went off with the laundry.

'I would like to examine the baby,' Nefret said, watching them go. 'It appears to be healthy enough, but its nose was running.'

'Babies' noses always run,' I said authoritatively (hoping I was right). 'You can do that another time. Emerson is waiting for you.'

'Aren't you coming?'

'Not just yet. It is time I made one of my little lists.'

I ruled the paper according to my usual scheme, with columns headed: 'Questions' and 'What to do about them.' For reasons which will be apparent as my narrative proceeds, I did not keep a copy of the list. As I recall, the questions went something like this:

1. Who is Plato Panagopolous?
2. Who killed him?
3. Where is the man Mansur and what is his mission?
4. What has become of Mme von Eine and what is her aim?
5. Why did Major Morley increase the speed of his work?

I had taken the first step to identifying Panagolopous. He had avoided having a photograph taken, and he had avoided meeting certain individuals. I would show David's sketch, after it had been modified by me, to those individuals. Once I discovered his real identity, I might have the answer to the second question.

I couldn't think what to do about Mansur, or even decide whether I needed to do anything. The answer to the second part of the question might be connected to the fifth question. Perhaps some sort of deadline for the completion of that mission was approaching, and perhaps Morley's assistance was necessary. However, that was as yet only surmise, and interrogating Morley would almost certainly be a waste of time.

Which left me with question number four.

Vanity, alas, affects even the best of us. I took a little time to smooth my hair and change my shirt for a clean one before I selected a rather becoming broad-brimmed hat, with crimson ribbons that tied under my chin. After slipping my little pistol into one of my pockets and a few other useful items into another, I took my heaviest parasol and went forth.

Clouds hid the sun and a brisk breeze tugged at my hat brim. It would have taken more than inclement weather to stop me. The autumn rainy season, with its heavy downpours – the inundation of the river in the sky – was still a month away. If a shower were to occur, it would be brief, and I had my useful parasol.

I had hoped to find Ali Bey on duty at the barricade, but he was nowhere to be seen. I asked the fellow on duty where he had gone and got only a stare and a shrug; but the invocation of that mighty name got me past the ropes. I made my way to Morley's tent, observing with some surprise that the toiling workmen were not at their task. The windlass hung empty from its support. Was that an indication that Morley had found what he sought, or that he sought it elsewhere?

It is not possible to knock at the flap of a tent. I called out. At first there was no response except for sounds of movement within. Someone was there, then, probably Morley himself. He could – and would – tell me where the lady was staying. I called again, announcing myself by name.

The flap was drawn aside, just far enough to show Mme von Eine herself. She was dressed with her usual elegance, not a hair on her fair head ruffled. 'Mrs Emerson! What a surprise. If you are looking for Major Morley, he is not here.'

'I am looking for you,' I said, clutching my hat. 'I was not expecting to see you, but I hoped to get your address from the major.'

'I see.' It was clear she wanted me to go away. Naturally, that made me all the more determined to stay.

In retrospect, that might not have been one of my wisest decisions.

After several long seconds she said, 'Come in, then.'

She drew the flap farther aside. Not until I was inside the tent did I see the man sitting at a table to the right of the entrance. I had never beheld him before, but I knew at once who he must be, for his appearance matched Ramses's description. The first part of my third question had received an answer.

Discretion, perhaps, would have dictated a speedy withdrawal. With the speed of light, alternatives raced through my mind. The lady stood between me and the exit, and Mansur had risen to his feet. They could easily prevent my departure. The only hope, it seemed to me, was to feign ignorance of Mansur's identity and pretend that my motive for seeking Mme von Eine was purely social.

'I apologize for intruding,' I said. 'I did not know you were entertaining a friend. I will come another time.'

'I cannot possibly let you go,' Madame said. 'Without offering you a cup of tea. May I present Mr. Abdul Mohammed.'

'How do you do?' I produced my best social smile and inclined my head, without taking my eyes off his face. It was worthy of attention, with the combined delicacy and strength of a master carving. Only the shape of his mouth spoiled the nobility of his countenance. It had curved into a thin-lipped smile. He wore a robe of creamy-white wool, embroidered at the neck and around the sleeves, and when he acknowledged my greeting by raising his hands in salute, I noticed he moved one arm stiffly.

Mme von Eine seated herself behind the tea service and waved me to a chair. 'Do you take milk? Sugar?'

'Neither, thank you.'

The tea was tepid. I sipped it while I examined my surroundings. The tent was fitted out with all the luxuries money can buy, including several crates labeled 'Fortnum and Mason' and another that bore the mark of a famous winery. Nothing I saw inspired an idea, or the means, of a daring escape. The silence of my companions, and Mansur's fixed smile, persuaded me that there was little chance of their letting me go. I would have to make a dash for it.

Under cover of the table I slipped my hand into my pocket. When I jumped up I was holding my little pistol.

'I must make my excuses,' I said, pointing the gun at them. 'Don't move, either of you.'

I began backing toward the exit. The wind had risen; the tent shook and creaked and a blast of air tugged at my hat.

'Why, Mrs. Emerson,' said the lady, opening her eyes wide. 'What has come over you?'

Mansur only smiled more broadly. He lifted his left hand and brought it down in a chopping motion. Pain blossomed through my head, and my eyes went blind.

When I came to my senses I was lying on one of the beautiful oriental rugs, with my hands and feet tied. Bending over me was Mme von Eine, her face set in a look of hypocritical concern.

'Gott sei Dank,' she exclaimed. 'You are not seriously injured.'

'There was a guard,' I muttered. 'He was not on duty when I came in . . .'

Mansur looked up from the paper he was reading. I recognized it as my list; I must have put it in my pocket without realizing it. 'Most illuminating,' Mansur said with a tight smile. His voice was as deep and his English as excellent as Ramses had described. 'If I had entertained any doubts as to your involvement, this would remove them. As for the guard, the fellow must have gone off on a – er – private errand, but he has redeemed himself by returning in time to obey my orders.'

'You forced us to act,' Madame said. 'Your behavior was most extraordinary.'

'The conventional excuse of the villain – "You made me do it,"' I said. 'What am I going to make you do next?'

'Why, nothing, except to keep you comfortable and safe until we are certain you have recovered from your fit of hysteria. Mansur will watch over you. Good afternoon, Mrs. Emerson.'

Only pride prevented me from begging she would remain. She would never commit an act of violence with her own hands, or even watch its being done. She would only authorize such an act, explicitly or by her silence. All down the centuries evil men – and a few women, I admit – had maintained their innocence of murder and torture by remaining aloof from the actuality. I doubted that Mansur would be deterred by those hypocritical excuses.

However, if I could keep him talking, something might yet turn up!

'What precisely is it you hope to accomplish here?' I asked.

He looked up from his examination of my pistol and an expression of genuine amusement transformed his face.

'You live up to your reputation for forthrightness, Mrs. Emerson. Do you really expect me to answer that question?'

'It never hurts to try,' I said, squirming about in an effort to find a more comfortable position. The ropes were not tight, but my surreptitious efforts to loosen them had had no effect. 'If you are planning to dispose of me, there can be no harm in satisfying my curiosity before you do so.'

'Believe me,' he said earnestly, 'I don't want to kill you.'

'It is against your principles as a civilized man?'

'You heard that from your son, didn't you? What else did he tell you?'

'Quite a lot. The other members of my family know everything he knows.'

Mansur shook his head. 'They know it secondhand, as do you. The only person who threatens my cause is your son. If he is willing to exchange himself for you, you will be released unharmed.'

'No,' I exclaimed. 'Impossible. I won't permit it.'

'You cannot prevent it. Nor can the other members of your group. We have our methods, Mrs. Emerson. The message has already been sent. It will be delivered to him in private, and if he is as wily as I know him to be, he will respond to it without letting anyone else know.'

'O God,' I whispered. It was a prayer, not an expletive. Having made that appeal, knowing it would be understood, I said, 'But how can you reach him without . . . Ah. The Sons of Abraham? You have been expelled from that group, you have no more power over its members.'

'The word of that event has not yet spread to all the persons involved.' He smiled. 'You amaze me, Mrs. Emerson. Your powers of concentration function under the most adverse situations. I do hope my little scheme succeeds, for it would distress me, personally as well as philosophically, to be forced to harm you.'

'There it is again,' I said scornfully. 'The specious reasoning of the villain. No one is forcing you to do anything. You are the master of your destiny and you bear the responsibility for your acts.'

His face darkened, and he turned away without replying.

I had struck a nerve of some kind, but I did not pursue the conversation. Continuing to tug at my bonds, I strained my ears for the sound of someone approaching. How long had I been unconscious? How long would it take the message to reach Ramses? That he would respond instantly I did not doubt. If I could shout loudly enough, call out a warning . . .

Time seemed to stretch out forever. Mansur sat brooding over his cold tea. The wind had subsided somewhat. I thought I heard movement outside and drew a deep breath, but hesitated. It might have been the guard I heard. If I cried out, Mansur might decide to gag me.

There was no further sound, no warning. The tent flap lifted and Ramses entered. His eyes found me where I lay, my lips parted but incapable of speech. He held a knife. The blade was darkly stained.

'All right, are you, Mother?' he inquired. 'I came as soon as I could.'

Mansur got slowly to his feet. 'You killed the guards. Very civilized. The poor devils were only doing their duty.'

'Obeying orders,' Ramses corrected, with a curl of the lip. 'It went against my instincts, of course, but –'

'You had to do it,' said Mansur, curling his lip. He didn't do it as well as Ramses.

'No. I didn't have to. I had a choice and I made it. You see, Mansur, I can't trust you to keep your word. Now it's between you and me. Free her and I'll stay here.'

Mansur took a step toward me. Ramses was quicker. With two deft slashes he cut the ropes that held me. I felt the warm stickiness of blood against my wrists. I knew it was not my blood.

'A bit stiff, are you?' he asked, extending a hand to help me rise. 'Go now, Mother. With celerity, as you might say.'

He smiled at me. I felt an odd pang in that region of the anatomy that is often mistaken for the heart. His eyes were bright and his cheeks were flushed. Haste or excitement might be responsible, but I doubted it. I spun round, not toward the exit but toward the table where my little pistol . . .

Had lain. It was now in Mansur's hand, and it was pointed at me.

'I'm afraid I cannot allow that,' he said, attempting to emulate Ramses's coolness. 'I will keep my word, but she must stay here until morning.'

'So it's for tonight, is it?' Ramses inquired, trying to get in front of me.

'What?' I asked, avoiding the attempt.

'I'm beginning to get a vague idea,' Ramses said. He glanced at an object I had not noticed before – a prettily carved box that stood on a nearby table. 'I see she left the job to you, Mansur. I wouldn't recommend it. You could just as easily –'

Suddenly he flung himself at me. We both fell to the floor, with Ramses on top, and the gun went off, two, three times. I felt Ramses flinch and tried to free myself from his weight. Desperation lent strength to my limbs; I pushed him off me and sat up. His eyes were open and his lips were moving. I assumed he was swearing until he found his voice and gasped, 'Run, Mother. Now!'

I snatched up the knife that had fallen from his hand and turned on Mansur. His lips were moving too, and I felt fairly certain he *was* swearing.

'There were only three bullets left in the gun,' I said. 'I neglected to refill it after I used it last time. Now put your hands behind you and turn round.'

Mansur's face was distorted with rage. Having come so close to accomplishing his desire, he was maddened by failure. Spinning round, he dropped the gun, snatched up the carved box, and ran, not toward the entrance to the tent, but toward the back, where one of the pegs had been pulled out, leaving a space below.

'Stop me if you can!' he shouted, and ducked under the loosened section of canvas.

Ramses staggered to his feet and took the knife from me. I read his intent in his grim face and tried to catch hold of him.

'Let him go!' I shrieked. 'He wants you to follow him! It is an ambush!'

'I have to finish this,' Ramses gasped. 'He won't leave us alone, it's a matter of personal revenge now . . . Mother, stay here. Just for once, will you please do as I ask?'

He pulled away from me and ducked under the canvas.

Naturally I followed at once. The pistol was useless to me now, but the Reader may well believe I did not forget my parasol.

The wind had died; the stillness had an ominous quality, like some mighty force holding its breath. The sky was black except for a few streaks of violent crimson on the western horizon, but I was able to make out a column of white, in rapid movement, which could only be Mansur's snowy robe. Ramses, in drab work shirt and trousers, was virtually invisible.

I was running as fast as I dared, over uneven and unfamiliar ground, trying to keep the moving whiteness in sight, when suddenly it disappeared. I ran faster, brandishing my parasol and shouting. Almost at once I tripped and fell.

'Haste makes waste,' said a familiar voice. I could see Ramses now, bending over me. 'Are you hurt?'

'Only bruised knees,' I replied, accepting the hand he offered.

'Damn,' said Ramses, so softly I could barely hear him. I knew what he was thinking, and moved back a little in case he decided to take steps to prevent me from going on. I doubted, however, that he would have the temerity to imitate his father, who had once struck me unconscious in the hope of removing me from the scene of the action. (It had not succeeded.)

I recognized my surroundings now. The object that had tripped me up was one of Morley's rope barricades. Beyond, lingering light reflected off a gently moving surface. It was water. We had reached the Pool of Siloam.

'Where did he go?' I asked. I thought I knew the answer, though, and my heart beat faster with excitement.

'Back that way,' Ramses said, pointing.

'No, I would have seen him. He has gone into the tunnel! Hezekiah's tunnel!'

We had a little discussion. Ramses was twitching with impatience to get on lest his quarry elude him, and I refused to yield, so in the end he was forced to give in.

'Stay behind me,' he said sternly. 'Perhaps you are safer here with me than you would be stumbling into open pits. But please – please! – if I tell you to go back, assume that I have good reason to say so.'

The pool was low, since this was the end of summer, and owing to the lateness of the hour, water carriers and pilgrims had gone. There were only a few inches of water in the tunnel itself. It was very narrow; my outstretched hands measured barely two feet from side to side.

'Would you like a candle?' I inquired. I certainly wanted one, since I couldn't see a cursed thing.

'I might have known you'd have one. Thank you.'

He held it while I lit it with one of the matches from my waterproof box. The wavering light gave his face an eerie look, with deep shadows framing his tight mouth and turning his eye sockets into holes of darkness.

'The roof is quite high,' I said encouragingly. 'We needn't fear bumping our heads.'

'It is lower farther on. What other useful items do you have with you?'

'In addition to my parasol, only a roll of bandages and a little bottle of brandy.'

'Is that all? Let's hope we don't need either.'

He sounded quite calm, but I was close enough to him to realize he was shivering. The water was icy cold and the tunnel itself dank and chilly.

'Perhaps the candle was not a good idea,' I said uneasily. 'He will be waiting for you, won't he?'

'So I assume.'

'Here.' I offered him my parasol. 'If you hold this upright it will warn you when the roof begins to lower. I will extinguish the candle.'

Ramses, who had eyed the parasol askance, let out a sputter of laughter. The sound echoed uncannily and I put my finger to my lips.

'He knows we're here,' Ramses said, taking the parasol. 'If he's standing still he will hear our movements through the water. There's nothing we can do about it, so let us go on.'

He paid me the compliment of not bothering to advise me to keep one hand on the wall to one side. The sides were of solid rock, rough hewn and winding. I rested my other hand lightly on his back so that I would not run into him if he halted.

Had it not been for the absence of light and the fact that there was an assassin lying (or standing) in wait, I would have considered this one of the most thrilling moments of my life. I had given up hope of Emerson allowing me to explore the tunnel, and now Fate had presented me the opportunity.

Our progress was slow, for obvious reasons. Every now and then Ramses stopped, presumably to listen for sounds of movement ahead. I, too, strained my ears in vain. The water was a little deeper here, but not deep enough to produce splashing noises unless the person was running fast. Keeping track of elapsed time was impossible. I did count my steps, which gave a rough indication of the distance we had traveled. As I recalled, the tunnel was approximately 1,750 feet long. There was quite a distance yet to go.

A low-voiced warning from Ramses informed me that the roof had lowered. It was still high enough not to incommode my five feet and a bit, but had it not been for the parasol, Ramses might have been in danger of hitting his head. On, and yet farther on; I too had begun to shiver in the dank air and my feet were icy, even through my boots. I began to hope that I had been mistaken about Mansur's motives, that he meant to escape through the exit when a light suddenly flared just ahead. It was bright enough to blind me after that intense darkness. I flung up my hand to shield my eyes and saw that Ramses had done the same.

Standing squarely in the center of the tunnel was Mansur. One arm was folded across the breast of his robe. His hand held a torch. In the other hand was a knife. The backlight from his torch displayed a countenance fixed in a stare of disbelief. Then he let out a high-pitched cackle of laughter.

'Is that your weapon?' he asked. 'A lady's parasol?'

Ramses straightened slowly. The tunnel was only six feet high here. The top of his unkempt black head brushed the roof. 'Give it up,' he said.

Mansur mistook his meaning. His arm tightened protectively over the object in the breast of his robe. When he spoke again I knew from his voice and his wild-eyed look that he had crossed the border between mania and sanity.

'Turn now, Sitt Hakim,' he crooned. 'Go back. I will not follow. I am a man of honor. This is not the place I would have chosen, but I will fight fairly, man to man.'

He made a sudden rush at Ramses, who lowered the parasol and thrust, at the full length of his arm. The result proved what I have always maintained, that as a defensive weapon a parasol cannot be too highly commended. The point struck Mansur full in the stomach while his knife hand was a foot or more from Ramses's body. Mansur doubled over and staggered back.

I heard it before I saw it – a sound that can be described only in metaphor. A waterfall, a great wave crashing down on the shore, a flood, a torrent! I had only a glimpse of a wall of water filling the tunnel from side to side and floor to ceiling before it enveloped us all. The spring of Gihon had overflowed. The winter rains had come a month early.

I do not dislike adventure, but that was an experience I would not care to repeat. The first rush swept me off my feet. I was aware of moving rapidly back down the tunnel in the direction from which we had come and of wondering how much longer I could hold my breath. I do not think I prayed, but like an answer to prayer, my head suddenly rose above the water and I was jerked to a stop by an arm round my waist. Impenetrable darkness surrounded me, but I realized we had reached the part of the tunnel that was at its highest and that Ramses had kept hold of me the whole time, towing me along with the current. The current was still extremely swift, but the water was only up to my chest.

'Hold on to me,' he called. 'We are almost out.'

When we emerged from the tunnel it was into a downpour so heavy one could scarcely distinguish the air from the pool itself. We got to the side and Ramses hauled me out. For a little time we stood without speaking, holding each other tightly, choking and gasping, and, of course, soaked to the skin.

The darkness was almost as intense as it had been inside the tunnel. It would be futile to try to light a candle. We had to get to shelter, as quickly as possible. I squinted, trying to make out a landmark – when what should I see but a light, like that of a torch – what should I hear but a voice whose sheer volume rose over even the thunder of the rain.

'Peabody! Peeeeabody! Curse it, where are you?'

The body was found next morning, floating in the Pool of Siloam. The news reached us via the usual channels (gossip and the village grapevine) at about eight. We were breakfasting late, an indulgence to which at least some of us were entitled. Safika, the maidservant, delivered the news along with the eggs and toast.

'Wait,' I said as Ramses put down his fork and rose. 'There is no need for you to go there. You don't look well, and furthermore –'

'The police will want an identification,' Ramses said. 'I am one of the few who can provide it. Excuse me, Mother.'

The argument was logical, but I knew he had another reason. He wanted to be sure his nemesis was dead.

In point of fact, he had a third reason, which I did not learn until he returned an hour later. He found the rest of us still at the table, waiting. It was impossible to go on with our daily tasks until doubt had been removed.

'Well?' I said anxiously.

'It was he. The police have removed him.' Ramses put an object down on the table. 'This was still inside his robe.'

At first I did not recognize the carved box, it was so warped and battered. Cracks ran the length of the sides and base, but the ornate brass clasp had held.

'What is it?' Nefret asked.

'The motive behind Mansur's actions,' Ramses said. He wrenched the lid open. We crowded round, heads together, inspecting the contents. For those of us who still had hopes of a jeweled reliquary or golden ornaments, the result was, to say the least, disappointing. The entire box was filled with a layer of mud or clay less than two inches deep.

'A box filled with mud?' Nefret said.

'Clay,' Ramses corrected. 'Until a thorough soaking dissolved it, this was a clay tablet like the ones found at Amarna and in the Hittite archives. It bore a long inscription in cuneiform. I found a broken-off corner at Frau von Eine's campsite at Sebaste, with a few signs intact.'

Emerson's expressive countenance displayed a degree of distress it had not shown at the news of Mansur's death. 'It was a valuable artifact, now lost forever.'

'No,' Ramses said. 'It was a forgery. My discovery of that scrap, which Mansur found on my person, made it necessary – at least in his opinion – for him to silence me.'

'Do you mean that all this,' Nefret said incredulously, 'your kidnapping, his remorseless pursuit, his attempt to kill you – all because of a miserable scrap of clay tablet?'

'Not initially. Initially they reeled me in because I had learned a little too much from Macomber. Mansur was quite candid about that. Unfortunately it wasn't enough to make a solid case against them, but it might have interfered temporarily with their plans. Once they had accomplished their aim I could pass on the information without damaging them. But that aim had everything to do with the clay tablet. We assumed they wanted to find some talisman or icon under the temple. What they wanted to do was *plant* an artifact there – a written record dating from the period of Abraham. It might even have contained a prophecy, mentioning a kindly emperor from across the sea who would eventually free the land from its oppressors. Morley would find it, the location verified not only by Madame but by Morley's workmen.'

'That is absurd,' I exclaimed. 'No one would have believed such a preposterous claim, and any reputable scholar would have recognized the tablet as a forgery.'

Emerson had resorted to his pipe for comfort. 'Reputable scholars might have denied its authenticity, but there are always other scholars who disagree – and people believe what they want to believe, never mind the evidence. If there is anything life has taught me, it is that there is no idea so absurd that someone will not accept it as truth, and no action so bizarre that it will not be justified in the eyes of a true believer.'

'And it would have been an excellent fake,' Ramses added. 'She knew her cuneiform and her history. I don't doubt she went to Boghazkoy on this expedition to collect enough of the right sort of clay, so even the material would be authentic. She was working on the tablet while she was at Samaria and a corner got broken off. That wouldn't have destroyed the value of the tablet itself, but my testimony, that I had found the broken bit miles from Jerusalem and weeks before Morley was due to discover the tablet, would have been a devastating blow.'

'What about the box?' David asked, staring at the dismal object. 'It's obviously modern – or at least, recently made.'

'By a skilled craftsman in Sebaste,' said Ramses. 'They'd have had an answer to that, though; the original container would have to be replaced not once but many times over the centuries.'

'It's one of the wildest plots we've ever encountered,' David remarked.

'I wouldn't say that,' Emerson grunted. 'Several of Sethos's little schemes were almost as bizarre. That is one thing we have to be thankful for, at any rate. No Sethos.'

The rain had begun to fall more heavily, so when Emerson dropped hints about his excavation I firmly forbade his leaving the house. 'And Ramses,' I said, 'must rest. No, Ramses, don't argue. If you will not allow me to take your temperature, I must assume it is above normal. Nefret, is there any of the herb left?'

'Not much.' Nefret made a sudden lunge at Ramses and pressed her hand to his brow. 'Yes, he is running a slight fever. I will prepare another dose. We may need more, though.'

Ramses had tried several times to get a word in. Realizing the impossibility of overriding both Nefret and me, he confined his response to a scowl worthy of his father's best.

'I'll ride to the castle,' David offered. 'The medicine came from one of the villages nearby. I'm sure I can track down the man who guided us or one of the other villagers who assisted him.'

'I don't believe that will be necessary,' I said.

'But, Aunt Amelia –'

'There may be an easier way. I have invited a number of people to tea this afternoon. I want you all to be present. It is time we settled the questions that yet remain.'

I kept myself busy all day, instructing the cook how to prepare cucumber sandwiches and brew a proper pot of tea, and getting my notes in order. Emerson had gone to his study, from which Panagopolous's body had been removed by the police.

He emerged from it later that afternoon demanding to know where our visitors were. I deduced he had been working on a report of some sort, probably making notes about his excavation, since he was rumpled and ink-stained.

'The first should be arriving at any moment,' I replied, inspecting the table to make sure everything was in order. 'Go and wake Ramses and bring him here.'

Shaking his head, Emerson went off. When he returned he was accompanied not only by Ramses but by David and Nefret.

'Ramses should be in bed,' said the latter, inspecting him.

'I am sorry to have disturbed you, my boy,' I said. He was heavy-eyed and flushed. 'But I will need you. Ah, I believe the first visitor is here. Come in, Rabbi. I regret having brought you out on such a day. Ramses, will you translate for us?'

Rabbi Ben Ezra was as shabby as ever, but I thought there was a new look about him. Ramses repeated what I had said in Hebrew.

I gestured to the rabbi to take a chair and some refreshment, and the others settled down round the table.

The rabbi eyed the cucumber sandwiches doubtfully but accepted a cup of tea. Then he removed a small packet from a pocket. 'I understand you are in need of this.'

'Thank you,' I replied. 'We are grateful for your kindness in this as in so many other ways. I have only one more favor to ask.'

Nefret examined the packet, which of course contained a quantity of the medicinal herb. 'How . . .' she burst out.

'I sent word to the rabbi through a member of his organization,' I replied impatiently. 'Never mind that now, Nefret. We must not keep Rabbi Ben Ezra. He seems impatient to be gone.'

Ramses translated the last two sentences, and the rabbi nodded. He had finished his tea and was shifting uneasily in his chair. 'What else do you want of me, Mrs. Emerson? I will do it if I can. You have rendered us a service and we always pay our debts.'

'We pay our debts, too, and in this case the debt is still on our side. How can we assist the aims of your group? For if I understand them correctly, they are noble ideals with which we are in sympathy.'

The rabbi inclined his head and rose to his feet. 'Only continue as you have begun. Foil the plots of the predators who would use us for their own selfish ends. Leave us alone. We will work out our own destiny. Good day to you all.'

The finality in his voice precluded further questioning. Ramses said quietly, 'And peace to you. Give my thanks to Ismail.'

Ben Ezra stopped on his way to the door. 'I will do that. But he is no longer the leader. His term has finished.'

'Who is the leader, then?' I asked.

The rabbi shook his head. He smiled sweetly at me and trotted out. I thought I had received my answer, though, in his smile and his new air of confidence.

'Well!' said Emerson, drawing a long breath. 'We will respect his request, of course, but I wish we could learn more about the Sons of Abraham. They are an amazingly diverse bunch of people, aren't they? A rabbi, a rapscallion Egyptian ex-smuggler, some simple villagers –'

'And the madam of a house of prostitution,' Ramses finished. 'They do not discriminate on the basis of gender or religion. We can only wish them well and hope they succeed.'

'Amen,' said Emerson.

'Why, Emerson!' I exclaimed.

'It slipped out,' Emerson said quickly. 'Your influence, Peabody. Hmph. Where are the rest of our mysterious visitors?'

They were soon at the door, demanding admittance, and in a surly mood. Handing his wet coat to Safika, Mr. Glazebrook said, 'I am always happy to accept your invitations, Mrs. Emerson, but on this occasion I admit I would have preferred to stay home. What is this important matter that needs my attention?'

'All in due time, Mr. Glazebrook, all in due time. Have a cucumber sandwich. You too, Mr. Page.'

As I had expected, this culinary reminder of home put both visitors in a happier mood. The head of the BSEP (British Society for the Exploration of Palestine, in case the Reader has forgotten) wiped his glasses on his handkerchief. Sipping his tea, Mr. Page said, 'Well, this is pleasant. Have you anything to report, Professor?'

I had not expected him to come to the point quite so suddenly. The point being, in this case, the iniquities of Major Morley, which, I was somewhat embarrassed to recall, we had promised to end. I was trying to think of a way to get round the embarrassing fact that so far we had been unable to do so, when Emerson said, 'If you are referring to Major Morley, the problem is in hand and will soon be resolved to our mutual satisfaction. Ours, not his.'

'How soon?' Mr. Page demanded.

'Within forty-eight hours.'

'That would certainly be a relief,' said Glazebrook. 'If I may say so, Page and his associates have been driving me – er, that is to say . . .'

'My husband's word is his bond,' I said, wondering what the devil Emerson was up to. His ordinary way of dealing with difficulties like Morley was to threaten, harass, and, if necessary, physically remove them. So far as I knew he hadn't been anywhere near Morley in recent days.

'That is not why I asked you gentlemen here,' I said. 'David, did you bring your sketching pad and pencils?'

'As you asked, Aunt Amelia.'

David opened his sketch pad to a page that bore an excellent likeness of Plato Panagopolous, as he had appeared in death.

'Very good,' I said. 'Now, David, take your pencils, remove his beard and give him a full head of fair hair.'

'Good Gad,' said Emerson. 'He looks entirely different. I had no idea a thick head of hair could alter a person's appearance so drastically.' He ran his hand complacently over his own black locks.

'He shaved his cranium,' I said. 'I noticed the stubble when I examined him after he was attacked on the street, and then I remembered he was careful to wear a hat whenever he could. It was a clear indication that he needed to disguise himself from someone here in Jerusalem who might recognize him in his earlier incarnation. He was conspicuously absent when we visited you, Mr. Page. Do you recognize him?'

'I cannot say that I do,' Mr. Page admitted.

'Then he had another reason for being elsewhere that day. Mr. Glazebrook?'

Glazebrook's eyes had opened wide. 'Good heavens, yes! Though I might not have known him as Papapa – er –'

'Panagopolous,' I said.

'Herbert Jenkins,' the consul exclaimed. 'That was the name under which I knew him two years ago, when I had the pleasure of expelling him from Palestine. He had been the subject of innumerable complaints from tourists he had swindled by selling them faked antiquities, but it was not until he seduced a young native girl that I found sufficient grounds for diplomatic action. He went willingly, in fact, since the girl's family was after his blood and his only hope was to leave the country.'

'I doubt we will be able to trace his subsequent movements,' I said. 'Since he was in the habit of changing his appearance as well as his name. We must assume, however, that he ended up in Greece, where he encountered the original Plato Panagopolous and realized that that unfortunate man's wild theories could provide him with the means for a new swindle, one that suited his knowledge of and interest in antiquities.'

'Are you saying he murdered the poor fellow?' Emerson demanded.

'We may never know. In a way, Jenkins is a tragic figure; had he but turned his talents to honest labor he might have been an authority in the field of biblical history. His memory was phenomenal, his ingenuity superb. The inscription he produced when you challenged him to reproduce part of his scroll was a copy of the inscription found in the Siloam tunnel. It is now in Constantinople and has been reproduced in various books.'

'How do you know that?' Emerson demanded skeptically.

'I showed it to Ramses.'

'Oh,' said Emerson.

'At any rate, Jenkins has received his just deserts. I do not doubt that the girl he seduced was not the first or the last. A man of base appetites and no morals, he may have pursued other victims during the hours he was not in our company. Finally he became careless. The vengeance of an outraged parent or betrothed caught up with him. Let us hope it occurred before this poor girl was ruined, like Ghada.'

'Like who?' Emerson said in bewilderment.

He can never remember the servants' names, but in this case I couldn't blame him. She had not been often in his presence. Nefret remembered, though.

'Ghada? Do you mean that Plato' – she choked on the name – 'was her seducer?'

'Herbert Jenkins,' I corrected. 'I rather think so. The baby is fair-skinned, and you recall Plato's behavior when he saw her. He fled precipitately and never came here with us again. He knew he could not count on his disguise rendering him unrecognizable, for the eyes of love – or hate – are not easily deceived.'

'Hate, surely,' Nefret muttered. 'He took me in completely, Aunt Amelia. We must do something for Ghada.'

'We will discuss it later, Nefret.'

Which we did, as soon as the gentlemen had left. I had, of course, considered the problem of Ghada and arrived at a solution, which I proposed at once.

'A sizable dowry would probably be sufficient inducement for a young man to overlook her – er – other deficiency. You might consult Kamir. He seems to have a soft spot for her, otherwise he would not have sent her to us. He can suggest some suitable candidates, and make sure the chosen suitor treats her well.'

Nefret's jaw was set at an angle I was more accustomed to see from Emerson. 'Are you actually suggesting I purchase a husband for her? I cannot believe you mean it.'

'It is the only thing you can do for her,' I said sadly but firmly, 'and probably the thing she would choose for herself. Don't let your kind heart and romantic notions overcome your common sense. You cannot snatch her away from her home and her people and try to turn her into someone other than who she is. In time, let us hope, her daughter or granddaughter or great-granddaughter will have other choices.'

'Let us hope.' Nefret turned her head away for a moment. 'It is such a sweet baby.'

'A very sweet baby.'

'I will interview the candidates personally.'

'You might give Ghada a voice in the decision too,' I suggested.

Nefret gave me a watery smile and a hearty hug. 'You are always right, Aunt Amelia.'

I did not need to make a new list of 'Things to Be Done.' All the pressing issues on the original list had been dealt with, except for two. I decided to confront the least difficult first.

I had determined that Frau von Eine was staying at the Grand Hotel, the best in Jerusalem. The effrontery of the woman was amazing! Her plot had been thwarted, her influence ended. It must be pure arrogance that kept her here. In fact, we would have had a difficult time proving she was guilty of a crime. The Turkish authorities would never have arrested a prominent citizen of a nation whose influence with the Sublime Porte was so high.

I sent up my card and received an immediate response. A veiled servant opened the door and was dismissed with a wave of Frau von Eine's hand.

'Please sit down, Mrs. Emerson. I will order tea.'

'No, thank you, I prefer to stand. I will not keep you long.'

'Have you come to revel in your triumph?'

In fact, I had, but it was an unworthy motive, one I preferred not to admit. 'Only to settle a few details,' I said.

'It is only a temporary triumph, you know. This particular strategy failed, but I have laid the groundwork for a movement that will win in the end.' Her chin lifted proudly and her pale eyes glittered. 'I work for my country, Mrs. Emerson, as you do for yours. The Ottoman Empire will crumble, it is rotten to the core. And when it does it will be replaced by a firm yet benevolent government that will give these poor people the security they deserve.'

'They don't want it, not from another occupying power,' I said in some exasperation. 'They want independence and the right to make their own mistakes instead of suffering from the mistakes of others. Good Gad, you are as bad as the British imperialists like Mr. Hogarth.'

'We will never agree on that, Mrs. Emerson.'

'No. I did not expect my reasonable arguments to prevail, but I felt obliged to make them. Good day, Frau von Eine.'

'Give my regards to your son. Making his acquaintance has been an interesting experience.'

I did not linger. As I made my way to the lift I pondered her last speech and the faint enigmatic smile that had accompanied it. Was it possible that Ramses . . . No, I told myself. I decided, however, that I would not pass on her regards.

Emerson and I were first at the breakfast table next morning. In fact, Emerson had been first, which was unusual enough to get me out of bed and dressed when I discovered he was absent. He greeted me with a nod and then retired behind a book. I was accustomed to that version of rudeness; taking a few papers from my coat pocket, I spread them out on the table.

Emerson's eyes appeared over the top of the book. 'One of your little lists, Peabody?'

I did not like the look of those blue eyes. They had a sparkle that seldom appeared at that hour of the morning.

'Yes,' I said.

'Surely,' said Emerson, still behind the book except for his eyes, 'you have by now ticked off all the items on that particular list. You have been even more efficient than usual, my dear.'

I had already begun to suspect he was up to something. His present behavior confirmed the suspicion. 'As you know perfectly well, Emerson, there is one major item that has not been dealt with: the reason we came to Palestine in the first place. Major Morley is still working.'

Emerson chuckled. 'Very good, my dear. Major item indeed.'

Now I *knew* he was up to something. 'We must make one more attempt to confront him, Emerson.'

'That won't be necessary,' said Emerson, continuing to chuckle in a particularly annoying manner. 'Major Morley has been dealt with.'

I snatched the book from his hands. His smug smile showed almost all his teeth.

'By you,' I said.

'By me.' Emerson reached for the coffee jug and poured into both our cups. 'Now don't be a dog in the manger, Peabody. You have taken care of everything and everybody else. Allow me one small triumph.'

'Well . . .' He was quite right, and I did not even blame him for teasing me a little. 'Tell me about it, Emerson.'

'It was rather clever, if I do say it as shouldn't. More along your line than mine, Peabody. It occurred to me, you see, that Morley must be getting rather frantic. His pits and tunnels have been flooded, he hasn't found a cursed thing. He would, I reasoned, be susceptible to any idea, no matter how chancy or illegal, if it gave him one final chance of success. So Ali Bey and I put our heads together. To make a long story short, Ali Bey got word to Morley that with the proper bribe he could gain admittance to the Noble Sanctuary itself and excavate under the floor.'

'Good Gad,' I exclaimed. 'That is outrageous, Emerson.'

'That's where every archaeologist who comes here wants to dig, Peabody. The majority, I daresay, would have better sense or better principles than to respond to such a proposition, but not Morley. He was getting desperate and he believes money will buy anything.'

Emerson paused and took out his pipe.

'Go on,' I urged. 'You have me on pins and needles.'

'Really?' Emerson beamed. 'Well, up to the Mount he went last night, after midnight, with one companion. The custodian was not there. Believing that the fellow had been bribed to stay away, Morley began work. Before he had struck more than a single blow, a horrible cry burst out, and there was the custodian, wringing his hands and screaming. He picked up a mattock Morley had brought, and went after Morley, leaving the latter in no doubt that his plan had misfired. He fled, leaving his tools – all the evidence any court would need as to his intentions. By the time he reached the foot of the Mount, a small mob was on his heels. It soon became a huge mob. Ali Bey, who had been watching the entire performance from hiding, distracted the infuriated worshippers long enough for Morley to get away. He didn't want a mob tearing a foreigner to bits, whatever the offense. A splendid fellow, Ali Bey.'

'Yes, indeed. Where is Morley now?'

Emerson gestured. 'In hiding, in Kamir's donkey shed. I met him, as planned, and took him there. Kamir has agreed to smuggle him out of Jerusalem and set him on his way to Jaffa in exchange for most of Morley's remaining funds. He will reach England impoverished – and, as soon as word of this affair reaches the English press, disgraced.'

'Emerson,' I said sincerely, 'I did not think it possible, but you have excelled yourself. How did you persuade Kamir to overcome his religious scruples to assist a heretic?'

Emerson snorted. 'Kamir has no scruples, religious or otherwise. How is Ramses this morning?'

'Sleeping soundly. He seems fully recovered. However –'

'I know, I know.' The incessant drumbeat of rain on the roof never stopped. Emerson sighed. 'You are going to tell me he should not be working in this weather.'

'No one can work under these conditions, Emerson. Everyone shuts down his excavation during the rainy season. I know what a blow it is to you, my dear, to admit defeat, but it is already too late to salvage anything. What the rain has not swept away the local thieves have found. Let us go home.'

'Back to England?' His heavy black brows drew together. 'Now?'

'No, my dear. Home. To Egypt.'